THE MYSTERIES OF LONDON

Editor's Acknowledgement

I would like to record my gratitude to many colleagues in the Department of English and History at Manchester Metropolitan University with whom I have discussed this project, and to Dr Bronwen Thomas for her invaluable editorial assistance with some of the work.

THE Mysteries OF London

G.W.M. Reynolds

Edited and with an Introduction by
Trefor Thomas

KEELEUNIVERSITY**PRESS**

First published in 1996 by
Keele University Press
Keele, Staffordshire

Introductory material and notes
© Trefor Thomas

Composed by KUP
Printed on acid-free paper
by Hartnolls, Bodmin,
Cornwall, England

ISBN 1 85331 111 1

Contents

G.W. M. Reynolds's *The Mysteries of London*: An Introduction   vii

Bibliography   xxv

The Mysteries of London   Series I, Volume I

		Prologue	3
Chapter	I	The Old House in Smithfield	5
	II	The Mysteries of the Old House	9
	III	The Trap-Door	11
	IV	The Two Trees	15
	V	Eligible Acquaintances	18
	VII	The Boudoir	20
	IX	A City Man.—Smithfield Scenes	25
	XIII	The Hell	32
	XVII	A Den of Horrors	37
	XIX	Morning	41
	XXIII	The Old House in Smithfield again	46
	XXVI	Newgate	48
	XXVII	The Republican and the Resurrection Man	50
	XXVIII	The Dungeon	54
	XXIX	The Black Chamber	64
	XLII	"The Dark House"	66
	XLIV	The Body-Snatchers	68
	LV	Miserrima!!!	73
	LVI	The Road to Ruin	83
	LVIII	New Year's Day	90
	LIX	The Royal Lovers	99
	LX	Revelations	105
	LXII	The Resurrection Man's History	107
	LXV	The Wrongs and Crimes of the Poor	118
	LXX	The Image, the Picture, and the Statue	125
	LXXI	The House of Commons	130
	LXXII	The Black Chamber again	133
	LXXXVII	The Professor of Mesmerism	137

LXXXVIII	The Figurante	144
XC	Markham's Occupations	147
XCI	The Tragedy	149
XCVII	Another New Year's Day	156
CIV	Female Courage	156
CV	The Combat	160
CVIII	The Exhumation	162
CXIII	The Lovers	167
CXVI	The Rattlesnake's History	172
CXXIX	The Fall	187
CXXXI	The Statue	191
CXXXIV	The Palace in the Holy Land	195
	Epilogue	197

The Mysteries of London   Series I, Volume II

CXXXVIII	A Public Functionary	201
CXL	Incidents in the Gipsy Palace	207
CXLVI	The Bath.—The Housekeeper	209
CXLIX	The Masquerade	212
CLV	Patriotism	218
CLXIII	The Zingarees	223
CLXVIII	The Plague Ship	228
CLXXI	Mr. Greenwood's Dinner-party	234
CLXXII	The Mysteries of Holmesford House	237
CLXXX	The "Boozing-Ken" once more	242
CLXXXI	The Resurrection Man again	243
CLXXXV	Another New Year's Day	248
CLXXXVI	The New Cut	250
CLXXXVII	The forged Bills	253
CLXXXIX	The Battle of Montoni	254
CXCI	Crankey Jem's History	259
CXCII	The Mint.—The Forty Thieves	272
CXCIII	Another Visit to Buckingham Palace	275
CXCIV	The Royal Breakfast	279
CCXI	The Deed	285
CCXXIII	The Marriage	289
CCXXXIX	The Resurrection Man's Return Home	294
CCLII	Death of the Marquis of Holmesford	297
CCLIII	The Ex-Member for Rottenborough	303
CCLVII	The Revenge	309
CCLVIII	The Appointment kept	316
CCLIX	Conclusion	326
	Epilogue	328
Appendix: complete chapter titles from the original edition		331

G. W. M. Reynolds's
The Mysteries of London
An Introduction

George William MacArthur Reynolds's novel The *Mysteries of London*, with its continuation *The Mysteries of the Court of London*, was a phenomenon of Victorian book production. This monumental work comprised a total of approximately four and a half million words, and was a best seller in its most characteristic format, the penny number, from its commencement in October 1844 to its conclusion in 1856. As a weekly literary soap opera, it was shrewdly designed to appeal to a newly literate lower-class readership in the cities; the combination of populist politics, dramatic illustration, voyeuristic revelation of high and low life depravity in the metropolis, and the exploitation of established conventional motifs from the Gothic horror canon produced sales figures which dwarfed those of rivals in this rapidly evolving market and brought national celebrity to its author. By 1847, Reynolds himself was able to refer to the 'immense circulation' of the weekly numbers, 'exceeding', he claimed, 'that of any novel published in the last twenty years', and to assert its status as a 'national tale'.[1] Total sales of the title in English and the other languages into which it was rapidly translated have been estimated at over a million.

    The complete original text has never been reprinted in the twentieth century. Although the odd bound volume occasionally surfaces in the antiquarian book trade, the full set of twelve can now only be consulted in specialist libraries. The purpose of this edition, therefore, is to put back into circulation substantial extracts from a novel that once had considerable cultural, political, and social significance. Its historical placing in the mid-1840s, at a moment when Europe was riven by pre-revolutionary tensions and when a new market for cheap popular fiction with values radically unlike those of the improving and moralistic penny magazines of the 1830s was evolving in the cities, gave it an almost emblematic status in the raging cultural battle for the minds of the working classes. In spite of, or perhaps even because of, its many crudities and contradictions, the text conveys insights into aspects of nineteenth-century urban life and culture often denied to more finished or literary fiction. Taken with Henry Mayhew's recording of the detail of street life in his *Morning Chronicle* letters of 1849, and with Dickens's apocalyptic vision of London in *Bleak House*, the text completes a literary triptych representing the culture of the metropolis from three distinctive perspectives at an epochal moment of social and political transition. The exceptional narrative variety and energy of the writing should also enable most modern readers to find some 'pleasures of the text' to celebrate in this edition.

The complete work, *The Mysteries of London* (Series One and Two, four volumes) and *The Mysteries of the Court of London* (Series One, Two, Three and Four, eight volumes), first appeared in the format with which it is most typically associated – weekly penny numbers – beginning in October 1844 and finally ceasing in 1856.[2] In a postscript at the conclusion of the final volume Reynolds remarked that for twelve years he had issued a number every week, 'without any intermission'. Each number occupied him 'an average of seven hours' in the composition; he explicitly denied the claim sometimes made that an 'army' of writers was employed. There is a total of 624 weekly penny numbers in the finished work, which Reynolds described as 'a complete Encyclopedia of tales'. Each number consists of 8 pages of small-print, double-column text, with a wood engraving, usually of a climactic moment in the narrative, on the first page.[3] The text often breaks off in the middle of a sentence, to be continued in the next number. The material could also be purchased as monthly parts for the price of sixpence: the parts consisted of 4 weekly numbers stitched into a specially engraved cover. At the end of each year, unsold weekly numbers were collected and bound up for sale in volume form: a title page and list of contents was available, at the cost of one penny, for purchasers who wished to make their own binding arrangements. In a complete bound set, there are 12 double-columned, small-print, 400-page volumes, one for each year of publication, each including 52 weekly numbers. There was also a substantial trade in back numbers, and the whole series was reissued from its commencement several times, once its commercial success became apparent. Advertisements in the *London Journal* reassured anxious readers that missing numbers could be reprinted from the stereotype plates without difficulty, and this was clearly done on a regular basis to satisfy demand. The full set of 12 volumes was also reissued by John Dicks in undated versions at least twice after the end of the series in 1856. Dicks also published a 36-volume, undated *Complete Works* of Reynolds later in the century. There was a later condensed, simplified and undated version in Milner's *Cottage Library* series, with the sub-title *Stories of Life in the Modern Babylon*. A few episodes from the novel have been included in modern anthologies, but the mass of the material has never been reprinted.

In a letter addressed to the 'industrious classes' in *Reynolds's Miscellany*, Reynolds himself gave an account of the 'mysteries' cult which developed in England after the publication of Eugene Sue's *The Mysteries of Paris* in an English translation in 1845:

> *The Mysteries of London* have been reprinted in America, and translations have been published in four languages of Europe – French,

Spanish, Italian, German. The German edition has sold to the extent of 8,000 copies, great numbers of which have found their way into Russia, despite the vigilance of the police. The book is literally devoured in Russia, and large sums are given for the loan of it.[4]

By 1846, according to advertisements in *Reynolds's Miscellany of Romance, General Literature, Science and Art*, at least two dramatic versions were in performance on the London stage and numerous imitations and variations on the 'mysteries' theme were published.[5] Anne Humpherys argues that the 'mysteries' novel at this time was evolving as a distinctive urban genre, and she identifies a dozen contemporary fictions which use the motif in their titles; she remarks that the plural form 'refers linguistically to the fragmented and hence incoherent experience of the modern city, as well as to the resulting feeling of disconnectedness'.[6] Richard Maxwell's recent *The Mysteries of Paris and London*[7] also discusses the 'mystery mania' of the 1840s. The genre represents an urbanization of eighteenth-century Gothic, and a new consciousness of the city as inexplicable and impenetrable.

The Mysteries of London itself was rapidly successful; its weekly sales were variously reported as 30,000 to 40,000 shortly after commencement in 1844. Even after its cessation, the fame of the title lived on: J. A. Berger's *New Mysteries of London* (1861) was a chapter-by-chapter parody of Reynolds's text, in which the infamous Resurrection Man rises once more from the dead.

Although publication in volume form was a significant factor in the sales figures, it was the weekly penny number which lay at the heart of Reynolds's fame. This format was exploited by a number of entrepreneurial publishers in the 1840s, notably Edward Lloyd, who issued many 'penny bloods' from his Salisbury Square offices, but Reynolds was distinguished from this group by both the relative quality of his writing and the radical thrust of his social and political comment. The distinctive qualities of *The Mysteries of London* made it a key element in the dramatic literary moment of the 1840s, when the mass market for cheap serial publications, created above all by Charles Knight's *Penny Magazine* and William Chambers's *Chambers's Journal* in the 1830s, moved towards entertainment rather than improvement. The national debate which raged around the emblematic penny – if the working classes were to be educated, what should they read? – gives some indication of the cultural and political anxieties associated with the evolution of cheap popular fiction in the cities in the decade of English Chartism and European revolution.[8] The middle-class sponsorship of improving weekly penny magazines such as the *Working Man's Friend and Family Instructor*, with its explicit programme of 'elevating the taste of the male and female operatives of England', was a direct response to fears about the effect of sensational fiction. Many derogatory accounts of cheap popular literature at this time are centred around the key terms 'sensational' and 'exciting'; it was the treatment of gender and sexuality, as much as populist political rhetoric, which aroused middle-class anxieties. Dickens's decision at the end of the decade to found a weekly magazine, significantly entitled *Household Words*, was a further instance of this opposition of sexual licence to domestic order; his references in the opening number to some 'tillers of the field' of cheap fiction as 'Bastards of the Mountain, draggled fringe on the Red Cap', who 'pander to the basest passions of the basest natures – whose existence is a national reproach', were widely taken as a direct reference to Reynolds.

The extracts chosen in this collection represent only a proportion of the whole work. Even the original first series of *The Mysteries of London*, published between 1844 and 1846, when the characteristics of the form were most sharply defined and from which this selection is chosen, includes an estimated 800,000 words and 104 weekly numbers. The narrative of the first series is complete in itself, although one of the central protagonists, Richard Markham, is reintroduced in the second series; later volumes show some decline from the quality of the earlier productions. After completion of the first and second series of *The Mysteries of London* (four volumes, 1844–8), Reynolds prepared a mass of material for a continuation, but quarrelled with both the original publisher, George Vickers, and with George Stiff, the proprietor of the *London Journal*, who also engraved the blocks for the first four volumes. Reynolds set up an independent publishing house with John Dicks, who had been a clerk in the Vickers office.[9] The later series were published by Dicks under the changed title of *The Mysteries of the Court of London*, while Stiff employed first Thomas Miller and later E. J. Blanchard to continue the original title, which was less successful after Reynolds severed his connection with it. The final number of the second series of *The Mysteries of London* announced that the first number of a new serial of the same title, written by Miller, would appear on 20 September 1848. This arrangement was, not unnaturally, angrily contested by Reynolds, who immediately began a continuation of his own under the modified title of *The Mysteries of the Court of London*.

In the original first series of *The Mysteries of London,* there are 259 chapters. This edition reproduces substantial extracts from 60 of those chapters, about 140,000 of the 800,000 words. The Appendix provides a complete list of the chapter titles in the first edition and references to the original page numbers. Where chapters have been abridged, this is indicated in the text by ellipses in square brackets. The reduction in size has been achieved by the complete omission of a number of the sub-plots which are appended to the main narrative line. The selections have also been chosen to contrast episodes of 'low' and 'high' London life, as happened in the original numbers, and to follow out the experiences of the central characters: Richard Markham; his brother Eugene (under one or other of his many pseudonyms); Anthony Tidkins, the Resurrection Man; his sworn enemy, James Cuffin, or Crankey Jem; and the two women, Ellen Monroe and Isabella Alteroni, who marry the brothers. Although this is not a complete version of the first series, every effort has been made, within the limits outlined above, to include a representative selection of the contents. Where possible, long extracts or complete chapters have been included, rather than briefer episodes. A dagger (†) has been used in the text to indicate those points at which the first and second penny numbers ceased. Most of the extracts chosen are illustrated by the wood-engravings so typical of this literary mode: the technique evolved by Thomas Bewick and his followers of engraving on the end-grain of a boxwood block allowed the representation of a high level of detail, and produced durable and cheap blocks which could withstand long print runs without wear. Many of the blocks for the first series of *The Mysteries of London* were drawn and engraved by George Stiff, who was also, briefly, the owner of the *London Journal* and later director of the '*Illustrated London News* Engraving Establishment'. Some of the woodcuts are unsigned and can only be attributed to Stiff on stylistic grounds. Later series used a variety of other artists and engravers; the first volume of *The Mysteries of the Court of London* (1847) includes 52 woodcuts 'drawn by Henry Anelay and engraved by E. Hooper'.[10]

G. W. M. Reynolds: biography and politics

George Reynolds was born in Sandwich on 23 July 1814, the son of a flag-officer in the Royal Navy. He inherited a substantial sum on his mother's death in 1830 (his father had died earlier) and left the Sandhurst Royal Military College, where he had been preparing for a military career, for Paris, to begin his career as a journalist. Here he acquired the knowledge of French popular fiction which he was able to use to good effect, edited an English-language newspaper published in Paris, and came in contact with revolutionary political ideas. His book *The Modern Literature of France* (London: 1839) contains an account of the major French writers of the time and their innovations. His reading of Eugene Sue's *The Mysteries of Paris* was of especial importance, as it suggested the idea for a similar novel of London life and demonstrated the potential of the *roman feuilleton*, a novel specifically designed for serial publication in newspapers.

After the failure of some business enterprises, Reynolds was declared bankrupt and he returned to England. In London he continued his journalistic career and contributed to a number of periodicals. His novel *Pickwick Abroad*, published in the *Monthly Magazine* from 1837, was a successful if plagiaristic attempt to emulate Dickens's commercial success, as was his *Master Timothy's Bookcase* (1841). At this time he also edited a crusading magazine, the *Teetotaller* (1840–1), having signed the pledge in 1840. He was briefly editor of the *London Journal* in 1845; this was a pioneering and important attempt to identify and exploit a new market for a weekly popular magazine among the urban working class. Simultaneously, he edited a highly successful family magazine, *Reynolds's Miscellany of Romance, General Literature, Science and Art*, which combined fiction with improving and informative articles. Between 1845 and 1855 Reynolds wrote at least 36 novels and short tales, all of which appeared either in magazines or as penny numbers. Many, but perhaps not all, of these titles were included in the *Complete Works* published later in the century by John Dicks. In 1848 he married Susanna Pearson, who was also a successful popular novelist. They had three children, one of whom was, significantly, christened Kossuth Mazzini.[11] After 1860 he wrote little and, according to Frederic Boase's *Modern Biographies*, became a churchwarden at St Andrew's, Well Street. He died in his Woburn Square house on 17 June 1879.

By 1848, Reynolds's reputation as a successful popular author and editor, exploiting the new technologies of steam press, cheap paper, and national distribution through the developing railway network, was firmly established. It was at this point, in the winter of 1848 – the year of revolution – that his active political career began, although his interest in radicalism and republicanism had been apparent throughout the 1840s. In its edition of 11 March 1848, the Chartist newspaper, the *Northern Star,* carried a report of a 'great open-air meeting' which had been held a few days previously in Trafalgar Square. Police attempts to disperse this illegal gathering of 'an immense assemblage', which was inflamed by the recent news of the successful revolutionary overthrow of Louis Philippe in Paris, had led to sporadic street violence. A mob surged down the Mall and through St James's Park, egged on by cries of 'To the Palace!', as far as the gates of the royal residence itself. A week later, the same paper triumphantly reported a further great mass meeting at Kennington Common.

At the first of these meetings, in Trafalgar Square, the chairman, selected by acclaim, was a man described by the *Northern Star* as 'the popular author Mr. G. W. M. Reynolds'. At the conclusion of the demonstration, Reynolds was carried in triumph back to his house in Wellington Street, where he addressed the crowd from a balcony. A week later, at Kennington Common, Reynolds once more took the chair and presided beneath a revolutionary tricolour banner. In his speech, he fiercely attacked the profligacy of the monarchy and the callousness of the aristocracy – they enjoyed untold luxury in their private lives while ignoring the plight of the poor, who existed 'herded together in the dens and cellars of the metropolis'.[12] He also attacked those elements in the press which referred to the Chartists as 'a mob, ruffians or rifraff'.

Although he was elected as representative for Derby on the Chartist convention in 1848 and continued to be a member of the National Charter Association, Reynolds played only a minor role in the later history of the movement. After four years he quarrelled with a number of its leaders, and was involved in a libel case with Ernest Jones. It is, however, his work as a journalist, editor, and popular novelist, advocating the cause of the poor against the rich in the crucial transitional decade between 1844 and 1854, rather than his engagement in public politics, which is central to his reputation. The Chartist newspaper which he founded and edited in 1849,

Reynolds's Political Instructor, was short-lived, but *Reynolds's Weekly Newspaper*, which he founded in 1850, played an important part in the formation and publicizing of radical thought in England throughout the nineteenth century.

The assessment of the significance of Reynolds's political career has always divided critics. Many of his contemporaries, including E. J. Blanchard, who called him a 'professional democrat' and a 'political humbug all round', Karl Marx, who thought him 'a rich and able speculator', and Charles Dickens, regarded him mainly as a commercially motivated and plagiaristic exploiter of the new mass market for leisure reading. For these critics, his radicalism was largely a matter of expediency, more to do with a shrewd commercial assessment of the market than with social analysis. Anne Humpherys, whose recent articles contain the most serious and sustained attempt to come to terms with the paradoxes of Reynolds's career, argues that his strength lay precisely in the capacity of his writing to represent the divergent and conflicting elements which formed popular consciousness at this transitional epoch, without any striving for formal resolution or aesthetic consistency. Thus, *The Mysteries of London* is constructed out of a series of unresolved and even contradictory elements. At one level, it belongs to a formative historical moment of transition, when a mass market for sensational popular entertainment was coming into being, but its language and attitudes are also influenced by the newer, radical vocabulary of class conflict. Equally, an older cultural inheritance from the romantic populism of 'old radicalism', with its attacks on a profligate aristocracy and effete monarchy, is set against 'traditional' puritan values of restraint and temperance. As Patrick Joyce remarks in his *Visions of the People*, Reynolds serves as 'a crucially important bridge between the old radicalism and the new'.[13] Thus the text includes elements from the older traditions of street ballad and broadside, as well as the newer voice of the radical unstamped and Chartist press. Indeed, the very success of *The Mysteries of London* is inextricably related to the question of popular or class consciousness; the weekly penny-number format ensured that publisher and author could respond positively and quickly to readership reaction expressed through sales figures, and the existence of active correspondence columns dealing with queries in both the *London Journal* and *Reynolds's Miscellany* was a further example of this almost reciprocal process. In a letter addressed to 'The Industrious Classes' in *Reynolds's Miscellany*, 30 January 1847, the point is explicitly made by Reynolds himself:

> I have received, both in my capacity as editor and author, innumerable letters from the correspondents among you... This interchange of communications has led to results extremely gratifying to myself. Not only have I been able to ascertain that my humble efforts to entertain and instruct have experienced success, but I have also received many valuable hints and suggestions which I have never failed to adopt and follow...[14]

Although Reynolds's Chartist career might indicate that *The Mysteries of London* should be read as a new, radical, urban fictional genre, organically linked to the working-class identity that E. P. Thompson and others argue was established by the 1830s, a close reading of the novel suggests that the situation is more complex. The text stands at a moment of transition between 'old' and 'new' languages of class, and both elements surface in its political rhetoric. The 'enemies of the people' identified and attacked in its passages of explicit political rhetoric include such traditional figures of popular hatred as the hangman, the body-snatcher and the rake, but also the 'new' figures of the City man, the crooked financier and the corrupt politician. Indeed, one striking feature of the novel is its revelation of the venal connections between Government, Church, the City of London, and the aristocracy.

The Mysteries of London and its readers

On 18 October 1849, the London-based radical newspaper the *Morning Chronicle* announced its intention of publishing, in weekly instalments, a major social survey of the 'moral, intellectual, material, and physical condition of the industrial poor throughout England'. The contributions dealing with London were written and researched by Henry Mayhew and formed the basis of his famous sociological work, later published as *London Labour and the London Poor*.[15] Many of the less well-known articles describing the conditions of the poor in the north of England were written by a young Scottish journalist, Angus Bethune Reach. His accounts of the area appeared in the *Morning Chronicle* in October and November 1849. Reach was interested in the cultural as well as the material life of the Lancashire working classes and, as part of his investigations into the literary market in the industrial city, he visited a working-class bookshop owned by a Manchester trader, Abel Heywood. Heywood, who had been imprisoned in the 1830s for selling unstamped radical newspapers, was a key figure in the process by which cheap, London-published literature was made available to the emergent working classes in the north-west. Reach provided a careful and detailed description of Heywood's Oldham Street shop and its contents in 1849, offering a unique insight into reading habits among the Lancashire working class. His perceptive account of the 'literary chaos' of the shop can be taken as a emblem of the different elements which formed popular consciousness at this conjuncture:

> Masses of penny novels and comic song and recitation books are jumbled with sectarian pamphlets and democratic essays. Educational books abound in every variety. Loads of cheap reprints of American authors, seldom or never heard of among the upper reading classes here, are mingled with editions of the early puritan divines. Double-

columned translations from Sue, Dumas, George Sand, Paul Feval and Frederic Soulie jostle with dream-books, scriptural commentaries, Pinnock's Guides, and quantities of cheap music ... altogether, the literary chaos is very significant of the restless and all-devouring literary appetite which it supplies.[16]

Among this mass of material, Reach observed that a 'species of novel, adorned with woodcuts, and published in weekly penny parts, claims the foremost place'. He found these 'utterly beneath criticism', and remarked that they reflected all the 'most abominable features of the French Feuilleton Roman'. He identified two sources for the penny fiction: the 'mass of literary garbage' published by Edward Lloyd, with total sales of 6,000 a week in the Manchester region, and those produced by smaller publishers, totalling 5,000 a week. In the latter group, two titles by the 'popular author' G. W. M. Reynolds, *The Mysteries of London* and its sequel *The Mysteries of the Court of London,* had sales of 1,000 and 1,500 copies each week in the Manchester region. The readership was predominately working class; Reach noted that 'operative taste' called for the 'links of a story' in its leisure reading.

A further detailed insight into the important Lancashire market in weekly penny-number fiction is given in Abel Heywood's evidence to the Parliamentary Commission on Newspaper Stamps in 1851.[17] He was concerned to impress the Commission with the respectability of his business, and put the total sales of all periodicals imported by him from London into the north-west at 80,000 a week. Of these, he remarked, most were of 'a good tendency', morally improving or educational in content. Of those which had an 'exciting tendency', he noted that Reynolds's *The Mysteries of the Court of London* was still, in 1851, the most popular of its kind, selling 1,500 copies each week. Heywood remarked that the novel was available to readers in a number of different formats: most sales were of the characteristic weekly penny number, but the monthly version, consisting of four weekly numbers bound in an illustrated cover, was, he recorded, often bought by regular subscribers rather than casual purchasers. Some purchasers collected the numbers and had them bound annually in volume form when complete, a service provided by Heywood's shop. Heywood also recorded a substantial demand for back numbers. He identified purchasers of penny fiction as 'a spreeing sort of young man', the type who visit taverns and 'put cigars in their mouths in a flourishing way', but he also claimed that 'a great many females' were buying *The Mysteries of London.*

Evidence from other sources suggests that the popularity of *The Mysteries of London* with a working-class readership was a national phenomenon. Advertisements in *Reynolds's Miscellany* claimed national sales of 30,000 copies a week very soon after the commencement of publication. The dangers posed by this success were rapidly recognized, and a national debate about the potentially corrupting effects of cheap sensational literature ensued.

An article in the *London Journal,* 18 April 1845, defended the genre and defined a new category of 'Economic Literature' which was replacing old forms: its energy, the author argued, 'is electric' and would 'burst through the veil of ignorance, and break into the inmost recesses of all institutions, social, moral, and political'.[18]

In a key chapter of *London Labour and the London Poor,* Henry Mayhew gave an account of the 'literature of costermongers', although, he remarks, 'it may seem anomalous to speak of the literature of an uneducated body'. He reported that, in an informant's view, the costermongers were tired of the 'blood-stained' stories of Lloyd, and that, among them, Reynolds was the most popular man in all London. His anti-aristocratic politics and support for popular causes created a readership 'most eager' for the weekly numbers. Mayhew's informant also identified a significant practice of collective reading. Ten or twelve young men and women, he observed, would gather after work to have the text narrated by a literate working man. The group engaged actively in the reading and maintained a barrage of query and comment:

> 'Here all my audience', said the narrator to me 'broke out with :—
> 'Aye, that's how the harristocrats hooks it! There's nothing of that sort among us; the rich has all that barrikin to themselves!' 'Yes! that's the b— way the taxes goes in!' shouted a woman.[19]

He also noted that the costermongers were 'very fond of illustrations', and that men who could not read would sometimes buy numbers for the woodcuts alone. They would then request explanations from a reader: '"... but about the picture?" they would say, and this is a very common question put by them whenever they see an engraving'.

Here there is evidence for the existence of a popular collective process of interpretation which implicitly challenges many conventional assumptions about the essentially domestic and individual nature of Victorian readership. Behind Mayhew's account lies an inherited demotic tradition of collective reading of radical prints and tracts, which may produce interpretations quite different from those of the educated élite. The active and collective reading that Mayhew describes also has direct links with popular melodrama, its conventions of audience participation and support for the poor and oppressed, and with the practice of public readings at Chartist and Union meetings. The collaborative fusing of text and illustration so characteristic of this publishing mode was clearly helpful to semi-literate readers; the illustrations are a democratizing force in this text. It is a mistake, however, to assume that the lower-class urban readership of *The Mysteries of London* was incapable of a more complex or sophisticated response to the text: at one level, it was surely read as a generic parody, mocking the standard conventions of Gothic terror. The faintly ridiculous naming of the horrific Resurrection Man as 'Tidkins' is a trivial example of this aspect of the novel, one commonly overlooked by literary critics. The constable who remarks to Richard Markham at one point that 'Lord, Sir, if I arrested all imposters, half London would be in prison', is making a similar point about the self-conscious mockery of Gothic motifs in this novel. There is certainly some evidence here for the view that *The Mysteries of London* is related to popular consciousness in ways that more sophisticated writing could not achieve. Both the *London Journal* and *Reynolds's Miscellany* published regular series of articles aimed at the 'industrious classes', which clearly identified the targeted readership as the class of respectable but productive poor — the cotton spinner, the clerk, the skilled artisan. Many of Reynolds's own magazine articles from this time show this equivalence clearly: sensational fiction appears side by side with detailed informative accounts of etiquette, popular history, temperance tracts, and family reading.

Although it is difficult to adduce further precise information about readerships, there is some evidence to support the view that, despite the explicit definitions contained in the magazines and the implied readership constructed within the text, a taste for Reynolds's sensational fiction in fact extended more widely across the classes than might be thought. Some surviving sets of the novels have original inscriptions which indicate a respectable middle-class, or even aristocratic, ownership of the volumes. Further evidence for the view that a taste for Reynolds was not wholly restricted to the working classes can be found in the observation that some of the more lurid or salacious illustrations which appeared in early numbers published by George Vickers were completely replaced when reissued in volume form by John Dicks. The 'Boudoir' and 'Dungeon' wood engravings are reproduced in this edition in both early and late forms. Other engravings were subject to major revision and improvement, usually on aesthetic grounds, in the later reissues. The differences between these illustrations may indicate that Dicks and Reynolds recognized that the social groups able to purchase the text in volume form were likely to be more concerned with taste and respectability than purchasers of the weekly penny numbers.

Reading *The Mysteries of London*

Between May 1847 and April 1848 *Reynolds's Miscellany* published a plagiarized version of William Hogarth's moral series *Industry and Idleness*, entitled *Days of Hogarth*, or *Mysteries of Old London*.[20] This was illustrated with thirty-six large wood-engravings directly copied from Hogarth and included a commentary written by Reynolds which provided an elucidation of their meanings. Reynolds's interest in Hogarth was not accidental; the combination of a popular graphic narrative genre with a simple moralized plot-structure has clear parallels in *The Mysteries of London*. At the surface level, this text, too, functions as a morality tale in a populist mode well suited to the urban readerships of the early nineteenth century.

The tale concerns two brothers, Richard and Eugene Markham, who set off as young men on separate journeys into the moral and material mazes of metropolitan life. They agree to meet in twelve years' time at a spot between two ash trees which they have known from childhood. Eugene, the elder, has quarrelled with his father and leaves home penniless to seek his fortune. Richard remains at home but, after the death of his father, he too is adrift in the city. Eugene is represented as self-seeking and corrupt, while Richard stands for all that is heroic and honourable. Eugene, who is active in the narrative under a series of pseudonyms, becomes a seducer, a crooked financier, and a Member of Parliament before his inevitable fall. Richard, after many trials and tribulations, including a period of wrongful imprisonment in Newgate Gaol, becomes involved in a struggle for freedom in the Italian state of Castelcicala, and marries Isabella, daughter of the rightful ruler. When the brothers finally meet again after a series of adventures and misfortunes, Eugene is stabbed by his valet, whom he has cheated, and dies in the arms of his brother. Other characters, too, meet a fitting retribution for their lives of crime or debauchery: Anthony Tidkins, the Resurrection Man and murderer, dies in a cellar in which he has been trapped by his enemy Crankey Jem, blinded by an explosion caused in an attempt to escape; the dissolute Marquis of Holmesford expires horribly in the arms of his 'houris'.[21] The Epilogue which appeared at the conclusion of the first series makes the point clearly: "Tis done. Virtue is rewarded—Vice has received its punishment.' Of the two main protagonists, Eugene 'sleeps in an early grave', his reputation and fortune ruined, while Richard is fêted as a popular hero of the Italian republican movement, finally marries the woman he loves, and becomes rich. Thus, at one level, the text may be read as a fable in a familiar idiom of moral accountancy: virtue rewarded; vice punished.

Reynolds himself is anxious to reassure sceptics that the purpose of the work is moral. In the 'Address to the Reader' included in the Epilogue he explicitly refers to 'fugitive reports' that the mind may be shocked more than it can be improved by the story, and argues that its 'raking among the filth' is balanced by attention to the 'bright and glorious phases' of English life. The social morality asserted here is that of an implied readership which is identified with what Reynolds often calls, in a significant phrase, 'the industrious classes'. 'The problem with England', the author replied to a correspondent who had accused him of making the poor discontented, 'is that the poor are too poor, and the rich too rich'.[22] The enemies of this central morality are both traditional – by the 1840s, the body-snatcher was no longer an active threat to the poor, but remained a potent source of superstitious dread within the folk-memory; the Regency rake was a symbol of 'old corruption' – and contemporary. The enigmatic figure of Montague Greenwood, the corrupt financier who 'devotes his attention to commercial speculation of all kinds, and whose sphere is chiefly the City', represents a new threat to the traditional values of thrift, moderation, and sexual and material puritanism. In a number of episodes the 'old corruption' of the aristocracy and the new threat of the unscrupulous financier are combined. In the chapter entitled 'The Mysteries of Holmesford House' Greenwood is introduced by the Marquis of Holmesford into the life of sensual excess. In this context, too, the treatment of the young Queen Victoria is significant. In a genre of royal revelations only too familiar to modern readers, a pot-boy, Henry Holford, breaks into Buckingham Palace and, from a hiding-place beneath a sofa, overhears love-making and conversations between Albert and Victoria. When they retire, Holford creeps into the Throne Room itself and symbolically 'places himself in the seat of England's Monarch'. Although there is an account of the overheard 'secret' of inherited madness in the Hanoverian dynasty, and of the depressions into which the Queen falls as a result, the truth about the state of the poor is concealed from her by advisers who deny her access to the real facts. Thus, the Queen is ignorant rather than callous in her attitudes to the condition of the poor. Although the Queen as an individual is represented sympathetically, as are the difficulties that she has in her relations with Albert, who is denied his 'natural' right of power within the marriage because of her status as monarch, the luxury and excesses of the Court which surrounds her are attacked.

Although the overt values represented in the text are those associated with a puritan social centre-ground broadly identified with the 'industrious classes', there are few, if any, characters who are themselves within this social grouping. Richard Markham, the heroic and romanticized figure at the centre of the narrative, is the son of an affluent merchant and inherits a large mansion and estate in North London, while other characters are either depraved criminals or corrupt aristocrats. At a structural level, the text defines its social centre not by explicit assertion, but through a more complex process involving the construction of a symbolic 'other' of high- and low-life depravity. In this way, the text demonstrates its most striking paradox: an obsessive interest in the cartography of the very same social 'other' of depravity and excess that it ostensibly seeks to deny or reject. The thematic tensions between the overt puritan morality and the barely concealed fascination with, on the one hand, the detail of criminal culture in its most lurid and depraved forms and, on the other, with the excesses of aristocratic sensual indulgence provide the text with much of its characteristic energy, openness, and ambiguity. The concealed sub-text revealed by close attention to many of the illustrations and episodes exploits strategies often deployed in the Gothic convention: in a classical use of the *doppelgänger*, or double motif, Richard Markham is pursued from the commencement by his monstrous shadow, the Resurrection Man. Tidkins is stabbed, blown up, imprisoned, abandoned for dead on a plague ship, but continually returns to haunt Markham's every step. 'By God', he curses when Richard Markham thwarts him, 'I will be revenged!' The illustrations of Tidkins reinforce his association with animality and appetite, as opposed to culture and order. At one level, the relationship can only usefully be read in Freudian terms – Markham and Tidkins are two elements in a single but divided self. The numerous voyeuristic scenes which dwell on the detail of female *toilettes*, and the scenes of gratuitous violence which abound, are a further aspect of this mapping of a hidden 'other' of desire and illicit fascination. The symbolic topography of London itself, as it appears in the text, is part of this process. There are 'plague-spots' in the city – the Mint, the Holy Land, Smithfield – where violence and depravity rule. In the Holy Land[23] 'everything that is squalid, hideous, debauched and immoral makes its dwelling'. The area between Shoreditch Church and Wentworth Street, however, sinks even beneath the Holy Land: there, 'the most intense pangs of poverty, the most profligate morals, the most odious crimes, rage with the fury of a pestilence'. These districts had been ungovernable centres of vice and criminality for decades, and were regarded with fascinated fear by the respectable classes. Stedman Jones remarks that they had been 'embellished with surreal horror' by the literary imagination, although the processes of clearance were in fact well advanced by the mid-1840s.[24] The low taverns called the Dark House and the Boozing-Ken, where thieves and prostitutes gathered, are also part of this hidden culture of the 'other', as are the cellars and dungeons which recur in the text and the gipsies who occupy a 'palace' in the middle of the Holy Land. Gypsies, with their distinctive culture outside the rule of law and freedom from the constrictions of convention, were at once repellent and attractive to the settled industrious classes.

In the case of the representation of gender, too, a profound ambivalence can be identified in the text. At the overt level, gender is a clear and unproblematic category. The binary division is validated and unquestioned. Richard Markham, after a series of misunderstandings, eventually marries Isabella, daughter of the rightful ruler of the Italian state of Castelcicala. At her marriage, and earlier, she is represented through a series of highly conventional images. She is a paradigm of chastity and purity: eyes like stars, teeth of ivory, dress of virgin white. At her marriage to Richard Markham, 'there was an air of purest chastity in her appearance which showed how nearly allied her heart was to the guilelessness of angels'. The images associated with her are static and literary; she is denied activity in the text and has no being outside her place as Richard's consort. After marriage, she finds complete fulfilment in husband and children.

However, at another level, the text recognizes the flawed and problematic nature of these social definitions of gender: the first number of the novel is illustrated by a striking engraving showing a young woman in the clothing of a youth, posing dramatically against a background of city scenes. In the engraving illustrating the Boudoir episode, the same woman is represented surrounded by a mixture of male and female clothing, giving the curious impression to the observer that 'this elegant boudoir was occupied by a man of strangely feminine tastes, or a woman of extraordinary masculine ones'. The trajectory followed by Ellen Monroe provides a further example of this exploration of gender.[25] She is the daughter of the man who acts as Richard Markham's guardian after the death of his father. While Richard is in prison, Mr Monroe takes the advice of the crooked financier, Greenwood, and loses his own money and Richard's inheritance. To escape from poverty, Ellen takes employment as a seamstress and, when that fails, determines to sell her remaining asset – physical beauty – on the market. She enters the burgeoning world of Victorian popular commercial entertainment and obtains positions as a mesmerist's assistant, a model for a sculptor, a photographer, an artist, a figurante or dancer and, finally, as an actress. She has a secret illegitimate child by Greenwood, and later forces him to marry her by threatening to reveal the truth about his activities. Although these events are conventionally read as moral decline, at another level she is celebrated as a figure of remarkable energy and enterprise, who learns to exploit the new commercial possibilities of the city and is unafraid of its challenges. In a remarkable passage in the chapter entitled 'Female Courage', Ellen purchases male clothing from a shop in Holywell Street, a locality notorious for its connections with the pornographic book trade, and walks the streets of London disguised as a man. In these ways, the socially dominant accounts of gender divisions as natural and determining are undercut by the sub-text of this novel, which actually derives much of its energy from an exploration of the tension between the surface signs of gender and the more complex and contradictory psychological realities which the signs may conceal.

Many of the gaps, inconsistencies, silences, and ambiguities identified above are ultimately related to questions of representation and form. At the level of moral fable, the text works in an established convention in which a powerful narrative rhetoric carries the official moralized 'reading' of the action as 'improving'. The narrative voice is constantly interpolated into the plot as comment and judgement and also appears in the structuring patterns of reward and punishment which provide a formal resolution to the social and political conflicts articulated in the text. At the surface level, this pressure to conventional resolution – rewarding the honourable and punishing the reprobate – meets the needs of the reader for orderly conclusion, psychological consolation, and reassurance. However, the text itself is in fact far less coherent and unified at a structural and linguistic level than reference to the 'official' narrative voice alone might suggest.

It is possible to identify a number of distinct generic influences which surface at the level of language and produce the characteristically fragmented series of 'voices' which constitute the text. The interpolated first-person 'histories' of low-life characters (the 'Resurrection Man's History', 'The Rattlesnake's History') are an attempt to record directly in fiction lives which are usually hidden;[26] the statistical footnotes and references to government reports that are incorporated into the text belong to a wider discourse in which 'facts' are used to validate social analysis; the use of motifs from the Gothic convention and from popular melodrama, and the incorporation of material from other genres – poetry, letters, inscriptions, graphic art – provide a further indication of the fractures and fissures which characterize the linguistic surfaces of this text. Syntactical and stylistic features – the short sentences placed on a single line, the repetition of key phrases, the use of simple diagrams, the double-column format itself – undercut the power of the controlling narrative voice and create a sub-text which is fragmented and elliptical in its effect. The obsessive and recurrent narrative interest in masks, disguises, mirrors, portraits, pseudonyms, cross-dressing and false identities suggests that a further powerful sub-text of the fiction is concerned with the relations of surface appearance and psychological identity. In *The Mysteries of London*, surfaces conceal more than they reveal.

Although the novel can be read simply as an enduring monument to the commercial acumen of author and publisher, more remarkable for its shrewd marketing and its cynical insights into the formations of popular consciousness than for its purely literary attainments, it has as its themes, in common with *Bleak House* and other novels of the period, a new awareness of urban crisis and class alienation. Paradoxically, its very lack of literary sophistication, the fragmentation of its literary strategies and its openness to interpretation may allow the text to represent cultural relations and urban life at a historical moment of crisis in ways closed to more complex and orderly writing. At the heart of the novel is a representation of the metropolis itself, seen as a 'mystery' in need of a solution. The metaphorical structures outlined earlier – the moral cartography of centre and 'other', and the symbolic topography of surfaces and depths – are both part of this fictional attempt to 'read' the city in new ways. Working-class readers of the period could also purchase for a penny the weekly numbers of Charles Knight's *London* (5 vols., 1841–6), which offered a more technological and celebratory account of the city as productive and socially dynamic. As Asa Briggs remarks, 'the world of Victorian cities was fragmented, intricate, eclectic, messy, and no single approach to their understanding provides us with all the right questions and answers.'[27] This characterization of the Victorian city can readily be applied, without amendment, to the complexities and confusions of *The Mysteries of London*.

Notes

1. *Reynolds's Miscellany* II (26), 15 May 1847, p. 159.
2. *London Journal* I (12), 24 May 1845, p. 192 (advertisement for *The Mysteries of London*), states that the original intention had been to publish the novel in one-shilling monthly parts, but author and publisher decided instead to 'render it more accessible to all classes' by adopting the weekly penny-number format.
3. The double-column format was a feature of cheap magazine and newspaper publication. While it is not appropriate to reproduce this aspect of the layout here, other visual characteristics of the form have been retained.

INTRODUCTION   xxiii

4. *Reynolds's Miscellany* I (13), 30 January 1847, p. 200. Sue's *Mystères de Paris*, the novel which began the 'urban mysteries' cult, was first published in a Paris newspaper, *Le Journal de Débats*, from June 1842 to October 1843. English translations rapidly followed in 1844 (Harper Brothers, New York), and 1845 (Chapman and Hall, London). By 1847, most major European and American cities had a 'mysteries' novel to their name.
5. The 'mysteries' cult took some odd forms: L. Wright, *Clean and Decent* (London, 1960), p. 121, illustrates a contemporary commode consisting of four dummy volumes labelled 'Mysteries of Paris'.
6. A. Humpherys, 'Generic strands and urban twists', *Victorian Studies* 34 (4), Summer 1991, pp. 463–72.
7. R. Maxwell, *The Mysteries of Paris and London* (University of Virginia Press, 1992).
8. As late as July 1868, an anonymous contributor to the *Bookseller* wrote a long article entitled 'Mischievious Literature' attacking Reynolds, in particular, for exploitation of the sensational and exciting topics of love and seduction.
9. Little useful biographical information about Vickers, Stiff or Dicks survives. F. Boase, *Modern Biographies* (London, 1913) contains short entries for each.
10. R. K. Engen, *A Dictionary of Victorian Wood Engravers* (London, 1986), has a full bibliography covering the craft and its practitioners. G. Wakeman, *Victorian Book Illustration* (1973), has technical information.
11. *Reynolds's Miscellany* III (60), 1 September 1849, carried a detailed biography of Louis Kossuth, the 'master-spirit' of the 1848 Hungarian Revolution. The Italian political exile Mazzini was in London from 1837, and may well have met Reynolds.
12. The *Northern Star*, 18 March 1848. For a fierce attack on Reynolds's personal and political integrity, see Thomas Clark, *A Letter to G. W. M. Reynolds* (T. Clark, London, 1850). This public letter provides much detail concerning Reynolds's finances and the sales of his books, as revealed at his several bankruptcy hearings, and attacks him as 'an unprincipled and mountebank demagogue' who profits from indecent literature and damages the good name of Chartism. Clark was secretary to the National Charter League in 1850.
13. P. Joyce, *Visions of the People* (Cambridge, 1991), p. 66.
14. *Reynolds's Miscellany* I (13), 30 January 1847, p. 199.
15. H. Mayhew, *London Labour and the London Poor* (London, 1861–2).
16. J. G. Ginswick (ed.), *Labour and the Poor in England and Wales 1849–1851*, (London, 1983), Vol. 1, pp. 61–2.
17. Evidence is given by Abel Heywood to the Parlimentary Select Committee on Newspaper Stamps, 30 May 1851 (reprinted in Irish University Press Nineteeth-Century Parlimentary Papers, *Newspapers*, Vol. 1, pp. 371–89 (original reference, sess. 1851 (558)).
18. J. W. Ross, 'The influence of cheap literature', *London Journal* I, 18 April 1845, p. 115. This important article defends the new form of 'economic literature', arguing that it brings the benefits of imagination into the poorest homes in the land.
19. Mayhew, *London Labour and the London Poor*, Vol. I, p. 25.
20. *Days of Hogarth* was available in the same format and binding as *The Mysteries of London*.
21. The Marquis of Hertford, a notorious rake, had recently died after a fit of debauchery with a group of prostitutes.

22. G. W. M. Reynolds, 'Letter to the industrious classes', *Reynolds's Miscellany* I (13), 30 January 1847, p. 199.
23. The 'Holy Land' was part of the great rookery of St Giles. It had been a criminal refuge for centuries, and was interwoven with an impenetrable network of tunnels, back-alleys, trap-doors and secret passages which provided a defence against the forces of law.
24. G. Stedman Jones, *Outcast London* (London, 1971), p. 179.
25. Some indication of the interest of this figure can be found in the existence of an American piracy which extracted and published the episodes, in which she appeared under the title of *Ellen Monroe*.
26. Reynolds seems to have undertaken some original research into criminal culture and language for these purposes. His techniques may have had some influence on the later work of Henry Mayhew.
27. A. Briggs, 'The Human Aggregate', in H. G. Dyos and M. Wolff (eds), *The Victorian City* (London, 1973), p. 83.

Bibliography

There is as yet no full account of Reynolds's life and career, nor any completely satisfactory bibliography of his work. A brief outline of events in his life is included in *The Dictionary of Labour Biography* (London: 1976), pp. 146–51, and E. F. Bleiler's edition of Reynolds's *Wagner the Wehrwolf* (New York: 1975) contains a detailed bibliography and some biographical background. Much general information concerning the day-to-day publishing history of *The Mysteries of London* can be obtained from advertisements and correspondence columns in the *London Journal* and *Reynolds's Miscellany*. The recent articles by Anne Humpherys contain the most serious and sustained attempts to come to terms with the problems of interpretation posed by this text. Richard Maxwell's *The Mysteries of Paris and London* is an imaginative analysis of the 'Urban Mystery' sub-genre which includes discussion of Reynolds as well as Sue, Dickens, Hugo and Ainsworth. With these exceptions, there is little critical material which focuses directly on *The Mysteries of London*, although cultural historians often refer generally to its importance. The following books and articles include some discussion of the novel or its socio-historical background: the best source of general information about the period is still Louis James's pioneering *Fiction for the Working Man, 1830–50*, cited below.

Books

R. D. Altick, *The English Common Reader* (Chicago: 1957).

C. Baldick, *In Frankenstein's Shadow: Myth, Monstrosity, and Nineteenth-Century Writing* (Clarendon Press, Oxford: 1987).

M. Dalziel, *Popular Fiction a Hundred Years Ago* (London: 1958).

U. Eco, *The Rise of The Reader: Explorations in the Semiotics of Texts* (Bloomington University Press: 1979); see, in particular, the chapter on Eugene Sue, *The Mysteries of Paris*.

R. K. Engen, *Dictionary of Victorian Wood Engravers* (London: 1985), includes brief biographical details of engravers and a bibliography.

C. Gallagher, *The Industrial Reformation of English Fiction, 1832–1867* (University of Chicago Press, Chicago: 1985).

G. Himmelfarb, *The Idea of Poverty* (Faber and Faber, London: 1984), Chapter XVIII, 'The Gothic Poor'.

K. Hollingworth, *The Newgate Novel, 1830–1847* (Wayne State University Press, Detroit, 1963).

A. Humpherys, *Travels into the Poor Man's Country* (University of Georgia Press, Athens: 1977).

L. James, *Fiction for the Working Man, 1830–1850* (Oxford University Press, London: 1963). This pioneering study includes a comprehensive bibliography of secondary sources and contemporary responses to Reynolds.

L. James, *Print and the People, 1819–1851* (Allen Lane, London: 1976).

R. Maxwell, *The Mysteries of Paris and London* (Virginia University Press, Virginia: 1992).

R. Richardson, *Death, Dissection and the Destitute* (Routledge and Kegan Paul, London: 1988).

J. Shattock and M. Wolff (eds), *The Victorian Periodical Press: Samplings and Soundings* (Leicester University Press, Leicester: 1982).

G. Wakeman, *Victorian Book Illustration* (David and Charles, Newton Abbot, 1973). Includes a wealth of technical information about the process of wood-engraving.

R. K. Webb, *The British Working Class Reader, 1790–1848* (Allen & Unwin Ltd, London: 1955).

S. A. Williams, *The Rich Man and the Diseased Poor in Early Victorian Literature* (London, 1987).

Articles

V. Berridge, 'Popular Sunday Papers and Mid-Victorian Society', in *Newspaper History from the Seventeeth Century to the Present Day*, ed. G. Boyce, J. Curran, P. Wingate (London, 1978).

D. S. Burt, 'A Victorian gothic: G. W. M. Reynolds's *The Mysteries of London*', *New York Literary Forum*, 7 (1980), pp. 141–58.

Abel Heywood, jun., 'Newspapers and periodicals: their circulation in Manchester', *Papers of the Manchester Literary Club* (1876), pp. 42–57. This account of the history of the local press by the son of Abel Heywood, who was a major distributor of *The Mysteries of London* in the 1840s, gives more information about the market for cheap popular fiction in nineteenth-century Lancashire.

A. Humpherys, 'G. W. M. Reynolds: Popular Literature and Popular Politics', *Victorian Periodicals Review* 16 (1983), pp. 79–89.

A. Humpherys, 'The Geometry of the modern city: G. W. M. Reynolds and *The Mysteries of London*', *Browning Institute Studies* 11 (1983), pp. 69–80.

A. Humpherys, 'Generic Strands and Urban Twists: The Victorian Mysteries Novel', *Victorian Studies* 34 (4) (Summer 1991), pp. 463–72.

J. V. B. S. Hunter, 'George Reynolds', *Book Handbook* 4 (1947), pp. 225–36.

L. James, 'The view from Brick Lane: contrasting perspectives in working-class and middle-class fiction of the early Victorian period', *Yearbook of English Studies* 11 (1981), pp. 87–101.

R. C. Maxwell, 'G. W. M. Reynolds, Dickens, and *The Mysteries of London*', *Nineteenth Century Fiction* 32 (1977), pp. 185–213.

V. McKendry, '*The Illustrated London News* and the invention of tradition', *Victorian Periodicals Review* 27 (1) (1994), pp. 1–23.

J. D. Nodal, 'Newspapers and Periodicals: their circulation in Manchester', *Papers of the Manchester Literary Club* (1875).

J. Springall, '"A life story for the people?" Edwin J. Brett and the London "Low-Life" Penny Dreadfuls of the 1860s', *Victorian Studies* 33 (2) (Winter 1990), pp. 223–46.

S. J. Tindall, 'Victorian popular fiction and the condition of England question', *Publications of the Mississippi Philological Assocation* (1987), pp. 154–63.

THE

MYSTERIES OF LONDON.

BY

GEORGE W. M. REYNOLDS.

WITH NUMEROUS ILLUSTRATIONS.

VOLUME I.

[In the Prologue Reynolds identifies the broad patterns which structure the narrative of *The Mysteries of London*. Within the context of an exploration of the extraordinary social contrasts characteristic of early nineteenth-century London – the extremes of poverty and wealth – two young men set out on trajectories which first separate them, and at the conclusion bring them together in a melodramatic denouement. One brother, Richard Markham, follows the path of 'rectitude and virtue' and the other, Eugene Markham, that of 'chicanery, dissipation, and voluptuousness'. The use of short, staccato sentences and simple diagrams illustrating the ideas is derived in part from the model of French popular serial fiction.]

PROLOGUE.

BETWEEN the 10th and 13th centuries Civilisation withdrew from Egypt and Syria, rested for a little space at Constantinople, and then passed away to the western climes of Europe.

From that period these climes have been the grand laboratory in which Civilisation has wrought out refinement in every art and every science, and whence it has diffused its benefits over the earth. It has taught commerce to plough the waves of every sea with the adventurous keel; it has enabled handfuls of disciplined warriors to subdue the mighty armaments of oriental princes; and its daring guns have planted its banners amidst the eternal ice of the poles. It has cut down the primitive forests of America; carried trade into the interior of Africa; annihilated time and distance by the aid of steam; and now contemplates how to force a passage through Suez and Panama.

The bounties of Civilisation are at present almost everywhere recognised.

Nevertheless, for centuries has Civilisation established, and for centuries will it maintain, its headquarters in the great cities of Western Europe: and with Civilisation does Vice go hand-in-hand.

Amongst these cities there is one in which contrasts of a strange nature exist. The most unbounded wealth is the neighbour of the most hideous poverty; the most gorgeous pomp is placed in strong relief by the most deplorable squalor; the most seducing luxury is only separated by a narrow wall from the most appalling misery.

The crumbs which fall from the tables of the rich would appear delicious viands to starving millions; and yet those millions obtain them not!

In that city there are in all districts five prominent buildings: the church, in which the pious pray; the gin-palace, to which the wretched poor resort to drown their sorrows; the pawnbroker's, where miserable creatures pledge their raiment, and their children's raiment, even unto the last rag, to obtain the means of purchasing food, and—alas! too often—intoxicating drink; the prison, where the victims of a vitiated condition of society expiate the crimes to which they have been driven by starvation and despair; and the workhouse, to which the destitute, the aged, and the friendless hasten to lay down their aching heads—and die!

And, congregated together in one district of this city, is an assemblage of palaces, whence emanate by night the delicious sounds of music; within whose walls the foot treads upon rich carpets; whose sideboards are covered with plate; whose cellars contain the choicest nectar of the temperate and torrid zones; and whose inmates recline beneath velvet canopies, feast at each meal upon the collated produce of four worlds, and scarcely have to breathe a wish before they find it gratified.

Alas! how appalling are these contrasts!

And, as if to hide its infamy from the face of heaven, this city wears upon its brow an everlasting cloud, which even the fresh fan of the morning fails to disperse for a single hour each day!

And in one delicious spot of that mighty city—whose thousand towers point upwards, from horizon to horizon, as an index of its boundless magnitude—stands the dwelling of one before whom all knees bow, and towards whose royal footstool none dares approach save with downcast eyes and subdued voice. The entire world showers its bounties upon the head of that favoured mortal; a nation of millions does homage to the throne whereon that being is exalted. The dominion of this personage so supremely blest extends over an empire on which the sun never sets—an empire greater than Genghis Khan achieved or Mohammed conquered.

This is the parent of a mighty nation; and yet around that parent's seat the children crave for bread!

Women press their little ones to their dried-up breasts in the agonies of despair; young delicate creatures waste their energies in toil from the dawn of day till long past the hour of midnight, perpetuating their unavailing labour from the hour of the brilliant sun to that when the dim candle sheds its light around the attic's naked walls; and even the very pavement groans beneath the weight of grief which the poor are doomed to drag over the rough places of this city of sad contrasts.

For in this city the daughter of the peer is nursed in enjoyments, and passes through an uninterrupted avenue of felicity from the cradle to the tomb; while the daughter of poverty opens her eyes at her birth upon destitution in all its most appalling shapes, and at length sells her virtue for a loaf of bread.

There are but two words known in the moral alphabet of this great city; for all virtues are summed up in the one, and all vices in the other: and those words are

WEALTH. | POVERTY.

Crime is abundant in this city: the lazarhouse, the prison, the brothel, and the dark alley, are rife with all kinds of enormity; in the same way as the palace, the mansion, the clubhouse, the parliament, and the parsonage, are each and all characterised by their different degrees and shades of vice. But wherefore specify crime and vice by their real names, since in this city of which we speak they are absorbed in the multi-significant words—WEALTH and POVERTY?

Crimes borrow their comparative shade of enormity from the people who perpetrate them: thus is it that the wealthy may commit all social offences with impunity; while the poor are cast into dungeons and coerced with chains, for only following at a humble distance in the pathway of their lordly precedents.

From this city of strange contrasts branch off two roads, leading to two points totally distinct the one from the other.

One winds its tortuous way through all the noisome dens of crime, chicanery, dissipation, and voluptuousness: the other meanders amidst rugged rocks and wearisome acclivities, it is true, but on the wayside are the resting-places of rectitude and virtue.

Along those roads two youths are journeying.

They have started from the same point; but one pursues the former path, and the other the latter.

Both come from the city of fearful contrasts; and both follow the wheels of fortune in different directions.

Where is that city of fearful contrasts?

Who are those youths that have thus entered upon paths so opposite the one to the other?

And to what destinies do those separate roads conduct them?

[Chapters I, II and III, with their Gothic backdrop of dramatic storm, and their exploitation of the classic theme of innocence at risk in the great metropolis, set the scene for the action to follow. Many standard popular motifs – the darkened house, the ominous trap-door in the floor, the ambiguities of sexual identity, the nocturnal setting – are deployed. The striking illustration of a 'youth' of feminine aspect self-consciously posing among scenes of poverty in the city, with the dome of St Paul's in the background, provides an early indication to the reader of the importance of the sub-textual exploration of gender boundaries so characteristic of this narrative. The opening also echoes that of Sue's *Mysteries of Paris*.]

CHAPTER I.
THE OLD HOUSE IN SMITHFIELD.

OUR narrative opens at the commencement of July, 1831.

The night was dark and stormy. The sun had set behind huge piles of dingy purple clouds, which, after losing the golden hue with which they were for awhile tinged, became sombre and menacing. The blue portions of the sky that here and there had appeared before the sunset, were now rapidly covered over with those murky clouds which are the hiding places of the storm, and which seemed to roll themselves together in dense and compact masses, ere they commenced the elemental war.

In the same manner do the earthly squadrons of cavalry and mighty columns of infantry form themselves into one collected armament, that the power of their onslaught may be the more terrific and irresistible.

That canopy of dark and threatening clouds was formed over London; and a stifling heat, which there was not a breath of wind to allay or mitigate, pervaded the streets of the great metropolis.

Everything portended an awful storm.

In the palace of the peer and the hovel of the artisan the windows were thrown up; and at many, both men and women stood to contemplate the scene—timid children crowding behind them.

The heat became more and more oppressive.

At length large drops of rain fell, at intervals of two or three inches apart, upon the pavement.

And then a flash of lightning, like the forked tongue of one of those fiery serpents of which we read in oriental tales of magic and enchantment, darted forth from the black clouds overhead.

At an interval of a few seconds the roar of the thunder, reverberating through the arches of heaven—now sinking, now exalting its fearful tone, like the iron wheels of a chariot rolled over a road with patches of uneven pavement here and there—stunned every ear, and struck terror into many a heart—the innocent as well as the guilty.

It died away, like the chariot, in the distance; and then all was solemnly still.

The interval of silence which succeeds the protracted thunder clap is appalling in the extreme.

A little while—and again the lightening illuminated the entire vault above: and again the thunder, in unequal tones,—amongst which was one resembling the rattling of many vast iron bars together,—awoke every echo of the metropolis from north to south, and from east to west.

This time the dread interval of silence was suddenly interrupted by the torrents of rain that now deluged the streets.

There was not a breath of air; and the rain fell as perpendicularly straight as a line. But with it came a sense of freshness and of a pure atmosphere, which formed an agreeable and cheering contrast to the previously suffocating heat. It was like the spring of the oasis to the wanderer in the burning desert.

But still the lightening played, and the thunder rolled, above.

At the first explosion of the storm, amidst the thousands of men and women and children, who were seen hastening hither and thither, in all directions, as if they were flying from the plague, was one person on whose exterior none could gaze without being inspired with a mingled sentiment of admiration and interest.

He was a youth, apparently not more than sixteen years of age, although taller than boys usually are at that period of life. But the tenderness of his years was divined by the extreme effeminacy and juvenile loveliness of his countenance, which was as fair and delicate as that of a young girl. His long, luxuriant hair, of a beautiful light chestnut colour, and here and there borrowing dark shades from the frequent undulations in which it rolled, flowed not only over the collar of his closely-buttoned blue frock coat, but also upon his shoulders. Its extreme profusion, and the singular manner in which he wore it, were, however, partially concealed by the breadth of the brim of his hat, that was placed as it were entirely upon the back of his head, and, being thus thrown off his countenance, revealed the high, intelligent, and polished forehead above which that rich hair was carefully parted.

His frock coat, which was single-breasted, and buttoned up to the throat, set off his symmetrical and elegant figure to the greatest advantage. His shoulders were broad, but were characterised by that fine fall or slope which is so much admired in the opposite sex. He wore spurs upon the heels of his diminutive polished boots; and in his hand he carried a light riding-whip. But he was upon foot and alone; and, when the first flash of lightning dazzled his expressive hazel eyes, he was hastily traversing the foul and filthy arena of Smithfield-market.

An imagination poetically inspired would suppose a similitude of a beautiful flower upon a fetid manure heap.

He cast a glance, which may almost be termed one of affright, around; and his cheek became flushed. He had evidently lost his way, and was uncertain where to obtain an asylum against the coming storm.

The thunder burst above his head; and a momentary shudder passed over his frame. He accosted a man to inquire his way; but the answer he received was rude, and associated with a ribald joke.

He had not courage to demand a second time the information he sought; but, with a species of haughty disdain at the threatening storm, and a proud reliance upon himself, proceeded onwards at random.

[...]

To one so young, so delicate, and so frank in appearance, the mere fact of losing his way by night in a disgusting neighbourhood, during an impending storm, and insulted by a low-life ruffian, was not the mere trifle which it would have been considered by the hardy and experienced man of the world.

Not a public conveyance was to be seen; and the doors of all the houses around appeared inhospitably closed: and every moment it seemed to grow darker.

Accident conducted the interesting young stranger into that labyrinth of narrow and dirty streets which lies in the immediate vicinity of the north-western angle of Smithfield-market.

It was in this horrible neighbourhood that the youth was now wandering. He was evidently shocked at the idea that human beings could dwell in such fetid and unwholesome dens; for he gazed with wonder, disgust, and alarm upon the houses on either side. It seemed as if he had never beheld till now a labyrinth of dwellings whose very aspect appeared to speak of hideous poverty and fearful crime.

Meantime the lightning flashed, and the thunder rolled; and at length the rain poured down in torrents. Obeying a mechanical impulse, the youth rushed up the steps of a house at the end of one of those dark, narrow, and dirty streets the ominous appearance of which was every now and then revealed to him by a light streaming from a narrow window, or the glare of the lightning. The framework of the door projected somewhat, and appeared to offer a partial protection from the rain. The youth drew as closely up to it as possible; but to his surprise it yielded behind him, and burst open. With difficulty he saved himself from falling backwards into the passage with which the door communicated.

Having recovered from the sudden alarm with which this incident had inspired him, his next sentiment was one of pleasure to think that he had thus found a more secure asylum against the tempest. He, however, felt wearied— desperately wearied; and his was not a frame calculated to bear up against the oppressive and crushing feeling of fatigue. He determined to penetrate, amidst the profound darkness by which he was surrounded, into the dwelling; thinking that if there were any inmates they would not refuse him the accommodation of a chair; and if there were none, he might find a seat upon the staircase.

He advanced along the passage, and groped about. His hand encountered the lock of a door: he opened it, and entered a room. All was dark as pitch. At that moment a flash of lightning, more than usually vivid and prolonged, illuminated the entire scene. The glance which he cast around was as rapid as the glare which made objects visible to him for a few moments. He was in a room entirely empty; but in the middle of the floor—only three feet from the spot where he stood—there was a large square of jet blackness.

The lightning passed away: utter darkness again surrounded him; and he was unable to ascertain what that black square, so well defined and apparent upon the dirty floor, could be.

An indescribable sensation of fear crept over him; and the perspiration broke out upon his forehead in large drops. His knees bent beneath him; and, retreating a few steps, he leaned against the door-posts for support.

He was alone—in an uninhabited house, in the midst of a horrible neighbourhood; and all the fearful tales of midnight murders which he had ever heard or read, rushed to his memory: then, by a strange but natural freak of the fancy, those appalling deeds of blood and crime were suddenly associated with that incomprehensible but ominous black square upon the floor.

He was in the midst of this terrible waking dream—this more than ideal nightmare—when hasty steps approached the front door from the street; and, without stopping, entered the passage. The youth crept silently towards the farther end, the perspiration oozing from every pore. He felt the staircase with his hands; the footsteps advanced; and, light as the fawn, he hurried up the stairs. So noiseless were his motions, that his presence was not noticed by the new comers, who in their turns also ascended the staircase.

The youth reached a landing, and hastily felt for the doors of the rooms with which it communicated. In another moment he was in a chamber, at the back part of the house. He closed the door, and placed himself against it with all his strength—forgetful, poor youth! that his fragile form was unavailing, with all its power, against even the single arm of a man of only ordinary strength.

Meanwhile the new-comers ascended the stairs.

CHAPTER II.
THE MYSTERIES OF THE OLD HOUSE.

FORTUNATELY for the interesting young stranger, the individuals who had just entered the house did not attempt the door of the room in which he had taken refuge. They proceeded straight—and with a steadiness which seemed to indicate that they knew the locality well—to the front chamber upon the same floor.

In a few moments there was a sharp grating noise along the wall; and then a light suddenly shone into the room where the young stranger was concealed. He cast a terrified glance around, and beheld a small square window in the wall, which separated the two apartments. It was about five feet from the floor—a height which permitted the youth to avail himself of it, in order to reconnoitre the proceedings in the next room.

By means of a candle which had been lighted by the aid of a lucifer-match, and which stood upon a dirty deal table, the young stranger beheld two men, whose outward appearance did not serve to banish his alarm. They were dressed like operatives of the most humble class. One wore a gabardine and coarse leather gaiters, with laced-up boots; the other had on a fustian shooting-jacket and long corduroy trousers. They were both dirty and unshaven. The one with the shooting-jacket had a profusion of hair about his face, but which was evidently not well acquainted with a comb: the other wore no whiskers, but his beard was of three or four days' growth. Both were powerful, thick-set, and muscular men; and the expression of their countenances was dogged, determined, and ferocious.

The room to which they had betaken themselves was cold, gloomy, and dilapidated. It was furnished with the deal table before mentioned, and three old crazy chairs, upon two of which the men now seated themselves. But they were so placed that they commanded, their door being open, a full view of the landing-place; and thus the youthful stranger deemed it impolitic to attempt to take his departure for the moment.

"Now, Bill, out with the bingo," said the man in the gabardine to his companion.

"Oh! you're always for the lush, you are, Dick," answered the latter in a surly tone, producing at the same time a bottle of liquor from the capacious pocket of his fustian coat. "But I wonder how the devil it is that Crankey Jem ain't come yet. Who the deuce could have left that infernal door open?"

"Jem or some of the other blades must have been here and left it so. It don't matter; it lulls suspicion."

"Well, let's make the reglars all square," resumed the man called Bill, after a moment's pause; "we'll then booze a bit, and talk over this here new job of our'n."

[...]

The alarm of the poor youth in the next chamber, as he contemplated these extraordinary proceedings, may be better conceived than depicted. His common sense told him that he was in a den of lawless thieves—perhaps murderers; in a house abounding with the secret means of concealing every kind of infamy. His eye wandered away from the little window that had enabled him to observe the above-described proceedings, and glanced fearfully around the room in which he was concealed. He almost expected to see the very floor open beneath his feet. He looked down mechanically as this idea flitted through his imagination; and to his horror and dismay he beheld a trap-door in the floor. There was no mistaking it: there it was—about three feet long and two broad, and a little sunken beneath the level of its framework.

Near the edge of the trap-door lay an object which also attracted the youth's attention and added to his fears. It was a knife with a long blade pointed like a dagger. About three inches of this blade was covered with a peculiar rust: the youth shuddered; could it be human blood that had stained that instrument of death?

[The youth overhears the criminals planning a robbery at the house of a Mr. Markham, a 'swell' with two sons, but is accidentally seen by the criminals through a small window.]

The man stopped short, turned ghastly pale, and fell back stupified and speechless in his chair. His pipe dropped from between his fingers, and broke to pieces upon the floor.

"What the devil's the matter now?" demanded his companion, casting an anxious glance around.

"There! there! don't you see—," gasped the terrified ruffian, pointing towards the little window looking into the next room.

"It's only some d—d gammon of Crankey Jem," ejaculated Dick, who was more courageous in such matters than his companion. "I'll deuced soon put that to rights!"

Seizing the candle, he was hurrying towards the door, when his comrade rushed after him, crying, "No—I won't be left in the dark! I can't bear it! Damme, if you go, I'll go with you!"

The two villains accordingly proceeded together into the next room.

CHAPTER III.
THE TRAP-DOOR.

THE youthful stranger had listened with ineffable surprise and horror to the conversation of the two ruffians. His nerves had been worked up by all the circumstances of the evening to a tone bordering upon madness—to that pitch, indeed, when it appeared as if there were no alternative left save to fall upon the floor and yield to the *delirium tremens* of violent emotions.

He had restrained his feelings while he heard the burglary at Mr. Markham's dwelling coolly planned and settled; but when the discourse of those two monsters in human shape developed to his imagination all the horrors of the fearful place in which he had sought an asylum,—when he heard that he was actually standing upon the very verge of that staircase down which innumerable victims had been hurled to the depths of the slimy ditch beneath, —and when he thought how probable it was that his bones were doomed to whiten in the dark and hidden caverns below, along with the remains of other human beings who had been barbarously murdered in cold blood,—reason appeared to forsake him. A cold sweat broke forth all over him; and he seemed about to faint under the impression of a hideous nightmare.

He threw his hat upon the floor—for he felt the want of air. That proud forehead, that beautiful countenance were distorted with indescribable horror; and an ashy pallor spread itself over his features.

Death, in all its most hideous forms, appeared to follow—to surround—to hem him in. There was no escape: a trap-door here—a well, communicating with the ditch, there—or else the dagger;—no matter in what shape—still Death was before him—behind him—above him—below him—on every side of him.

It was horrible—most horrible!

Then was it that a sudden thought flashes across his brain: he resolved to attempt a desperate effort to escape. He summoned all his courage to his aid, and opened the door so cautiously that, though the hinges were old and rusted, they did not creak.

The crisis was now at hand. If he could clear the landing unperceived, he was safe. It was true that, seen or unseen, he might succeed in escaping from the house by means of his superior agility and nimbleness; but he reflected that these men would capture him again, in a few minutes, in the midst of a labyrinth of streets with which he was utterly unacquainted, but which they knew so well. He remembered that he had overheard their secrets and witnessed their mysterious modes of concealment; and that, should he fall into their power, death must inevitably await him.

These ideas crossed his brain in a moment, and convinced him of the necessity of prudence and extreme caution. He must leave the house unperceived, and dare the pitiless storm and pelting rain; for the tempest still raged without.

He once more approached the window to ascertain if there were any chance of stealing across the landing-place unseen. Unfortunately he drew too near the window: the light of the candle fell full upon his countenance, which horror and alarm had rendered deadly pale and fearfully convulsed.

It was at this moment that the ruffian, in the midst of his unholy vaunts, had caught sight of that human face—white as a sheet—and with eyes fixed upon him with a glare which his imagination rendered stony and unearthly.

The youth saw that he was discovered; and a full sense of the desperate peril which hung over him, rushed to his mind. He turned, and endeavoured to fly away from the fatal spot; but, as imagination frequently fetters the limbs in a nightmare, and involves the sleeper in danger from which he vainly attempts to run, so did his legs now refuse to perform their office.

His brain whirled—his eyes grew dim: he grasped at the wall to save himself from falling—but his senses were deserting him—and he sank fainting upon the floor.

He awoke from the trance into which he had fallen, and became aware that he was being moved along. Almost at the same instant his eyes fell upon the sinister countenance of Dick, who was carrying him by the feet. The other ruffian was supporting his head.

They were lifting him down the staircase, upon the top step of which the candle was standing.

All the incidents of the evening immediately returned to the memory of the wretched boy, who now only too well comprehended the desperate perils that surrounded him.

The bottom of the staircase was reached: the villains deposited their burden for a moment in the passage, while Dick retraced his steps to fetch down the candle.

And then a horrible conflict of feelings and inclinations took place in the bosom of the unhappy youth. He shut his eyes; and for an instant debating within himself whether he should remain silent or cry out. He dreamt of immediate—instantaneous death; and yet he thought that he was young to die—oh! so young—and that men could not be such barbarians—

But when the two ruffians stooped down to take him up again, fear surmounted all other sentiments, feelings, and inclinations; and his deep—his profound—his heartfelt agony was expressed in one long, loud, and piercing shriek!

And then a fearful scene took place.

The two villains carried the youth into the front room upon the ground-floor, and laid him down for a moment.

It was the same room to which he had first found his way upon entering that house.

It was the room in which, by the glare of the evanescent lightning, he had seen that black square upon the dirty floor.

For a few instants all was dark. At length the candle was brought by the man in the fustian coat.

The youth glanced wildly around him, and speedily recognised that room.

He remembered how deep a sensation of horror seized him when that black square upon the floor first caught his eyes.

He raised himself upon his left arm, and once more looked around.

Great God! was it possible?

That ominous blackness—that sinister square was the mouth of a yawning gulf, the trap-door of which was raised.

A fetid smell rose from the depths below, and the gurgling of a current was faintly heard.

The dread truth was in a moment made apparent to that unhappy boy—much more quickly than it occupies to relate or read. He started from his supine posture, and fell upon his knees at the feet of those merciless villains who had borne him thither.

"Mercy, mercy! I implore you! Oh! do not devote me to so horrible a death! Do not—*do not murder me*!"

"Hold your noisy tongue, you fool," ejaculated Bill, brutally. "You have heard and seen too much for our safety; we can't do otherwise."

"No, certainly not," added Dick. "You are now as fly to the fakement as any one of us."

"Spare me, spare me, and I will never betray you! Oh! do not send me out of this world, so young—so very young! I have money, I have wealth, I am rich, and I will give you all I possess!" ejaculated the agonized youth; his countenance wearing an expression of horrible despair.

"Come; here's enough. Bill, lend a hand!" and Dick seized the boy by one arm, while his companion took a firm hold of the other.

"Mercy, mercy!" shrieked the youth, struggling violently; but struggling vainly. "You will repent when you know—I am not what I—"

He said no more: his last words were uttered over the mouth of the chasm ere the ruffians loosened their hold;—and then he fell.

The trap-door was closed violently over the aperture, and drowned the scream of agony which burst from his lips.

The two murderers then retraced their steps to the apartment on the first floor.

★   ★   ★   ★   ★

On the following day, about one o'clock, Mr. Markham, a gentleman of fortune residing in the northern environs of London, received the following letter:—

"The inscrutable decrees of Providence have enabled the undersigned to warn you, that this night a burglarious attempt will be made upon your dwelling. The wretches who contemplate this infamy are capable of a crime of much blacker die. Beware!

"AN UNKNOWN FRIEND."

This letter was written in a beautiful feminine hand. Due precaution was adopted at Mr. Markham's mansion; but the attempt alluded to in the warning epistle was, for some reason or another, not made.

[Chapters IV and V introduce the two brothers, Richard and Eugene Markham, sons of a 'Gentleman of fortune' who occupies a large estate in 'the environs of north London'. Markham Place is the mansion referred to by the thieves in the previous chapter. Eugene has quarrelled with his father over the payment of debts of honour, and determines to leave home penniless to seek his fortune in the city. After the death of his father, four years later in 1835, Richard too is alone in the city. He is befriended by the Honourable Arthur Chichester, an aristocrat of dubious antecedants, who introduces him to a gambling den. The two ash trees beneath which Richard and Eugene have their final conversation reappear several times in the text as an organizing motif: at intervals the brothers inscribe messages for each other on the bark, and agree to meet on the twelfth anniversary of their parting at the same spot.]

CHAPTER IV.
THE TWO TREES.

IT was between eight and nine o'clock, on a delicious evening, about a week after the events related in the preceding chapters, that two youths issued from Mr. Markham's handsome, but somewhat secluded dwelling, in the northern part of the environs of London, and slowly ascended the adjacent hill. There was an interval of four years between the ages of these youths, the elder being upwards of nineteen, and the younger about fifteen; but it was easy to perceive by the resemblance which existed between them that they were brothers. They walked at a short distance from each other, and exchanged not a word as they ascended the somewhat steep path which conducted them to the summit of the eminence that overlooked the mansion they had just left. The elder proceeded first; and from time to time he clenched his fists, and knit his brows, and gave other silent but expressive indications of the angry passions which were concentrated in his breast. His brother followed him with downcast eyes, and with a countenance denoting the deep anguish that oppressed him. In this manner they arrived at the top of the hill, where they seated themselves upon a bench, which stood between two young ash saplings.

For a long time the brothers remained silent; but at length the younger of the two suddenly burst into tears, and exclaimed, "Oh! why, dearest Eugene, did we choose this spot to say farewell—perhaps for ever?"

"We could not select a more appropriate one, Richard," returned the elder brother. "Four years ago those trees were planted by our hands; and we have ever since called them by our own names. When we were wont to separate, to repair to our respective schools, we came hither to talk over our plans, to arrange the periods of our correspondence, and to anticipate the pursuits that should engage us during the vacations. And when we returned from our seminaries, we hastened hither, hand-in-hand, to see how our trees flourished; and he was most joyous and proud whose sapling appeared to expand the more luxuriantly. If ever we quarrelled, Richard, it was here that we made our peace again; and, seated upon this bench, we have concocted plans for the future; which, haply, will never now be realised!"

"You are right, my dear brother," said Richard, after a pause, during which he appeared to reflect profoundly upon Eugene's words; "we could not have selected a better spot. Still it is all those happy days to which you allude that now render this moment the more bitter. Tell me, must you depart? Is there no alternative? Can I not intercede with our father? Surely, surely, he will not discard one so young as you, whom he has loved—must still love—so tenderly?"

"Intercede with my father!" repeated Eugene, with an irony which seemed extraordinary in one of his tender age; "no, never! He has signified his desire, he has commanded me no longer *to pollute his dwelling*—those were his very words, and he shall be obeyed."

"Our father was incensed, deeply incensed, when he spoke," urged Richard, whose voice was rendered almost inaudible by his sobs; "and to-morrow he will repent of his harshness towards you."

"Our father had no right to blame me," said Eugene violently; "all that has occurred originated in his own conduct towards me. The behaviour of a parent to his son is the element of that son's ruin or success in after life."

"I know not how you can reproach our father, Eugene," said Richard, somewhat reproachfully, "for he has ever conducted himself with tenderness towards us; and since the death of our dear mother—"

"You are yet too young, Richard," interrupted Eugene impatiently, "to comprehend the nature of the accusation which I bring against my father. I will, however, attempt to enable you to understand my meaning, so that you may not imagine that I am acting with duplicity when I endeavour to find a means of extenuation, if not of justification, for my own conduct. My father lavished his gold upon my education, as he also did upon yours; and he taught us from childhood to consider ourselves the sons of wealthy parents, who would enable their children to move with *éclat* in an elevated sphere of life. It was just this day year that I joined my regiment at Knightsbridge. I suddenly found myself thrown amongst gay, dissipated, and wealthy young men—my brother officers. Many of them were old acquaintances, and had been my companions at the Royal Military College at Sandhurst. They speedily enlisted me in all their pleasures and debaucheries, and my expenditure soon exceeded my pay and my allowance. I became involved in debts, and compelled to apply to my father to relieve me from my embarrassments. I wrote a humble and submissive letter, expressing contrition for my faults, and promising to avoid similar pursuits in future. Indeed, I was wearied of the dissipation into which I had plunged, and should have profited well by the experience my short career of pleasure and folly had enabled me to acquire. I trembled upon that verge when my father could either ruin or save me. He did not reply to my letter, and I had not courage to seek an interview with him. Again did I write to him: no answer. I had lost money at private play, and had contracted debts in the same manner. Those, Richard, are called *debts of honour*, and must be paid in full to your creditor, however wealthy he may be, even though your servants and tradesmen should be cheated out of their hard-earned and perhaps much-needed money altogether. I wrote a third time to our father, and still no notice was taken of my appeal. The officers to whom I owed the money lost at play began to look coldly upon me, and I was reduced to a state of desperation. Still I waited for a few days, and for a fourth time wrote to my father. It appears that he was resolved to make me feel the inconvenience of the position in which I had placed myself by my follies; and he sent me no answer. I then called at the house, and he refused to see me. This you know, Richard. What could I do? Driven mad by constant demands for money which I could not pay, and smarting under the chilling glances and taunting allusions of my brother officers, I sold my commission. You are acquainted with the rest. I came home, threw myself at my father's feet, and he spurned me away from him! Richard, was my crime so very great? and has not the unjust, the extreme severity of my father been the cause of all my afflictions?"

"I dare not judge between you," said Richard mildly.

"But what does common sense suggest?" demanded Eugene.

"Doubtless our father knows best," returned the younger brother.

"Old men are often wrong, in spite of their experience—in spite of their years," persisted Eugene.

"My dear brother," said Richard, "I am afraid to exercise my judgment in a case where I stand a chance of rebelling against my father, or questioning his wisdom; and, at the same time, I am anxious to believe everything in your justification."

"I knew that you would not comprehend me," exclaimed Eugene, impatiently. "It is ridiculous not to dare to have an opinion of one's own! My dear brother," he added, turning suddenly round, "you have been to Eton to little purpose: I thought that nearly as much of the world was to be seen there as at Sandhurst. I find that I was mistaken".

And Eugene felt and looked annoyed at the turn which the conversation had taken.

Richard was unhappy, and remained silent.

In the meantime the sun had set; and the darkness was gradually becoming more intense.

Suddenly Eugene grasped his brother's hand, and exclaimed, "Richard, I shall now depart!"

"Impossible!" cried the warm-hearted youth: "you will not leave me thus—you will not abandon your father also, for a hasty word that he has spoken, and which he will gladly recal to-morrow? Oh! no—Eugene, you will not leave the dwelling in which you were born, and where you have passed so many happy hours! What will become of you? What do you purpose? What plan have you in view?"

"I have a few guineas in my pocket," returned Eugene; "and many a princely fortune has been based upon a more slender foundation."

"Yes," said Richard hastily; "you read of fortunes being easily acquired in novels and romances; and in past times persons may have enriched themselves suddenly; but in the great world of the present day, Eugene, I am afraid that such occurrences are rare and seldom seen."

"You know nothing of the world, Richard," said Eugene, almost contemptuously. "There are thousands of persons in London who live well, and keep up splendid establishments, without any apparent resources; and I am man of the world enough to be well aware that those always thrive the best in the long run who have the least to lose at starting. At all events I shall try *my* fortune. I will not, cannot succumb to a parent † who has caused my ruin at my first entrance into life."

"May God prosper your pursuits, and send you the fortune which you appear to aim at!" ejaculated Richard fervently. "But once again—and for the last time let me implore you—let me entreat you not to push this rash and hasty resolve into execution. Do stay—do not leave me, my dearest, dearest brother!"

"Richard, not all the powers of human persuasion shall induce me to abandon my present determination," cried Eugene emphatically, and rising from the bench as he spoke. "It is growing late, and I must depart. Now listen, my dear boy, to what I have to say to you."

"Speak! speak!" murmured Richard, sobbing as if his heart would break. [...]

"All remonstrances—all objections are vain," interrupted Eugene impatiently. "We must say adieu! But one word more," he added, after an instant's pause, as a sudden thought seemed to strike him; "*you* doubt the possibility of my success in life, and *I* feel confident of it. Do *you* pursue your career under the auspices of that parent in whose wisdom you so blindly repose: I will follow *mine*, dependent only on mine own resources. This is the 10th of July, 1831; twelve years hence, on the 10th of July, 1843, we will meet again upon this very spot, between the two trees, if they be still standing. Remember the appointment: we will *then* compare notes relative to our success in life!"

The moment he had uttered these words, Eugene hastily embraced his brother, who struggled in vain to retain him; and having wrung the hand of the old butler, who was now sobbing like a child, the discarded son threw his little bundle over his shoulder, and hurried away from the spot.

[...]

CHAPTER V.
ELIGIBLE ACQUAINTANCES.

FOUR years passed away.

During that interval no tidings of the discarded son reached the disconsolate father and unhappy brother; and all the exertions of the former to discover some trace of the fugitive were fruitless. Vainly did he lavish considerable sums upon that object: uselessly did he dispatch emissaries to all the great manufacturing towns of England, as well as to the principal capitals of Europe, to endeavour to procure some information of him whom he would have received as the prodigal son, and to welcome whose return he would have "killed the fatted calf:"—all his measures to discover his son's retreat were unavailing.

At length, after a lapse of four years, he sank into the tomb—the victim of a broken heart!

A few days previous to his death, he made a will in favour of his remaining son, the guardianship of whom he intrusted to a Mr. Monroe, who was an opulent City merchant, and an old and sincere friend.

Thus, at the age of nineteen, Richard found himself his own master, with a handsome allowance to meet his present wants, and with a large fortune in the perspective of two years more.

[...]

The ancient abode of the family of Markham was a spacious and commodious building, but of heavy and sombre appearance. This gloomy aspect of the architecture was increased by the venerable trees that formed a dense rampart of verdure around the edifice. The grounds belonging to the house were not extensive, but were tastefully laid out; and within the enclosure over which the dominion of Richard Markham extended, was the green hill surmounted by the two ash trees. From the summit of that eminence the mighty metropolis might be seen in all its vastitude—that metropolis whose one single heart was agitated with so many myriads of conflicting passions, warring interests, and opposite feelings.

Perhaps a dozen pages of laboured description will not afford the reader a better idea of the characters and dispositions of the two brothers than that which has already been conveyed by their conversation and conduct detailed in the preceding chapter. Eugene was all selfishness and egotism, Richard all generosity and frankness: the former deceitful, astute, and crafty; the latter honourable even to a fault.

With Eugene, for the present, we have little to do; the course of our narrative follows the fortunes of Richard Markham.

[...]

It was, nevertheless, upon a beautiful afternoon in the month of August, 1835, that Richard appeared amongst the loungers in Hyde Park. He was on foot, and attired in deep mourning; but his handsome countenance, symmetrical form, and thoroughly genteel and unassuming air attracted attention.

Parliament had been prorogued a fortnight before; and all London was said to be "out of town."

[...]

Richard, wearied with his walk, seated himself upon a bench, and contemplated with some interest the moving pageantry before him. He was thus occupied when he was suddenly accosted by a stranger, who seated himself by his side in an easy manner, and addressed some common-place observation to him.

This individual was a man of about two-and-thirty, elegantly attired, agreeable in his manners, and prepossessing in appearance. Under this superficial tegument of gentility a quicker eye than Richard Markham's would have detected a certain swagger in his gait and a kind of dashing recklessness about him which produced an admirable effect upon the vulgar or the inexperienced, but which were not calculated to inspire immediate confidence in the thorough man of the world. Richard was, however, was all frankness and honour himself, and he did not scruple to return such an answer to the stranger's remark as was calculated to encourage farther conversation.

[Richard Markham's chance acquaintance is the Honourable Arthur Chichester, who introduces him to London's night life.]

[Chapter VII reveals to the reader the true identity of the youth who appears in the first episodes. The 'strange being' who now appears in her boudoir is, in fact, a woman – Eliza Sydney. The passage dwells on the oddness of the decor: it is 'either inhabited by a man of strange feminine tastes, or a woman of extraordinary masculine ones'. It provides an early example of a theme of cross-dressing which recurs in the narrative. A further mystery here is the true identity of the 'Mr Stephens', who has persuaded the young woman to maintain a deception by impersonating her lost brother Walter, in return for some undefined benefit to follow. Mr Stephens introduces a third person of mysterious origins, George Montague, to share in the conspiracy. The original illustration of this scene, which appeared in early penny issues was replaced in later volume re-issues by a less obviously salacious version.]

CHAPTER VII.
THE BOUDOIR.

IT was the morning after the events related in the last chapter.

The scene changes to a beautiful little villa in the environs of Upper Clapton.

[...]

The villa stood in the midst of a small garden, beautifully laid out in the French style of Louis XV.; and around it—interrupted only by the avenue leading to the front door of the dwelling—was a grove of evergreens. This grove formed a complete circle, and bounded the garden; and the entire enclosure was protected by a regular paling, painted white.

This miniature domain, consisting of about four acres, was one of the most beautiful spots in the neighbourhood of London; and behind it—far as the eye could reach—stretched the green fields, smiling and cultivated like those of Tuscany.

[...]

[First version of the wood engraving, published by George Vickers]

The windows of the villa were embellished with flowers in pots and vases of curious workmanship; and outside the casements of the chambers upon the first floor were suspended cages containing beautiful singing birds.

To the interior of one of these rooms must we direct the attention of the reader. It was an elegant *boudoir:* and yet it could scarcely justify the name; for by a *boudoir* we understand something completely feminine, whereas this contained articles of male and female use and attire strangely commingled—pell-mell—together.

Upon the toilet-table were all the implements necessary for the decoration and embellishment of female beauty; and carelessly thrown over a chair were a coat, waistcoat, and trousers. A diminutive pair of patent-leather Wellington boots kept company with delicate morocco shoes, to which sandals were affixed. A huge press, half-open, disclosed an array of beautiful dresses—silk, satin, and precious stuffs of all kinds, and on a row of pegs were hung a scarlet hunting coat, a shooting-jacket, a jockey-cap, and other articles of

[Later version of the wood engraving, published by John Dicks]

attire connected with field sports and masculine recreations. Parasols, foils †
single-sticks, dandy-canes, and hunting whips, were huddled together in one
corner of that bureau. And yet all the confusion of these various and discrepant objects was so regular in appearance—if the phrase can be understood—
that it seemed as if some cunning hand had purposely arranged them all so
as to strike the eye in a manner calculated to encourage the impression that
this elegant boudoir was inhabited by a man of strange feminine tastes, or a
woman of extraordinary masculine ones.

There was no pompous nor gorgeous display of wealth in this boudoir: its
interior, like that of the whole villa throughout, denoted competence and
ease—elegance and taste, but no useless luxury nor profuse expenditure.

The window of the boudoir was half open. A bowl of chrystal water, containing gold and silver fish, stood upon a table in the recess of the casement.
The chirrup of the birds echoed through the room, which was perfumed
with the odour of sweet flowers.

By the wall facing the window stood a French bed, on the head and foot of which fell pink satin curtains, flowing from a gilt-headed arrow fixed near the ceiling.

It was now nine o'clock, and the sun shed a flood of golden light through the half-open casement upon that couch which was so voluptuous and so downy.

A female of great beauty, and apparently about five-and-twenty years of age, was reading in that bed. Her head reposed upon her hand, and her elbow upon the pillow: and that hand was buried in a mass of luxuriant light chestnut hair, which flowed down upon her back, her shoulders, and her bosom; but not so as altogether to conceal the polished ivory whiteness of the plump fair flesh.

The admirable slope of the shoulders, the swan-like neck, and the exquisite symmetry of the bust, were descried even amidst those masses of luxuriant and shining hair.

A high and ample forehead, hazel eyes, nose perfectly straight, small but pouting lips, brilliant teeth, and a well rounded chin, were additional charms to augment the attractions of that delightful picture.

[A servant enters, and warns the lady that a visitor has arrived, and cautions her against imprudence.]

"Imprudent!" hastily exclaimed the lady: "how am I imprudent? Do I not follow all *his* directions—all *your* advice? Have I not even learned to talk to the very groom in his own language about the horses and the dogs? and do I not scamper across the country, upon my chestnut mare, with him following upon the bay horse at my heels, as if we were both mad? And then you say that I am imprudent, when I have done all I can to sustain the character which I have assumed? And with the exception of these rides, how seldom do I go abroad? Half-a-dozen names include all my acquaintances: and no one—no one ever comes here! This is, indeed, a hermit's dwelling! How can you say that I am imprudent?"

"Without going out of this very room," began Louisa, with a smile, "I could—"

"Ah! the eternal remonstrances against these habiliments of my sex!" exclaimed the lady, drawing back the satin curtain at the head of the bed with her snow-white arm, and glancing towards the bureau that contained the female dresses: "ever those remonstrances! Alas! I should die—I could not support this appalling deceit—were I not to gratify my woman's feelings from time to time. Do you think that I can altogether rebel against nature, and not experience the effects? [...] But if it be desired that I should altogether forget my sex—and cling to the garb of a man; if I may never—not even for an hour in the evening—follow my fantasy, and relieve my mind by resuming the garb which is natural to me—within these four walls—unseen by a soul save you—"

"Yes, yes, you shall have your way," interrupted Louisa soothingly. "But Mr. Stephens waits: will you not rise and see him?"

"It is my duty," said the lady resignedly. "He has surrounded me with every comfort and every luxury which appetite can desire or money procure; and, however he may ultimately benefit by this proceeding, in the meantime my gratitude is due to him."

"The delicacy of his conduct towards you equals his liberality," observed Louisa pointedly.

[...]

"Oh! how happy, thrice happy shall I be, when, the period of my emancipation being arrived, I may escape to some distant part of my own native country, or to some foreign clime, resume the garb belonging to my sex, and live in a way consistent with nature, and suitable to my taste."

[...]

Then followed the mysterious toilet.

Stays, curiously contrived, gave to that exquisitely modelled form as much as possible the appearance of the figure of a man. The swell of the bosom, slightly compressed, was rendered scarcely apparent by padding skilfully placed, so as to fill up and flatten the undulating bust. The position of the waist was lowered; and all this was effected without causing the subject of so strange a transformation any pain or uneasiness.

The semi-military blue frock coat, buttoned up to the throat, completed the disguise.

[...]

The toilet being thus completed, this strange being to whom we have introduced our readers, descended to a parlour on the ground floor.

[...]

[In Chapter IX, we make the acquaintance of one of the central and most original characters, George Montague. He is an early representation in fiction of the dubious financial speculator, one of the 'new' enemies of the people who were replacing the aristocracy as the natural targets of radical rhetoric. His unscrupulous interest in 'commercial speculations of all shapes' leads him to great wealth, to Parliament, and later to disgrace, when his financial machinations are revealed. Here, his antecedents, and indeed his lifestyle, are presented as shrouded in mystery, although hints concerning his real identity are given to the careful reader. 'Walter Sydney', the 'youth' who appeared in the opening scenes, explains, after a four-year time-lapse, how 'he' escaped from the Old House. Both the reader and Mr Montague are by now aware of the real gender of 'Walter', and Montague is party to a complicated deception which is being practised for financial gain, in which Eliza Sydney impersonates her dead brother.]

CHAPTER IX.
A CITY MAN.—SMITHFIELD SCENES.

GEORGE MONTAGUE was a tall, good-looking young man of about three or four-and-twenty. His hair and eyes were black, his complexion rather dark, and his features perfectly regular.

His manners were certainly polished and agreeable; but there was, nevertheless, a something reserved and mysterious about him—an anxiety to avert the conversation from any topic connected with himself—a studied desire to flatter and gain the good opinions of those about him, by means of compliments at times servile—and an occasional betrayal of a belief in a code of morals not altogether consistent with the well-being of society, which constituted features in his character by no means calculated to render him a favourite with all classes of persons. He was, however, well-informed upon most topics; ambitious of creating a sensation in the world, no matter by what means; resolute in his pursuit after wealth, and careless whether the paths leading to the objects which he sought were tortuous or straightforward. He was addicted to pleasure, but never permitted it to interfere with his business or mar his schemes. *Love* with him was merely the blandishment of beauty; and *friendship* was simply that bond which connected him with those individuals who were necessary to him. He was utterly and completely selfish; but he was somehow or another possessed of sufficient tact to conceal most of his faults—of the existence of which he was well aware. The consequence was that he was usually welcomed as an agreeable companion; some even went so far as to assert that he was a "devilish good fellow;" and all admitted that he was a thorough man of the world. He must have commenced his initiation early, thus to have acquired such a character ere he had completed his four-and-twentieth year!

London abounds with such precocious specimens of thorough heartlessness and worldly mindedness. The universities and great public schools let loose upon society every half-year a cloud of young men, who think only how soon they can spend their own property in order to prey upon that of others. These are your "young men *about* town:" as they grow older they become "men *upon* the town." In their former capacity they graduate in all the degrees of vice, dissipation, extravagance, and debauchery; and in the latter they become the tutors of the novices who are entering in their turn upon the road to ruin. The transition from the young man about town to the man upon the town is as natural as that of a chrysalis to a butterfly. These men *upon* the town constitute as pestilential a section of male society as the women *of* the town do of the female portion of the community. They are alike the reptiles produced by the great moral dung-heap.

We cannot, however, exactly class Mr. George Montague with the men upon the town in the true meaning of the phrase, inasmuch as he devoted his attention to commercial speculations of all kinds and under all shapes, and his sphere was chiefly the City; whereas men upon the town seldom entertain an idea half "so vulgar" as mercantile pursuits, and never visit the domains of the Lord Mayor save when they want to get a bill discounted, or to obtain cash for a check of too large an amount to be entrusted to any of their high-born and aristocratic companions.

Mr. George Montague was, therefore, one of that multitudinous class called "City men," who possess no regular offices, but have their letters addressed to the Auction Mart or Garraway's, and who make their appointments at such places as "the front of the Bank," "the Custom-house Wharf," and "under the clock at the Docks."

City men are very extraordinary characters. They all know "a certain speculation that would make a sure fortune, if one had but the capital to work upon;" they never fail to observe, while making this assertion, that they *could* apply to a friend if they chose, but that they do not choose to lay themselves under the obligation; and they invariably affirm that nothing is more easy than to make a fortune in the City, although the greater portion of them remain without that happy consummation until the day of their deaths. Now and then, however, one of these City men *does* succeed in "making a hit" by some means or other; and then his old friends, the very men who are constantly enunciating the opinion relative to the facility with which fortunes are obtained in the City, look knowing, wink at each other, and declare "that it never could have been done unless he'd had somebody with plenty of money to back him."

Now Mr. Montague was one of those who adopted a better system of logic than the vulgar reasoning. He knew that there was but little merit in producing bread from flour, for instance: but he perceived that there was immense credit due to those who could produce their bread without any flour at all. Upon this principle he acted, and his plan was not unattended with success. He scorned the idea "that money was necessary to beget money;" he began his "City career," as he sometimes observed, without a farthing; and he was seldom without gold in his pocket.

No one knew where he lived. He was sometimes seen getting into a Hackney omnibus at the Flower Pot, a Camberwell one at the Cross Keys; or running furiously after a Hammersmith one along Cheapside; but as these directions were very opposite, it was difficult to deduce from them any idea of his domiciliary whereabouts.

He was young to be a City man; the class does not often include members under thirty; but of course there are exceptions to all rules; and Mr. George Montague was one.

He was then a City man: but if the reader be anxious to know what sort of *business* he transacted to obtain his living; whether he dabbled in the funds, sold wines upon commission, effected loans and discounts, speculated in shares, got up joint-stock companies, shipped goods to the colonies, purchased land in Australia at eighteen-pence an acre and sold it again at one-and-nine, conducted compromises for insolvent tradesmen, made out the accounts of bankrupts, arbitrated between partners who disagreed, or bought in things in a friendly way at public sales; whether he followed any of these pursuits, or meddled a little with them all, we can no more satisfy our readers than if we attempted the biography of the Man in the Moon,—all we can say is, that he was invariably in the City from eleven to four; that he usually had "an excellent thing in hand just at that moment;" and, in a word, that he belonged to the class denominated *City Men*!

We have taken some pains to describe this gentleman; for reasons which will appear hereafter.

Having been duly introduced to Walter Sydney by Mr. Stephens, and after a few observations of a general nature, Mr. Montague glided almost imperceptibly into topics upon which he conversed with ease and fluency.

Presently a pause ensued; and Mr. Stephens enquired "if there were anything new in the City?"

"Nothing particular," answered Montague. "I have not of course been in town this morning; but I was not away till late last night. I had a splendid thing in hand, which I succeeded in bringing to a favourable termination. By-the-by, there was a rumour on 'Change yesterday afternoon, just before the close, that Alderman Dumkins is all wrong"

"Indeed," said Stephens; "I thought he was wealthy."

"Oh! no; *I* knew the contrary eighteen months ago! It appears he has been starting a joint-stock company to work the Ercalat tin-mines in Cornwall—"

"And I suppose the mines do not really exist?"

"Oh! yes; they do—upon his maps! However, he has been exhibiting certain specimens of tin, which he has passed off as Ercalat produce; and it is now pretty generally known that the article was supplied him by a house in Aldgate."

"Then he will be compelled to resign his gown?"

"Not he! On the contrary, he stands next in rotation for the honours of the civic chair; and he intends to go boldly forward as if nothing had happened. You must remember that the aldermen of the City of London have degenerated considerably in respectability during late years; and that none of the really influential and wealthy men in the City will have anything to do with the corporation affairs. You do not see any great banker nor merchant wearing the aldermanic gown. The only alderman who really possessed what may be called a large fortune, and whose pecuniary position was above all doubt, resigned his gown the other day in disgust at the treatment which he received from his brother authorities, in consequence of his connexion with the *Weekly Courier*—the only newspaper that boldly, fearlessly, and effectually advocates the people's cause."

"And Dumkins will not resign, you think?"

"Oh! decidedly not. But for my part," added Montague, "I feel convinced that the sooner some change is made in the City administration the better. Only conceive the immense sums which the corporation receives from various sources, and the uses to which they are applied. Look at the beastly guzzling at Guildhall, while there are in the very heart of the City Augean stables of filth, crime, and debauchery to be cleansed—witness Petticoat-lane, Smithfield—"

A species of groan or stifled exclamation of horror issued from the lips of Walter as Montague uttered these words: her countenance grew deadly pale, and her entire frame appeared to writhe under a most painful reminiscence or emotion.

"Compose yourself, compose yourself," said Stephens, hastily. "Shall I ring for a glass of water, or wine, or anything—"

"No, it is past," interrupted Walter Sydney; "but I never think of that horrible—that appalling adventure without feeling my blood curdle in my veins. The mere mention of the word Smithfield—"

"Could I have been indiscreet enough to give utterance to anything calculated to annoy?" said Montague, who was surprised at this scene.

"You were not aware of the reminiscence you awoke in my mind by your remark," answered Walter, smiling; "but were you acquainted with the particulars of that fearful night, you would readily excuse my weakness."

"You have excited Mr. Montague's curiosity," observed Stephens, "and you have now nothing to do but to gratify it."

"It is an adventure of a most romantic kind—an adventure which you will scarcely believe— and yet one that will make your hair stand on end."

"I am now most anxious to learn the details of this mysterious occurrence," said Montague, scarcely knowing whether these remarks were made in jest or earnest.

Walter Sydney appeared to reflect for a few moments; and then commenced the narrative in the following manner:—

"It is now a little more than four years ago—very shortly after I first arrived at this house—that I rode into town, attended by the same groom who is in my service now. I knew little or nothing of the City, and felt my curiosity awakened to view the emporium of the world's commerce. I accordingly determined to indulge in a ramble by myself amidst the streets and the thoroughfares of a place of which such marvellous accounts reach those who pass their youth in the country. I left the groom with the horses at a livery-stable in Bishopsgate-street, with a promise to return in the course of two or three hours. I then roved about to my heart's content, and never gave the lapse of time a thought. Evening came, and the weather grew threatening. Then commenced my perplexities. I had forgotten the address of the stables where the groom awaited my return; and I discovered the pleasing fact that I had lost my way just at the moment when an awful storm seemed ready to break over the metropolis. When I solicited information concerning the right path which I should pursue, I was insulted by the low churls to whom I applied. To be brief, I was overtaken by darkness and by the storm, in a place which have since ascertained to be Smithfield market. I could not have conceived that so filthy and horrible a nuisance could have been allowed to exist in the midst of a city of so much wealth. But, oh! the revolting streets which branch off from that Smithfield. It seemed to me that I was wandering amongst all the haunts of crime and appalling penury of which I had read in romances, but which I never could have believed to exist in the very heart of the metropolis of the world. Civilisation appeared to me to have chosen particular places which it condescended to visit, and to have passed others by without even leaving a foot-print to denote its presence."

"But this horrible adventure?" said Montague.

"Oh! forgive my digression. Surrounded by darkness, exposed to the rage of the storm, and actually sinking with fatigue, I took refuge in an old house, which I am sure I could never find again; but which was situated nearly at the end, on the right-hand side of the way, of one of those vile narrow streets branching off from Smithfield. That house was the den of wild beasts in human shape! I was compelled to hear a conversation of a most appalling nature between two ruffians, who made that place the depôt for their plunder. They planned, amongst other atrocious topics, the robbery of a country-seat, somewhere to the north of Islington, and inhabited by a family of the name of Markham."

"Indeed! What—how strange!" ejaculated Montague: then immediately afterwards, he added, "How singular that you should have heard so vile a scheme!"

"Oh! those villains," continued Walter, "were capable of crimes of a far deeper dye. They discussed horror upon horror, till I thought that I was going raving mad. I made a desperate attempt to escape, and was perceived. What then immediately followed I know not, for I became insensible: in a word, Mr. Montague, I fainted!"

A deep blush suffused her countenance, as she made this avowal—for it seemed to have a direct relation to her sex; and she was well aware that the secret connected therewith had been revealed by her benefactor to George Montague. On his part, he gazed upon her with mingled interest and admiration.

"I awoke to encounter a scene of horror," she continued, after a short pause, "which you must fancy; but the full extent of which I cannot depict. I can only *feel* it even now. Those wretches were conveying me to a room upon the ground-floor—a room to which the cells of the Bastille or the Inquisition could have produced no equal. It had a trap-door communicating with the Fleet Ditch! I begged for mercy—I promised wealth—for I knew that my kind benefactor," she added, glancing towards Mr. Stephens, "would have enabled me to fulfil my pledge to them; but all was in vain. The murderers hurled me down the dark and pestiferous hole!"

"Merciful heavens!" ejaculated Montague.

"It would appear that the house in question," proceeded Walter, "stood upon the side of, and not over the Ditch. There can be, however, no doubt that the trap-door was contrived for the horrible purpose of disposing of those victims who fell into the merciless hands of the occupants of the dwelling; for when I had fallen some distance, instead of being immersed in black and filthy mud, I was caught upon a sloping plank which shelved towards a large aperture in the wall of the Ditch. I instinctively clung to this plank, and lay stretched upon it for some moments until I had partially recovered my presence of mind. The circumstance of having thus escaped a dreadful death gave me an amount of courage at which I myself was astonished. At length I began to reason whether it would be better to remain there until morning, and then endeavour to reach the trap-door above my head, or to devise some means of immediate escape. I decided upon the latter proceeding; for I reflected that the morning would not afford light to that subterranean hole to enable me to act with certainty; and I, moreover, dreaded the extreme vengeance of those ruffians who had already given me a sample of their brutality, should I happen to encounter them on emerging from the trap-door. Lastly, I considered that it was also probable that I might not succeed in raising the trap-door at all."

"What a fearful situation!" observed Montague.

"Horrible even to think of," added Stephens, who listened with the deepest attention to this narrative, although he had heard it related on former occasions.

"With my hands and legs I groped about," continued Walter, "and I speedily ascertained my exact position with regard to the locality. My feet were close to a large square aperture in the perpendicular wall overhanging the Ditch; and the floor of the cellar was only a couple of feet below the aperture. I accordingly got cautiously off the board, and stood upon the damp ground. After the lapse of several minutes, during which I nerved myself to adopt the idea that had struck me, I passed my head through the aperture, and looked out over the Ditch. The stream appeared rapid, to judge by its gurgling sound; and the stench that exhaled from it was pestiferous in the extreme. Turning my head to the left I saw hundreds of lights twinkling in the small narrow windows of two lines of houses that overhung the Ditch. The storm had now completely passed away—the rain had ceased—and the night was clear and beautiful. In a few minutes I was perfectly acquainted with the entire geography of the place. The means of escape were within my reach. About three feet above the aperture through which I was now looking, a plank crossed the Ditch; and on the opposite side—for the Ditch in that part was not above two yards wide from wall to wall—was a narrow ledge running along the side of the house facing the one in which I was, and evidently communicating with some lane or street close by. I can scarcely tell you how I contrived to creep through the aperture and reach the plank overhead. Nevertheless, I attempted the dangerous feat, and I accomplished it. I crossed the plank, and reached the ledge of which I have spoken: it terminated in the very street where stood the terrible den from which I had just so miraculously escaped. Indeed, I emerged upon that street only at a distance of a few yards from the door of that detestable place. To hurry away in a contrary direction was my first and most natural impulse; but I had not proceeded far when the door of a house was suddenly thrown violently open, and out poured a crowd of men and women, among whom I was, as it were, immediately hemmed in."

"What! another adventure?" exclaimed Montague.

"One calculated to inspire feelings of deep disgust, if not of alarm," answered Walter. "It appeared that two women had been quarreling and had turned out to fight. They fell upon each other like wild cats, or as you would fancy that tigers would fight. A clear and lovely moon lighted this revolting scene. A circle was formed round the termagants, and for ten minutes did they lacerate themselves with fists and nails in a fearful manner. Their clothes were torn into ribands—their countenances were horribly disfigured with scratches—the blood poured from their noses—and their hair, hanging all dishevelled over their naked shoulders, gave them a wild, ferocious, and savage appearance, such as I never could have expected to encounter in the metropolis of the civilised world."

"And in the very heart of the City," added Mr. Montague.

"Suddenly a cry of ' *The Bluebottles*!' was raised, and the crowd, belligerents and all, rushed pell-mell back again into the house. In spite of all my endeavours to escape I was hurried in with that hideous mob of ferocious-looking men and brazen-faced women. In a few moments I found myself in a large room, in which there were at least thirty wretched beds huddled close together, and so revoltingly dirty that the cold pavement or a hedge-side would have seemed a more preferable couch. And, oh! how can I describe the inmates of that den, many of whom were crowding round a fire cooking provender, which filled the place with a sickening and most fetid odour. There were young girls almost naked, without clothes or stockings, and whose sunken cheeks, dimmed eyes, and miserable attire contrasted strangely with their boisterous mirth. [...] On the third floor and in the attics were the most horrible scenes of wretchedness which I had yet beheld. Those dens were filled with straw beds, separated from each other only by pieces of plank about eight or ten inches in height. Men, women, and children were all crowded together—sleeping pell-mell. Oh! it was a horrible, horrible spectacle. To be brief, I escaped from that moral plague-house; and in a few moments was traversing Smithfield once more." [...]

[Chapters XIII, XVII and XIX provide an example of the social documentary mode, in which the extremes of low and high life depravity in London are explored and described in detail, as part of the mapping of the 'other' so characteristic of this text. The upper-class gambling den to which Richard Markham is introduced by his aristocratic 'friend', the Honourable Arthur Chichester, is the scene of an horrific suicide, while the following episodes, in which the thief Bill Bolter brutally murders his wife after first blinding her, are among the most violent and sadistic to be found in any Victorian fiction. The 'fearful mysteries' of the 'hideous districts' around Smithfield, one of the 'moral plague spots' of London revealed by this account, include incest, murder, and rotting corpses.]

CHAPTER XIII.
THE HELL.

AFTER having taken a few turns in Regent-Street, the baronet observed "that it was devilish slow work;" Mr. Talbot suggested the propriety of "a spree;" and Mr. Chichester declared "that as his friend Markham was anxious to see *life,* the best thing they could all do was to drop in for an hour at No.—, Quadrant."

"What place is that?" demanded Markham.

"Oh; only an establishment for cards and dice, and other innocent diversions," carelessly answered Chichester.

The Quadrant of an evening is crowded with loungers of both sexes. Beneath those arcades walk the daughters of crime, by ones and twos—dressed in the flaunting garb that tells so forcibly the tale of broken hearts, and blighted promise, and crushed affections,—to lose an hour amidst the haunts of pleasure and vice, and to court the crime by which alone they live. The young men that saunter arm-in-arm up and down, and the hoary old sinners, whose licentious glances seem to plunge down into the depths of the boddices of those frail but beauteous girls, little think of the amount of mental suffering which is contained beneath those gay satins and rustling silks. They mark the heaving of the voluptuous bosom, but dream not of the worm that gnaws eternally within:—they behold smiles upon the red lips, and are far from suspecting that the hearts of those who laugh so joyfully are all but broken!

Thus is it that in the evening the Quadrant has a characteristic set of loungers of its own:—or, at least, it is frequented after dusk by a population whose characters are easily to be defined.

A bright lamp burnt in the fan-light over the door of No.—. Mr. Chichester gave a loud and commanding knock; and a policeman standing by, who doubtless had several golden reasons for not noticing anything connected with that establishment, instantly ran across the road after a small boy whom he suspected to be a thief, because the poor wretch wore an uncommonly shabby hat. The summons given by Mr. Chichester was not immediately answered. Five minutes elapsed ere any attention was paid to it; and then the door was only opened to the small extent allowed by a chain inside. A somewhat repulsive looking countenance was at the same time protruded from behind the door.

"Well?" said the man to whom the countenance belonged.

"All right," returned Chichester.

The chain was withdrawn, and the door was opened to its full extent. The party was thereupon admitted, with some manifestations of impatience on the part of the porter, who no doubt thought that the door was kept open too long, into a passage at the end of which was a staircase covered with a handsome carpet.

Chichester led the way, and his companions followed, up to a suite of rooms on the first floor. These were well furnished, and brilliantly lighted, and red moreen curtains, with heavy and rich fringes, were carefully drawn over the windows. Splendid mirrors stood above the mantels, which were also adorned with French timepieces in *or molu*, and candelabra of the same material. On one side of the front room stood a bouffet covered with wines and liquors of various descriptions.

In the middle of that same front apartment was the *rouge et noir* table. On each side sate a *Croupier*, with a long rake in his hand, and a green shade over his eyes. Before one of them was placed a tin case: this was the *Bank*;—and on each side of that cynosure of all attention, stood little piles of markers, or counters.

Two or three men—well but flashily dressed, and exhibiting a monstrous profusion of Birmingham jewellery about their persons—sate at the table. These were the *Bonnets*—individuals in reality in the pay of the proprietor of the establishment, and whose duties consist in enticing strangers and visitors to play, or in maintaining an appearance of playing deeply when such strangers and visitors first enter the room.

The countenances of the croupiers were cold, passionless, and totally devoid of any animation. They called the game, raked up the winnings, or paid the losings, without changing a muscle of their features. For all that regarded animation or excitement, they might have been easily passed off as automatons.

Not so was it with the Bonnets. These gentlemen were compelled to affect exuberant joy when they won, and profound grief or rage when they lost. From time to time they paid a visit to the sideboard, and helped themselves to wine or spirits, or regaled themselves with cigars. These refreshments were supplied gratuitously to all comers by the proprietor: this apparent liberality was upon the principle of throwing out a sprat to catch a whale.

When none save the Croupiers and Bonnets are present, they throw aside their assumed characters, and laugh, and joke, and chatter, and smoke, and drink; but the moment steps are heard upon the staircase, they all relapse with mechanical exactitude into their business aspect. The Croupiers put on their imperturbable countenances as easily as if they were masks; and the Bonnets appear to be as intent upon the game, as if its results were to them perspective life or death.

The Croupiers are usually trustworthy persons well-known to the proprietor, or else shareholders themselves in the establishment. The Bonnets are young men of education and manners, who have probably lost the ample fortunes wherewith they commenced life, in the very whirlpool to which, for a weekly stipend, they are employed to entice others.

In one of the inner rooms there was a roulette-table; but this was seldom used. A young lad held the almost sinecure office of attending upon it.

The front room was tolerably crowded on the evening when Chichester, Markham, the baronet, and Talbot, honoured the establishment with a visit.

The moment they entered the apartment, Richard instinctively drew back, and, catching hold of Chichester's arm, whispered to him in a hurried and anxious manner, "Tell me, is this a Gambling-House? is it what I have heard called a Hell?"

"It is a Gambling-House, if you will, my dear fellow," was the reply; "but a most respectable one. Besides—you must see life, you know!"

With these words he took Markham's arm, and conducted him up to the *rouge et noir* table.

A young officer, whose age could not have exceeded twenty, was seated at the further end of the green-baize covered board. A huge pile of notes and gold lay before him; but at rapid intervals one of the Croupiers raked away the stakes which he deposited; and thus his heap of money was gradually growing smaller.

"Well, this is extraordinary!"ejaculated the young officer: "I never saw the luck set so completely in against me. However—I can afford to lose a little; for I broke your bank for you last night, my boys?"

"What does that mean?" demanded Richard in a whisper.

"He won all the money which the proprietor deposited in that tin case, he means," replied Chichester.

"And how much do you suppose that might be?"

"About fifteen hundred to two thousand pounds."

"Here—waiter!"exclaimed the young officer, who had just lost another stake,—"a glass of claret."

The waiter handed him a glass of the wine so demanded. The young officer did not notice him for a moment, but waited to see the result of the next chance.

He lost again.

He turned round to seize the glass of wine; but when his eyes caught sight of it, his countenance became almost livid with rage.

"Fool! idiot!" he ejaculated, starting from his seat:"bring me a tumbler—a large tumbler full of claret; my mouth is as parched as h—l, and my stomach is like a lime-kiln."

The waiter hastened to comply with the wishes of the young gambler. The tumbler of claret was supplied; and the game continued.

Still the officer lost.

"A cigar!" he shouted, in a fearful state of excitement—"bring me a cigar!"

The waiter handed him a box of choice Havannahs, that he might make his selection.

"Why the devil don't you bring a light at the same time, you d—d infernal rascal?" cried the gamester; and while the domestic hastened to supply this demand also, he poured a volley of most horrible oaths at the bewildered wretch's head.

Again the play proceeded.

And again the young officer lost.

His pile of gold was gone: the Croupier who kept the bank changed one of his remaining notes.

"That makes three thousand that I have lost already, by G—d!" ejaculated the young officer.

"Including the amount you won last night, I believe," said one of the Bonnets.

"Well, sir, and suppose it is—what the deuce is that to you?" demanded the officer fiercely."Have I not been here night after night for these six weeks? and have I not lost thousands—thousands? When did I ever get a vein of good luck until last night? But never mind—I'll play on—I'll play till the end: I will either win all back, or lose everything together. And then—in the latter case—"

He stopped: he had just lost again. His countenance grew ghastly pale, and he bit his lips convulsively.

"Claret—more claret!" he exclaimed, throwing away the Havannah:"that cigar only makes me the more thirsty."

And again the play proceeded.

"I am really afraid to contemplate that young man's countenance," whispered Markham to Chichester.

"Why so?"

"I have an idea that if he should prove unsuccessful he will commit suicide. I have a great mind just to mention my fears to those men in the green shades, who seem to be winning all his money."

"Pray be quiet. They will only laugh at you."

"But the life of a fellow-creature?"

"What do they care?"

"Do you mean to say they are such wretches—"

"I mean that they do not care one fig what may happen so long as they get the money."

Markham was struck speechless with horror as he heard this cold-blooded announcement. Chichester had, however, stated nothing but the truth.

The proceedings were now fearfully interesting. The young officer was worked up to a most horrible state of excitement: his losses continued to be unvaried by a single gleam of good fortune. Still he persisted in his ruinous career: note after note was changed. At length his last was melted into gold. He now became absolutely desperate: his countenance was appalling;—the frenzy of gambling and the inflammatory effects of the liquors he had been drinking, rendered his really handsome features positively hideous.

Markham had never beheld such a scene before, and felt afraid. His companions surveyed it with remarkable coolness.

The play proceeded; and in a few moments the officer's last stake was swept away.

Then the croupiers paused, as it were, by common consent; and all eyes were directed towards the object of universal interest.

"Well—I said I would play until I won all or lost all," he said;"and I have done so. Waiter, give me another tumbler of claret: it will compose me."

He laughed bitterly as he uttered these words.

The claret was brought: he drained the tumbler, and threw it upon the table, where it broke into a dozen pieces.

"Clear this away, Thomas," said one of the Croupiers, completely unmoved.

"Yes, sir;" and the fragments of the tumbler disappeared forthwith.

The Bonnets, perceiving the presence of other strangers, were now compelled to withdraw their attention from the ruined gambler, and commence playing.

And so the play again proceeded.

"Where is my hat, waiter?" demanded the young officer, after a pause, during which he had gazed vacantly upon the game.

"In the passage, sir—I believe."

"No—I remember, it is in the inner room. But do not trouble yourself— I will fetch it myself."

"Very good, sir;" and the waiter did not move.

The young officer sauntered, in a seemingly leisurely manner, into the innermost room of the suite.

"What a shocking scene!" whispered Markham to Chichester. "I am glad I came hither this once: it will be a lesson for me which I can never forget."

At this instant the report of a pistol echoed sharply through the rooms.

There was a simultaneous rush to the inner apartment:—Markham's presentiments were fulfilled—the young officer had committed suicide.

His brains were literally blown out, and he lay upon the carpet weltering in his blood.

A cry of horror burst from the strangers present; and then, with one accord, they hastened to the door. The baronet, Chichester, and Talbot, were amongst the foremost who made this movement, and were thereby enabled to effect their escape.

Markham stood rivetted to the spot, unaware that his companions had left him, and contemplating with feelings of supreme horror the appalling spectacle before him.

Suddenly the cry of "The police" fell upon his ears; and heavy steps were heard hurrying up the staircase.

"The Bank!" ejaculated one of the Croupiers.

"All right!" cried the other; and in a moment the lights were extinguished, as by magic, through the entire suite of rooms.

Obeying a natural impulse, Markham hastened towards the door; but his progress was stopped by a powerful hand, and in an instant the bull's-eye of a lantern glared upon his countenance.

He was in the grasp of a police officer.

CHAPTER XVII.
A DEN OF HORRORS.

HOWEVER filthy, unhealthy, and repulsive the entire neighbourhood of West Street (Smithfield), Field Lane, and Saffron Hill, may appear at the present day, it was far worse some years ago. There were then but few cesspools; and scarcely any of those which did exist possessed any drains. The Knacker's yards of Cow Cross, and the establishment in Castle Street where horses' flesh is boiled down to supply food for the dogs and cats of the metropolis, send forth now, as they did then, a fœtid and sickening odour which could not possibly be borne by a delicate stomach. At the windows of those establishments the bones of the animals are hung to bleach, and offend the eye as much the horrible stench of the flesh acts repugnantly to the nerves. Upward of sixty horses a day were frequently slaughtered in each yard; and many of them are in the last stage of disease when sent to their "long home." Should there not be a rapid demand for the "meat" on the part of the itinerant purveyors of that article for canine and feline favourites, it speedily becomes putrid; and a smell, which would alone appear sufficient to create pestilence, pervades the neighbourhood.

As if nothing should be wanting to render that district as filthy and unhealthy as possible, water is scarce. There is in this absence of a plentiful supply of that wholesome article, an actual apology for dirt. Some of the houses have small back yards, in which the inhabitants keep pigs. A short time ago, an infant belonging to a poor widow, who occupied a back room on the ground-floor of one of these hovels, died, and was laid upon the sacking of the bed while the mother went out to make arrangements for its interment. During her absence a pig entered the room from the yard, and feasted upon the dead child's face!

In that densely populated neighbourhood that we are describing, hundreds of families each live and sleep in one room. When a member of one of these families happens to die, the corpse is kept in the close room where the rest still continue to live and sleep. Poverty frequently compels the unhappy relatives to keep the body for days—aye, and weeks. Rapid decomposition takes place;—animal life generates quickly; and in four-and-twenty hours myriads of loathsome animalculæ are seen crawling about. The very undertakers' men fall sick at these disgusting—these revolting spectacles.

The wealthy classes of society are far too ready to reproach the miserable poor for things which are really misfortunes and not faults. The habit of whole families sleeping together in one room destroys all sense of shame in the daughters: and what guardian then remains for their virtue? But, alas! a horrible—an odious crime often results from that poverty which thus huddles brothers and sisters, aunts and nephews, all together in one narrow room— the crime of incest!

When a disease—such as the small-pox or scarlatina—breaks out in one of those crowded houses, and in a densely populated neighbourhood, the consequences are frightful: the mortality is as rapid as that which follows the footsteps of the plague!

These are the fearful mysteries of that hideous district which exists in the very heart of this great metropolis. From St. John-street to Saffron Hill—from West-street to Clerkenwell Green, is a maze of narrow lanes, choked up with dirt, pestiferous with nauseous odours, and swarming with a population that is born, lives, and dies, amidst squalor, penury, wretchedness, and crime.

Leading out of Holborn, between Field Lane and Ely Place, is Upper Union Court—a narrow lane forming a thoroughfare for only foot passengers. The houses in this court are dingy and gloomy: the sunbeams never linger long there; and should an Italian-boy pass through the place, he does not stop to waste his music upon the inhabitants. The dwellings are chiefly let out in lodgings; and through the open windows upon the ground-floor may occasionally be seen the half-starved families of mechanics crowding round the scantily-supplied table. A few of the lower casements are filled with children's book, pictures of actors and highwaymen glaringly coloured, and lucifer-matches, twine, sweet-stuff, cotton, &c. At one door there stands an oyster-stall, when the comestible itself is in season: over another hangs a small board with a mangle painted upon it. Most of the windows on the ground-floors announce rooms to let, or lodgings for single men; and perhaps a notice may be seen better written than the rest, that artificial flower makers are required at that address.

It was about nine o'clock in the evening when two little children—a boy of seven and a girl of five—walked slowly up this court, hand in hand, and crying bitterly. They were both clothed in rags, and had neither shoes nor stockings upon their feet.

[The children return home, and are beaten for failing to beg successfully.]

The woman caught hold of the boy, and dealt him a tremendous blow upon the back with her thin bony fist. He fell upon his knees, and begged for mercy. His unnatural parent levelled a volley of abuse at him, mingled with oaths and filthy expressions, and then beat him—dashed him upon the floor —kicked him—all but stamped on his poor body as he writhed at her feet.

His screams were appalling.

Then came the turn of the girl.

[…]

At length the mother sate down, exhausted; and the poor lad drew his little sister into a corner, and endeavoured to soothe her.

The husband of that vile woman had remained unmoved in his seat, quietly smoking his pipe, while this horrible scene took place; and if he did not actually enjoy it, he was very far from disapproving of it.

[Their mother throws two pieces of bread to the children.]

The little boy gave the larger piece of bread to his sister; and, having divested her of her rags, he made her as comfortable as he could on the filthy mattress, covering her over not only with *her* clothes but also with *his own*. He kissed her affectionately, but without making any noise with his lips, for fear that *that* should irritate his mother; and then lay down beside her.

Clasped in each other's arms, those two children of poverty—the victims of horrible and daily cruelties—repulsed by a father whose neck they had longed to encircle with their little arms, and whose hand they had vainly sought to cover with kisses; trembling even at the looks of a mother whom they loved in spite of all her harshness towards them, and from whose lips one word—one single word of kindness would have gladdened their poor hearts;

—under such circumstances, we say, did these persecuted but affectionate infants, still smarting with the pain of cruel blows, and with tears upon their cheeks,—thus did they sink into slumber in each other's arms!

Merciful God! it makes the blood boil to think that this is no over-drawn picture—that there is no exaggeration in these details; but that there really exist monsters in a human form—wearing often, too, the female shape—who make the infancy and early youth of their offspring one continued hell—one perpetual scene of blows, curses, and cruelties! Oh! for how many of our fellow-creatures have we to blush:—how many demons are there who have assumed our mortal appearance, who dwell amongst us, and who set us examples the most hideous—the most appalling!

As soon as the children were in bed, the woman went out, and returned in a few minutes with two pots of strong beer—purchased with the alms that day bestowed by the charitable upon her suffering offspring.

She and her husband then partook of some cold meat, of which there was a plentiful provision—enough to have allowed the boy and the girl each a good slice of bread.

And the bread which this man and this woman ate was new and good; but the morsels thrown to the children were stale and mouldy.

"I tell you what," said the woman, whispering in a mysterious tone to her husband, "I have thought of an excellent plan to make Fanny useful."

"Well, Polly, and what's that?" demanded the man.

"Why," resumed his wife, her countenance wearing an expression of demoniac cruelty and cunning, "I've been thinking that Harry will soon be of use to you in your line. He'll be so handy to shove through a window, or to sneak down a area and hide himself all day in a cellar to open the door at night,—or a thousand things."

"In course he will," said Bill, with an approving nod.

"Well, but then there's Fanny. What good can she do for us for years and years to come? She won't beg—I know she won't. It's all that boy's lies when he says she does: he is very fond of her, and only tells us that to screen her. Now I've a very great mind to do someot that will make her beg—aye, and be glad to beg, and beg too in spite of herself".

"What the hell do you mean?"

"Why, doing *that* to her which will put her entirely at our mercy, and at the same time render her an object of such interest that the people *must* give her money. I'd wager that with my plan she'd get her five bob a day; and what a blessin' that would be."

"But how?" said Bill impatiently.

"And then," continued the woman, without heeding this question, "she wouldn't want Henry with her; and you might begin to make him useful some how or another. All we should have to do would be to take Fanny every day to some good thoroughfare, put her down there of a mornin,' and go and fetch her agen at night; and I'll warrant she'd keep us in beer—aye, and in brandy too."

"What the devil are you driving at?" demanded the man.

"Can't you guess?"

"No—blow me if I can."

"Do you fancy the scheme?"

"Am I a fool? Why, of course I do: but how the deuce is all this to be done? You never could learn Fanny to be so fly as that?"

"I don't want to learn her anything at all. What I propose is to force it on her."

"And how is that?" asked the man.

"By putting her eyes out," returned the woman.

Her husband was a robber—yes, and a murderer: but he started when this proposal met his ear.

"There's nothin' like a blind child to excite compassion," added the woman coolly. "I know it for a fact," she continued, after a pause, seeing that her husband did not answer her. "There's old Kate Betts, who got all her money by travelling about the country with two blind girls; and she made 'em blind herself too—she's often told me how she did it; and that has put the idea into my head."

"And how did she do it?" asked the man, lighting his pipe, but not glancing towards his wife; for although her words had made a deep impression upon him, he was yet struggling with the remnant of a parental feeling, which remained in his heart in spite of himself.

"She covered the eyes over with cockle shells, the eye-lids, recollect, being wide open; and in each shell there was a large black beetle. A bandage tied tight round the head, kept the shells in their place; and the shells kept the eyelids open. In a few days the eyes got quite blind, and the pupils had a dull white appearance."

"And you're serious, are you?" demanded the man.

"Quite," returned the woman, boldly: "why not?"

"Why not indeed?" echoed Bill, who approved of the horrible scheme, but shuddered at the cruelty of it, villain as he was.

"Ah! why not?" pursued the female: "one must make one's children useful somehow or another. So, if you don't mind, I'll send Harry out alone tomorrow morning and keep Fanny at home. The moment the boy's out of the way, I'll try my hand at Kate Betts's plan."

The conversation was interrupted by a low knock at the attic-door.

CHAPTER XIX.
MORNING.

THE orgie lasted throughout the night in the "boozing-ken." There were plenty of kind guests who, being flush with money, treated those that had none; and thus Tom the Cracksman, Dick Flairer, and Bill Bolter, were able to indulge, to their heart's content, in the adulterated liquors sold at the establishment.

The cold raw November morning was ushered in with a fine mizzling rain. The gas-lights were extinguished in the parlour; and the dawn of day fell upon countenances inflamed with debauchery, and rendered hideous by dirt and dark bristling beards.

[…]

In the parlour there were several men occupied in warming beer, toasting herrings, and frying sausages. The tables were smeared over with a rag as black as a hat, by a dirty slip-shod drab of a girl […] Totally regardless of her presence, the men continued their obscene and filthy discourse; and she proceeded with her work as coolly as if nothing offensive met her ears.

[…]

There are, thank God! thousands of British women who constitute the glory of their sex—chaste, virtuous, delicate-minded, and pure in thought and action,—beings who are but one remove from angels now, but who will be angels hereafter when they succeed to their inheritance of immortality. It must be to such as these that the eyes of the poet are turned when he eulogises, in glowing and impassioned language, the entire sex comprehended under the bewitching name of WOMAN! For, oh! how would his mind be shocked, were he to wander for a few hours amidst those haunts of vice and sinks of depravity which we have just described;—his spirit, towering on eagle-wing up into the sunny skies of poesy, would flutter back again to the earth, at the aspect of those foul and loathsome wretches, who, in the female shape, are found in the dwelling-places of poverty and crime!

But to continue.

Bill Bolter took leave of his companions at about eight o'clock in the morning, after a night of boisterous revelry; and rapidly retraced his steps homewards.

Field Lane was swarming with life. The miserable little shops were all open; and their proprietors were busy in displaying their commodities to the best advantage. Here Jewesses were occupied in suspending innumerable silk handkerchiefs to wires and poles over their doors: there the "translators" of old shoes were employed in spreading their stock upon the shelves that filled the place where the windows ought to have been. In one or two low dark shops women were engaged in arranging herrings, stockfish, and dried haddocks: in another, coals, vegetables, and oysters were exposed for sale; and not a few were hung with "old clothes as good as new." To this we may add that in the centre of the great metropolis of the mightiest empire in the world—in a city possessing a police which annually costs the nation thousands of pounds—and in a country whose laws are vaunted as being adapted to reach and baffle all degrees of crime—numbers of receivers of stolen goods were boldly, safely, and tranquilly exposing for sale the articles which their agents had "picked up" during the preceding night.

There was, however, nothing in the aspect of Field Lane at all new to the eyes of Bill Bolter. Indeed he merely went down that Jew's bazaar, in his way homewards, because he was anxious to purchase certain luxuries in the shape of red-herrings for his breakfast, he having borrowed a trifle of a friend at the "boozing-ken" to supply his immediate necessities.

When he arrived at his lodgings in Lower Union Court, he was assailed with a storm of reproaches, menaces, and curses, on the part of his wife, for having stayed all night at the "boozing ken." At first that cruel and remorseless man trembled—actually turned pale and trembled in the presence of the virago who thus attacked him. But at length his passion was aroused by her taunts and threats; and after bandying some horrible abuse and foul epithets with the infuriate woman, he was provoked to blows. With one stroke of his enormous fist, he felled her to the ground, and then brutally kicked her as she lay almost senseless at his feet.

He then coolly sate down by the fire to cook his own breakfast, without paying the least attention to the two poor children, who were crying bitterly in the corner of the room where they had slept.

In a few minutes the woman rose painfully from the floor. Her features were distorted and her lips were livid with rage. She dared not, however, attempt to irritate her furious husband any farther: still her passion required a vent. She looked round, and seemed to reflect for a moment.

Then, in the next instant, all her concentrated rage burst upon the heads of her unhappy offspring.

With a horrible curse at their squalling, the woman leapt, like a tiger-cat, upon the poor little boy and girl. Harry, as usual, covered his sister with his own thin and emaciated form as well as he could; and a torrent of blows rained down upon his naked flesh. The punishment which that maddened wretch thus inflicted upon him, was horrible in the extreme.

A thousand times before that day had Polly Bolter treated her children with demoniac cruelty; and her husband had not attempted to interfere. On the present occasion, however, he took it into his head to meddle in the matter—for the simple reason that, having quarrelled with his wife, he hated her at the moment, and greedily availed himself of any opportunity to thwart or oppose her.

Starting from his chair, he exclaimed, "Come, now—I say, leave those children alone. They haven't done nothing to you."

"You mind your own business," returned the woman, desisting for an instant from her attack upon the boy, and casting a look of mingled defiance and contempt at her husband.

That woman's countenance, naturally ugly and revolting, was now absolutely frightful.

"I say, leave them children alone," cried Bill. "If you touch 'em again, I'll drop down on you."

"Oh, you coward! to hit a woman! I wish I was a man, I'd pay you off for this: and if I was, you wouldn't dare strike me."

"Mind what you say, Poll; I'm in no humour to be teased this morning. Keep your mawleys off the kids, or I'm blessed if I don't do for you."

"Ugh—coward! This is the way I dare you;" and she dealt a tremendous blow upon her boy's shoulder.

The poor lad screamed piteously: the hand of his mother had fallen with the weight of a sledge hammer upon his naked flesh.

But that ferocious blow was echoed by another, at scarcely a moment's interval. The latter was dealt by the fist of Bill Bolter, and fell upon the back part of the ruthless mother's head with stunning force.

The woman fell forward, and struck her face violently against the corner of the deal table.

Her left eye came in contact with the angle of the board, and was literally crushed in its socket—an awful retribution upon her who only a few hours before was planning how to plunge her innocent and helpless daughter into the eternal night of blindness.

She fell upon the floor, and a low moan escaped her lips. She endeavoured to carry her right hand to her now sightless eye; but her strength failed her, and her arm fell lifeless by her side. She was dying.

The man was now alarmed, and hastened to raise her up. The children were struck dumb with unknown fears, and clasped each other in their little arms.

The woman recovered sufficient consciousness during the two or three seconds which preceded the exhalation of her last breath, to glance with her remaining eye up into her husband's face. She could not, however, utter an articulate sound—not even another moan.

But no pen could depict, and no words describe, the deadly—the malignant—the fiendish—hatred which animated her countenance as she thus met her husband's gaze.

The tigress, enveloped in the folds of the boa-constrictor, never darted such a glance of impotent but profound and concentrated rage upon the serpent that held it powerless in its fatal clasp.

She expired with her features still distorted by that horrible expression of vindictive spite.

A few moments elapsed before the man was aware that his wife was dead—that he had murdered her!

He supported her mechanically, as it were; for he was dismayed and appalled by the savage aspect which her countenance had assumed—that countenance which was rendered the more hideous by the bleeding eye-ball crushed in its socket.

At length he perceived that she was no more; and, with a terrible oath, he let her head drop upon the floor.

For a minute he stood and contemplated the corpse:—a whirlwind was in his brain.

The voices of his children aroused him from his reverie.

"Father, what's the matter with mother?" asked the boy, in a timid and subdued tone.

"Mother's hurt herself," said Fanny: "poor mother!"

"Look at mother's eye, father," added the boy: "do look at it! I'm sure something dreadful is the matter."

"Damnation!" ejaculated the murderer: and, after another minute's hesitation, he hurried to the door.

"O, father, father, don't leave us—don't go away from us!" cried the little boy, bursting into an agony of tears: "pray don't go away, father! I think mother's dead," added he with a glance of horror and apprehension towards the corpse: "so don't leave us, father—and I and Fanny will go out and beg, and do anything you like; only pray don't leave us; don't, don't, leave us!"

[…]

In another moment the two children were alone with the corpse of their mother; while the murderer was rapidly descending the stairs to escape from the contemplation of that scene of horror.

CHAPTER XXIII.
THE OLD HOUSE IN SMITHFIELD AGAIN.

The visitor to the Polytechnic Institution or the Adelaide Gallery, has doubtless seen the exhibition of the microscope. A drop of the purest water, magnified by that instrument some thousands of times, appears filled with horrible reptiles and monsters of revolting forms.

Such is London.

Fair and attractive as the mighty metropolis may appear to the superficial observer, it swarms with disgusting, loathsome, and venomous objects, wearing human shapes.

Oh! London is a city of strange contrasts!

The bustle of business, and the smile of pleasure,—the peaceful citizen, and the gay soldier,—the splendid shop, and the itinerant pastry-stall,—the gorgeous equipage, and the humble market-cart,—the palaces of nobles, and the hovels of the poor,—the psalm from the chapel, and the shout of laughter from the tavern,—the dandies lounging in the west-end streets, and the paupers cleansing away the mud,—the funeral procession, and the bridal cavalcade,—the wealthy and high-born lady whose reputation is above all cavil, and the lost girl whose shame is below all notice, [...] in a word, grandeur and squalor, wealth and misery, virtue and vice,—honesty which has never been tried, and crime which yielded to the force of irresistible circumstances,—all the features, all the characteristics, all the morals, of a great city, must occupy the attention of him who surveys London with microscopic eye.

And what a splendid subject for the contemplation of the moralist is a mighty city which, at every succeeding hour, presents a new phase of interest to the view;—in the morning, when only the industrious and the thrifty are abroad, and while the wealthy and the great are sleeping off the night's pleasure and dissipation:—at noon, when the streets are swarming with life, as if some secret source without the walls poured at that hour myriads of animated streams into the countless avenues and thoroughfares;—in the evening, when the men of pleasure again venture forth, and music, and dancing, and revelry prevail around;—and at night, when every lazar-house vomits forth its filth, every den lets loose its horrors, and every foul court and alley echoes to the footsteps of crime!

It was about two o'clock in the morning, [...] that a man, drenched by the rain which continued to pour in torrents, with his hat drawn over his eyes, and his hands thrust in his pockets to protect them against the cold, crept cautiously down West Street, from Smithfield, dodged past the policeman, and entered the old house which we have described at the beginning of our narrative.

[...]

This man—so wet, so cold, and so miserable—was Bill Bolter, the murderer.

[The murderer Bolter seeks refuge in the Old House, and drinks rum with his fellow criminals, one of whom sings the Thieves' Alphabet.]

THE THIEVES' ALPHABET

A was an Area-sneak, leary and sly;
B was a Buzgloak, with fingers so fly;
C was a Cracksman, that forked all the plate;
D was a Dubsman, who kept the jug-gate.
  For we are rollicking chaps,
   All smoking, singing, boozing;
  We care not for the traps,
   But pass the night carousing!

E was an Efter, that went to the play;
F was a Fogle he knapped on his way;
G was a Gag, which he told to the beak;
H was a Hum-box, where parish-prigs speak.
       CHORUS.

I was an Ikey, with swag all encumbered;
J was a Jug, in whose cell he was lumbered;
K was a Kye-bosh, that paid for his treat;
L was a Leaf that fell under his feet.
       CHORUS.

M was a Magsman, frequenting Pall-Mall;
N was a Nose that turned chirp on his pal;
O was an Onion, possessed by a swell;
P was a Pannie, done niblike and well.
       CHORUS.

Q was a Queer-screen, that served as a blind;
R was a Reader, with flimsies well-lined;
S was a Smasher, so nutty and spry;
T was a Ticker, just faked from a cly.
       CHORUS.

U was an Up-tucker, fly with the cord;
V was a Varnisher, dressed like a lord;
Y was a Yoxter that eat caper sauce:
Z was a Ziff who was flashed on the horse.
  For we are rollicking chaps
   All smoking, singing, boozing:
  We care not for the traps,
   But pass the night carousing.

[Efter: a thief who frequents theatres; Hum-box: pulpit; Ikey: a Jew fence, receiver of stolen goods; Kye-bosh: one shilling and sixpence; Leaf: the drop; Onion: a watch seal; Queer-screen: served to deceive the unwary; Reader: pocket book; Ticker: watch; Up-tucker: Jack Ketch; Varnisher: utterer of false sovereigns; Yoxter: a convict returned fron transportation before his time; To 'eat caper sauce': hanged; Ziff: juvenile thief; Flashed on the horse: privately whipped in prison.]

In this manner did the three thieves pass the first hours of morning at the old house in Chick Lane.

[Bolter hides in a concealed cellar in the House.]

[Richard Markham is arrested after the incident in the gambling den, accused of possessing a counterfeit note which has, in fact, been planted on him by the Honourable Arthur Chichester, and remanded to Newgate Gaol. Here, he meets members of the criminal gang who form one polarity in the narrative: Anthony Tidkins – the Resurrection Man – and his sworn enemy Jem Cuffin, known as Crankey Jem because of his unpredictable behaviour. He also meets Thomas Armstrong, a 'famous republican', imprisoned for his political beliefs, who relates that he has been betrayed by a man he trusted, George Montague. The contrast between Tidkins and Armstrong – one imprisoned for unspeakable crimes, and the other for his democratic ideals – makes an obvious political point. Richard Markham's friendship with Armstrong leads directly to his later involvement with the republican movement in Italy, while he is dogged by Tidkins until the conclusion of the tale. The episode derives some of its power from the horrific popular reputation of the old Newgate Gaol for atrocities of all kinds, and its almost mythic status within street literature of the period.]

CHAPTER XXVI.
NEWGATE.

NEWGATE! what an ominous sound has that word.

And yet the horror exists not in the name itself; for it is a very simple compound, and would not grate upon the ear nor produce a shudder throughout the frame, were it applied to any other kind of building.

It is, then, its associations and the ideas which it conjures up that render the word NEWGATE fearful and full of dark menace.

At the mere mention of this name, the mind instantaneously becomes filled with visions of vice in all its most hideous forms, and crime in all its most appalling shapes;—wards and court-yards filled with a population peculiar to themselves,—dark gloomy passages, where the gas burns all day long, and beneath the pavement of which are interred the remains of murderers and other miscreants who have expiated their crimes upon the scaffold,—shelves filled with the casts of the countenances of those wretches, taken the moment after they were cut down from the gibbet,—condemned cells,—the chapel in which funeral sermons are preached upon men yet alive to hear them, but who are doomed to die on the morrow,—the clanking of chains, the banging of huge doors, oaths, prayers, curses, and ejaculations of despair!

Oh! if it were true that the spirits of the departed are allowed to revisit the earth for certain purposes and on particular occasions,—if the belief of superstition were well founded, and night could be peopled with the ghosts and spectres of those who sleep in troubled graves,—what a place of ineffable horrors—what a scene of terrible sights, would Newgate be at midnight! The huge flag-stones of the pavement would rise, to permit the phantoms of the murderers to issue from their graves. Demons would erect a gibbet at the debtor's door; and, amidst the sinister glare of torches, an executioner from hell would hang those miscreants over again. This would be part of their posthumous punishment, and would occur in the long—long nights of winter. There would be no moon; but all the windows of Newgate looking upon the court-yards (and there are none commanding the streets) would be brilliantly lighted with red flames, coming from an unknown source. And throughout the long passages of the prison would resound the orgies of hell; and skeletons wrapped in winding sheets would shake their fetters; and Greenacre and Good—Courvoisier and Pegsworth—Blakesley and Marchant, with all their predecessors in the walks of murder, would come in fearful procession from the gibbet, returning by the very corridors which they traversed in their way to death on the respective mornings of their execution. Banquets would be served up to them in the condemned cells; demons would minister to them; and their food should be the flesh, and their drink the gore, of the victims whom they had assassinated upon earth!

All would be horrible—horrible!

But, heaven be thanked! such scenes are impossible; and never can it be given to the shades of the departed to revisit the haunts which they loved or hated—adored or desecrated, upon earth!

NEWGATE!—fearful name!

And Richard Markham was now in Newgate.

He found, when the massive gates of that terrible prison closed behind him, that the consciousness of innocence will not afford entire consolation, in the dilemma in which unjust suspicions may involve the victim of circumstantial evidence. He scarcely knew in what manner to grapple with the difficulties that beset him;—he dared not contemplate the probability of a condemnation to some infamous punishment;—and he could scarcely hope for an acquittal in the face of the testimony that conspired against him.

He recalled to mind all the events of his infancy and his boyish years, and contrasted his present position with that which he once enjoyed in the society of his father and Eugene.

His brother?—aye—what had become of his brother?—that brother, who had left the paternal roof to seek his own fortunes, and who had made so strange an appointment for a distant date, upon the hill-top where the two trees were planted? Four years and four months had passed away since the day on which that appointment was made; and in seven years and eight months it was to be kept.

They were then to compare notes of their adventures and success in life, and decide who was the more prosperous of the two,—Eugene, who was dependent upon his own resources, and had to climb the ladder of fortune step by step;—or Richard, who, placed by his father's love half-way up that ladder, had only to avail himself, it would have seemed, of his advantageous position to reach the top at his leisure?

But, alas! probably Eugene was a miserable wanderer upon the face of the earth; perhaps he was mouldering beneath the sod that no parental nor fraternal tears had watered;—or haply he was languishing in some loathsome dungeon the doors of which served as barriers between him and all communion with his fellow-men!

It was strange—passing strange that Eugene had never written since his departure; and that from the fatal evening of his separation on the hill-top all traces of him should have been so suddenly lost.

[...]

Such were the topics of Markham's thoughts, as he walked up and down the large paved court-yard belonging to that department of the prison to which he had been consigned;—and, of a surety, they were of no pleasurable description.

[...]

CHAPTER XXVII.
THE REPUBLICAN AND THE RESURRECTION MAN.

As Richard was walking up and down the yard, an hour or two after his interview with Mr. Monroe, he was attracted by the venerable appearance of an elderly gentleman who was also parading that dismal place to and fro.

This individual was attired in a complete suit of black; and his pale countenance, and long grey hair flowing over his coat-collar, were rendered the more remarkable by the mournful nature of his garb. He stooped considerably in his gait, and walked with his hands joined together behind him. His eyes were cast upon the ground; and his meditations appeared to be of a profound and soul-absorbing nature.

Markham immediately experienced a strange curiosity to become acquainted with this individual, and to ascertain the cause of his imprisonment. He did not, however, choose to interrupt that venerable man's reverie.

Accident presently favoured his wishes, and placed within his reach the means of introduction to the object of his curiosity. The old gentleman changed his line of walk in the spacious yard, and tripped over a loose flagstone. His head came suddenly in contact with the ground. Richard hastened to raise him up, and conducted him to a bench. The old gentleman was very grateful for these attentions; and, when he was recovered from the effects of his fall, he surveyed Markham with the utmost interest.

"What circumstance has thrown you into this vile den?" he inquired, in a pleasant tone of voice.

Richard instantly related, from beginning to end, those particulars with which the reader is already acquainted.

[…]

"And now, permit me to ask you what has plunged you into a gaol? No crime, I feel convinced before you speak!"

"Never judge hastily, young man," returned the old gentleman. "My conviction of your innocence was principally established by the very circumstance which would have led others to pronounce in favour of your guilt. You blushed—deeply blushed; but it was not the glow of shame: it was the honest flush of conscious integrity unjustly suspected. Now, with regard to myself, I know why you imagine me to be innocent of any crime; but, remember that a mild, peaceable, and venerable exterior frequently covers a heart eaten up with every evil passion, and a soul stained with every crime. You were, however, right in your conjecture relative to myself. I am a person accused of a political offence—a libel upon the government, in a journal of considerable influence which I conduct. I shall be tried next session, my sentence will not be severe, perhaps; but it will not be the less unjust. I am the friend of my fellow countrymen and my fellow-creatures: the upright and the enlightened denominate me a philanthropist: my enemies denounce me as a disturber of the public peace, a seditious agitator, and a visionary. You have undoubtedly heard of Thomas Armstrong?"

"I have not only heard of you, sir," said Richard, surveying the great Republican writer with profound admiration and respect, "but I have read your works and your essays with pleasure and interest."

[…]

Markham gazed upon that venerable gentleman with profound respect. He remembered to have seen the daily Tory newspapers denounce that same old man as "an unprincipled agitator—the enemy of his country—the foe to morality—a political ruffian—a bloody-minded votary of Danton and Robespierre:"—and he now heard the sweetest and holiest sentiment of Christian morality emanate from the lips of him who had thus been fearfully represented. […]

Presently the conversation was resumed; and the more that Markham saw of the Republican, the more did he respect and admire him.

In the course of the afternoon, Markham was accosted by one of his fellow-prisoners, who beckoned him aside in a somewhat mysterious manner. This individual was a very short, thin, cadaverous-looking man, with coal-black hair and whiskers, and dark piercing eyes half concealed beneath shaggy brows of the deepest jet. He was apparently about five-and-thirty years of age. His countenance was downcast; and when he spoke, he seemed as if he could not support the glance of the person whom he addressed. He was dressed in a seedy suit of black, and wore an oil-skin cap with a large shade.

 This person, who was very reserved and retired in his habits, and seldom associated with his fellow prisoners, drew Markham aside, and said, "I've taken a liberty with your name; but I know you won't mind it. In a place like this we must help and assist each other."

"And in what way—" began Markham.

"Oh! nothing important; only it's just as well to tell you in case the turnkey says a word about it. The fact is, I haven't half enough to eat with this infernal gruel and soup that they give those who, like me, are forced to take the gaol allowance, and my old mother—who is known by the name of the Mummy—has promised to send me in presently a jolly good quartern loaf and three or four pound of Dutch cheese."

"But I thought that those who took the gaol allowance were not permitted to receive any food from outside?" said Markham.

"That's the very thing," said the man: "so I have told the Mummy to direct the parcel to you, as I know that you grub yourself at your own cost."

"So long as it does not involve me—"

"No—not in the least, my good fellow," interrupted the other. "And, in return," he added, after a moment's pause, "if I can ever do you a service, outside or in, you may reckon upon the Resurrection Man."

"The Resurrection Man!" ejaculated Richard, appalled, in spite of himself, at this ominous title.

"Yes—that's my name and profession," said the man. "My godfathers and godmothers called me Anthony, and my parents had previously blessed me with the honourable appellation of Tidkins: so you may know me as Anthony Tidkins, the Resurrection Man."

"And are you really—" began Richard, with a partial shudder; "are you really a—"

"A body snatcher?" cried Anthony; "of course I am—when there's any work to be done; and when there isn't, then I do a little in another line."

"And what may that be?" demanded Markham.

This time the Resurrection Man *did* look his interlocutor full in the face; but it was only for a moment; and he again averted his glance in a sinister manner, as he jerked his thumb towards the wall of the yard, and exclaimed, "Crankey Jem on t'other side will tell you if you ask him. They would not put us together: no—no," he added with a species of chuckle; "they know a trick worth two of that. We shall both be tried together: fifteen years for him—freedom for me! That's the way to do it."

With these words the Resurrection Man turned upon his heels, and walked away to the farther end of the yard.

We shall now take leave of Markham for the present: when we again call the reader's attention to his case, we shall find him standing in the dock of the Central Criminal Court, to take his trial upon the grave accusation of passing forged notes.

[In this scene, illustrated by a graphic wood engraving, the murderer Bill Bolter is in hiding in a dungeon where he is haunted by horrific phantasms, including the avenging ghost of his dead wife.]

CHAPTER XXVIII.
THE DUNGEON.

RETURN we now to Bill Bolter, the murderer, who had taken refuge in the subterranean hiding-place of the Old House in Chick Lane.

Heavily and wearily did the hours drag along. The inmate of that terrible dungeon was enabled to mark their lapse by the deep-mouthed bell of St. Sepulchre's Church, on Snow Hill, the sound of which boomed ominously at regular intervals upon his ear.

That same bell tolls the death-note of the convict on the morning of his execution at the debtors' door of Newgate.

The murderer remembered this, and shuddered.

A faint—faint light glimmered through the little grating at the end of the dungeon; and the man kept his eyes fixed upon it so long, that at length his imagination began to conjure up phamtoms to appal him. That small square aperture became a frame in which hideous countenances appeared; and then, one gradually changed into another—horrible dissolving views that they were!

But chiefly he beheld before him the tall gaunt form of his murdered wife—with one eye smashed and bleeding in her head:—the other glared fearfully upon him.

This phantasmagoria became at length so fearful and so real in appearance, that the murderer turned his back towards the little grating through which the light struggled into the dungeon in two long, narrow, and oblique columns.

But then he imagined that there were goblins behind him; and this idea soon grew as insupportable as the first;—so he rose, and groped his way up and down that narrow vault—a vault which might become his tomb!

This horrible thought never left his memory. Even while he reflected upon other things,—amidst the perils which enveloped his career, and the reminiscences of the dread deeds of which he had been guilty,—amongst the reasons which he assembled together to convince himself that the hideous countenances at the grating did not exist in reality,—there was that one idea —unmixed—definite—standing boldly out from all the rest in his imagination,—*that he might be left to die of starvation*!

At one time the brain of this wretch was excited to such a pitch that he actually caught his head in his two hands, and pressed it with all his force— to endeavour to crush the horrible visions which haunted his imagination.

Then he endeavoured to hum a tune; but his voice seemed to choke him. He lighted a pipe, and sate and smoked; but as the thin blue vapour curled upwards, in the faint light of the grating, it assumed shapes and forms appalling to behold. Spectres, clad in long winding sheets—cold grisly corpses, dressed in shrouds, seemed to move noiselessly through the dungeon.

He laid aside the pipe; and, in a state of mind bordering almost upon frenzy, tossed off the brandy that had remained in the flask.

[First version of the wood engraving, published by George Vickers]

But so full of horrible ideas was his mind at that moment, that it appeared to him as if he had been drinking blood!

He rose from his seat once more, and groped up and down the dungeon, careless of the almost stunning blows which he gave his head, and the violent contusions which his limbs received, against the uneven walls.

Hark! suddenly voices fell upon his ears.

He listened with mingled fear and joy,—fear of being discovered, and joy at the sound of human tones in the midst of that subterranean solitude.

Those voices came from the lower window of the dwelling on the other side of the ditch.

"How silent and quiet everything has been lately in the old house opposite," said a female.

"Last night—or rather early this morning, I heard singing there," replied another voice, which was evidently that of a young woman.

[Later version of the wood engraving, published by John Dicks]

Oh! never had the human tones sounded so sweet and musical upon the murderer's ears before!

"It is very seldom that any one ever goes into that old house now," said the first speaker.

"Strange rumours are abroad concerning it: I heard that there are subterranean places in which men can conceal themselves, and no power on earth could find them save those in the secret."

"How absurd, I was speaking to the policeman about that very thing a few days ago; and he laughed at the idea. He says it is impossible; and of course he knows best."

"I am not so sure of that. Who knows what fearful deeds have those old walls concealed from human eye? For my part, I can very well believe that there are secret cells and caverns. Who knows but that some poor wretch is hiding there this very moment?"

"Perhaps the man that murdered his wife up in Union Court."

"Well—who knows? But at this rate we shall never get on with our work."

The noise of a window being shut down fell upon the murderer's ears: and he heard no more.

But he had heard enough! Those girls had spoken of him:—they had mentioned him as *the man who had murdered his wife*.

The assassination, then, was already known: the dread deed was bruited abroad:—thousands and thousands of tongues had no doubt repeated the tale here and there—conveying it hither and thither—far and wide!

And throughout the vast metropolis was he already spoken of as *the man who had murdered his wife!*

And in a few hours more, would millions in all parts hear of *the man who had murdered his wife!*

And already were the officers of justice actively in search of *the man who had murdered his wife!*

Heavily—heavily passed the hours.

At length the dungeon became pitch dark; and then the murderer saw sights more appalling than when the faint gleam stole through the grating.

In due time the sonorous voice of St. Sepulchre proclaimed the hour of nine.

Scarcely had the last stroke of that iron tongue died upon the breeze, when a noise at the head of the spiral staircase fell upon the murderer's ears. The trap-door was raised, and the well-known voice of Dick Flairer was heard.

"Well, Bill—alive or dead, eh—old fellow!" exclaimed the burglar.

"Alive—and that's all, Dick," answered Bill Bolter, ascending the staircase.

"My God! how pale you are, Bill," said Dick, the moment the light of the candle fell upon the countenance of the murderer, as he emerged from the trap-door.

"Pale, Dick!" ejaculated the wretch, a shudder passing over his entire frame; "I do not believe I can stand a night in that infernal hole."

"You must, Bill—you must," said Flairer: "all is discovered up in Union Court there, and the police are about in all directions."

"When was it found out? Tell me the particulars—speak!" said the murderer, with frenzied impatience.

"Why, it appears that the neighbours heard a devil of a noise in your room, but didn't think nothink about it, cos you and Polly used to spar a bit now and then. But at the last the boy—Harry, I mean—went down stairs, and said that his mother wouldn't move, and that his father had gone away. So up the neighbours went—and then everything was blown. The children was sent to the workus, and the coroner held his inquest this afternoon at three. Harry was had up before him; and—"

"And what?" demanded Bolter, hastily.

"And, in course," added Dick, "the Coroner got out of the boy all the particklars: so the jury returned a verdict—"

"Of *Wilful Murder*, eh?" said Bill, sinking his voice almost to a whisper.

"*Wilful Murder against William Bolter*," answered Dick, coolly.

"That little vagabond Harry!" cried the criminal—his entire countenance distorted with rage; "I'll be the death on him!"

"There's no news at all about t'other affair up at Clapton, and no stir made in it at all," said Dick. after a moment's pause: "so that there business is all right. But here's a lot of grub and plenty of lush, Bill: that'll cheer ye, if nothink else will."

"Dick!" exclaimed the murderer, "I cannot go back into that hole—I had rather get nabbed at once. The few hours I have already been there have nearly drove me mad; and I can't—I won't attempt the night in that infernal cold damp vault. I feel as if I was in my coffin."

"Well, you know best," said Dick, coolly. "A hempen neckcloth at Tuck-up fair, and a leap from a tree with only one leaf, is what you'll get if you're perverse."

"My God—my God!" ejaculated Bolter, wringing his hands, and throwing glances of extreme terror around the room; "what am I to do? what am I to do?"

"Lie still down below for a few weeks, or go out and be scragged," said Dick Flairer. "Come, Bill, be a man; and don't take on in this here way. Besides, I'm in a hurry, and must be off. I've brought you enough grub for three days, as I shan't come here too often till the business has blowed over a little."

Bill Bolter took a long draught from a quart bottle of rum which his friend had brought with him; and he then felt his spirits revive. Horrible as the prospect of a long sojourn in the dungeon appeared, it was still preferable to the fearful doom which must inevitably follow his capture; and, accordingly, the criminal once more returned to his hiding-place.

Dick Flairer promised to return on the third evening from that time; and the trap-door again closed over the head of the murderer.

Bolter supped off a portion of the provisions which his friend had brought him, and then lay down upon the hard stone bench to sleep. A noisome stench entered the dungeon from the Ditch, and the rats ran over the person of the inmate of that subterranean hole. Repose was impossible: the miserable wretch therefore sat up, and began to smoke.

By accident he kicked his leg a little way beneath the stone bench: the heel of his boot encountered something that yielded to the touch; and a strange noise followed.

That noise was like the rattling of bones!

The pipe fell from the man's grasp; and he himself was stupefied with sudden terror.

At length, exercising immense violence over his feelings, he determined to ascertain whether the horrible suspicions which had entered his mind were well-founded or not.

He thrust his hand beneath the bench, and encountered the mouldering bones of a human skeleton.

With indescribable feelings of agony and horror he threw himself upon the bench—his hair on end, and his heart palpitating violently.

Heaven only can tell how he passed that long weary night—alone, in the darkness of the dungeon, with his own thoughts, the skeleton of some murdered victim, and the vermin that infected the subterranean hole.

He slept not a wink throughout those live-long hours, the lapse of which was proclaimed by the voice of Saint Sepulchre's solemn and deep-toned bell.

And none who heard the bell during that night experienced feelings of such intense anguish and horror as the murderer in his lurking-hole. Not even the neighbouring prison of Newgate, nor the hospital of Saint Bartholomew, nor the death-bed of a parent, knew mental suffering so terrible as that which wrung the heart of this guilty wretch.

The morning dawned; and the light returned to the dungeon.

The clock had just struck eight, and the murderer was endeavouring to force a mouthful of food down his throat, when the voice of a man in the street fell upon his ear. He drew close up to the grating, and clearly heard the following announcement:—

"*Here is a full and perfect account of the horrible assassination committed by the miscreant William Bolter, upon the person of his wife; with a portrait of the murderer, and a representation of the room as it appeared when the dead was first discovered by a neighbour. Only one Penny! The fullest and most perfect account—only one Penny!*"

A pause ensued, and then the voice, bawling more lustily than before, continued thus:—

"*A full and perfect account of the bloody and cruel murder in Upper Union Court; shewing how the assassin first dashed out one of his victim's eyes, and then fractured her skull upon the floor. Only one Penny, together with a true portrait of the murderer, for whose apprehension a reward of One Hundred Pounds is offered! Only one Penny!*"

"A reward of one hundred pounds!" cried another voice: "my eye! how I should like to find him!"

"Wouldn't I precious soon give him up!" ejaculated a third.

"I wonder whereabouts he is," said a fourth. "No doubt that he has run away—perhaps to America—perhaps to France."

"That shews how much you know about such things," said a fifth speaker. "It is a very strange fact, that murderers always linger near the scene of their crime; they are attracted towards it, seemingly, as the moth is to the candle. Now, for my part, I shouldn't at all wonder if the miscreant was within a hundred yards of us at the present moment."

"*Only one Penny! The fullest and most perfect account of the horrible and bloody murder—*"

The itinerant vender of pamphlets passed on, followed by the crowd which his vociferations had collected; and his voice soon ceased to break the silence of the morning.

Bolter sank down upon the stone bench, a prey to maddening feelings and fearful emotions.

A hundred pounds were offered for his capture! Such a sum might tempt even Dick Flairer or Tom the Cracksman to betray him.

Instinctively he put his fingers to his neck, to feel if the rope were there yet, and he shook his head violently to ascertain if he were hanging on a gibbet, or could still control his motions.

The words "miscreant," "horrible and bloody murder," and "portrait of the assassin," still rang in his ears—loud—sonorous—deep—and with a prolonged echo like that of a bell!

Already were men speculating upon his whereabouts, and anxious for his apprehension—some for the reward, others to gratify a morbid curiosity: already were the newspapers, the cheap press, and the pamphleteers busy with his name.

None now mentioned him save as *the miscreant William Bolter.*

Oh! if he could but escape to some foreign land,—if he could but avoid the ignominious consequences of his crime in this,—he would dedicate the remainder of his days to penitence,—he would toil from the dawn of morning till sunset to obtain the bread of honesty,—he would use every effort, exert every nerve to atone for the outrage he had committed upon the laws of society!

But—no! it was too late. The blood-hounds of the law were already upon his track.

An hour passed away; and during that interval the murderer sought to compose himself by means of his pipe and the rum-bottle: but he could not banish the horrible ideas which haunted him.

Suddenly a strange noise fell upon his ear.

The blood appeared to run cold to his very heart in a refluent tide; for the steps of many feet, and the sounds of many voices, echoed through the old house.

The truth instantly flashed to his mind: the police had entered the premises.

With hair standing on end, eye-balls glaring, and forehead bathed in perspiration, the murderer sate motionless upon the cold stone bench—afraid even to breathe. Every moment he expected to hear the trap-door at the head of the spiral staircase move: but several minutes elapsed, and his fears in this respect were not accomplished.

At length he heard a sound as of a body falling heavily; and then a voice almost close to him fell upon his ear.

The reader will remember that the vault in which he was concealed, joined the cellar from whence Walter Sydney had escaped. The officers had entered that cellar by means of the trap-door in the floor of the room immediately above it. Bolter could overhear their entire conversation.

"Well, this is a strange crib, this is," said one. "Show the bull's-eye up in that farther corner: there may be a door in one of them dark nooks."

"It will jist end as I said it would," exclaimed another: "the feller wouldn't be sich a fool as to come to a place that's knowed to the Force as one of bad repute."

"I didn't think, myself, there was much good in coming to search this old crib: but the inspector said *yes*, and so we couldn't say *no*."

"Let's be off: the cold of this infernal den strikes to my very bones. But I say—that there shelving board that we first lighted on in getting down, isn't made to help people to come here alive."

"Turn the bull's-eye more on it."

"Now can you see?"

"Yes—plain enough. It leads to a hole that looks on the ditch. But the plank is quite old and rotten; so I dare say it was put there for some purpose or another a long time ago. Pr'aps the thieves used to convey their swag through that there hole into a boat in the ditch, and—"

"No, no," interrupted the other policeman: "it wasn't swag that they tumbled down the plank into the Fleet: it was stiff 'uns."

"Very likely. But there can't be any of that kind of work ever going on now: so let's be off."

The murderer in the adjoining vault could hear the policemen climb up the plank towards the trap-door; and in a few minutes profound silence again reigned throughout the old house.

This time he had escaped detection; and yet the search was keen and penetrating.

The apparent safety of his retreat restored him to something like good spirits; and he began to calculate the chances which he imagined to exist for and against the probability of his escape from the hands of justice.

"There is but five men in the world as knows of this hiding-place," he said to himself; "and them is myself, Dick Flairer, Crankey Jem, the Resurrection Man, and Tom the Cracksman. As for me, I'm here—that's one what won't blab. Dick Flairer isn't likely to sell a pal: Tom the Cracksman I'd rely on even if he was on the rack. Crankey Jem is staunch to the backbone; besides, he's in the Jug: so is the Resurrection Man. They can't do much harm there. I think I'm tolerably safe; and as for frightening myself about ghosts and goblins—"

He was suddenly interrupted by the rattling of the bones beneath the stone-bench. He started; and a profuse perspiration instantly broke out upon his forehead.

A huge rat had disturbed those relics of mortality; but this little incident tended to hurl the murderer back again into all that appalling gloominess of thought from which he had for a moment seemed to be escaping.

Time wore on: and heavily and wearily still passed the hours. At length darkness again came down upon the earth: the light of the little grating disappeared; and the vault was once more enveloped in the deepest obscurity.

The murderer ate a mouthful, and then endeavoured to compose himself to sleep, for he was worn out mentally and bodily.

The clock of Saint Sepulchre's proclaimed the hour of seven, as he awoke from a short and feverish slumber.

He thought he heard a voice calling him in his dreams; and when he started up he listened with affright.

"Bill—are you asleep?"

It was not, then, a dream: a human voice addressed him in reality.

"Bill—why don't you answer?" said the voice. "It's only me!"

Bolter suddenly felt relieved of an immense load; it was his friend Dick who was calling him from the little trap-door. He instantly hurried up the staircase, and was surprised to find that there was no light in the room.

"My dear feller," said Dick, in a hurried tone, "I didn't mean to come back so soon again, but me and Tom is a-going to do a little business together down Southampton way—someot that he has been told of; and as we may be away a few days, I thought I'd better come this evenin' with a fresh supply. Here's plenty of grub, and rum, and bakker."

"Well, this is a treat—to hear a friendly voice again so soon," said Bill;— "but why the devil don't you light the candle?"

"I'm a-going to do it now," returned Dick; and he struck a lucifer-match as he spoke. "I thought I wouldn't show a light here sooner than was necessary; and we must not keep it burning too long; cos there may be chinks in them shutters, and I des say the blue-bottles is on the scent."

"They come and searched the whole place this mornin'," said Bill: "but they didn't smell me though."

"Then you're all safe now, my boy," cried Dick. "Here, look alive—take this basket, and pitch it down the stairs: it's well tied up, and chock full of cold meat and bread. Put them two bottles into your pocket: there—that's right. Now—do you want anythink else?"

"Yes—a knife. I was forced to gnaw my food like a dog for want of one."

"Here you are," said Dick; and, taking a knife from the secret cupboard between the windows, he handed it to his friend. "Now are you all right?"

"Quite—that is, as right as a feller in my sitivation can be. You won't forget to come—"

Bolter was standing within two or three steps from the top of the staircase; and the greater part of his body was consequently above the trap-door.

He stopped suddenly short in the midst of his injunction to his companion, and staggered in such a way that he nearly lost his footing.

His eye had caught sight of a human countenance peering from behind the half-open door of the room.

"Damnation!" exclaimed the murderer: "I'm sold at last!"—and, rushing up the steps, he fell upon Dick Flairer with the fury of a tiger.

At the same moment four or five officers darted into the room:—but they were too late to prevent another dreadful deed of blood.

Bolter had plunged the knife which he held in his hand, into the heart of Dick Flairer, the burglar.

The blow was given with fatal effect: the unfortunate wretch uttered a horrible cry, and fell at the feet of his assassin, stone dead.

"Villain! what have you done?" ejaculated the serjeant who headed the little detachment of police.

"I've drawn the claret of the rascal that nosed upon me," returned Bolter doggedly.

"You were never more mistaken in your life," said the serjeant.

"How—what do you mean? Wasn't it that scoundrel Dick that chirped against me?"

"No—ten thousand times *No!*" cried the officer: "it was a prisoner in Newgate who split upon this hiding place. Somehow or another he heard of the reward offered to take you; and he told the governor the whole secret of the vault. Without knowing whether we should find you here or not, we came to search it."

"Then it was the Resurrection Man who betrayed me after all!" exclaimed Bolter; and, dashing the palms of his two hands violently against his temples, he added, in a tone of intense agony, "I have murdered my best friend—monster, miscreant that I am!"

The policeman speedily fixed a pair of manacles about his wrists; and in the course of a quarter of an hour he was safely secured in one of the cells at the station-house in Smithfield.

On the following day he was committed to Newgate.

[Bolter is found guilty of murder, and hanged.]

[As often, Reynolds incorporates contemporary controversy into his text: the discovery that private letters of the Italian political exile Mazzini had been opened by the Post Office on behalf of the Government led to a national scandal in the 1840s. There are documentary accounts of this in a number of the magazines edited by Reynolds (see *The London Journal*, 15 March 1845).]

CHAPTER XXIX.
THE BLACK CHAMBER.

ONCE more does the scene change.

The reader who follows us through the mazes of our narrative, has yet to be introduced to many strange places—many hideous haunts of crime, abodes of poverty, dens of horror, and lurking-holes of perfidy—as well as many seats of wealthy voluptuousness and aristocratic dissipation.

It will be our task to guide those who choose to accompany us, to scenes and places whose very existence may appear to belong to the regions of romance rather than to a city in the midst of civilisation, and whose characteristic features are as yet unknown to even those that are the best acquainted with the realities of life.

About a fortnight had elapsed since the events related in the preceding chapter.

In a small, high, well-lighted room five individuals were seated at a large round oaken table. One of these persons, who appeared to be the superior, was an elderly man with a high forehead, and thin white hair falling over the collar of his black coat. He was short and rather corpulent: his countenance denoted frankness and good-nature; but his eyes, which were small, grey, and sparkling, had a lurking expression of cunning, only perceptible to the acute observer. The other three individuals were young and gentlemanly-looking men, neatly dressed, and very deferential in their manners towards their superior.

The door of this room was carefully bolted. At one end of the table was a large black tray covered with an immense quantity of bread-seals of all sizes. Perhaps the reader may recall to mind that, amongst the pursuits and amusements of his school-days, he diverted himself with moistening the crumb of bread, and kneading it with his fingers into a consistency capable of taking and retaining an accurate impression of a seal upon a letter. The seals—or rather blank bread-stamps—now upon the tray, were of this kind, only more carefully manufactured, and well consolidated with thick gum-water.

Close by this tray, in a large wooden bowl, were wafers of all sizes and colours; and in a box also standing on the table, were numbers of wafer-stamps of every dimension used. A second box contained thin blades of steel, set fast in delicate ivory handles, and sharp as razors. A third box was filled with sticks of sealing-wax of all colours, and of foreign as well as British manufacture. A small glass retort fixed over a spirit-lamp, was placed near one of the young men. A tin-box containing a little cushion covered with printer's red ink in one compartment, and several stamps such as the reader may have seen used in post-offices, in another division, lay open near the other articles mentioned. Lastly, an immense pile of letters—some sealed, and others wafered—stood upon that end of the table at which the elderly gentleman was seated.

The occupations of these five individuals may be thus described in a few words.

The old gentleman took up the letters one by one, and bent them open, as it were, in such a way, that he could read a portion of their contents when they were not folded in such a manner as effectually to conceal all the writing. He also examined the addresses, and consulted a long paper of an official character which lay upon the table at his right hand. Some of the letters he threw, after as careful a scrutiny as he could devote to them without actually breaking the seals or wafers, into a large wicker basket at his feet. From time to time, however, he passed a letter to the young man who sate nearest to him.

If the letters were closed with wax, an impression of the seal was immediately taken by means of one of the bread stamps. The young man then took the letter and held it near the large fire which burnt in the grate until the sealing-wax became so softened by the heat that the letter could be easily opened without tearing the paper. The third clerk read it aloud, while the fourth took notes of its contents. It was then returned to the first young man, who re-sealed it by means of the impression taken on the bread stamp, and with wax which precisely matched that originally used in closing the letter. When this ceremony was performed, the letter was consigned to the same basket which contained those that had passed unopened through the hands of the Examiner.

If the letter were fastened with a wafer, the second clerk made the water in the little glass retort boil by means of the spirit-lamp; and when the vapour gushed forth from the tube, the young man held the letter to its mouth in such a way that the steam played full upon the identical spot where the wafer was placed. The wafer thus became moistened in a slight degree; and it was only then necessary to pass one of the thin steel blades skilfully beneath the wafer, in order to open the letter. The third young man then read this epistle, and the fourth took notes, as in the former instance. The contents being thus ascertained, the letter was easily fastened again with a very thin wafer of the same colour and size as the original; and if the job were at all clumsily done, the tin-box before noticed furnished the means of imprinting a red stamp upon the back of the letter, in such a way that a portion of the circle fell precisely over the spot beneath which the wafer was placed.

These processes were accomplished in total silence, save when the contents of the letters were read; and then, so accustomed were those five individuals to hear the revelations of the most strange secrets and singular communications, that they seldom appeared surprised or amused—shocked or horrified, at anything which those letters made known to them. Their task seemed purely of a mechanical kind: indeed, automatons could not have shewn less passion or excitement.

Oh! vile—despicable occupation,—performed, too, by men who went forth, with heads erect and confident demeanour, from their atrocious employment—after having violated those secrets which are deemed most sacred, and broken the seals which merchants, lovers, parents, relations, and friends, had placed upon their thoughts!

Base and diabolical outrage—perpetrated by the commands of the Ministers of the Sovereign!

Reader, this small, high, well-lighted room, in which such infamous scenes took place with doors all secured by bolts and bars, was the *Black Chamber of the General Post-Office, St. Martin's-le-Grand*.

And now, reader, do you ask whether all this be true;—whether, in the very heart of the metropolis of the civilized world, such a system and such a den of infamy can exist;—whether, in a word, the means of transferring thought at a cheap and rapid rate, be really made available to the purposes of government and the ends of party policy? If you ask these questions, to each and all do we confidently and boldly answer "Yes."

[…]

[After two years, both Eliza Sydney, who has been committed to prison for her part in the deception planned by Greenwood, and Richard Markham, are released from their respective gaols on the same day. Richard discovers that almost all his money has been lost by Mr Monroe, his guardian, who also acted on the advice of Montague Greenwood. Richard courts Isabella, the daughter of an Italian Count, to whom he has been introduced by Thomas Armstrong, the republican he met in Newgate. He is blackmailed by Tidkins, who threatens to reveal the truth about his past. They agree to meet in the 'Dark House', a tavern frequented by criminals.]

CHAPTER XLII.
"THE DARK HOUSE".

MARKHAM did not forget his appointment with the Resurrection Man.

[…]

There is probably not in all London—not even in Saint Giles's nor the Mint—so great an amount of squalid misery and fearful crime huddled together, as in the joint districts of Spitalfields and Bethnal Green. Between Shoreditch Church and Wentworth Street the most intense pangs of poverty, the most profligate morals, and the most odious crimes, rage with the fury of a pestilence.

Entire streets that are nought but sinks of misery and vice,—dark courts, fœtid with puddles of black slimy water,—alleys, blocked with heaps of filth, and nauseating with unwholesome odours, constitute, with but little variety, the vast district of which we are speaking.

The Eastern Counties' Railway intersects Spitalfields and Bethnal Green. The traveller upon this line may catch, from the windows of the carriage in which he journeys, a hasty, but alas! too comprehensive glance of the wretchedness and squalor of that portion of London. He may actually obtain a view of the interior and domestic misery peculiar to the neighbourhood; —he may penetrate, with his eyes, into the secrets of those abodes of sorrow, vice, and destitution. In summer time the poor always have their windows open, and thus the hideous poverty of their rooms can be readily descried from the summit of the arches on which the railroad is constructed.

And in these rooms may be seen women half naked,—some employed in washing the few rags which they possess,—others ironing the linen of a more wealthy neighbour,—a few preparing the sorry meal,—and numbers scolding, swearing, and quarrelling. At many of the windows, men out of work, with matted hair, black beards, and dressed only in filthy shirts and ragged trousers,—lounge all the day long, smoking.

[...]

The *Dark House* was a tavern of the lowest description in Brick Lane, a little north of the spot where the railway now intersects the street. The parlour of the *Dark House* was dirty and repulsive in all respects; the gas-lights formed two enormous black patches upon the ceiling; the tables were occupied by ill-looking men, whose principal articles of consumption were tobacco and malt liquor, and the atmosphere was filled with a dense volume of smoke.

[Richard Markham meets the Resurrection Man in the *Dark House*, as arranged. The Resurrection Man attempts to blackmail him.]

"This gammon won't do for me," cried the Resurrection Man. "You want to stall me off; but I'm too wide awake. Give me the tin, or I'll start off to-morrow morning to Richmond, and see the count upon—*you* know what subject."

[...]

"No", returned Richard in a resolute manner.

[...]

"You do not think I would have done what I said?" cried the Resurrection Man.

"I believe you to be capable of any villany. But we have already conversed too long. I was anxious to show you how a virtuous resolution would enable me to triumph over your base designs;—and I have now nothing more to say to you. Our ways lie in different directions, both at present and in future. Farewell."

With these words Markham continued his way up Brick Lane; but the Resurrection Man was again by his side in a moment.

"You refuse to assist me?" he muttered in a hoarse and savage tone.

"I do. Molest me no further."

"You refuse to assist me?" repeated the villain, grinding his teeth with rage: "then you may mind the consequences! I will very soon show you that you will bitterly—bitterly repent your determination. By God, I will be revenged!"

[...]

[The body-snatcher was a figure of horror in popular literature from the eighteenth century onwards, and the details provided in the following passage place the Resurrection Man in context as a folk-devil in this tradition. In the contemporary idiom, however, he is also represented as a 'new' urban entrepreneur, applying business efficiency and technological skill to his grisly trade. The Anatomy Act of 1832 had replaced the old tradition, in which the bodies of murderers were provided for dissection with a new provision, that the corpses of paupers and inhabitants of workhouses who were unable to pay for their funerals should be sent to hospitals. Although the trade was defunct by the mid-1830s, when this episode takes place, the Resurrectionist lived on as a bogey-man in popular consciousness.]

CHAPTER XLIV.
THE BODY-SNATCHERS.

THE Resurrection Man, the Cracksman, and the Buffer hastened rapidly along the narrow lanes and filthy alleys leading towards Shoreditch Church. They threaded their way in silence, through the jet-black darkness of the night, and without once hesitating as to the particular turnings which they were to follow. Those men were as familiar with that neighbourhood as a person can be with the rooms and passages in his own house.

At length the body-snatchers reached the low wall surmounted with a high railing which encloses Shoreditch churchyard. They were now at the back part of that burial ground, in a narrow and deserted street, whose dark and lonely appearance tended to aid their designs upon an edifice situated in one of the most populous districts in all London.

For some minutes before their arrival an individual, enveloped in a long cloak, was walking up and down beneath the shadow of the wall.

This was the surgeon, whose thirst after science had called into action the energies of the body-snatchers that night.

The Cracksman advanced first, and ascertained that the surgeon had already arrived, and that the coast was otherwise clear.

He then whistled in a low and peculiar manner; and his two confederates came up.

"You have got all your tools?" said the surgeon in a hasty whisper.

"Every one that we require," answered the Resurrection Man.

"For opening a vault inside the church, mind?" added the surgeon, interrogatively.

"You show us the vault, sir, and we'll soon have out the body," said the Resurrection Man.

"All right," whispered the surgeon, "and my own carriage will be in this street at three precisely. We shall have plenty of time—there's no one stirring till five, and it's dark till seven."

The surgeon and the body-snatchers then scaled the railing, and in a few moments stood in the churchyard.

The Resurrection Man addressed himself to his two confederates and the surgeon, and said, "Do you lie snug under the wall here while I go forward and see how we must manage the door." With these words he crept stealthily along, amidst the tomb-stones, towards the church.

The Surgeon and the Cracksman seated themselves upon a grave close to the wall; and the Buffer threw himself flat upon his stomach, with his ear towards the ground. He remained in this position for some minutes, and then uttered a species of low growl as if he were answering some signal which caught his ears alone.

"The skeleton-keys won't open the side-door, the Resurrection Man says," whispered the Buffer, raising his head towards the surgeon and the Cracksman.

He then laid his ear close to the ground once more, and resumed his listening posture.

In a few minutes he again replied to a signal; and this time his answer was conveyed by means of a short sharp whistle.

"It appears there is a bolt; and it will take a quarter of an hour to saw through the padlock that holds it," observed the Buffer in a whisper.

Nearly twenty minutes elapsed after this announcement. The surgeon's teeth chattered with the intense cold; and he could not altogether subdue certain feelings of horror at the idea of the business which had brought him thither. The almost mute correspondence which those two men were enabled to carry on together—the methodical precision with which they performed their avocations—and the coolness they exhibited in undertaking a sacrilegious task, made a powerful impression upon his mind. He shuddered from head to foot:—his feelings of aversion were the same as he would have experienced had a loathsome reptile crawled over his naked flesh.

"It's all right now!" suddenly exclaimed the Buffer, rising from the ground. "Come along."

The surgeon and the Cracksman followed the Buffer to the southern side of the church where there was a flight of steps leading up to a side-door in a species of lobby, or lodge. This door was open; and the Resurrection Man was standing inside the lodge.

As soon as they had all entered the sacred edifice, the door was carefully closed once more.

We have before said that the night was cold: but the interior of the church was of a chill so intense, that an icy feeling appeared to penetrate to the very back-bone. The wind murmured down the aisle, and every footstep echoed, like a hollow sound in the distance, throughout the spacious pile.

"Now, sir," said the Resurrection Man to the surgeon, "it is for you to tell us whereabouts we are to begin."

The surgeon groped his way towards the communion-table, and at the northern side of the railings which surrounded it he stopped short.

"I must now be standing," he said, "upon the very stone which you are to remove. You can, however, soon ascertain; for the funeral only took place yesterday morning, and the mortar must be quite soft."

The Resurrection Man stooped down, felt with his hand for the joints of the pavement in that particular spot, and thrust his knife between them.

"Yes," he said, after a few minutes' silence: "this stone has only been put down a day or two. But do you wish, sir, that all traces of our work should disappear?"

"Certainly! I would not for the world that the family of the deceased should learn that this tomb has been violated. Suspicion would immediately fall upon me; for it would be remembered how earnestly I desired to open the body, and how resolutely my request was refused."

"We must use a candle, then, presently," said the Resurrection Man; "and that is the most dangerous part of the whole proceeding."

"It cannot be helped," returned the surgeon, in a decided tone. "The fact that the side-door has been opened by unfair means must transpire in a day or two; and search will then be made inside the church to ascertain whether those who have been guilty of the sacrilege were thieves or resurrection-men. You see, then, how necessary it is that there should remain no proofs of the violation of a tomb."

"Well and good, sir," said the Resurrection Man. "You command—we obey. Now, then, my mates, to work."

In a moment the Resurrection Man lighted a piece of candle, and placed it in the tin shade before alluded to. The glare which it shed was thereby thrown almost entirely downwards. He then carefully, and with surprising rapidity, examined the joints of the large flag-stone which was to be removed, and on which no inscription had yet been engraved. He observed the manner in which the mortar was laid down, and noticed even the places where it spread a little over the adjoining stones or where it was slightly deficient. This inspection being completed, he extinguished the light, and set to work in company with the Cracksman and the Buffer.

The eyes of the surgeon gradually became accustomed to the obscurity; and he was enabled to observe to some extent the proceedings of the body-snatchers.

These men commenced by pouring vinegar over the mortar round the stone which they were to raise. They then took long clasp-knives, with very thin and flexible blades, from their pockets; and inserted them between the joints of the stones. They moved these knives rapidly backwards and forwards for a few seconds, so as effectually to loosen the mortar, and moistened the interstices several times with the vinegar.

This operation being finished, they introduced the thin and pointed end of a lever between the end of the stone which they were to raise and the one adjoining it. The Resurrection Man, who held the lever, only worked it very gently; but at every fresh effort on his part, the Cracksman and the Buffer introduced each a wedge of wood into the space which thus grew larger and larger. By these means, had the lever suddenly given way, the stone would not have fallen back into its setting. At length it was raised to a sufficient height to admit of its being supported by a thick log about three feet in length.

While these three men were thus proceeding as expeditiously as possible with their task, the surgeon, although a man of a naturally strong mind, could not control the strange feelings which crept upon him. It suddenly appeared to him as if he beheld those men for the first time. That continuation of regular and systematic movements—a silent perseverance, faintly shadowed forth amidst the obscurity of the night, at length assumed so singular a character, that the surgeon felt as if he beheld three demons disinterring a doomed one to carry him off to hell!

He was aroused from this painful reverie by the Resurrection Man, who said to him, "Come and help us remove the stone."

The surgeon applied all his strength to this task; and the huge flag-stone was speedily moved upon two wooden rollers away from the mouth of the grave.

"You are certain that this is the place?" said the Resurrection Man.

"As certain as one can be who stood by the grave for a quarter of an hour in day-light, and who has to recognise it again in total darkness," answered the surgeon. "Besides, the mortar was soft—"

"There might have been another burial close by," interrupted the Resurrection Man; "but we will soon find out whether you are right or not, sir. Was the coffin a wooden one?"

"Yes! an elm coffin, covered with black cloth," replied the surgeon. "I gave the instructions for the funeral myself, being the oldest friend of the family."

The Resurrection Man took one of the long flexible rods which we have before noticed, and thrust it down into the vault. The point penetrated into the lid of a coffin. He drew it back, put the point to his tongue, and tasted it.

"Yes," he said, smacking his lips, "the coffin in this vault is an elm one, and is covered with black cloth."

"I thought I could not be wrong," observed the surgeon.

The body-snatchers then proceeded to raise the coffin, by means of ropes passed underneath it. This was a comparatively easy portion of their task; and in a few moments it was placed upon the flag-stones of the church.

The Resurrection Man took a chisel and opened the lid with considerable care. He then lighted his candle a second time; and the glare fell upon the pale features of the corpse in its narrow shell.

"This is the right one," said the surgeon, casting a hasty glance upon the face of the dead body, which was that of a young girl of about sixteen.

The Resurrection Man extinguished the light; and he and his companions proceeded to lift the corpse out of the coffin.

The polished marble limbs of the deceased were rudely grasped by the sacrilegious hands of the body-snatchers; and, having stripped the corpse stark naked, they tied its neck and heels together by means of a strong cord. They then thrust it into a large sack made for the purpose.

The body-snatchers then applied themselves to the restoration of the vault to its original appearance.

The lid of the coffin was carefully fastened down; and that now tenantless bed was lowered into the tomb. The stone was rolled over the mouth of the vault; and one of the small square boxes previously alluded to, furnished mortar wherewith to fill up the joints. The Resurrection Man lighted his candle a third time, and applied the cement in such a way that even the very workman who laid the stone down after the funeral would not have known that it had been disturbed. Then, as this mortar was a shade fresher and lighter than that originally used, the Resurrection Man scattered over it a thin brown powder, which was furnished by the second box brought away from his house on this occasion. Lastly, a light brush was swept over the scene of these operations, and the necessary precautions were complete.

The clock struck three as the surgeon and the body-snatchers issued from the church, carrying the sack containing the corpse between them.

They reached the wall at the back of the church-yard, and there deposited their burden, while the Cracksman hastened to see if the surgeon's carriage had arrived.

In a few minutes he returned to the railing, and said in a low tone, "All right!"

The body was lifted over the iron barrier and conveyed to the vehicle.

The surgeon counted ten sovereigns into the hands of each of the body-snatchers; and, having taken his seat inside the vehicle, close by his strange freight, was whirled rapidly away towards his own abode.

[...]

[Chapters LV, LVI and LVIII relate the story of Ellen Monroe. She was a childhood friend of Richard Markham, and the daughter of the Mr Monroe who was appointed Richard's guardian after the death of his father. Ellen takes up a career as a model, first for a sculptor, and then for a photographer. This is perhaps the earliest fictional record of the new technology of the daguerreotype. The description of the photographer may well be based on the studio of Antoine Claudet, whose attic premises in St Martin's Fields were established in 1841. Ellen, who has been seduced by George Montague, by whom she has an illegitimate child, later has an active career in the rapidly developing entertainment industry in London. These chapters form an unusual addition to the better-known 'Seamstress' literature of the period, in which conditions in the East End sweat-shops received wide publicity: Ellen's escape from poverty by the marketing of her physical attractions is treated with some sympathy in the text, rather than condemned. She appears as a figure of energy and enterprise, able to exploit the possibilities of city life in ways forbidden to more conventional heroines. Her history is prefaced by the remark that it contains 'less romance and more truth' than others in the story.]

CHAPTER LV.
MISERRIMA!!!

WE now come to a sad episode in our history—and yet one in which there is perhaps less romance and more truth than in any scene yet depicted.

We have already warned our reader that he will have to accompany us amidst appalling scenes of vice and wretchedness:—we are now about to introduce him to one of destitution and suffering—of powerful struggle and unavailing toil—whose details are so very sad, that we have been able to find no better heading for our chapter than *miserrima*, or "very miserable things."

The reader will remember that we have brought our narrative, in preceding chapters, up to the end of 1838:—we must now go back for a period of two years, in order to commence the harrowing details of our present episode.

In one of the low dark rooms of a gloomy house in a court leading out of Golden Lane, St. Luke's, a young girl of seventeen sate at work. It was about nine o'clock in the evening; and a single candle lighted the miserable chamber, which was almost completely denuded of furniture. The cold wind of December whistled through the ill-closed casement and the broken panes, over which thin paper had been pasted to repel the biting chill. A small deal table, two common chairs, and a mattress were all the articles of furniture which this wretched room contained. A door at the end opposite the window opened into another and smaller chamber: and this latter one was furnished with nothing, save an old mattress. There were no blankets—no coverlids in either room. The occupants had no other covering at night than their own clothes;—and those clothes—God knows they were thin, worn, and scanty enough!

Not a spark of fire burned in the grate;—and yet that front room in which the young girl was seated was as cold as the nave of a vast cathedral in the depth of winter.

The reader has perhaps experienced that icy chill which seems to strike to the very marrow of the bones, when entering a huge stone edifice:—the cold which prevailed in that room, and in which the young creature was at work with her needle, was more intense—more penetrating—more bitter—more frost-like than even that icy chill!

Miserable and cheerless was that chamber: the dull light of the candle only served to render its nakedness the more apparent, without relieving it of any of its gloom. And as the cold draught from the wretched casement caused the flame of that candle to flicker and oscillate, the poor girl was compelled to seat herself between the window and the table, to protect her light from the wind. Thus, the chilling December blast blew upon the back of the young sempstress, whose clothing was so thin and scant—so very scant!

The sempstress was, as we have before said, about seventeen years of age. She was very beautiful; and her features, although pale with want, and wan with care and long vigils, were pleasing and agreeable. The cast of her countenance was purely Grecian—the shape of her head eminently classical—and her form was of a perfect and symmetrical mould. Although clothed in the most scanty and wretched manner, she was singularly neat and clean in her appearance; and her air and demeanour were far above her humble occupation and her impoverished condition.

She had, indeed, seen better days! Reared in the lap of luxury by fond, but too indulgent parents, her education had been of a high order; and thus her qualifications were rather calculated to embellish her in prosperity than to prove of use to her in adversity. She had lost her mother at the age of twelve; and her father—kind and fond, and proud of his only child—had sought to make her shine in that sphere which she had then appeared destined to adorn. But misfortunes came upon them like a thunderbolt: and when poverty—grim poverty stared them in the face—this poor girl had no resource, save her needle! Now and then her father earned a trifle in the City, by making out accounts or copying deeds;—but sorrow and ill-health had almost entirely incapacitated him from labour or occupation of any kind;—and his young and affectionate daughter was compelled to toil from sun-rise until a late hour in the night to earn even a pittance.

One after another, all their little comforts, in the shape of furniture and clothing, disappeared; and after vainly endeavouring to maintain a humble lodging in a cheap but respectable neighbourhood, poverty compelled them to take refuge in that dark, narrow, filthy court leading out of Golden Lane.

Such was the sad fate of Mr. Monroe and his daughter Ellen.

At the time when we introduce the latter to our readers, her father was absent in the City. He had a little occupation in a counting-house, which was to last three days, which kept him hard at work from nine in the morning till eleven at night, and for which he was to receive a pittance so small we dare not mention its amount! This is how it was:—an official assignee belonging to the Bankruptcy Court had some heavy accounts to make up by a certain day: he was consequently compelled to employ an accountant to aid him; the accountant employed a petty scrivener to make out the balance-sheet; and the petty scrivener employed Monroe to ease him of a portion of the toil. It is therefore plain that Monroe was not to receive much for his three days' labour.

And so Ellen was compelled to toil and work, and work and toil—to rise early, and go to bed late—so late that she had scarcely fallen asleep, worn out with fatigue, when it appeared time to get up again;—and thus the roses forsook her cheeks—and her health suffered—and her head ached—and her eyes grew dim—and her limbs were stiff with the chill!

And so she worked and toiled, and toiled and worked.

We said it was about nine o'clock in the evening.

Ellen's fingers were almost paralysed with cold and labour; and yet the work which she had in her hands must be done that night; else no supper then—and no breakfast on the morrow; for on the shelf in that cheerless chamber there was not a morsel of bread!

And for sixteen hours had that poor girl fasted already; for she had eaten a crust at five in the morning, when she had risen from her hard cold couch in the back chamber. She had left the larger portion of the bread that then remained, for her father; and she had assured him that she had a few halfpence to purchase more for herself—but she had therein deceived him! Ah! how noble and generous was that deception;—and how often—how very often did that poor girl practise it!

Ellen had risen at five that morning to embroider a silk shawl with eighty flowers. She had calculated upon finishing it by eight in the evening; but, although she had worked, and worked, and worked hour after hour, without ceasing, save for a moment at long intervals to rest her aching head and stretch her cramped fingers, eight had struck—and nine had struck also—and still the blossoms were not all embroidered.

It was a quarter to ten when the last stitch was put into the last flower.

But then the poor creature could not rest:—not to her was it allowed to repose after that severe day of toil! She was hungry—she was faint—her stomach was sick for want of food; and at eleven her father would come home, hungry, faint, and sick at stomach also!

Rising from her chair—every limb stiff, cramped, and aching with cold and weariness—the poor creature put on her modest straw bonnet with a faded riband, and her thin wretched shawl, to take home her work.

Her employer dwelt upon Finsbury Pavement; and as it was now late, the poor girl was compelled to hasten as fast as her aching limbs would carry her.

The shop to which she repaired was brilliant with lamps and gas-lights. Articles of great variety and large value were piled in the windows, on the counters, on the shelves. Upwards of twenty young men were busily employed in serving the customers. The proprietor of that establishment was at that moment entertaining a party of friends up stairs, at a champagne supper!

The young girl walked timidly into the vast magazine of fashions, and, with downcast eyes, advanced towards an elderly woman who was sitting at a counter at the farther end of the shop. To this female did she present the shawl.

"A pretty time of night to come!" murmured the shopwoman. "This ought to have been done by three or four o'clock."

"I have worked since five this morning, without ceasing." answered Ellen; "and I could not finish it before."

"Ah! I see," exclaimed the shopwoman, turning the shawl over, and examining it critically; "there are fifty or sixty flowers, I see."

"Eighty," said Ellen; "I was ordered to embroider that number."

"Well, Miss—and is there so much difference between sixty and eighty?"

"Difference, ma'am!" ejaculated the young girl, the tears starting into her eyes; "the difference is more than four hours' work!"

"Very likely, very likely, Miss. And how much do you expect for this?"

"I must leave it entirely to you, ma'am."

The poor girl spoke deferentially to this cold-hearted woman, in order to make her generous. Oh! poverty renders even the innocence of seventeen selfish, mundane, and calculating!

"Oh! you leave it to me, do you?" said the woman, turning the shawl over and over, and scrutinising it in all points; but she could not discover a single fault in Ellen's work. "You leave it to me? Well, it isn't so badly done—very tolerably for a girl of your age and inexperience! I presume," she added, thrusting her hand into the till under the counter, and drawing forth sixpence, "I presume that this is sufficient."

"Madam," said Ellen, bursting into tears. "I have worked nearly seventeen hours at that shawl—"

She could say no more: her voice was lost in sobs.

"Come, come," cried the shopwoman harshly, "no whimpering here! Take up your money, if you like it—and if you don't, leave it. Only decide one way or another, and make haste!"

Ellen took up the sixpence, wiped her eyes, and hastily turned to leave the shop.

"Do you not want any more work?" demanded the shopwoman abruptly.

The fact was that the poor girl worked well, and did not "shirk" labour; and the woman knew that it was the interest of her master to retain that young creature's services.

Those words, "Do you not want any more work?" reminded Ellen that she and her father must live—that they could not starve! She accordingly turned towards that uncouth female once more, and received another shawl, to embroider in the same manner, and at the same price!

Eighty blossoms for sixpence!

Sixteen hours' work for sixpence!!

A farthing and a half per hour!!!

The young girl returned to the dirty court in Golden Lane, after purchasing some food, coarse and cheap, on her way home.

On the ground-floor of a house in the same court dwelt an old woman—one of those old women who are the moral sewers of great towns—the sinks towards which flow all the impurities of the human passions. One of those abominable hags was she who dishonour the sanctity of old age. She had hideous wrinkles upon her face; and as she stretched out her huge, dry, and bony hand, and tapped the young girl upon the shoulder, as the latter hurried past her door, the very touch seemed to chill the maiden even through her clothes.

Ellen turned abruptly round, and shuddered—she scarcely knew why—when she found herself confronting that old hag by the dim lustre of the lights which shone through the windows in the narrow court.

That old woman, who was the widow of crime, assumed as pleasant an aspect as her horrible countenance would allow her to put on, and addressed the timid maiden in a strain which the latter scarcely comprehended. All that Ellen could understand was that the old woman suspected how hardly she toiled and how badly she was paid, and offered to point out a more pleasant and profitable mode of earning money.

Without precisely knowing why, Ellen shrank from the contact of that hideous old hag, and trembled at the words which issued from the crone's mouth.

"You do not answer me," said the wretch. "Well, well; when you have no bread to eat—no work—no money to pay your rent—and nothing but the workhouse before you, you will think better of it and come to me."

Thus saying, the old hag turned abruptly into her own den, the door of which she banged violently.

With her heart fluttering like a little bird in its cage, poor Ellen hastened to her own miserable abode.

She placed the food upon the table, but would not touch it until her father should return. She longed for a spark of fire, for she was so cold and so wretched—and even in warm weather misery makes one shiver! But that room was as cold as an ice-house—and the unhappiness of that poor girl was a burden almost too heavy for her to bear.

She sate down, and thought. Oh! how poignant is meditation in such a condition as hers. Her prospects were utterly black and hopeless.

When she and her father had first taken those lodgings, she had obtained work from a "middle-woman." This middle-woman was one who contracted with great drapery and upholstery firms to do their needle-work at certain low rates. The middle-woman had to live, and was therefore compelled to make a decent profit upon the work. So she gave it out to poor creatures like Ellen Monroe, and got it done for next to nothing.

Thus for some weeks had Ellen made shirts—with the collars, wristbands, and fronts all well stitched—for four-pence the shirt.

And it took her twelve hours, without intermission, to make a shirt: and it cost her a penny for needles, and thread, and candle.

She therefore had three-pence for herself!

Twelve hours' unwearied toil for three-pence!!

One farthing an hour!!!

Sometimes she had made dissecting-trousers, which were sold to the medical students at the hospitals; and for those she was paid two-pence half-penny each.

It occupied her eight hours to make one pair of those trousers!

At length the middle-woman had recommended her to the linen-draper's establishment on Finsbury Pavement; and there she was told that she might have plenty of work, and be well paid.

Well paid!

At the rate of a farthing and a half per hour!!

Oh! it was a mockery—a hideous mockery, to give that young creature gay flowers and blossoms to work—she, who was working her own winding-sheet!

She sate, shivering with the cold, awaiting her father's return. Ever and anon the words of that old crone who had addressed her in the court, rang in her ears. What could she mean? How could she—stern in her own wretchedness herself, and perhaps stern to the wretchedness of others—how could that old hag possess the means of teaching her a pleasant and profitable mode of earning money? The soul of Ellen was purity itself—although she dwelt in that low, obscene, filthy, and disreputable neighbourhood. She seemed like a solitary lily in the midst of a black morass swarming with reptiles!

The words of the old woman were therefore unintelligible to that fair young creature of seventeen:—and yet she intuitively reproached herself for pondering upon them. Oh! mysterious influence of an all-wise and all-seeing Providence, that thus furnishes warnings against dangers yet unseen!

She tried to avert her thoughts from the contemplation of her own misery, and of the tempting offer made to her by the wrinkled harridan in the adjoining house; and so she busied herself with thinking of the condition of the other lodgers in the same tenement which she and her father inhabited. She then perceived that there were others in the world as wretched and as badly off as herself; but, in contradiction to the detestable maxim of Rochefoucauld—she found no consolation in this conviction.

In the attics were Irish families, whose children ran all day, half naked, about the court and lane, paddling with their poor cold bare feet in the puddle or the snow, and apparently thriving in dirt, hunger, and privation. Ellen and her father occupied the two rooms on the second floor. On the first floor, in the front room, lived two families—an elderly man and woman, with their grown-up sons and daughters; and with one of those sons were a wife and young children. Eleven souls thus herded together, without shame, in a room eighteen feet wide! These eleven human beings, dwelling in so swine-like a manner, existed upon twenty-five shillings a week, the joint earnings of all of them who were able to work. In the back chamber on the same floor was a tailor, with a paralytic wife and a complete tribe of children. This poor wretch worked for a celebrated "Clothing Mart," and sometimes toiled for twenty hours a-day—never less than seventeen, Sunday included—to earn—what?

Eight shillings a week.

He made mackintoshes at the rate of one shilling and three-pence each; and he could make one each day. But then he had to find needles and thread; and the cost of these, together with candles, amounted to nine-pence a week.

He thus had eight shillings remaining for himself, after working like a slave, without recreation or rest, even upon the sabbath, seventeen hours every day.

A week contains a hundred and sixty-eight hours.

And he worked a hundred and nineteen hours each week!

And earned eight shillings!!

A decimal more than three farthings an hour!!!

On the ground floor of the house the tenants were no better off. In the front room dwelt a poor costermonger, or hawker of fruit, who earned upon an average seven shillings a week, out of which he was compelled to pay one shilling to treat the policeman upon the beat where he took his stand. His wife did a little washing, and perhaps earned eighteen-pence. And that was all this poor couple with four children had to subsist upon. The back room on the ground floor was occupied by the landlady of the house. She paid twelve shillings a week for rent and taxes, and let the various rooms for an aggregate of twenty-one shillings. She thus had nine shillings to live upon, supposing that every one of her lodgers paid her—which was never the case.

Poor Ellen, in reflecting in this manner upon the condition of her neighbours, found herself surrounded on all sides by misery. Misery was above—misery below: misery was on the right and on the left. Misery was the genius of that dwelling, and of every other in that court. Misery was the cold and speechless companion of the young girl as she sate in that icy chamber: misery spread her meal, and made her bed, and was her chambermaid at morning and at night!

Eleven o'clock struck by St. Luke's church; and Mr. Monroe returned to his wretched abode. It had begun to rain shortly after Ellen had returned home; and the old man was wet to the skin.

"Oh! my dear father!" exclaimed the poor girl, "you are wet, and there is not a morsel of fire in the grate!"

"And I have no money, dearest," returned the heart-broken father, pressing his thin lips upon the forehead of his daughter. "But I am not cold, Nell—I am not cold!"

Without uttering a word, Ellen hastened out of the room, and begged a few sticks from one lodger, and a little coal from another. It would shame the affluent great, did they know how ready are the miserable—miserable poor to assist each other!

With her delicate taper fingers—with those little white hands which seemed never made to do menial service, the young girl laid the fire; and when she saw the flame blazing cheerfully up the chimney, she turned towards the old man—and smiled!

She would not for worlds have begged any thing for herself—but for her father—oh! she would have submitted to any degradation!

And then for a moment a gleam of something like happiness stole upon that hitherto mournful scene, as the father and daughter partook of their frugal—very frugal and sparing meal together.

As soon as it was concluded, Ellen rose, kissed her parent affectionately, wished him "good night," and retired into her own miserable, cold, and naked chamber.

She extinguished her candle in a few moments, to induce her father to believe that she had sought repose; but when she knew that the old man was asleep, she lighted the candle once more, and seated herself upon the old mattress, to embroider a few blossoms upon the silk which had been confided to her at the establishment in Finsbury.

From the neighbouring houses the sounds of boisterous revelry fell upon her ears. She was too young and inexperienced to know that this mirth emanated from persons perhaps as miserable as herself, and that they were only drowning care in liquor, instead of encountering their miseries face to face. The din of that hilarity and those shouts of laughter, therefore made her sad.

Presently that noise grew fainter and fainter; and at length it altogether ceased. The clock of St. Luke's church struck one; and all was then silent around.

A lovely moon rode high in the heavens; the rain had ceased, and the night was beautiful—but bitter, bitter cold.

Wearied with toil, the young maiden threw down her work, and, opening the casement, looked forth from her wretched chamber. The gentle breeze, though bearing on its wing the chill of ice, refreshed her; and as she gazed upwards to the moon, she wondered within herself whether the spirit of her departed mother was permitted to look down upon her from the empyrean palaces on high. Tears—large tears trickled down her cheeks; and she was too much overcome by her feelings even to pray.

While she was thus endeavouring to divert her thoughts from the appalling miseries of earth to the transcendant glories of heaven, she was diverted from her mournful reverie by the sound of a window opening in a neighbouring house; and in a few moments violent sobs fell upon her ears. Those sobs, evidently coming from a female bosom, were so acute, so heart-rending, so full of anguish, that Ellen was herself overcome with grief. At length those indications of extreme woe ceased gradually, and then these words—" Oh my God! what will become of my starving babes!" fell upon Ellen's ears. She was about to inquire into the cause of that profound affliction, when the voice of a man was heard to exclaim gruffly, " Come—let's have no more of this gammon: we must all go to the workus in the morning—that's all!" And then the window was closed violently.

The workhouse! That word sounded like a fearful knell upon Ellen's ears.

Oh! for hours and hours together had that poor girl meditated upon the sad condition of her father and herself, until she had traced, in imagination, their melancholy career up to the very door of the workhouse. And there she had stopped: she dared think no more—or she would have gone mad, raving mad! For she had heard of the horrors of those asylums for the poor; and she knew that she should be separated from her father on the day when their stern destinies should drive them to that much-dreaded refuge. And to part from him—from the parent whom she loved so tenderly, and who loved her so well;—no—death were far preferable!

The workhouse! How was it that the idea of this fearful home—more dreaded than the prison, less formidable than the grave—had taken so strong a hold upon the poor girl's mind? Because the former tenant of the miserable room which now was hers had passed thence to the workhouse: but ere she went away, she left behind her a record of her feelings in anticipation of that removal to the pauper's home!

Impelled by an influence which she could not control—that species of impulse which urges the timid one to gaze upon the corpse of the dead, even while shuddering at the aspect of death—Ellen closed the window, and read for the hundredth time the following lines, which were pencilled in a neat hand upon the whitewashed wall of the naked chamber:—

"I HAD A TENDER MOTHER ONCE."

I had a tender mother once,
    Whose eyes so sad and mild
Beamed tearfully yet kindly on
    Her little orphan child.
A father's care I never knew;
    But in that mother dear,
Was centred every thing to love
    To cherish, and revere!

[...]

Ah! we shall ne'er be blessed again
    Till death has closed our eyes,
And we meet in the pauper's ground
    Where my poor mother lies.—
Though sad this chamber, it is bright
    To what must be our doom;
The portal of the workhouse is
    The entrance of the tomb!

Ellen read these lines till her eyes were dim with tears. She then retired to her wretched couch; and she slept through sheer fatigue. But dreams of hunger and of cold filled up her slumbers;—and yet those dreams were light beside the waking pangs which realised the visions!

The young maiden slept for three hours, and then arose, unrefreshed, and paler than she was on the preceding day. It was dark: the moon had gone down; and some time would yet elapse ere the dawn. Ellen washed herself in water upon which the ice floated; and the cold piercing breeze of the morning whistled through the window upon her fair and delicate form.

[...]

CHAPTER LVI.
THE ROAD TO RUIN.

ABOUT two months after the period when we first introduced Ellen Monroe to our readers, the old woman of whom we have before spoken, and who dwelt in the same court as that poor maiden and her father, was sitting at work in her chamber.

The old woman was ill-favoured in countenance, and vile in heart. Hers was one of those hardened dispositions which know no pity, no charity, no love, no friendship, no yearning after anything proper to human fellowship.

She was poor and wretched;—and yet *she*, in all her misery, had a large easy chair left to sit upon, warm blankets to cover her at night, a Dutch clock to tell her the hour, a cupboard in which to keep her food, a mat whereon to set her feet, and a few turves burning in the grate to keep her warm. The walls of her room were covered with cheap prints, coloured with glaring hues, and representing the exploits of celebrated highwaymen and courtezans; scenes upon the stage in which favourite actresses figured, and execrable imitations of Hogarth's "Rake's Progress." The coverlid of her bed was of patchwork, pieces of silk, satin, cotton, and other stuffs, all of different patterns, sizes, and shapes, being sewn together—strange and expressive remnants of a vicious and faded luxury! Upon the chimney-piece were two or three scent-bottles, which for years had contained no perfume; and in the cupboard was a champagne-bottle, in which the hag now kept her gin. The pillow of her couch was stuffed neither with wool nor feathers—but with well-worn silk stockings, tattered lace collars, faded ribands, a piece of a muff and a boa, the velvet off a bonnet, and old kid gloves. And—more singular than all the other features of her room—the old hag had a huge Bible, with silver clasps, upon a shelf!

This horrible woman was darning old stockings, and stooping over her work, when a low knock at the door of her chamber fell upon her ear. That knock was not imperative and commanding, but gentle and timid; and therefore the old woman did not hurry herself to say, "Come in!" Even after the door had opened and the visitor had entered the room, the old hag proceeded with her work for a few moments.

At length raising her head, she beheld Ellen Monroe.

She was not surprised: but as she gazed upon that fair thin face whose roundness had yielded to the hand of starvation, and that blue eye whose fire was subdued by long and painful vigils, she said, "And so you have come at last? I have been expecting you every day!"

"Expecting me! and why?" exclaimed Ellen, surprised at these words, which appeared to contain a sense of dark and mysterious import that was ominous to the young girl.

"Yes—I have expected you," repeated the old woman. "Did I not tell you that when you had no money, no work, and no bread, and owed arrears of rent, you would come to me?"

"Alas! and you predicted truly," said Ellen, with a bitter sigh. "All the miseries which you have detailed have fallen upon me;—and more! for my father lies ill upon the *one mattress* that remains to us!"

"Poor creature!" exclaimed the old woman, endeavouring to assume a soothing tone; then, pointing to a foot-stool near her, she added, "Come and sit near me that we may talk together upon your sad condition."

[...]

Suddenly a thought struck the hag.

"I can do nothing for you, miss, since you will not follow my advice," she said, after a while: "and yet I am acquainted with a statuary who would pay you well for casts of your countenance for his Madonnas, his actresses, his Esmeraldas, his queens, his princesses, and his angels."

These words sounded upon the ears of the unhappy girl like a dream; and parting, with her wasted fingers, the ringlets that clustered round her brow, she lifted up her large moist eyes in astonishment towards the face of the aged hag.

But the old woman was serious in her offer.

"I repeat—will you sell your countenance to a statuary?" she said. "It is a good one; and you will obtain a handsome price for it."

Ellen was literally stupefied by this strange proposal; but when she had power to collect her ideas into one focus, she saw her father pining upon a bed of sickness, and surrounded by all the horrors of want and privation;— and she herself—the unhappy girl—had not tasted food for nearly thirty hours. Then, on the other side, was her innate modesty;—but this was nothing in the balance compared to the poignancy of her own and her parent's sufferings.

So she agreed to accompany the old hag to the house of the statuary in Leather Lane, Holborn.

[...]

Up two flights of narrow and dark stairs, precipitate as ladders, did the trembling and almost heartbroken girl follow the hag. They then entered a spacious depository of statues modelled in plaster of Paris. A strange assembly of images was that! Heathen gods seemed to fraternize with angels, Madonnas, and Christian saints; Napoleon and Wellington stood motionless side by side; George the Fourth and Greenacre occupied the same shelf; William Pitt and Cobbett appeared to be contemplating each other with silent admiration; Thomas Paine elbowed a bishop; Lord Castlereagh seemed to be extending his hand to welcome Jack Ketch; Cupid pointed his arrow at the bosom of a pope; in a word, that strange pell-mell of statues was calculated to awaken ideas of a most wild and ludicrous character, in the imagination of one whose thoughts were not otherwise occupied.

The statuary was an Italian; and as he spoke the English language imperfectly, he did not waste much time over the bargain. With the cool criticism of a sportsman examining a horse or a dog, the statuary gazed upon the young maiden; then, taking a rule in his hand, he measured her head; and with a pair of blunt compasses he took the dimensions of her features. Giving a nod of approval, he consulted a large book which lay open upon a desk; and finding that he had orders for a queen, an opera-dancer, and a Madonna, he declared that he would take three casts of his new model's countenance that very morning.

The old woman whispered words of encouragement in Ellen's ear, as they all three repaired to the workshop, where upwards of twenty men were employed in making statues. Some were preparing the clay models over which the plaster of Paris was to be laid: others joined legs and arms to trunks;—some polished the features of the countenances: others effaced the seams that betrayed the various joints in the complete statues. One fixed wings to angels' backs—another swords to warriors' sides: a third repaired a limb that had been broken; a fourth stuck on a new nose in the place of an old one knocked off.

Ellen was stretched at full length upon a table; and a wet cloth was placed over her face. The statuary then covered it with moist clay;—and the process was only complete when she was ready to faint through difficulty of breathing. She rested a little while; and then the second cast was taken. Another interval to recover breath—and the third and last mould was formed.

The statuary seemed well pleased with this trial of his new model; and placing a sovereign in the young maiden's hand, he desired her to return in three days, as he should require her services again. The poor trembling creature's eyes glistened with delight as she balanced the gold in her little hand; and she took her departure, accompanied by the hag, with a heart comparatively light.

[...]

Thus for three months did Ellen earn the means of a comfortable subsistence, by selling her countenance to the statuary. And that countenance might be seen belonging to the statues of Madonnas in catholic chapels; opera dancers, and actresses in theatrical clubs; nymphs holding lamps in the halls of public institutions; and queens in the staircase windows of insurance offices.

[...]

Three months passed away; and already had a little air of comfort succeeded to the former dismal aspect of those two chambers which the father and daughter occupied, when the statuary died suddenly.

Ellen's occupation was once more gone; and, after vainly endeavouring to obtain needle-work—for that which she did in the presence of her father was merely a pretence to make good her tale to him—she again repaired to the abode of the old hag who had introduced her to the statuary.

The aged female was, if possible, more wrinkled and hideous than before; the contrast between her and her fair young visitant was the more striking, inasmuch as the cheeks of the latter had recovered their roundness, and her form its plumpness by means of good and sufficient food.

"You have come to me again," said the hag. "Doubtless I should have never seen you more if you had not wanted my services."

"The statuary is dead," returned Ellen, "and has left behind him an immense fortune. His son has therefore declined the business, and has discharged every one in the employment of his late father."

"And what would you have me do for you, miss?" demanded the old woman. "I am not acquainted with another statuary."

Ellen heaved a deep sigh.

The hag contemplated her for some time in silence, and then exclaimed, "Your appearance has improved; you have a tinge of the carnation upon your cheeks; and your eyes have recovered their brightness. I know an artist of great repute, who will be glad of you as a copy for his shepherdesses, his huntresses, his sea-nymphs, and heathen goddesses. Let us lose no time in proceeding to his residence."

This proposal was far more agreeable to the maiden than the one which had led her into the service of the statuary; and she did not for a moment hesitate to accompany the old woman to the abode of the artist.

The great painter was about forty years of age, and dwelt in a splendid house in Bloomsbury Square. The rooms on the third floor were his *studio*, as he required a clear and good light. He accepted the services of Ellen Monroe as a copy, and remunerated the old woman out of his own pocket, for the introduction. But he required the attendance of his copy every day from ten till four; and she was accordingly compelled to tell her father another story to account for these long intervals of absence. She now assured him that she was engaged to work at the residence of a family in Bloomsbury Square; and the old man believed her.

Her countenance having embellished statues, was now transferred to canvass. Her Grecian features and classic head appeared surmounted with the crescent of Diana, the helmet of Minerva, and the crown of Juno. The painter purchased dresses suitable to the characters which he wished her to adopt; and, although she was frequently compelled to appear before him, in a state which at first was strongly repugnant to her modesty—with naked bust, and naked arms, and naked legs—the feeling of shame gradually wore away. Thus, though in body she remained pure and chaste, yet in soul was she gradually hardened to the sentiments of maiden delicacy and female reserve!

It is true that she retained her virtue—because it was not tempted. The artist saw not before him a lovely creature of warm flesh and blood; he beheld nothing but a beautiful and symmetrical statue which served as an original for his heathen divinities and pastoral heroines. And in this light did he treat her.

He paid her handsomely; and her father and herself were enabled to remove to better lodgings, and in a more respectable neighbourhood, than those which had been the scene of so much misery in Golden Lane.

The artist whom Ellen served was a portrait-painter as well as a delineator of classical subjects. When he was employed to paint the likeness of some vain and conceited West End daughter of the aristocracy, it was Ellen's hand—or Ellen's hair—or Ellen's eyes—or Ellen's bust—or some feature or peculiar beauty of the young maiden, in which the fashionable lady somewhat resembled her, that figured upon the canvass. Then when the portrait was finished, the artist would assemble his friends at the same that the lady and *her* friends called to see it; and the artist's friends—well tutored beforehand—would exclaim, one, "How like is the eye!" another, "The very mouth!" a third, "The hair to the life itself!" a fourth, "The exact profile!"—and so on. And all the while it was Ellen's eye, or Ellen's mouth, or Ellen's hair, or Ellen's profile, which the enthusiasts admired. Then the lady, flattering herself that *she* alone was the original, and little suspecting that the charms of another had been called in to enhance the beauty of *her* portrait, persuaded her fond and uxorious husband to double the amount of the price bargained for, and had the picture set in a very costly frame, to hang in the most conspicuous place in her mansion.

It happened one day that the artist obtained the favour of a marchioness of forty-six by introducing into her portrait the nose, eyes, and mouth of that fair young maiden of seventeen. The great lady recommended him to the Russian Ambassador as the greatest of English painters; and the ambassador immediately retained him to proceed to St. Petersburgh to transfer to canvass the physiognomy of the Czar.

Ellen thus lost her employment once more; and again did she repair to the den of the old hag who had recommended her to the statuary and the artist.

[...]

"I am acquainted with a French gentleman of science at the West End," answered the hag, "who has invented a means of taking likenesses by the aid of the sun. I do not know what the process is: all that concerns me and you is that the Frenchman requires a beautiful woman to serve as a pattern for his experiments."

"Give me his address," said Ellen, "and if he engages me I will pay you liberally. You know that you can rely upon me."

The old woman once more had recourse to her filthy drawer, in which her present memoranda were mingled with the relics of the luxury of former days; and taking thence a letter which she had only received that same morning, she tore off the address for the use of the young maiden.

Ellen, who a few months previously had been accustomed to work for seventeen or eighteen hours without ceasing, now took a cab to proceed from the neighbourhood of St. Luke's to Leicester Square. The French scientific experimentalist was at home; and Ellen was conducted up four flights of stairs to a species of belvidere, or glass cabinet, built upon the roof of the house. The windows of this belvidere, and the paper with which the woodwork of the interior was covered, were of a dark blue, in order to mitigate the strength of the sun's rays.

Within this belvidere the Frenchman was at work. He was a short, middle-aged, sallow-faced, sharp-featured person—entirely devoted to matters of science, and having no soul for love, pleasure, politics, or any kind of excitement save his learned pursuits. He was now busily employed at a table covered with copper plates coated with silver, phials of nitric acid, cotton wool, pounce, a camera obscura, several boxes, each of about two feet square, and other materials necessary for photography.

The Frenchman spoke English tolerably well; and eyeing his fair visitant from head to foot, he expressed himself infinitely obliged to the person who had sent her. He then entered into particulars; and Ellen found, to her surprise, that the photographer was desirous of taking full-length female portraits in a state of nudity. She drew her veil over her countenance, and was about to retire in disgust and indignation, when the Frenchman, who was examining a plate as he spoke, and therefore did not observe the effect his words had produced upon her, mentioned the price which he proposed to pay her. Now the artist paid better than the statuary; the sculptor better than the artist; and the photographer better than the sculptor. She therefore hesitated no longer; but entered the service of the man of science.

We shall not proceed to any details connected with this new avocation to which that lovely maiden lent herself. Suffice it to say, that having sold her countenance to the statuary, her likeness to the artist, and her bust to the sculptor, she disposed of her whole body to the photographer. Thus her head embellished images white and bronzed; her features and her figure were perpetuated in divers paintings; her bust was immortalized in a splendid statue; and her entire form is preserved, in all attitudes, and on many plates, in the private cabinet of a photographer at one of the metropolitan Galleries of Practical Science.

At length the photographer was satisfied with the results of his experiments regarding the action of light upon every part of the human frame; and Ellen's occupation was again gone.

A tainted soul now resided in a pure body. Every remaining sentiment of decency and delicacy was crushed—obliterated—destroyed by this last service. Pure souls have frequently resided in tainted bodies: witness Lucretia after the outrage perpetrated upon her :—but here was essentially a foul soul in a chaste and virgin form.

And what dread cause had consummated this sad result? Not the will of the poor girl; for when we first saw her in her cold and cheerless chamber, her mind was spotless as the Alpine snow. But dire necessity—that necessity which became an instrument in the old hag's hands to model the young maiden to her purposes. For it was with ulterior views that the designing harridan had introduced the poor girl to that career which, without being actually criminal, led step by step towards criminality. The wretch knew the world well, and was enabled to calculate the influence of exterior circumstances upon the mind and the passions. After the first conversation which she had with Ellen, she perceived that the purity of the virgin was not to be undermined by specious representations, nor by dazzling theories, nor by delusive sophistry: and the hag accordingly placed the confiding girl upon a path which, while it supplied her with the necessaries of life, gradually presented to her mind scenes which were calculated to destroy her purity of thought and chastity of feeling for ever!

[…]

[Chapters LVIII, LIX, LX describe how a pot-boy, Henry Holford, breaks into Buckingham Palace with the assistance of the Resurrection Man, eavesdrops on royal conversations from beneath a sofa, and sits on Victoria's throne. Victoria and Albert, who are engaged at this point, are generally treated with respect in this text. Victoria is represented as ignorant of the state of the poor in the country: the truth is concealed from her. This episode was successful with readers, and Holford's exploit is repeated in Volume II of *The Mysteries of London*. The mysterious conversation overheard by Henry Holford relates to the inherited diseases of scrofula and insanity associated with George the Third and his family. Reynolds is here exploiting a growing market for revelations about the domestic life of the royal family: representations of the monarchy were also a staple of the up-market *Illustrated London News* in this period. Reynolds's text seeks to demystify the monarchy by revealing the 'truth' about Palace life – a strategy familiar to modern readers.]

CHAPTER LVIII.
NEW YEAR'S DAY.

IT was the 1st of January, 1839.

The weather was cold and inclement;—Nature in nakedness appeared to recline upon the turfless grave of summer.

The ancient river which intersects the mightiest city upon the surface of the earth, was swollen; and in the country through which it wound its way, the fields were flooded in many parts.

The trees were stripped of their verdure: the singing of birds had ceased.

Gloomy and mournful was the face of nature; sombre and lowering the aspect of the proud city.

So pale—so faint were the beams of the mid-day sun, that the summit of St. Paul's, which a few months back was wont to glitter as if it were crowned with a diadem of gold, was now veiled in a murky cloud; and the myriad pinnacles of the modern Babylon, which erst were each tipped as with a star, pointed upwards to a sky ominous and foreboding.

Nevertheless, the ingenuity and wonderous perseverance of man had adopted all precautions to expel the cold from the palaces of the rich and powerful, and to surround the lordly owners of those splendid mansions with the most delicious wines and the most luxurious food, in doors, to induce them to forget that winter reigned without.

Soft carpets, thick curtains—satin, and velvet, and silk,—downy beds beneath gorgeous canopies,—warm clothing, and cheerful fires, combined to defy the approach of winter, and to render the absence of genial summer a matter of small regret.

Then, when the occupants of these palaces went abroad, there was no bold exertion required for them to face the nipping cold; for they stepped from their thresholds into carriages thickly lined with wool, and supplied with cushions, soft, luxurious, and warm.

But that cold which was thus expelled from the palaces of the rich took refuge in the dwellings of the poor; and there it remained, sharp as a razor, pitiless as an executioner, inexorable as a judge, and keen as the north-western wind that blows from the ice-bound coasts of Labrador.

No silks, nor satins, nor velvets, nor carpets, nor canopies, nor curtains, had the dwellings of the poor to defy, or even mitigate the freezing malignity of that chill which, engendered in the arctic regions of eternal snow, and having swept over the frozen rivers and the mighty forests of America, had come to vent its collected spite upon the islands of Europe.

Shivering, starving, in their miserable hovels, the industrious many, by the sweat of whose brow the indolent few were supplied with their silks, and their satins, and their velvets, wept bitter—bitter tears over their suffering and famished children, and cursed the day on which their little ones were born.

For the winter was a very hard one; and bread—bread was very dear!

Yes—bread, which thou, Almighty God! hast given to feed those whom thou didst create after thine own image,—even bread was too dear for the starving poor to buy!

How long, O Lord! wilt thou permit the few to wrest every thing from the many—to monopolize, accumulate, gripe, snatch, drag forth, cling to, the fruits of the earth, for their own behoof alone?

How long shall there exist such spells in the privilege of birth? how long must all happiness and all misery be summed up in the words—

WEALTH | POVERTY.

We said that it was New Year's Day, 1839.

In the palaces of the great were rejoicings, and music, and festivity; and diamonds glittered—and feathers waved—and silks rustled;—the elastic floors bent beneath the steps of the dancers; the wine flowed in crystal cups; and the fruits of summer were amongst the dainties spread to tempt the appetite of the aristocracy.

Ah! there was happiness indeed, in thus welcoming the new year; for those who there greeted its presence, were well assured that it would teem with the joys and blandishments which had characterized the one that had just sunk into the grave of Time!

And how was it with the poor of this mighty metropolis—the imperial city, to whose marts whole navies waft the commerce of the world!

The granaries were full; the pastures had surrendered up fat oxen to commemorate the season; the provision-shops teemed with food of the most luxurious and of the humblest kinds alike. A stranger walking through this great city would have wondered where the mouths were that could consume such vast quantities of food.

And yet thousands famished for want of the merest necessaries of life.

The hovels of the poor echoed not to the sound of mirth and music—but to the wail of hunger and the cry of misery. In those sad abodes there was no joviality to welcome a new year;—for a new year was a curse—a mere prolongation of the acute and poignant horrors of the one gone by.

Alas! that New Year's Day was one of strange contrasts in the social sphere of London.

And as London is the heart of this empire, the disease which prevails in the core is conveyed through every vein and artery over the entire national frame.

The country that contains the greatest wealth of all the territories of the universe, is that which also knows the greatest amount of hideous, revolting, heart-rending misery.

In England men and women die of starvation in the streets.

In England women murder their children to save them from a lingering death by famine.

In England the poor commit crimes to obtain an asylum in a gaol.

In England aged females die by their own hands, in order to avoid the workhouse.

There is one cause of all these miseries and horrors—one fatal scourge invented by the rich to torture the poor—one infernal principle of mischief and of woe, which has taken root in the land—one element of a cruelty so keen and so refined, that it outdoes the agonies endured in the Inquisition of the olden time.

And this fertile source of misery, and murder, and suicide, and crime, is—

THE TREATMENT OF THE WORKHOUSE.

Alas! when the bees have made the honey, the apiarist comes and takes all away, begrudging the industrious insects even a morsel of the wax!

Let us examine for a moment the social scale of these realms:

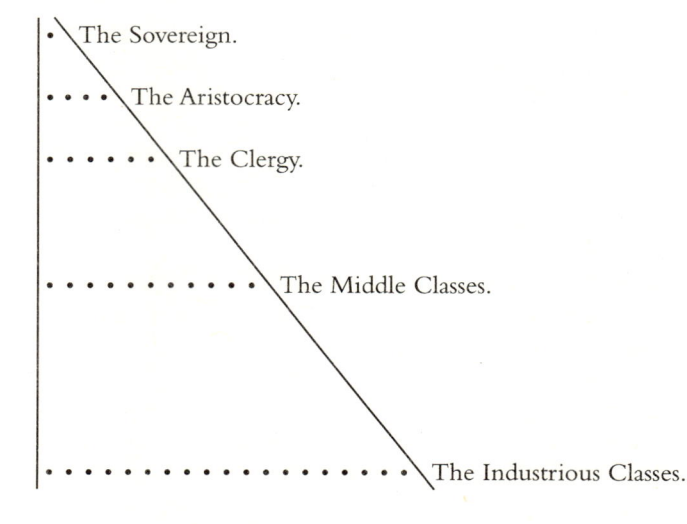

• The Sovereign.
• • • • The Aristocracy.
• • • • • • The Clergy.
• • • • • • • • • • • The Middle Classes.
• The Industrious Classes.

The lowest step in the ladder is occupied by that class which is the most numerous, the most useful, and which ought to be the most influential.

The average annual incomes of the individuals of each class are as follows:—

The Sovereign	£500,000.
The member of the Aristocracy	£30,000.
The Priest	£7,500.
The member of the middle classes	£300.
The member of the industrious classes	£20.

Is this reasonable? is this just? is this even consistent with common sense? It was New Year's Day, 1839.

The rich man sate down to a table crowded with every luxury: the pauper in the workhouse had not enough to eat. The contrast may thus be represented:—

Turtle, venison, turkey, hare, pheasant, perigord pie, plum-pudding, mince-pies, jellies, blancmanger, trifle, preserves, cakes, fruits of all kinds, wines of every description.	½ lb. bread. 4 oz. bacon. ½ lb. potatoes. 1½ pint gruel.

And this was New Year's Day, 1839!

But to proceed.

It was five o'clock in the evening. Three persons were conversing together on Constitution Hill, beneath the wall of the Palace Gardens.

Two of them, who were wrapped up in warm pilot coats, are well known to our readers: the third was a young lad of about sixteen or seventeen, and very short in stature. He was dressed in a blue jacket, dark waistcoat of coarse materials, and corduroy trousers. His countenance was effeminate and by no means bad-looking; his eyes were dark and intelligent; his teeth good. The name of this youth was Henry Holford.

"Well, my boy," said the Resurrection Man, for he was one of the lad's companions, the other being the redoubtable Cracksman,—"well, my boy, do you feel equal to this undertaking?"

"Quite," answered Holford in a decided tone.

"If we succeed, you know," observed the Cracksman, "it will be a jolly good thing for you; and if you happen to get nabbed, why—all the beaks can do to you will be to send you for a month or two upon the stepper. In that there case Tony and me will take care on you when you come out—won't we, Tony?"

"Certainly," replied the Resurrection Man.—"But if you get scented, Harry," he continued, addressing himself to the lad, "as you approach the big house, you must have a run for it, and we shall stay here and leave the rope over the wall for two hours. If you don't come back by that time, we shall suppose that you've either got into some quiet corner of the palace, or that you're taken; and then, whichever happens of these two events, we shan't be of any service to you."

"One thing I should like you to bear in mind, youngster," said the Cracksman, "and that is, that if you don't pluck up your courage well, and prepare for all kinds of dangers and difficulties, you'd much better give up the thing at once. We don't want you to run neck and heels into a business that you are afeard on."

"Afraid!" exclaimed the youth, contemptuously: "I shall not fail for want of courage. I have made up my mind to risk the venture; and let the result be what it will, I shall go through with it."

"That's what I call speaking like a man," said the burglar, "though you are but a boy. Take a drop of brandy before you begin."

"Not a drop," answered Holford: "I require a clear head and a quick eye, and dare not drink."

"Well, as you will," said the Cracksman; and he took a tolerably long draught from a case-bottle which he had produced from his pocket.

He then handed the bottle to the Resurrection Man, who also paid his respects to it with a hearty good will.

"I am ready," said Holford; "there is no use in delay."

"Not a bit," observed the Cracksman "Tony and me will help you over the wall in a jiffey."

By the aid of the Resurrection Man and the burglar, the youth scaled the wall of the Palace Gardens, and ere he dropped upon the inner side, he said in a low but firm tone, "Good night."

Holford was now within the enclosure of the royal demesne. The evening was very dark; but at a distance the windows of the palace shone with effulgence.

Thitherward did he proceed, advancing cautiously along, for he knew that there was a piece of water in the pleasure-grounds. This small lake he soon left on his right hand; and he was shortly within fifty yards of the back part of Buckingham Palace.

At that moment he was suddenly startled by hearing voices close to him. He stood still, and listened. Steps approached, and he heard a gardener issue some instructions to a subordinate. There was a tuft of trees near at hand: Holford had not a moment to lose;—he darted into the thicket of evergreens, where he concealed himself.

"What was that?" said the gardener, stopping short.

"I heard nothing," answered the man.

"Yes—there was a rustling of those trees."

"A cat, perhaps."

"Or one of the aquatic birds."

All was still, and the gardener, accompanied by his man, proceeded on his way. The sounds of their footsteps were soon lost in the distance; and Holford emerged from his hiding-place. Without any farther alarm he reached the back premises of the palace.

He now became involved in a maze of out-houses and offices, and was at a loss which direction to take. He was going cautiously along the wall of one of those buildings, when he suddenly ran against a man who was advancing rapidly in a contrary direction.

"Halloa! who the devil is this?" cried the man; and clutching hold of Holford's collar, he dragged him a few paces, until he brought him beneath a window whence streamed a powerful light. "I suppose you're the new boy that the head-gardener hired this morning?"

"Yes, sir," answered Holford, gladly availing himself of an excuse thus so conveniently suggested by the error of the man who had collared him.

"Then mind which way you go in future, young brocoli-sprout," exclaimed the other; and, dismissing the youth with a slight cuff on the head, he passed on.

Holford hastened away from the light of the window; and, crossing a small court, reached a glass door opening into the back part of the palace. The adventurous lad laid his hand upon the latch: the door was not locked; and he hesitated not a moment to enter the royal abode.

He was now in a low vestibule, well lighted, and at the extremity of which there was a staircase. In one corner of the vestibule was a marble table, on which lay several cloaks, the skirts of which hung down to the ground. This circumstance was particularly fortunate for the safety of the intruder, inasmuch as he had scarcely entered the vestibule, when the sound of footsteps, rapidly descending the staircase, fell upon his ears. He hastened to conceal himself beneath the table, the cloaks serving effectually to veil his person.

Two footmen in gorgeous liveries shortly made their appearance in the vestibule.

"Where did you say her Majesty is?" demanded one.

"In the Roman drawing-room," replied the other. "The Sculpture Gallery is to be lighted up this evening. You can attend to that duty at once, if you will,"

"Very well," said the first speaker; and he left the vestibule by means of a door on the right-hand side, but which door he neglected to close behind him.

The other servant advanced straight up to the marble table, and, sweeping off the cloaks, threw them all over his left arm. Holford's person was now exposed to the eyes of any one who might happen to glance beneath that table. The domestic was, however, a tall and stately individual, and kept his head elevated. Having taken the cloaks from the table, he slowly retraced his steps up the stairs, and disappeared from Holford's view.

The young adventurer started from his hiding-place. The door, by which one of the servants had left the vestibule for the purpose of repairing to the Sculpture Gallery, was open. It communicated with a long passage, only feebly lighted. Holford hesitated not a moment, but proceeded in this direction.

He advanced to the end of the passage, and entered a narrow corridor, branching off to the right, and lighted by lamps sustained in the hands of two tall statues.

[…]

He now gained access to the Sculpture Gallery; but there he found no means of concealment. He determined to explore elsewhere, and speedily found himself in a magnificent saloon, adjoining the library, and where he beheld sofas, with the drapery hanging down to the carpet.

It was beneath one of these downy sofas that the daring intruder into the royal dwelling took refuge; and there, comfortably extended at full length, he chuckled triumphantly at the success which had, up to this moment, attended his adventurous undertaking. We have before said that he was of very small stature; he was moreover thin and delicate, and easily packed away.

Some time passed, and no one appeared to interrupt the reflections of Henry Holford. Hour after hour glided by; and at length the palace-clock struck nine. Scarcely had the last chime died away, when the folding doors were thrown open, and a gorgeous procession of nobles and ladies entered the apartment. The magnificence of the dresses worn by England's peeresses and high-born dames—the waving plumes, the glittering jewels, the sparkling diamonds,—combined with a glorious assemblage of female loveliness, formed a spectacle, at once awe-inspiring, ravishing, and delightful. A little in advance of that splendid *cortège*,—conversing easily with the ladies who walked one pace behind her on either hand, and embellished with precious stones of regal price,—moved the sovereign of the mightiest empire in the universe.

Upon her high and polished brow, Victoria wore a tiara of diamonds: diamonds innumerable, and of immense value, studded her stomacher; diamond pendants adorned her ears; and diamonds also glistened upon her wrists. She walked with grace and dignity; and her noble bearing compensated for the shortness of her stature.

The queen advanced to the very sofa beneath which Holford lay concealed, and seated herself upon it. The ladies and nobles of the court, together with the guests present upon the occasion, stood at a respectful distance from the sovereign. The splendour of the scene was enhanced by the brilliant uniforms of several military officers of high rank, and the court-dresses of the foreign ambassadors. The blaze of light in which the room was bathed, was reflected from the diamonds of the ladies, and the stars and orders which the nobles wore upon their breasts.

At that time Victoria was yet a virgin-queen. If not strictly beautiful, her countenance was very pleasing. Her light brown hair was worn quite plain; her blue eyes were animated with intellect; and when she smiled, her lips revealed a set of teeth white as Oriental pearls. Her bust was magnificent, and her figure good, in spite of the lowness of her stature. Her manner was distinguished by somewhat of that impatience which characterised all the family of George the Third, and which seemed to result from a slightly nervous temperament. She appeared to require answers to her questions more promptly than court etiquette permitted those around her to respond to her inquiries. With regard to the condition of the humbler classes of her subjects, she was totally ignorant: she knew that they were suffering *some* distress; but the fearful amount of that misery was carefully concealed from her. She only read the journals favourable to the ministry; and they took care to report nothing which might offend or wound her. Thus, she who should have known every thing relative to her people, in reality scarcely knew any thing!

Foremost amid the chiefs of foreign diplomacy was the Ambassador from the court of Castelcicala. He was a man of advanced years; and on his breast glittered the stars of all the principal orders of knighthood in Europe—the Cross and Bath of England, the Legion of Honour of France, the Golden Fleece of Spain, the Black Eagle of Prussia, the Sword of Sweden, the Crescent of Turkey, Saint Nepomecenus of Austria, and the Lion Rampant of Castelcicala. The Ambassadors of France and Austria were also present upon this occasion,—Count Sebastiani, the representative of Louis-Philippe, being clad in the splendid uniform of a General in the French army, and wearing the grand cordon of the Legion of Honour,—and Prince Esterhazy, the Austrian Minister, and himself the possessor of estates more extensive than many a German principality, wearing a court dress covered with lace and glittering stars.

Several members of the English Cabinet were also present. There was one whose good-tempered and handsome countenance, gentlemanly demeanour, stout and sturdy form, and complacent smile, would hardly have induced a stranger to believe that this was Viscount Melbourne, the Prime Minister of England. Next was a short personage, with a refined and intelligent, though by no means an imposing air,—a something sharp and cunning in the curl of the mouth, and the flash of the eye,—and a weak disagreeable voice, frequently stammering and hesitating at a long sentence: this was Lord John Russell, the Secretary for the Home Department. Near Lord Russell was a tall man of about fifty,—very good-looking, with dark and well-curled locks, glossy whiskers, and an elegant figure,—but excessively foppish in his attire, and somewhat affected in manner;—and this was Lord Palmerston, Secretary for Foreign Affairs. Conversing with this nobleman was a personage with pale and sallow cheeks, luxuriant and naturally-curling locks,—dark and interesting in appearance, and in the prime of life,—whose conversation denoted him to be a man of elegant taste, whose manners were those of a finished gentleman; but who little suited the idea which a stranger would have formed of a great viceroy or a responsible minister:—nevertheless, this was the Marquis of Normanby, lately Lord-Lieutenant of Ireland, and at the time of which we are speaking, Secretary for the Colonies.

The conversation turned upon the specimens of art in the gallery of sculpture, which the noble company had just visited. In this manner an hour passed away; and at the expiration of that period, the queen and her numerous guests repaired to the drawing-rooms on the first floor, where arrangements had been made for a grand musical entertainment.

The entire pageantry was viewed with ease, and the conversation plainly heard, by the plebian intruder upon that scene of patrician splendour, glory, and wealth. The musical tones of the queen's voice had fallen upon his ears: he had listened to the words of great lords and high-born ladies. At that moment how little, how contemptible did he feel himself to be! Never had he entertained so humble an opinion of his own worth and value in society as he did at that period. He—a common pot-boy in a public-house—had for an hour been the unseen companion of a queen and her mightiest paladins and loveliest dames;—and had he been discovered in his retreat, he would have been turned ignominiously forth, like the man in the parable who went to the marriage-feast without a without a wedding-garment.

For two more mortal hours did Holford remain beneath the sofa, cramped by his recumbent and uneasy position, and already more than half inclined to regret the adventure upon which he had so precipitately entered.

At length the palace grew quiet, and servants entered the room in which Holford was concealed, to extinguish the lights. The moment that this duty was performed, and the domestics had withdrawn, Holford emerged from beneath the sofa, and seated himself upon it. He was proud to think that he now occupied the place where royalty had so lately been. The voice of the queen still seemed to ring in his ears; and he felt an unknown and unaccountable species of happiness in recalling to mind and pondering upon all that had fallen from her lips. At that moment how he envied those peers and highborn dames who were privileged to approach the royal presence and bask beneath the smile of the sovereign;—how he wished that his lot had been cast in a different sphere! But—no! it was useless to regret what could not be remedied; and, although he was now in a palace, and seated upon the very cushion which a few hours previously had been pressed by royalty, he was not one atom less Henry Holford, the pot-boy!

The reverie of this extraordinary youth was long. Visions the most wild and fantastical sustained a powerful excitement in his imagination. At length the clock struck two. Holford awoke from his strange meditations, and collected his scattered ideas.

He now felt the cravings of hunger, and determined to explore the palace in search of food. He had already seen enough of its geography to be enabled to guess the precise position of the servants' offices; and thither he now directed his steps. He reached the great marble hall, which was lighted by lamps: there was no one there. He crossed it, and proceeded along those passages which he had already threaded a few hours before. After wandering about for some time, and, to his infinite surprise and joy, without encountering a soul, he reached the servant's offices. A short search conducted him to a well-stored larder. Some of the dishes had evidently been put away in a hurry, for silver spoons and forks had been left in them. Holford might have possessed himself of property of considerable value: but such an idea never for a moment entered his head. He moreover contented himself with the simplest food he could find; then, remembering that four-and-twenty hours might elapse ere he should be enabled to return to the larder, he supplied himself with a sufficient amount of provender to last during that interval.

Having adopted this precaution, he stole back again to the room where the friendly sofa had already afforded a secure hiding-place. He once more crept beneath the costly drapery, extended himself upon his back, and fell asleep.

CHAPTER LIX.
THE ROYAL LOVERS.

HOLFORD awoke with a start.

At that moment the time-piece upon the mantel struck five. It was still quite dark.

The young man felt cold and nervous. He had dreamt that he was discovered and ejected from the palace amidst the jeers and taunts of the servants.

He now suddenly recollected that the domestics would most probably soon arrive to cleanse and arrange the apartment; and detection in that case must be certain.

It struck him that he had better endeavour to escape at once from the royal dwelling. Then he thought and fondly flattered himself that the same good fortune which had hitherto attended him in this adventure would still follow him. This idea has caused many a hesitating mind to decide upon pursuing a career of crime, or folly, or peril. So was it with Holford; and he resolved to remain in the palace at least a short time longer.

But he perceived the absolute necessity of seeking out a secure place of concealment; and it struck him that the highest storeys of the building were those best calculated for this purpose. Leaving the apartment in which he had availed himself of the friendly sofa, and which, as before stated, was in the immediate vicinity of the Sculpture Gallery upon the ground-floor, he passed through the Library, and returned to the great hall. Ascending a magnificent marble staircase, he reached the Picture Gallery. Every here and there lamps were burning, and thus he was enabled to inspect all the scenes of magnificence and splendour through which he passed.

The Picture Gallery in Buckingham Palace is immediately over the Sculpture Gallery, and forms a wide passage separating the Green Drawing Room, the Throne Room, and other state apartments from the Roman, the Yellow, and the little drawing rooms. The Yellow Drawing Room is the largest and most splendid of the suite. The furniture is all richly carved, and is overlaid with burnished gilding and covered with yellow satin. The wall is surrounded by polished pillars of syenite marble; and on each panel is painted a portrait of some royal personage.

The Dining Room also leads out of the Picture Gallery. This gallery itself is decorated and adorned upon classic models. The frames of the pictures are very plain, but neat, and appropriated to the style of the architecture. There is nothing gorgeous in this gallery: every thing is in good taste; and yet the mouldings and fret-work of the ceiling are of the most elaborate description. The pictures in the gallery are all originals by eminent masters, and are the private property of the sovereign.

It may be here observed that the Queen is passionately attached to the Fine Arts, in which, indeed, she is a proficient. In every room of the palace there are some excellent paintings; and in each apartment occupied by the queen, with the exception of the Throne Room, there is a grand pianoforte.

With a lamp in his hand, Henry Holford proceeded through those magnificent apartments which communicated with the Picture Gallery. He was astonished at the assemblage of wealth and splendour that met his eyes on every side. From time to time he seated himself upon the softest ottomans, and in the gilded chairs—in every place where he deemed it probable that the queen might have rested. At length he reached the Throne Room. The imperial seat itself was covered over with a velvet cloth, to protect it against the dust. Holford removed the cloth; and the splendours of the throne were revealed to him.

He hesitated for a moment: he felt as if he were committing a species of sacrilege;—then triumphing over this feeling—a feeling which had appeared like a remorse—he ascended the steps of the throne;—he placed himself in the seat of England's monarch!

Had the sceptre been there he would have grasped it;—had the crown been within his reach, he would have placed it upon his head!

But time pressed; and he was compelled to leave those apartments in which a strange and unaccountable fascination induced him to linger. He ascended a staircase leading to another storey; and now he proceeded with extreme caution, for he conceived that he must be in the immediate vicinity of the royal sleeping apartments. He hastened up to the highest storey he could reach, and entered several passages from which doors opened on either side. One of these doors was ajar; the light of a lamp in the passage enabled him to ascertain that the chamber into which it led was full of old furniture, trunks, boxes, bedding, and other lumber. This was precisely the place which suited the adventurous pot-boy; and he hastened to conceal himself amidst a pile of mattresses which formed a secure, warm, and comfortable berth.

Here he again fell asleep; and when he awoke the sun was shining brightly. He partook of his provisions with a good appetite, and then deliberated within himself what course he should pursue. He felt madly anxious to be near the person of the queen once more: he longed to hear her voice again; —he resolved to risk every thing to gratify these inclinations.

He began to understand that the vast extent of the palace, and the many different ways of reaching the various floors and suites of apartments, constituted the elements of his safety, and greatly diminished the risk of encountering any of the inmates of the royal dwelling. He was insane enough, moreover, to believe that some good genius or especial favour of fortune protected him; and these impressions were sufficiently powerful to induce him to attempt any fresh enterprise within the walls of the palace.

While he was debating within himself how he should proceed in order to satisfy his enthusiastic curiosity, the door suddenly opened, and two female servants of the royal household entered the lumber-room.

Holford's heart sank within him: his limbs seemed paralysed; his breath failed him.

"The entertainment takes place in the Yellow and Roman Drawing Rooms this evening," said one.

"The prince is expected at five o'clock," observed the other. "He and his father the Duke of Saxe Coburg Gotha, are to land at Woolwich between two and three."

"So I heard. the royal carriages have already left to meet her Majesty's guests."

"Have you ever seen the prince?"

"Once. He was in England, I remember, a short time previous to the accession of her Majesty."

"Is he good looking?"

"Very. Of course you believe as I do, and as every one else does that Prince Albert of Saxe Coburg will—"

"Soon be Prince Albert of England."

"Hush! walls have ears!"

The servants having discovered the article of furniture which was the object of their search, left the room—greatly to the relief of Henry Holford, whose presence they never for a moment suspected.

Holford had thus accidentally learnt some information which served to guide his plans. The evening's entertainment was to take place in the Yellow Drawing Room—an apartment which he could not fail to recognise by the colour, as one which he had visited before day-break that morning. He had heard of Prince Albert, whom rumour had already mentioned as the happy being who had attracted the queen's favour. Every circumstance now lent its aid to induce the enthusiastic lad to resolve upon penetrating into the Yellow Drawing Room, by some means or another, during the afternoon.

It struck the intruder that if the queen intended to receive company in the Yellow Drawing-room in the evening, she would most probably welcome her illustrious guests from Germany in some other apartment. He knew, from the conversation of the two female servants, that the Grand Duke of Saxe-Coburg Gotha and Prince Albert, were to arrive at five: he presumed that the inmates of the palace would assemble in those points where they could command a view of the ducal *cortège*; and he came to the conclusion that the coast would be most clear for his purposes, at five o'clock.

Nor was be wrong in his conjectures; for scarcely had two minutes elapsed after the clock had proclaimed the hour of five, when Henry Holford was safely ensconced beneath a sofa in the Yellow Drawing Room.

At eight o'clock the servants entered and lighted the lamps. The colour of the paper and the satin of the furniture enhanced the splendour of the effulgence thus created in that magnificent saloon.

At half-past nine the door opened again; and Holford's heart beat quickly, for he now expected the appearance of the sovereign and her guests. But, no—not yet. Two ladies attached to the court, entered the drawing-room, and seated themselves upon the sofa beneath which Holford lay concealed.

"Well—what think you of the young prince?" said one. "Your grace was seated next to him."

"Very handsome—and so unassuming," was the reply.

"Does your grace really believe that her Majesty is smitten?"

"No doubt of it. How fortunate for the family of the Grand Duke of Saxe-Coburg!"

"Yes—fortunate on the score of alliance."

"And in a pecuniary point of view."

"Not so much as your grace thinks. There has been an absurd report in circulation that the grand duke's revenues are so small, none of his family could venture to appear at the court of Vienna: and also, that the means of education for the younger branches were always excessively restricted."

"And are not these reports correct, countess?"

"By no means. Your grace probably is aware that the earl and myself visited Germany the year before last; and we remained six weeks at Gotha. The Duke of Saxe-Coburg possesses a considerable civil list, and a large private fortune. His brother Ferdinand espoused the wealthy Princess Kohary of Hungary; and another brother, Leopold, married our lamented Princess Charlotte. It has been stated that Prince Leopold himself was a simple major in the Austrian service, with nothing but his pay, when he was fortunate enough to obtain the favour of the Princess Charlotte: this is so far from being correct, that he never was in the Austrian service at all, but was a general officer in the Russian army, enjoying, in addition to his full pay, a princely allowance from his country."

"Your ladyship has greatly pleased me with these elucidations."

"Your grace honours me with this mark of satisfaction. Prince Albert was educated at Bonn, on the Rhine. His mental qualifications are said to be of a very high order; his disposition is amiable; and he has obtained the affections of all who know him in Germany."

"It is to be hoped that her most gracious Majesty will enjoy a long, prosperous, and happy reign," said the duchess, in a tone of unfeigned sincerity.

"Long and prosperous it may be," returned the countess, with a strange solemnity of voice and manner; "but happy for her—happy for the sovereign whom we all so much love,—no—that is impossible!"

"Alas! I know to what you allude," observed the duchess, her tone also changing. "Merciful heavens! is there, then, no perfect happinss in this world?"

"Where shall perfect happiness be found?" exclaimed the countess, in a voice of deep melancholy, and with a profound sigh. "Never did any sovereign ascend the throne under more favourable circumstances than Victoria. Enshrined in a nation's heart—beloved by millions of human beings,—wearing the proudest diadem in the universe, and swaying the sceptre of a dominion extensive as that of Rome, in her most glorious days,—oh! why should not Victoria be completely happy? Alas! she can command the affections of her people by her conduct:—the valour of her subjects, the prowess of her generals, and the dauntless courage of her admirals, can preserve her empire from all encroachment—all peril;—wealth can surround her with every luxury, and all the potentates of the earth may seek her friendship;—but no power— no dominion—no wealth—no luxury—no love, can exterminate the seeds—"

"Ah, countess! for God's sake, talk not in this manner!" ejaculated the duchess: "you make me melancholy—so melancholy, that I shall be dispirited the entire evening."

"Pardon me, my dear friend; but I know not how our discourse gradually turned upon so sad a subject. And yet the transition must have been natural," added the countess, in a mournful and plaintive voice; "for, most assuredly, I should not have voluntarily sought to converse upon so sad a theme."

"Sad!" cried the duchess; "'t is sufficient to make one's heart bleed. To think that a young creature whom millions and millions of beings idolize and adore—whose name is upon every lip—whose virtues and qualifications are the theme of every pen—whose slightest wish amounts to a command,—oh! to think that this envied and amiable being should be haunted, day and night—alone, or when surrounded by all that is most noble or most lovely in England's aristocracy,—haunted by that dread fear—that appalling alarm—that dismal apprehension,—oh, it is intolerable!"

[...]

It may be supposed that Holford had not lost one word of the above conversation. He had greedily drunk in every word;—but the concluding portion of it had filled him with the most anxious curiosity, and with wonder. To what did those dark, mysterious hints bear reference? And how could the happiness of the sovereign be incomplete? Those two noble ladies had detailed all the elements of felicity which formed the basis of the queen's position; and surely sufficient had been enumerated to prove the perfection of her happiness. And yet, allusion was made to one source of perpetual fear—one cause of unmixed alarm—one object of ever present dread, by which the queen was haunted on all occasions. What could this be? Conjecture was vain—imagination could suggest nothing calculated to explain this strange mystery.

Shortly after eleven o'clock the doors were thrown open, and the royal train made its appearance. On the queen's right hand walked Prince Albert, the sovereign leaning gently upon his arm. He was dressed in a court-garb, and wore a foreign order upon his breast. Of slight form and slender make, his figure was wanting in manliness; but his deportment was graceful. His eyes beamed kindness; and there was something peculiarly sweet and pleasant in his smile. His countenance was expressive of intellect; his conversation was amusing. He was evidently a very pleasant companion; and when Victoria and Albert walked down the saloon together, there appeared a certain fitness in their union which was calculated to strike the most common beholder.

The queen and the prince seated themselves upon the sofa beneath which the pot-boy was concealed; and their conversation was plainly overheard by him. The noble and beauteous guests—the lords and the ladies of the court—withdrew to a distance; and the royal lovers—for such already were Victoria and Albert—enjoyed the pleasures of a *tête-à-tête*. We shall not record any portion of their discourse—animated, interesting, and tender though it were: suffice it to say that, for a short time they seemed to forget their high rank, and to throw aside the trammels of court etiquette, in order to give vent to those natural feelings which the sovereign has in common with the peasant.

This *tête-à-tête* lasted for nearly an hour: music and dancing then ensued; and the entertainment continued until two o'clock in the morning.

The company retired—the lights were extinguished in the state apartments—and profound silence once more reigned throughout the palace.

Holford paid another visit to the larder, and then retraced his steps unobserved to the lumber-room, where he slept until a late hour in the morning.

CHAPTER LX.
REVELATIONS.

[Holford wakes up and decides to explore the Palace further. Concealed beneath a sofa, he overhears a conversation between two ladies-in-waiting. He later escapes over the wall, and returns to his criminal friends.]

[…]

Holford had seen much to surprise and astonish him. The image of the Queen ever haunted his imagination: her voice ever rang in his ears. He disliked Prince Albert: that low, vulgar, uneducated, despised, obscure pot-boy, entertained a feeling of animosity,—he scarcely knew wherefore—against the young German who was evidently destined to become the husband of England's queen. Again and again did he ponder upon the mysterious conversation between the two ladies of the court, which he had overheard; —and he felt an ardent and insuperable longing to fathom their meaning to the bottom. But how was this to be done? He determined to obtain access to the drawing-room once more, and trust to the chapter of accidents to elucidate the mystery.

Accordingly, he contrived that same afternoon, to obtain access to the royal apartments, without detection, once more; and once more, also, did he conceal himself beneath the sofa. Fortune appeared to favour his views and wishes. Not many minutes had elapsed after he had ensconsed himself in his hiding-place, when the two ladies, whose conversation had so much interested him on the preceding day, slowly entered the Yellow Drawing-Room.

The following dialogue then took place:—

[...]

"Have you heard when the royal intentions to contract a union with his Serene Highness Prince Albert, will be communicated to the country?"

"Not until the close of the year; and the marriage will therefore take place at the commencement of 1840. The Prince will pay but a short visit upon this occasion, and then return to Germany until within a short period of the happy day."

"God send that the union may be a happy one!" ejaculated the countess. "But—"

"Oh! my dear friend, do not relapse again into those gloomy forebodings which rendered me melancholy all yesterday evening," interrupted the duchess.

"Alas! your grace is well aware of my devoted attachment to our royal mistress; and if there be times when I tremble for the consequences of—"

"Breathe it not—give not utterance to the bare idea!" cried the duchess, in a tone of the most unfeigned horror. "Providence will never permit an entire empire to experience so great a misfortune as this!"

"Maladies of that kind are hereditary," said the countess, solemnly;— "maladies of that species descend through generations—unsparing—pitiless —regardless of rank, power, or position; oh! it is horrible to contemplate!"

"Horrible!—Most horrible!" echoed the duchess.

[...]

"The entire family of George the Third has inherited the seeds of disease —physical and mental—"

"Scrofula and insanity," said the duchess, with a cold shudder.

"Which were inherent in that monarch," added the countess.

[...]

[In Chapter LXII, Anthony Tidkins, the Resurrection Man, recounts his life history to the criminal gang which frequents the *Boozing Ken*, a low alehouse in the East End of London. The history or autobiography of the Resurrection Man is interpolated into the wider narration, and offers a perspective that contrasts with that of the controlling narrative voice of the text. Anthony Tidkins's account of his own life presents his crimes and antisocial behaviour as the product of social injustice. The attitudes of the wealthy inhabitants of Deal and its surrounding districts to poverty and suffering drive Tidkins to take revenge on society through incendiarism, and later to become a leader of criminal life in London. The account also offers some unusual detail concerning the practices of body-snatching, and the system of punishment.]

CHAPTER LXII.
THE RESURRECTION MAN'S HISTORY.

"I WAS born thirty-eight years ago, near the village of Walmer, in Kent. My father and mother occupied a small cottage—or rather hovel, made of the wreck of a ship, upon the sea-coast. Their ostensible employment was that of fishing: but it would appear that smuggling and body-snatching also formed a portion of my father's avocations. The rich inhabitants of Walmer and Deal encouraged him in his contraband pursuits, by purchasing French silks, gloves, and scent of him: the gentlemen, moreover, were excellent customers for French brandy, and the ladies for dresses and perfumes. The clergyman of Walmer and his wife were our best patrons in this way; and in consequence of the frequent visits they paid our cottage, they took a sort of liking to me. The parson made me attend the national school regularly every Sunday; and when I was nine years old he took me into his service to clean the boots and knives, brush the clothes, and so forth. I was then very fond of reading, and used to pass all my leisure time in studying books which he allowed me to take out of his library. This lasted till I was twelve years old, when my father was one morning arrested on a charge of smuggling, and taken to Dover Castle. The whole neighbourhood expressed their surprise that a man who appeared to be so respectable, should turn out such a villain. The gentlemen who used to buy brandy of him talked loudly of the necessity of making an example of him: the ladies, who were accustomed to purchase gloves, silks, and *eau-de-cologne*, wondered that such a desperate ruffian should have allowed them to sleep safe in their beds; and of course the clergyman and his wife kicked me ignominiously out of doors. As all things of this nature create a sensation in a small community, the parson preached a sermon upon the subject on the following Sunday, choosing for his text 'Render unto Cæsar the things that are Cæsar's, and unto God the things that are God's,' and earnestly enjoining all his congregation to unite in deprecating the conduct of a man who had brought disgrace upon a neighbourhood till then famed for its loyalty, its morality, and its devotion to the laws of the country.

"My father was acquitted for want of evidence, and returned home after having been in prison six months waiting for his trial. In the mean time my mother and myself were compelled to receive parish relief: not one of the fine ladies and gentlemen who had been the indirect means of getting my father into a scrape by encouraging him in his illegal pursuits, would notice us. My mother called upon several; but their doors were banged in her face. When I appeared at the Sunday School, the parson expelled me, declaring that I was only calculated to pollute honest and good boys; and the beadle thrashed me soundly for daring to attempt to enter the church. All this gave me a very strange idea of human nature, and set me a-thinking upon the state of society. Just at that period a baronet in the neighbourhood was proved to be the owner of a smuggling vessel, and to be pretty deep in the contraband business himself. He was compelled to run away: an Exchequer process, I think they call it, issued against his property; and every thing he possessed was swept away. It appeared that he had been smuggling for years, and had defrauded the revenue to an immense amount. He was a widower: but he had three children—two boys and a girl, at school in the neighbourhood. Oh! then what sympathy was created for these '*poor dear bereaved little ones,*' as the parson called them in a charity sermon which he preached for their benefit. And there they were, marshalled into the parson's own pew, by the beadle; and the parson's wife wept over them. Subscriptions were got up for them;—the mayor of Deal took one boy, the banker another, and the clergyman's wife took charge of the girl; and never was seen so much weeping, and consoling, and compassion before!

"Well, at that time my mother had got so thin, and weak, and ill, through want and affliction, that her neighbours gave her the name of the *Mummy*, which she has kept ever since. My father came home, and was shunned by every body. The baronet's uncle happened to die at that period, and left his nephew an immense fortune:—the baronet paid all the fines, settled the Exchequer matters, and returned to Walmer. A triumphal reception awaited him: balls, parties, concerts, and routs took place in honour of the event;—and the mayor, the banker and the clergyman and his wife were held up as the patterns of philanthropy and humanity. Of course the baronet rewarded them liberally for having taken care of his children in the hour of need.

"This business again set me a-thinking; and I began to comprehend that birth and station made an immense difference in the views that the world adopted of men's actions. My father, who had only higgled and fiddled with smuggling affairs upon a miserably small scale, was set down as the most atrocious monster unhung, because he was one of the common herd; but the baronet, who had carried on a systematic contraband trade to an immense amount, was looked upon as a martyr to tyrannical laws, because he was one of the upper classes and possessed a title. So my disposition was soured by these proofs of human injustice, at my very entrance upon life.

"Up to this period, in spite of the contemplation of the lawless trade carried on by my father, I had been a regular attendant at church and at the Sunday School; and I declare most solemnly that I never went to sleep at night, nor commenced my morning's avocations, without saying my prayers. But when my father got into trouble, the beadle kicked me out of church, and the parson drove me out of the school; and so I began to think that if my religion was only serviceable and available as long as my father remained unharmed by the law, it could not be worth much. From that moment I never said another prayer, and never opened a bible or prayer-book. Still I was inclined to labour to obtain an honest livelihood; and I implored my father, upon my knees, not to force me to assist in his proceedings of smuggling and body-snatching, to both which he was compelled by dire necessity to return the moment he was released from gaol. He told me I was a fool to think of living honestly, as the world would not let me; but he added that I might make the trial.

"Pleased with this permission, and sincerely hoping that I might obtain some occupation, however menial, which would enable me to eat the bread of honest toil, I went round to all the farmers in the neighbourhood, and offered to enter their service as a plough-boy or a stable-boy. The moment they found out who I was, they one and all turned me away from their doors. One said, '*Like father, like son*;'—another asked if I was mad, to think that I could thus thrust myself into an honest family;—a third laughed in my face;—a fourth threatened to have me taken up for wanting to get into his house to commit a felony;—a fifth swore that there was gallows written upon my countenance;—a sixth ordered his men to loosen the bulldog at me; —and a seventh would have had me ducked in his horse-pond, if I had not run away.

"Dispirited, but not altogether despairing, I returned home. On the following day, I walked into Deal, (which almost joins Walmer) and called at several tradesmen's shops to inquire if they wanted an errand boy. My reception by these individuals was worse than that which I had met with at the hands of the farmers. One asked me if I thought he would run the risk of having his house indicted as the receptacle for thieves and vagabonds;— a second pointed to his children, and said, '*Do you suppose I want to bring them up in the road to the gallows?*'—a third locked up his till in affright, and threatened to call a constable;—and a fourth lashed me severely with a horse whip.

"Still I was not totally disheartened. I determined to call upon some of those ladies and gentlemen who had been my father's best customers for his contraband articles. One lady upon hearing my business, seized hold of the poker with one hand and her salts-bottle with the other;—a second was also nearly fainting, and rang the bell for her maid to bring her some *eau-de-cologne*—the very *eau-de-cologne* which my father had smuggled for her; —a third begged me with tears in her eyes to retire, or my very suspicious appearance would frighten her lap-dog into fits;—and a fourth (an old lady, who was my father's best customer for French brandy), held up her hands to heaven, and implored the Lord to protect her from all sabbath-breakers, profane swearers, and drunkards.

"Finding that I had nothing to expect from the ladies, I tried the gentlemen who had been accustomed to patronise my father previous to his *misfortune*. The first swore at me like a trooper, and assured me that he had always prophesied I should go wrong:—the second spoke civilly, and regretted that his excellent advice had been all thrown away upon my father, whom he had vainly endeavoured to avert from his wicked courses (it was for smuggling things for this gentleman that my father had been arrested);—and the third made no direct answer, but shook his head solemnly, and wondered what the world was coming to.

"I was now really reduced to despair. I, however, resolved to try some of the very poorest tradesmen in the town. By these miserable creatures I was received with compassionate interest; and my case was fully comprehended by them. Some even gave me a few halfpence; and one made me sit down and dine with him, his wife, and his children. They, however, one and all declared *that they could not take me into their service, for, if they did, they would be sure to offend all their customers.* Thus was it that the overbearing conduct and atrocious tyranny of the more wealthy part of the community, compelled the poorer portion to smother all sympathy in my behalf.

"A sudden thought now struck me. I resolved to call next day upon the very baronet who had himself suffered so much in consequence of the customs-laws. Exhilarated by the new hope awakened within me, I repaired on the following morning to the splendid mansion which he now inhabited. I was shown into a magnificent room, where he received me, lounging before a cheerful fire. He listened very patiently to my tale, and then spoke, as nearly as I can recollect, as follows:—'My good lad, I have not the slightest doubt that you are anxious to eat the bread of honesty, as you very properly express it. But that bread is not within the reach of every body; and if we were all to pick and choose in this world, my God! what would become of us? My dear young man, I occupy a prominent position amidst the gentry of these parts, and I have also a duty to fulfil towards society. Society has condemned you— unheard, I grant you: nevertheless, society *has* condemned you. Under these circumstances I have no alternative, but to decline taking you into my service; and I must moreover request you to remember that if you are ever found loitering upon my grounds, I shall have you put in the stocks. I regret that my duty to society compels me thus to act.'

"You may conceive with what feelings I heard this long tirade. I was literally confounded, and retired without venturing upon a remonstrance. I knew not what course to adopt. To return home and inform my parents that I could obtain no work, was to lay myself under the necessity of becoming a smuggler and a body-snatcher at once. As a desperate resource I thought of calling upon the clergyman, and explaining all my sentiments to him. I hoped to be able to convince him that although my father was bad, or supposed to be bad, yet I abhorred vice in all its shapes, and was anxious only to pursue honest courses. As a Christian minister, he could not, I imagined, be so uncharitable as to infer my guilt in consequence of that of my parent; and, accordingly, to him did I repair. He had just returned to his own house from a funeral, and was in a hurry to be off on a shooting excursion, for he had on his sporting-garb beneath his surplice. He listened to me with great impatience, and asked if my father still pursued his contraband trade. Seeing that I hesitated how to reply, he exclaimed, turning his eyes up to heaven, '*Speak the truth, young man, and shame the devil!*' I answered in the affirmative; and he then said carelessly, 'Well, go and speak to my wife; she will act in the matter as she chooses.' Rejoiced at this hopeful turn in the proceeding, I sought his lady, as I was desired. She heard all that I had to say, and then observed, 'Not for worlds could I receive you into my house again; but if your father has any silks and gloves, very cheap and very good, I do not mind purchasing them. And remember,' she added, as I was about to depart, 'I do not want these things; I only offer to take them for the purpose of doing you a service. My motive is purely a Christian one.'

"I returned home. 'Well,' said my father, 'what luck this morning?'—'None,' I replied.—'And what do you mean to do, lad?'—'To become a smuggler, a body-snatcher, or any thing else that you choose,' was my reply; 'and the sooner we begin, the better, for I am sick and tired of being good.'

"So I became a smuggler and a resurrection man.

"You have heard, perhaps, that Deal is famous for its boatmen and pilots. It is also renowned for the beauty of the sailors' daughters. One of those lovely creatures captivated my heart—for I can even talk sentimentally when I think of those times; and she seemed to like me in return. Her name was Katharine Price—Kate Price, as she was called by her acquaintance; and a prettier creature the sun never shone upon. She was good and virtuous, too—and she alone understood my real disposition, which, even now that I had embarked in lawless pursuits, still panted to be good and virtuous also. At this time I was nineteen, and she was one year younger. We loved in secret—and we met in secret; for her parents would not for one moment have listened to the idea of our union. My hope was to obtain a good sum of money by one desperate venture in the contraband line, and run away with Kate to some distant part of the country, where we could enter upon some way of business that would produce us an honest livelihood. This hope sustained us!

"At this time there were a great many sick sailors in Deal Hospital, and numerous funerals took place in the burial-ground of that establishment. My father and I determined to have up a few of the corpses, for we always knew where to dispose of as many *subjects* as we could obtain. By these means I proposed to raise enough money to purchase in France the articles that I meant to smuggle into England and thereby obtain the necessary funds for carrying out the plans upon which Kate and myself were resolved.

"Good luck attended upon my father and myself in respect to the body-snatching business. We raised thirty pounds; and with that we set sail for France in the boat which we always hired for our smuggling expeditions. We landed at Calais, and made our purchases. We bought an immense quantity of brandy at tenpence a quart; gloves at eightpence a pair; three watches at two pound ten each; and some *eau-de-cologne*, proportionately cheap. Our thirty pounds we calculated would produce us a hundred and twenty. We put out to sea again at about ten o'clock at night. The wind was blowing stiff from the nor'-east; and by the time we had been an hour at sea it increased to a perfect hurricane. Never shall I forget that awful night. The entire ocean was white with foam; but the sky above was as black as pitch. We weathered the tempest until we reached the shore about a mile to the south'ard of Walmer, at a place called Kingsdown. We touched the beach—I thought every thing was safe. A huge billow broke over the stern of the lugger; and in a moment the boat was a complete wreck. My father leapt on shore from the bow at the instant this catastrophe took place: I was swallowed up along with the ill-fated bark. I was, however an excellent swimmer; and I combated, and fought, and struggled with the ocean, as a man would wrestle with a savage animal that held him in its grasp. I succeeded in gaining the beach; but so weak and enfeebled was I that my father was compelled to carry me to our hovel, close by.

"I was put to bed: a violent fever seized upon me—I became delirious—and for six weeks I lay tossing upon a bed of sickness.

"At length I got well. But what hope remained for me? We were totally ruined—so was the poor fisherman whose boat was wrecked upon that eventful night. I wrote a note to Kate to tell her all that had happened, and to make an appointment for the following Sunday evening, that we might meet and talk over the altered aspect of affairs. Scarcely had I despatched this letter to the care of Kate's sister-in-law, who was in our secret, and managed our little correspondence, when my father came in and asked me if I felt myself well enough to accompany him on a little expedition that evening. I replied in the affirmative. He then told me that a certain surgeon for whom we did business, and who resided in Deal, required a particular subject which had been buried that morning in Walmer Churchyard. I did not ask my father any more questions; but that night I accompanied him to the burial-ground between eleven and twelve o'clock. The surgeon had shown my father the grave in the afternoon; and we had a cart waiting in a lane close by. The church is in a secluded part, surrounded by trees, and at some little distance from any habitations. There was no danger of being meddled with:—moreover, we had often operated in the same ground before.

"To work we went in the usual manner. We shovelled out the soil, broke open the coffin, thrust the corpse into a sack, filled up the grave once more, and carried our prize safe off to the cart. We then set off at a round pace towards Deal, and arrived at the back door of the surgeon's house by two o'clock. He was up and waiting for us. We carried the corpse into the surgery, and laid it upon a table. 'You are sure it is the right one?' said the surgeon.—'It is the body from the grave that you pointed out,' answered my father.—'The fact is,' resumed the surgeon, 'that this is a very peculiar case. Six days ago, a young female rose in the morning in perfect health; that evening she was a corpse. I opened her, and found no traces of poison; but her family would not permit me to carry the examination any further. They did not wish her to be hacked about. Since her death some love-letters have been found in her drawer; but there is no name attached to any of them.'—I began to feel interested, I scarcely knew why; but this was the manner in which I was accustomed to write to Kate. The surgeon continued: 'I am therefore anxious to make another and more searching investigation than on the former occasion, into the cause of death. But I will soon satisfy myself that this is indeed the corpse I mean.' —With these words the surgeon tore away the shroud from the face of the corpse. I cast an anxious glance upon the pale, cold, marble countenance. My blood ran cold—my legs trembled—my strength seemed to have failed me. Was I mistaken? could it be the beloved of my heart?—'Yes; that is Miss Price,' said the surgeon, coolly. All doubt on my part was now removed. I had exhumed the body of her whom a thousand times I had pressed to my sorrowful breast—whom I had clasped to my aching heart. I felt as if I had committed some horrible crime—a murder, or other deadly deed!

"The surgeon and my father did not notice my emotions, but settled their accounts. The medical man then offered us each a glass of brandy. I drank mine with avidity, and then accompanied my father from the spot—uncertain whether to rush back and claim the body, or not. But I did not do so.

"For some days I wandered about scarcely knowing what I did—and certainly not caring what became of me. One morning I was roving amidst the fields, when I heard a loud voice exclaim, 'I say, you fellow there, open the gate, will you?' I turned round, and recognised the baronet on horseback. He had a large hunting whip in his hand.—'Open the gate!' said I; 'and whom for?' 'Whom for!' repeated the baronet; 'why, for me, to be sure, fellow.'—'Then open it yourself,' said I. The baronet was near enough to me to reach me with his whip; and he dealt me a stinging blow across the face. Maddened with pain, and soured with vexation, I leaped over the gate and attacked the baronet with a stout ash stick which I carried in my hand. I dragged him from his horse, and thrashed him without mercy. When I was tired, I walked quietly away, he roaring after me that he would be revenged upon me as sure as I was born.

"Next day I was arrested and taken before a magistrate. The baronet appeared against me, and—to my surprise—swore that I had assaulted him with a view to rob him, and that he had the greatest difficulty in protecting his purse and watch. [...] I was committed to gaol for trial at the next Maidstone assizes.

"For three months I lay in prison. I was not, however, completely hardened yet; nor did I associate with those who drank, and sang, and swore. [...]

"I was tried, and found guilty. The next two years of my life I passed at the hulks in Woolwich, dressed in dark grey, and wearing a chain around my leg. Even there I did not grow so corrupted, but that I sought for work the moment I was set at liberty again. [...] Turned away from the hulks one fine morning at ten o'clock, without a farthing in my pocket nor the means of obtaining a morsel of bread, my prospects were miserable enough. I could not obtain any employment in Woolwich: evening was coming on—and I was hungry. Suddenly I thought of enlisting. Pleased with this idea, I went to the barracks, and offered myself as a recruit. [...] The sergeant was delighted with me, because I could read and write well; but the surgeon would not pass me. He said to me, 'You have either been half-starved for a length of time, or you have undergone a long imprisonment, for your flesh is as flabby as possible.' Thus was this hope destroyed.

[...]

"Well—that night I wandered into the country and slept under a hedge. On the following morning I was compelled to satisfy the ravenous cravings of my hunger with Swedish turnips plucked from the fields.[...] A constable came up and took me into custody for robbing the turnip field. I was conducted before a neighbouring justice of the peace. He asked me what I meant by stealing the turnips? I told him that I had fasted for twenty-four hours, and was hungry. 'Nonsense, hungry!' he exclaimed; [...] And this excellent specimen of the 'Great unpaid' committed me forthwith to the treadmill for one month *as a rogue and vagabond*.

"The treadmill is a horrible punishment: it is too bad even for those that are really rogues and vagabonds. The weak and strong take the same turn, without any distinction; and I have seen men fall down fainting upon the platform, with the risk of having their legs or arms smashed by the wheel, through sheer exhaustion. [...]

"I had been two years at the hulks, and was not hardened: I had been a smuggler and a body-snatcher, and was not hardened:—but this one month's imprisonment and spell at the treadmill *did* harden me—and hardened me completely! I could not see any advantage in being good. I could not find out any inducement to be honest. [...] 'The legislature thinks that if it does not make the most grinding laws to keep down the poor, the poor will rise up and commit the most unheard-of atrocities. In fact the rich are prepared to believe any infamy which is imputed to the poor.' It was thus that I reasoned; and I looked forward to the day of my release with a burning—maddening—drunken joy!

"That day came. I was turned adrift, as before, without a shilling and without a crust. That alone was as bad as branding the words *rogue and vagabond* upon my forehead. How could I remain honest, even if I had any longer been inclined to do so, when I could not get work and had no money—no bread—no lodging? The legislature does not think of all this. It fancies that all its duty consists in punishing men for crimes, and never dreams of adopting measures to prevent them from committing crimes at all. But I now no more thought of honesty: I went out of prison a confirmed ruffian. I had no money—no conscience—no fear—no hope—no love—no friendship—no sympathy—no kindly feeling of any sort. My soul had turned to the blackness of hell!

"The very first thing I did was to cut myself a good tough ash stick with a heavy knob at one end. The next thing I did was to break into the house of the very justice who had sentenced me to the treadmill for eating a raw turnip; and I feasted jovially upon the cold fowl and ham which I found in his larder. I also drank success to my new career in a bumper of his fine old wine. This compliment was due to him: he had made me what I was!

"I carried off a small quantity of plate—all that I could find, you may be sure—and took my departure from the house of the justice. As I was hurrying away from this scene of my first exploit, I passed by a fine large barn, also belonging to my friend the magistrate. I did not hesitate a moment what to do. I owed him a recompense for my month at the treadmill; and I thought I might as well add *Incendiary* to my other titles of *Rogue and Vagabond*. Besides, I longed for mischief—the world had persecuted me quite long enough, the hour of retaliation had arrived. I fired the barn and scampered away as hard as I could. I halted at a distance of about half a mile, and turned to look. A bright column of flame was shooting up to heaven! Oh! how happy did I feel at that moment. Happy! this is not the word! I was mad—intoxicated—delirious with joy. I literally danced as I saw the barn burning. I was avenged on the man who would not allow me to eat a cold turnip to save me from starving:—that one cold turnip cost him dear! The fire spread, and communicated with his dwelling-house; and there was no adequate supply of water. The barn—the stacks—the out-houses—the mansion were all destroyed. But that was not all. The only daughter of the justice—a lovely girl of nineteen—was burnt to death. I read the entire account in the newspapers a few days afterwards!

"And the upper classes wonder that there are so many incendiary fires: my only surprise is, that there are so few! Ah! the Lucifer-match is a fearful weapon in the hands of the man whom for the laws, the aristocracy, and the present state of society have ground down to the very dust. I felt all my power—I knew all my strength—I was aware of all my importance as a man, when I read of the awful extent of misery and desolation which I had thus caused. Oh! I was signally avenged!

"I now bethought me of punishing the baronet in the same manner. He had been the means of sending me for two years to the hulks at Woolwich. Pleased with this idea, I jogged merrily on towards Walmer. It was late at night when I reached home. I found my mother watching by my father's death-bed, and arrived just in time to behold him breath his last. My mother spoke to me about a decent interment for him. I laughed in her face. Had he ever allowed any one to sleep quietly in his grave? No. How could *he* then hope for repose in the tomb? My mother remonstrated: I threatened to dash out her brains with my stout ash stick; and on the following night I sold my father's body to the surgeon who had anatomised poor Kate Price! This was another vengeance on my part.

"Not many hours elapsed before I set fire to the largest barn upon the baronet's estate. I waited in the neighbourhood and glutted myself with a view of the conflagration. The damage was immense. The next day I composed a song upon the subject, which I have never since forgotten. You may laugh at the idea of me becoming a poet; but you know well enough that I received some trifle of education—that I was not a fool by nature—and that in early life I was fond of reading. The lines were these:—

"THE INCENDIARY'S SONG.

"The Lucifer-match! the Lucifer-match!
    'Tis the weapon for us to wield.
How bonnily burns up rick and thatch,
    And the crop just housed from the field!
The proud may oppress and the rich distress,
    And drive us from their door;—
But they cannot snatch the Lucifer-match
    From the hand of the desperate poor!

"The purse proud squire and the tyrant peer
    May keep their Game Laws still;
And the very glance of the overseer
    May continue to freeze and kill.
The wealthy and great, and the chiefs of the state,
    May tyrannise more and more;—
But they cannot snatch the Lucifer-match
    From the hand of the desperate poor!

> "'*Oh! Give us bread!*' is the piteous wail
>   That is murmured far and wide;
> And echo takes up and repeats the tale—
>   But the rich man turns aside.
> The Justice of Peace may send his police
>   To scour the country o'er;
> But they cannot snatch the Lucifer-match
>   From the hand of the desperate poor!
>
> "Then, hurrah! hurrah! for the Lucifer match;
>   'Tis the weapon of despair—
> How bonnily blaze up barn and thatch—
>   The poor man's revenge is there!
> For the *worm* will turn on the feet that spurn—
>   And surely a *man* is more?—
> Oh! None can e'er snatch the Lucifer-match
>   From the hand of the desperate poor!

"The baronet suspected that I was the cause of the fire, as I had just returned to the neighbourhood; and he had me arrested and taken before a justice; but there was not a shadow of proof against me, nor a pretence to keep me in custody. I was accordingly discharged, with an admonition '*to take care of myself*'—which was as much as to say, '*If I can find an opportunity of sending you to prison, I will.*'

"Walmer and its neighbourhood grew loathsome to me. The image of Kate Price constantly haunted me; and I was moreover shunned by every one who knew that I had been at the hulks. I accordingly sold off all the fishing tackle, and other traps, and came up to London with the old Mummy."

"I need say no more."

"And there's enough in your history to set a man a-thinking," exclaimed the waiter of the boozing-ken; "there is indeed."

"Ah! I b'lieve you, there is," observed the Cracksman, draining the pot which had contained the egg-flip.

[…]

[The conversations in the *Dark-House*, a Tower Hamlets public house frequented by prostitutes and thieves, are part of a continuing narrative drive to demonstrate that crime and prostitution are the inevitable consequences of an unjust economic system. In Chapter LXV the system in which 'coal-whippers', or dockers employed to unload colliers, are forced to receive their wages in public houses whose owners are often in the pay of the employers, is exposed. Adulteration of drink by landlords was also a persistent popular grievance.]

CHAPTER LXV.
THE WRONGS AND CRIMES OF THE POOR.

THE parlour of the *Dark-House* was, as usual, filled with a very tolerable sprinkle of queer-looking customers. One would have thought, to look at their beards, that there was not a barber in the whole district of the Tower Hamlets; and yet it appears to be a social peculiarity, that the lower the neighbourhood, the more numerous the shaving-shops. Amongst the very rich classes, nobles and gentlemen are shaved by their valets: the males of the middle grade shave themselves; and the men of the lower orders are shaved at barber's shops. Hence the immense number of party-coloured poles projecting over the pavement of miserable and dirty streets, and the total absence of those signs in wealthy districts.

The guests in the *Dark-House* parlour formed about as pleasant an assemblage of scamps as one could wish to behold. The establishment was a notorious resort for thieves and persons of the worst character; and no one who frequented it thought it worth while to shroud his real occupation beneath an air of false modesty. The conversation in the parlour, therefore, usually turned upon the tricks and exploits of the thieves frequenting the place; and many entertaining autobiographical sketches were in this way delivered. Women often constituted a portion of the company in the parlour; and they were invariably the most noisy and quarrelsome of all the guests. Whenever the landlord was compelled to call in the police, to have a clearance of the house —a proceeding to which he only had recourse when his guests were drunk and penniless, and demanded supplies of liquor upon credit,—a woman was sure to be at the bottom of the row; and a virago of Spitalfields would think no more of smashing every window in the house, or dashing out the landlord's brains with one of his own pewter-pots, than of tossing off a tumbler of raw gin without winking.

On the evening of which we are writing there were several women in the parlour of the *Dark-House*. These horrible females were the "blowens" of the thieves frequenting the house, and the principal means of disposing of the property stolen by their paramours. They usually ended by betraying their lovers to the police, in fits of jealousy; and yet—by some strange infatuation on the part of those lawless men—the women who acted in this way speedily obtained fresh husbands upon the morganatic system. For the most part, these females are disfigured by intemperance; and their conversation is far more revolting than that of the males. Oh! there is no barbarism in the whole world so truly horrible and ferocious—so obscene and shameless—as that which is found in the poor districts of London!

Alas! what a wretched mockery it is to hold grand meetings at Exeter Hall, and proclaim, with all due pomp and ceremony, how many savages in the far-off islands of the globe have been converted to Christianity, when here—at home, under our very eyes—even London itself swarms with infidels of a more dangerous character:—how detestable is it for philanthropy to be exercised in clothing negroes or Red Men thousands of miles distant, while our own poor are cold and naked at our very doors:—how monstrously absurd to erect twelve new churches in Bethnal Green, and withhold the education that would alone enable the poor to appreciate the doctrines enunciated from that dozen of freshly-built pulpits!

But to return to the parlour of the *Dark-House*.

In one corner sate the Resurrection Man and the Cracksman, each with a smoking glass of gin-and-water before him. They mingled but little in the conversation, contenting themselves with laughing an approval of any thing good that fell upon their ears, and listening to the discourse that took place around them.

"Now, come, tell us, Joe," said a woman with eyes like saucers, hair like a bundle of tow, and teeth like dominoes, and addressing herself to a man who was dressed like a coal-heaver,—"tell us, Joe, how you come to be a prig?"

"Ah! do, Joe—there's a good feller," echoed a dozen voices, male and female.

"Lor' it's simple enough," cried the man thus appealed to: "every poor devil must become a thief in time."

"That's what you say, Tony," whispered the Cracksman to the Resurrection Man.

"Of course he must," continued the coal-heaver "more partickler them as follows my old trade—for though I've got on the togs of a whipper, I ain't one no longer. The dress is convenient—that's all."

"The Blue-bottles don't twig—eh?" cried the woman with the domino teeth.

"That's it: but you asked me how I come to be a prig—I'll tell you. My father was a coal-whipper, and had three sons. He brought us all up to be coal-whippers also. My eldest brother was drownded in the pool one night when he was drunk, after only drinking about two pots of the publicans' beer: my other brother died of hunger in Cold-Bath Fields prison, where he was sent for three months for taking home a bit of coal one night to his family when he could n't get his wages paid him by the publican that hired the gang in which he worked. My father died when he was forty—and any one to have seen him would have fancied he was sixty-five at least—so broke down was he with hard work and drinking. But no coal-whipper lives to an old age: they all die off at about forty—old men in the wery prime of life."

"And why's that?" demanded the large-toothed lady.

"Why not?" repeated the man. "Because a coal-whipper is n't a human being—or if he is, he is n't treated as such: and so I've always thought he must be different from the rest of the world."

"How is n't he treated like any one else?"

"In the first place, he does n't get paid for his labour in a proper way. Wapping swarms with low public-houses, the landlords of which act as middlemen between the owners of the colliers and the men that's hired to unload 'em. A coal-whipper can't get employment direct from the captain of the collier: the working of the collier is farmed by them landlords I speak of; and the whipper must apply at their houses. Those whippers as drinks the most always gets employment first; and whether a whipper chooses to drink beer or not, it's always sent three times a-day on board the colliers for the gangs. And, my eye! what stuff it is! Often and often have we throwed it away, 'cos we could'nt possibly drink it—and it must be queer liquor that a coal-whipper won't drink!"

"I should think so too. But go on."

"Well, I used to earn from fifteen to eighteen shillings a-week; and out of that, eight was always stopped for the beer; and if I didn't spend another or two on Saturday night when I received the balance, the landlord set me down as a stingy feller and put a cross agin my name in his book."

"What was that for?"

"Why, not to give me any more work till he was either forced to do so for want of hands, or I made it up with him by standing a crown bowl of punch. So what with one thing and another, I had to keep myself, my wife, and three children, on about seven or eight shillings a-week—after working from light to dark."

"And now your wife and children is better purvided for?" said the woman with the huge teeth.

"Yes—indeed! in the workus," answered the man, sharply. "So now you see what a coal-whipper's life is. He can't be a sober man if he wishes to—because he must pay for a certain quantity of drink; and so of course he won't throw it away, unless it's so bad he can't keep it on his stomach."

"And was that often the case?"

"Often and often. Well—he can't be a saving man, because he has no chance of getting his wages under his own management. He is the publican's slave—the publican's tool and instrument. Negro slavery is nothing to it. No tyranny is equal to the tyranny of them publicans."

"And why is n't the plan altered?"

"Ah! why? What do the owners of the colliers, or the people that the cargo's consigned to, care about the poor devils that unload? The publicans takes the unloading on contract, and employs the whippers in such a way as to get an enormous profit. Talk of appealing to the owners—what do they care? There has been meetings got up to change the system—and what's the consekvence? Why, them whippers as attended them became marked men, never got no more employment, and drownded themselves in despair, or turned prigs like me."

"Ah! that's better than suicide."

"Well—I don't know, now! But them meetings as I was a-speaking of, got up deputations to the Court of Aldermen, and the matter was referred to the Coal and Corn Committee—and there was, as usual, a great talk, but nothink done. Then an application was made to some Minister—I don't know which; and he sent back a letter with a seal as big as a crown-piece, just to say that he'd received the application, and would give it his earliest attention. Some time passed away, and no more notice was ever taken of it in that quarter; and so, I s'pose, a Minister's earliest attention means ten or a dozen years."

"What a shame to treat people so."

"It's only the poor that's treated so. And now I think I have said enough to show why I turned prig, like a many more whippers from the port of London. There is n't a more degraded, oppressed, and brutalised set of men in the world than the whippers. They are born with examples of drunken fathers afore their eyes; and drunken fathers makes drunken mothers; and drunken parents makes sons turn out thieves, and daughters prostitutes;—and that's the existence of the coal-whippers of Wapping. It ain't their fault: they haven't edication and self-command to refuse the drink that's forced upon them, and that they must pay for;—and their sons and daughters shouldn't be blamed for turning out bad. How can they help it? And yet one reads in the papers that the upper classes is always a-crying out about the dreadful immorality of the poor!"

"The laws—the laws, you see, Tony," whispered the Cracksman to his companion.

"Of course," answered the Resurrection Man. "Here we are, in this room, upwards of twenty thieves and prostitutes: I'll be bound to say that the laws and the state of society made eighteen of them what they are."

"Nobody knows the miseries of a coal-whipper's life," continued the orator of the evening, "but him that's been in it his-self. He is always dirty—always lurking about public-houses when not at work—always ready to drink

—always in debt—and always dissatisfied with his own way of living, which is n't, however, his fault. There s no hope for coal-whippers or their families. The sons that don't turn out thieves must lead the same terrible life of carthorse labour and constant drinking, with the certainty of dying old men at forty;—and the daughters that don't turn out prostitutes marry whippers, and draw down upon their heads all the horrors and sorrows of the life I have been describing."

"Well—I never knowed all this before!"

"No—and there's a deal of misery of each kind in London that is n't known to them as dwells in the other kinds of wretchedness: and if these things gets represented in Parliament, the cry is,'*Oh! the people's always complaining; they're never satisfied!*'

"Well, you speak of each person knowing his own species of misery, and being ignorant of the nature of the misery next door," said a young and somewhat prepossessing woman, but upon whose face intemperance and licentiousness had made sad havoc; "all I can say is, that people see girls like us laughing and joking always in public—but they little know how we weep and moan in private.

"Drink gin then, as I do," cried the woman with the large teeth.

"Ah! *you* know well enough," continued the young female who had previously spoken, "that we *do* drink a great deal too much of that! My father used to sell *jiggered gin* in George Yard, Whitechapel."

"And what the devil is jiggered gin?" demanded one of the male guests.

"It's made from molasses, beer, and vitriol. Lor', every one knows what jiggered gin is. Three wine glasses of it will make the strongest man mad drunk. I'll tell you one thing," continued the young woman, "which you do not seem to know—and that is, that the very, very poor people who are driven almost to despair and suicide by their sorrows, are glad to drink this jiggered gin, which is all that they can afford. For three halfpence they may have enough to send them raving; and then what do they think or care about their miseries?"

"Ah! very true," said the coal whipper. "I've heard of this before."

"Well—my father sold that horrid stuff," resumed the young woman; "and though he was constantly getting into trouble for it, he didn't mind; but the moment he came out of prison, he took to his old trade again. I was his only child; and my mother died when I was about nine years old. She was always drunk with the jiggered gin; and one day she fell into the fire and was burnt to death. I had no one then who cared any thing for me, but used to run about in the streets with all the boys in the neighbourhood. My father took in lodgers; and sixteen or seventeen of us, boys and girls all huddled together, used to sleep in one room not near so big as this. There was fifteen lodging houses of the same kind in George Yard at that time; and it was supposed that about two hundred and seventy-five persons used to sleep in those houses every night, male and female lodgers all pigging together. Every sheet, blanket, and bolster, in my father's house was marked with STOP

THIEF, in large letters. Well—at eleven years old I went upon the town; and if I didn't bring home so much money every Saturday night to my father, I used to be well thrashed with a rope's end on my bare back."

"Serve you right too, a pretty girl like you."

"Ah! you may joke about it—but it was no joke to me! I would gladly have done anything in an honest way to get my livelihood—"

"Like me, when I was young," whispered the Resurrection Man to his companion.

"Exactly. Let's hear what the gal has got to say for herself," returned the Cracksman; "the lush has made her sentimental;—she'll soon be crying drunk."

"But I was doomed, it seemed," continued the young woman, to live in this horrible manner. When I was thirteen or fourteen my father died, and I was then left to shift for myself. I moved down into Wapping, and frequented the long-rooms belonging to the public-houses there. I was then pretty well off; because the sailors that went to these places always had plenty of money and was very generous. But I was one night suspected of hocussing and robbing a sailor, and—though if I was on my death-bed I could swear that I never had any hand in the affair at all—I was so blown upon that I was forced to shift my quarters. So I went to a *dress-house* in Ada Street, Hackney Road. All the remuneration I received there was board and lodging; and I was actually a slave to the old woman that kept it. I was forced to walk the streets at night with a little girl following me to see that I did not run away; and all the money I received I was forced to give up to the old woman. While I was there, several other girls were turned out of doors, and left to die in ditches or on dunghills, because they were no longer serviceable. All this frightened me. And then I was so ill-used, and more than half starved. I was forced to turn out in all weathers—wet or dry—hot or cold—well or ill. Sometimes I have hardly been able to drag myself out of bed with sickness and fatigue—but, no matter, out I must go—the rain perhaps pouring in torrents, or the roads knee-deep in snow—and nothing but a thin cotton gown to wear! Winter and summer, always flaunting dresses—yellow, green, and red! Wet or dry, always silk stockings and thin shoes! Cold or warm, always short skirts and a low body, with strict orders not to fasten the miserable scanty shawl over the bosom! And then the little girl that followed me about was a spy with wits as sharp as needles. Impossible to deceive her! At length I grew completely tired of this kind of life; and so I gave the little spy the slip one fine evening. [...] But one day I met the old woman who kept the dress-house, and she gave me in charge for stealing wearing apparel—the clothes I had on my back when I ran away from her!"

"Always the police—the police—the police, when the poor and miserable are concerned," whispered the Resurrection Man to the Cracksman.

"But did the inspector take the charge?" demanded the coal-heaver.

"He not only took the charge," answered the unfortunate girl, "but the magistrate next morning committed me for trial, although I proved to him that the clothes were bought with the wages of my own prostitution! Well, I was tried at the Central Criminal Court—"

"And of course acquitted?"

"No—found *Guilty*—"

"What—by an English jury?"

"I can show you the newspaper—I have kept the report of the trial ever since."

"Then, by G—d, things are a thousand times worse than I thought they was!" ejaculated the coal-whipper, striking his clenched fist violently upon the table at which he was seated.

"But the jury recommended me to mercy," continued the unfortunate young woman, "and so the Recorder only sentenced me to twenty-one days' imprisonment. His lordship also read me a long lecture about the errors of my ways, and advised me to enter upon a new course of life; but he did not offer to give me a character, nor did he tell me how I was to obtain honest employment without one."

"That's the way with them beaks," cried one of the male inmates of the parlour: "they can talk for an hour; but supposing you'd said to the Recorder, '*My Lord, will your wife take me into her service as scullery-girl?*' he would have stared in astonishment at your imperence."

"When I got out of prison," resumed the girl who was thus sketching the adventures of her wretched life, "I went into Great Titchfield Street. My new abode was a dress-house kept by French people. Every year the husband went over to France, and returned with a famous supply of French girls, and in the mean time his wife decoyed young English women up from the country, under pretence of obtaining situations as nursery-governesses and lady's-maids for them. Many of these poor creatures were the daughters of clergymen and half-pay officers in the marines. The moment a new supply was obtained by these means, circulars was sent round to all the persons that was in the habit of using the house. Different sums, from twenty to a hundred pounds—"

"Ah! I understand," said the coal-whipper. "But did you ever hear say how many unfortunate gals there was in London?"

"Eighty thousand. From Titchfield Street I went into the Almonry, Westminster. The houses there are all occupied by *fences*, prigs, and gals of the town."

"And the parsons of Westminster Abbey, who is the landlords of the houses, does nothink to put 'em down," said the coal-whipper.

"Not a bit," echoed the young woman, with a laugh. "We had capital fun in the house where I lived—dog-fighting, badger-baiting, and drinking all day long. The police never visits the Almonry—"

"In course not, 'cos it's the property of the parsons. They wouldn't be so rude."

This coarse jest was received with a shout of laughter; and the health of the Dean and Chapter of Westminster was drunk amidst uproarious applause, by the thieves and loose women assembled in the *Dark-House* parlour.

[...]

[In Chapter LXX Ellen Monroe, who is now living in Markham Place, confronts Montague Greenwood, who has earlier seduced her, and by whom she is now pregnant. In his house Greenwood has pictures and a statue modelled on Ellen herself. These she calls 'emblems of phases in my life'. The episode provides a further example of a recurring motif in this text – the ambiguous relations between representation and reality.]

CHAPTER LXX.
THE IMAGE, THE PICTURE, AND THE STATUE.

Upon the sofa in Mr. Greenwood's elegantly-furnished drawing-room was seated the young lady who so anxiously sought an interview with the owner of that princely mansion.

Her face was very pale: a profound melancholy reigned upon her countenance, and was even discernible in her drooping attitude; her eyes expressed a sorrow bordering upon anguish; and yet, through that veil of dark foreboding, the acute observer might have seen a ray—a feeble ray of hope gleaming faintly, so faintly, that it appeared a flickering lamp burning at the end of a long and gloomy cavern.

Her elbow rested upon one end of the sofa, and her forehead was supported upon her hand, when Greenwood entered the room.

The doors of that luxurious dwelling moved so noiselessly upon their hinges, and the carpets spread upon the floors were so thick, that not a sound, either of door or footstep, announced to that pale and mournful girl the approach of the man whom she so deeply longed to see.

He was close by her ere she was aware of his presence.

With a start, she raised her head, and gazed stedfastly up into his countenance; but her tongue clave to the roof of her mouth, and refused utterance to the name which she would have spoken.

"Ellen!" ejaculated Greenwood, as his eyes met hers.—"What has brought you hither?"

[...]

As Greenwood uttered these words, he seated himself upon the sofa by the side of the young lady, and took her hand. We cannot say that her tears had moved him—for his was a heart that was moved by nothing regarding another: but she had looked pretty as she wept, and as her eyes glanced through their tears towards him; and the apparent kindness of his manner was the mechanical impulse of the libertine.

"Oh! if *you* would only smile thus upon me—now and then—" murmured Ellen, gazing tenderly upon him,—"how much of the sorrow of this life would disappear from before my eyes."

"How can one gifted with such charms as you be unhappy?" exclaimed Greenwood.

"What! do you imagine that beauty constitutes felicity?" cried Ellen, in an impassioned tone. "Are not the loveliest flowers exposed to the nipping frosts, as well as the rank and poisonous weeds? Do not clouds obscure the brightest stars, as well as those of a pale and sickly lustre? You ask me if I can be unhappy? Alas! it is now long—long since I knew what perfect happiness was! I need not tell you—*you*—how my father's fortune was swept away;—but I may detail to you the miseries which the loss of it raised up around him and me—and chiefly *me*!"

"But why dwell upon so sad a theme, Ellen? Did you come hither to divert me with a narrative of sorrows which must now be past, since—according to what I have heard—your father and yourself have found an asylum—"

"At Markham Place!" added Miss Monroe, emphatically. "Yes—we have found an asylum there—*there*, in the house of the individual whom my father's speculations and your agency—"

"Speak not of that—speak not of that, I conjure you!" hastily exclaimed Greenwood. "Tell me, Ellen—tell me, you have not breathed a word to your father, nor to that young man—"

"No—not for worlds!" cried Ellen, with a shudder: then, after a pause, during which she appeared to reflect deeply, she said, "But you ask me why I wish to narrate to you the history of all the miseries I have endured for two long years, and upwards: you demand of me why I would dwell upon so sad a theme. I will tell you presently. You shall hear me first. But pray, be not impatient: I shall not detain you long;—and, surely—surely, you can spare an hour to one who is so very—very miserable."

"Speak, Ellen—speak!"

"The loss of our fortune plunged us into the most frightful poverty. we were not let down gradually from affluence to penury;—but we fell—as one falls from a height—abruptly, suddenly, and precipitately into the depths of want and starvation. The tree of our happiness lost not its foliage leaf by leaf: it was blighted in an hour. This made the sting so much more sharp—the heavy weight of misfortune so much less tolerable. Nevertheless, I worked, and worked with my needle until my energies were wasted, my eyes grew dim, and my health was sinking fast. Oh! my God, I only asked for work;—and yet, at length, I lost even that resource! Then commenced a strange kind of life for me."

"A strange kind of life, Ellen—what mean you?" exclaimed Greenwood, now interested in the recital.

"I sold myself in detail," answered Ellen, in a tone of the deepest and most touching melancholy.

"I cannot understand you," cried Greenwood. "Surely—surely your mind is not wandering!"

"No: all I tell you is unhappily too true," returned the poor girl, shaking her head; then, as if suddenly recollecting herself, she started from her thoughtful mood, and said, "You have a plaster of Paris image as large as life, in the window of your staircase?"

"Yes—it is a Diana, and holds a lamp which is lighted at night," observed Greenwood. "But what means that strange question—so irrelevant to the subject of our discourse?"

"More—more than you can imagine," answered Ellen, bitterly "That statue explains one phase in my chequered life;"—then, sinking her tone almost to a whisper, grasping Greenwood's hand convulsively, and regarding him fixedly in the countenance, while her own eyes were suddenly lighted up with a strange wildness of expression, she added, "The face of your beautiful Diana is my own!"

Greenwood gazed upon her in speechless astonishment; he fancied that her reason was unhinged; and—he knew not why—he was afraid!

Ellen glanced around, and her eyes rested upon a magnificent picture that hung against the wall. The subject of this painting, which had no doubt struck her upon first entering that room, was a mythological scene.

Taking Greenwood by the hand, Ellen led him towards the picture.

"Do you see any thing that strikes you strangely there?" she said, pointing towards the work of art.

"The scene is Venus rising from the ocean, surrounded by nereids and nymphs," answered Greenwood.

"And you admire that picture much?"

"Yes—much; or else I should not have purchased it".

"Then have you unwittingly admired me," exclaimed Ellen; "for the face of your Venus is my own!"

Greenwood gazed earnestly upon the picture for a few moments; then, turning towards Ellen, he cried, "True—it is true! There are your eyes—your mouth—your smile—your forehead—your very hair! How strange that I never noticed this before. But—no—it is a dream: it is a mere coincidence. Tell me—how could this have taken place;—speak—is it not a mere delusion—an accidental resemblance which you noticed on entering this room?"

"Come with me," said Ellen in a soft and melancholy tone.

Still retaining him by the hand, she led him into the landing place communicating with the drawing-room and leading to the stairs.

A magnificent marble statue of a female, as large as life, stood in one corner. The model was naked down to the waist, one hand gracefully sustaining the drapery which enveloped the lower part of the form.

"Whence did you obtain that statue!" demanded Ellen, pointing towards the object of her inquiry.

"The ruin of a family long reputed rich, caused the sale of all their effects," answered Greenwood: "and I purchased that statue, amongst other objects of value which were sold, for a mere trifle."

"The lady has paid dearly for her vanity!" cried Ellen: "her fate—or rather the fate of her statue is a just reward for the contempt, the scorn—the withering scorn with which she treated me, when I implored her to take me into her service."

"What do you mean, Ellen?"

"I mean that the bust of your marble statue is my own," answered the young lady, casting down her eyes, and blushing deeply.

"Another enigma!" cried Greenwood.

They returned to the drawing-room, and resumed their seats upon the sofa. A long pause ensued.

"Will you tell me, Ellen," at length exclaimed Greenwood, deeply struck by all he had heard and seen within the last half hour,—"will you tell me, Ellen, whether you have lost your reason, or I am dreaming?"

"Lost my reason!" repeated Ellen, with fearful bitterness of tone; "no—that were perhaps a blessing; and naught save misery awaits me!"

"But the image—the picture—and the statue?" exclaimed Greenwood impatiently.

"They are emblems of phases in my life", answered Ellen. "I told you ere now that my father and I were reduced to the very lowest depths of poverty. And yet we could not die;—at least I could not see that poor, white-haired, tottering old man perish by inches—die the death of starvation. Oh! no—that was too horrible. I cried for bread—bread—bread! And there was one—an old hag—you know her—

"Go on—go on".

"Who offered me bread—bread for myself, bread for my father—upon strange and wild conditions. In a word I sold myself in detail."

"Again that strange phrase!" ejaculated Greenwood. "What mean you, Ellen?"

"I mean that I sold my face to the statuary—my likeness to the artist—my bust to the sculptor—my whole form to the photographer—and—"

"And—" repeated Greenwood, strangely excited.

"And my virtue to you!" added the young woman, whose tone, as she enumerated these sacrifices, had gradually risen from a low whisper to the wildness of despair.

[…]

"Then what, in the name of heaven, do you now require of me?" demanded the Member of Parliament impatiently.

"That you should do me justice," was the reply, while Ellen still remained upon her knees.

"Do you justice!" repeated Greenwood: "and how have I wronged you? If I deliberately set to work to seduce you—if, by art and treachery, I wiled you away from the paths of duty—if, by false promises, I allured you from a prosperous and happy sphere,—then might you talk to me of justice. But no: I knew not whom I was about to meet when the old hag came to me that day, and said—"

"Enough! enough! I understand you," cried Ellen, rising from her suppliant position, and clasping her hands despairingly together. "You consider that you purchased me as you would have bought any poor girl who, through motives of vanity, gain, or lust, would have sold her person to the highest bidder! Oh—now I understand you! But, one word, Mr. Greenwood! If there were no such voluptuaries—such heartless libertines as you in this world, would there be so many poor unhappy creatures like me? In an access of despair—of folly—and of madness, I rushed upon a path which men like you alone open to women placed as I then was! Perhaps you consider that I am not worthy to become your wife? Fool that I was to seek redress—to hope for consolation at your hands! Your conduct to others—to my father—to—"

"Ellen! I command you to be silent! Remember our solemn compact on that day when we met in so strange and mysterious a manner;—remember that we pledged ourselves to mutual silence—silence with respect to all we know of each other! Do you wish to break that compact?"

"No—no," ejaculated Ellen, convulsively clasping her hands together: "I would not have you publish my disgrace! Happily I have yet friends who will—but no matter. Sir, I now leave you: I have your answer. You refuse to give a father's name to the child which I bear? You may live to repent your decision. For the present, farewell."

And having condensed all her agonizing feelings into a moment of unnatural coolness—the awful calmness of despair—Ellen slowly left the room.

But Mr. Greenwood did not breathe freely until he heard the front door close behind her.

[In Chapter LXXI, Greenwood, now elected by corrupt practices to the constituency of Rottenborough, makes his maiden speech to the House of Commons. He presents the standard Tory view, that the complaints of the poor are unjustified. The passage also includes descriptions of several leading political figures of the time. More details concerning the interception of letters are given in the following chapter.]

CHAPTER LXXI.
THE HOUSE OF COMMONS.

THE building in which the representatives of the nation assemble at Westminster, is about as insignificant, ill-contrived, and inconvenient a place as can be well conceived. It is true that the edifices appropriated to both Lords and Commons are both only temporary ones; nevertheless, it would have been easy to construct halls of assembly more suitable for their purposes than those that now exist.

The House of Commons is an oblong, with rows of plain wooden benches on each side, leaving a space in the middle which is occupied by the table, whereon petitions are laid. At one end of this table is the mace: at the other, sit the clerks who record all proceedings that require to be noted. Close behind the clerks, and at one extremity of the apartment, is the Speaker's chair: galleries surround this hall of assembly;—the one for the reporters is immediately over the Speaker's chair; that for strangers occupies the other extremity of the oblong; and the two side ones are for the use of the members. The ministers and their supporters occupy the benches on the right of the speaker: the opposition members are seated on those to the left of that functionary. There are also cross-benches under the strangers' gallery, where those members who fluctuate between ministerial and opposition opinions, occasionally supporting the one side or the other according to their pleasure or convictions, take their places.

At each extremity of the house there is a lobby—one behind the cross-benches, the other behind the Speaker's chair, between which and the door of this latter lobby there is a high screen surmounted by the arms of the united kingdom. When the House divides upon any question, those who vote for the motion or bill pass into one lobby, and those who vote against the point in question proceed to the other. Each party appoints its *tellers*, who station themselves at the respective doors of the two lobbies, and count the members on either side as they return into the house.

The house is illuminated with bude-lights, and is ventilated by means of innumerable holes perforated through the floor, which is covered with thick hair matting.

According to the above-mentioned arrangements of benches, it is evident that the orator, in whatever part he may sit, almost invariably has a considerable number of members behind him, or, at all events, sitting in places extremely inconvenient for hearing. Then, the apartment itself is so miserably confined, that when there is a full attendance of members, at least a fourth cannot obtain seats.

It will scarcely be believed by those previously unaware of the fact, that the reporters for the public press are only allowed to attend and take notes of the proceedings *upon sufferance*. Any one member can procure the clearance of both the reporter's and the strangers' galleries, without assigning any reason whatever.

At half-past four o'clock the members began to enter the house pretty thickly.

Near the table stood a portly happy-looking man, with a somewhat florid and good-natured countenance, grey eyes, and reddish hair. He was well dressed, and wore enormous watch-seals and a massive gold guard-chain. He conversed in an easy and complacent manner with a few members who had gathered around him, and who appeared to receive his opinions with respect and survey him with profound admiration: this was Sir Robert Peel.

One of his principal admirers on this (as on all other occasions) was a very stout gentleman, with dark hair, prominent features, a full round face, eyes of a sleepy expression, and considerable heaviness of tone and manner: this was Sir James Graham.

Close by Sir James Graham, with whom he exchanged frequent signs of approval as Sir Robert Peel was conversing, was a small and somewhat repulsive looking individual, with red hair, little eyes that kept constantly blinking, a fair complexion, and diminutive features,—very restless in manner, and with a disagreeable and ill-tempered expression of countenance. When he spoke, there was far more of gall than honey in his language; and the shafts of his satire, though dealt at his political opponents, not unfrequently glanced aside and struck his friends. This was Lord Stanley.

Shortly before the Speaker took the chair, a stout burly man, accompanied by half-a-dozen representatives of the Emerald Isle, entered the house. He was enveloped in a cloak, which he proceeded to doff in a very leisurely manner, and then turned to make some observation to his companions. They immediately burst out into a hearty laugh—for it was a joke that had fallen upon their ears—a joke, too, purposely delivered in the richest Irish brogue, and, accompanied by so comical an expression of his round good-natured countenance that the jest was altogether irresistible. He then proceeded slowly to his seat, saying something good-natured to his various political friends as he passed along. His broad-brimmed hat he retained upon his head, but of his cloak he made a soft seat. His adherents immediately crowded around him; and while he told them some rich racy anecdote, or delivered himself of another jest, his broad Irish countenance expanded into an expression of the most hearty and heart-felt good-humour. And yet that man had much to occupy his thoughts and engage his attention; for he of whom we now speak was Daniel O'Connell.

Close by Mr. O'Connell's place was seated a gentleman of most enormously portly form, though little above the middle height. On the wrong side of sixty, he was as hale, robust, and healthy-looking a man as could be seen. His ample chest, massive limbs, ponderous body, and large head denoted strength of no ordinary kind. His hair was iron-grey, rough, and bushy; his eyes large, grey, and intelligent; his countenance rigid in expression, although broad and round in shape. This was Joseph Hume.

Precisely at a quarter to five the Speaker took the chair; Mr. Greenwood was then introduced by the Tory whipper-in, and (as the papers said next morning) "took the oaths and his seat for Rottenborough."

The Whig whipper-in surveyed him with a glance of indignant disappointment; but Mr. Greenwood affected not to notice the feeling which his conduct had excited. On the contrary, he passed over to the Opposition benches (for it must be remembered that the Whigs then occupied the ministerial seat) where his accession to the Tory ranks was very warmly greeted—being the more pleasant as it was totally unexpected—by Sir Robert Peel and the other leaders of that party.

Mr. Greenwood was not a man to allow the grass to grow under his feet. He accordingly delivered his "maiden speech" that very evening. The question before the House was connected with the condition of the poor. The new member was fortunate enough to catch the Speaker's eye in the course of the debate; and he accordingly delivered his sentiments upon the topic.

He declared that the idea of a diminution of duties upon foreign produce was a mere delusion. The people, he said, were in a most prosperous condition —they never were more prosperous; but they were eternal grumblers whom nothing could satisfy. Although some of the most enlightened men in the kingdom devoted themselves to the interests of the people—he alluded to the party amongst whom he had the honour to sit—the people were not satisfied. For his part, he thought that there was too much of what was called *freedom*. He would punish all mal-contents with a little wholesome exercise upon the tread-mill. What presumption, he would like to know, could be greater than that of the millions daring to have an opinion of their own, unless it were the audacity of attempting to make that opinion the rule for those who sate in that House? He was astounded when he heard the misrepresentations that had just met his ears from honourable gentlemen opposite relative to the condition of the working classes. He could prove that they ought to put money in the savings'-banks; and yet it was coolly alleged that in entire districts they wanted bread. Well—why did they not live upon potatoes? He could demonstrate, by the evidence of chemists and naturalists, that potatoes were far more wholesome than bread; and for his part he was much attached to potatoes. Indeed, he often ate his dinner without touching a single mouthful of bread. There was a worthy alderman at his right hand, who could no doubt prove to the House that bread spoilt the taste of turtle. Was it not, then, a complete delusion to raise such a clamour about bread? He (Mr. Greenwood) was really astonished at honourable gentlemen opposite; and he should give their measure his most strenuous opposition at every stage.

Mr. Greenwood sat down amidst loud cheers from the Tory party; and Sir Robert Peel turned round and gave him a patronising nod of most gracious approval. Indeed his speech must have created a very powerful sensation, for upwards of fifty members who had been previously stretched upon the benches in the galleries, comfortably snoozing, rose up in the middle of their nap to listen to him.

The Conservative papers next morning spoke in raptures of the brilliancy of the new talent which had thus suddenly developed itself in the political heaven; while the Liberal prints denounced Greenwood's language as the most insane farrago of anti-popular trash ever heard during the present century.

Mr. Greenwood cared nothing for these attacks. He had gained his aims: he had already taken a stand amongst the party with whom he had determined to act;—he had won the smiles of the leader of that party; and he chuckled within himself as he saw baronetcies and sinecures in the perspective.

That night he could not sleep. His ideas were reflected back to the time when, poor, obscure, and friendless, he had commenced his extraordinary career in the City of London. A very few years had passed;—he was now rich, and in a fair way to become influential and renowned. The torch of Fortune seemed ever to light him on his way, and never to shine obscurely for him in the momentous affairs of life:—like the fabled light of the Rosicrucian's ever-burning lamp, the halo of that torch appeared constantly to attend upon his steps.

Whether he thus prospered to the end, the sequel of our tale must show.

CHAPTER LXXII.
THE BLACK CHAMBER AGAIN.

IT was now the beginning of April, and the bleak winds had yielded to the genial breath of an early spring.

At ten o'clock, one morning, an elderly gentleman, with a high forehead, open countenance, thin white hair falling over his coat collar, and dressed in a complete suit of black, ascended the steps of the northern door, leading to the Inland Letter Department of the General Post Office, Saint Martin's-le-Grand.

He paused for a moment, looked at his watch, and then entered the building. Having ascended a narrow staircase, he stopped at a door in that extremity of the building which is the nearer to Aldersgate Street. Taking a key from his pocket, he unlocked the door, glanced cautiously behind him, and then entered the *Black Chamber*.

Having carefully secured the door by means of a bolt and chain, he threw himself into the arm-chair which stood near the large round oaken table.

The Examiner—for the reader has doubtless already recognised him to be the same individual whom we introduced in the twenty-ninth chapter of our narrative—glanced complacently around him; and a smile of triumph curled his thin pale lips. At the same time his small, grey, sparkling eyes were lighted up with an expression of diabolical cunning: his whole countenance was animated with a glow of pride and conscious power; and no one would have supposed that this was the same old man who meekly and quietly ascended the steps of the Post-Office a few minutes ago.

Bad deeds, if not the results of bad passions and feelings, soon engender them. This was the case with the Examiner. He was the agent of the Government in the perpetration of deeds which disgraced his white hair and his venerable years;—he held his appointment, not from the Postmaster-General, but direct from the Lords of the Treasury themselves;—he filled a situation of extreme responsibility and trust;—he knew his influence—he was well aware that he controlled an engine of fearful power—and he gloated over the secrets that had been revealed to him in the course of his avocation, and which he treasured up in his bosom.

He had risen from nothing; and yet his influence with the Government was immense. His friends, who believed him to be nothing more than a senior clerk in the Post-Office, were surprised at the great interest which he evidently possessed, and which was demonstrated by the handsome manner in which all his relatives were provided for. But the old man kept his secret. The four clerks who served in his department under him, were all tried and trustworthy young men; and their fidelity was moreover secured by good salaries. Thus every precaution was adopted to render the proceedings of the Black Chamber as secret as possible;—and, at the time of which we are writing, the uses to which that room was appropriated were even unknown to the greater number of the persons employed in the General Post-Office.

The Examiner was omnipotent in his inquisitorial tribunal. There alone the authorities of the Post-Office had no power. None could enter that apartment without his leave:—he was responsible for his proceedings only to those from whom he held his appointment. At the same time, he was compelled to open any letters upon a warrant issued and directed to him by the Secretaries of State for the Home and Foreign Departments, and for the Colonies, as well as in obedience to the Treasury. Thus did he superintend an immense system of *espionnage*, which was extended to every class of society, and had its ramifications through every department of the state.

It must be observed that, although the great powers of Europe usually communicated with their representatives at the English court by means of couriers, still the agency of post-offices was frequently used to convey duplicates of the instructions borne by these express-messengers; and many of the minor courts depended altogether upon the post-office for the transport of their despatches to their envoys and ambassadors. All diplomatic correspondence, thus transmitted, was invariably opened, and notes or entire copies were taken from the despatches, in the Black Chamber. Hence it will be perceived that the English Cabinet became possessed of the nature of the greater part of all the instructions conveyed by foreign powers to their representatives at the court of Saint James's.

But the Government carried its proceedings with regard to the violation of correspondence, much farther than this. It caused to be opened all letters passing between important political personages—the friends as well as the enemies of the Cabinet; and it thus detected party combinations against its existence ascertained private opinions upon particular measures, and became possessed of an immense mass of information highly serviceable to diplomatic intrigue and general policy.

Truly, this was a mighty engine in the hands of those who swayed the destinies of the British Empire;—but the secret springs of that fearfully complicated machine were all set in motion and controlled by that white-headed and aged man who now sat in the Black Chamber!

Need we wonder if he felt proud of his strange position? can we be astonished if he gloated, like the boa-constrictor over the victim that it retains in its deadly folds, over the mighty secrets stored in his memory?

That man knew enough to overturn a Ministry with one word.

That man could have set an entire empire in a blaze with one syllable of mystic revelation.

That man was acquainted with sufficient to paralyse the policy of many mighty states.

That man treasured in his mind facts a mere hint at which would have overwhelmed entire families—aye, even the noblest and highest in the land—with eternal disgrace.

That man could have ruined bankers—hurled down vast commercial firms—levelled mercantile establishments—destroyed grand institutions.

That man wielded a power which, were it set in motion, would have convulsed society throughout the length and breadth of the land.

Need we wonder if the government gave him all he asked? can we be astonished if all those in whom he felt an interest were well provided for?

When he went into society, he met the possessors of vast estates, whom he could prostrate and beggar with one word—a word that would proclaim the illegitimacy of their birth. He encountered fair dames and titled ladies, walking with head erect and unblushing brow, but whom he could level with the syllable that should announce their frailty and their shame. He conversed with peers and gentlemen who were lauded as the essence of honour and of virtue, but whose fame would have withered like a parched scroll, had his breath, pregnant with fearful revelations, only fanned its surface. There were few, either men or women, of rank and name, of whom he knew not something which they would wish to remain unknown.

Need we wonder if bad passions and feelings had been engendered in his mind? Can we be astonished if he had learnt to look upon human nature as a fruit resembling the apples of the Dead Sea, fair to gaze upon, but ashes at the heart?

Presently a knock at the door was heard. The Examiner opened it, and one of his clerks entered the room. He bowed respectfully to his superior, and proceeded to take his seat at the table. In like manner, at short intervals, the other three subordinates arrived; but the one who came last, brought with him a sealed parcel containing a vast number of letters, which he had received from the President of one of the sorting departments of the establishment. These letters were now heaped upon the table before the Examiner; and the business of this mysterious conclave commenced.

[...]

[The following chapters continue the stories of Ellen Monroe and Richard Markham. Ellen, who has secretly given birth to an illegitimate child as a result of her liason with Greenwood, moves further into the world of Victorian popular entertainment – there was a cult of 'Animal Magnetism' or Mesmerism in London in the 1840s. After a period as a figurante or ballet-dancer, she becomes an actress and appears under another name in a play written by Richard Markham. The Resurrection Man is in the audience at the first night and causes a riot when he identifies the author as 'Markham the Forger'. Also present in the audience is Isabella Alteroni, daughter of an Italian political exile to whom Richard has been introduced by Thomas Armstrong, the Republican of Newgate Prison. Count Alteroni is briefly incarcerated in a debtor's prison, from which he is released only after Richard secretly pays off the sum owed. The courtship of Richard and Isabella is continually undermined by the Resurrection Man, who intervenes at crucial moments.]

CHAPTER LXXXVII.
THE PROFESSOR OF MESMERISM.

ELLEN had already been long enough from home to incur the chance of exciting surprise or alarm at her absence; she was therefore compelled to postpone her visit to the Professor of Mesmerism until the following day.

On her return to the Place, after an absence of nearly three hours, her fears were to some extent realised, her father being uneasy at her disappearance for so long a period. She availed herself of this opportunity to acquaint Mr. Monroe with her anxiety to devote her talents to some useful purpose, in order to earn at least sufficient to supply them both with clothes, and thus spare as much as possible the purse of their benefactor. Her father highly approved of this laudable aim; and Ellen assured him that one of the families, for whom she had once worked at the West End, had promised to engage her as a teacher of music and drawing for a few hours every week. It will be recollected that the old man had invariably been led to believe that his daughter was occupied in private houses with her needle, when she was really in the service of the statuary, the artist, the sculptor, and the photographer: he therefore now readily put faith in the tale which Ellen told him, and even undertook not only to communicate her intention to Markham, but also to prevent him from throwing any obstacle in its way. This task the old man accomplished that very day: and thus Ellen triumphed over the chief difficulty which she had foreseen—namely, that of accounting for the frequent absence from home which her new pursuits would render imperative. And this duplicity towards her sire she practised without a blush. Oh! what a wreck of virtue and chastity had the mind of that young female become!

The Professor of Mesmerism occupied a handsome suite of apartments in New Burlington Street. He was a man of about fifty, of prepossessing exterior, elegant manners, and intelligent mind. He spoke English fluently, and was acquainted with many continental languages besides his own.

It was mid-day when Miss Monroe was ushered into his presence.

The Professor was evidently struck by the beauty of her appearance; but he held her virtue at no high estimation, in consequence of the source of her recommendation to him. Little cared he, however, whether she were a paragon of moral excellence, or an example of female degradation: his connexion with her was to be based upon a purely commercial ground; and he accordingly set about an explanation of his views and objects. Ellen listened with attention, and agreed to become the patient of the mesmerist.

Thus, having sold her countenance to the statuary, her likeness to the artist, her bust to the sculptor, her entire form to the photographer, and her virtue to a libertine, she disposed of her dreams to the mesmerist.

Several days were spent in taking lessons and studying her part, under the tutelage of the Professor. She was naturally quick of comprehension; and this practice was easy to her. Her initiation was therefore soon complete; and the Professor at length resolved upon giving a private exhibition of "the truths of Mesmerism practically illustrated" to a few friends. Ellen took a feigned name; and all the preliminary arrangements were settled.

The memorable evening arrived; and by eight o'clock the Professor's drawing-room was filled with certain select individuals, all of whom were favourably inclined towards the "science" of Mesmerism. Some of them, indeed, were perfectly enthusiastic in behalf of this newly-revived doctrine. The reporters of the press were rigidly excluded from this meeting, with two or three exceptions in favour of journals which were known to be friendly to the principle of Animal Magnetism.

When the guests were thus assembled, Ellen was led into the apartment. She was desired to seat herself comfortably in an easy arm-chair; and the Professor then commenced his manipulations, "with a view to produce *coma*, or mesmeric sleep." In about five minutes Ellen sank back, apparently in a profound sleep, with the eyes tightly closed.

The Professor then expatiated upon the truths of the science of Mesmerism; and the assembled guests eagerly drank in every word he uttered. At length he touched upon *Clairvoyance*, which he explained in the following manner:—

"*Clairvoyance*," he said, "is the most extraordinary result of Animal Magnetism. It enables the person magnetised to foretel events relating both to themselves and others; to describe places which they have never visited, and houses the interior of which they have never seen; to read books opened and held behind their heads; to delineate the leading points of pictures in a similar position; to read a letter through its envelope; to describe the motions or actions of a person in another room, with a wall intervening; and to narrate events passing in far distant places."

The Professor then proposed to give practical illustrations of the phenomena which he had just described.

The visitors were now all on the tiptoe of expectation; and the reporters prepared their note-books. Meantime Ellen remained apparently wrapped up in a profound slumber; and more than one admiring glance was turned upon her beautiful classic features and the exuberant richness of her bust.

"I shall now question the patient," said the Professor, "in a manner which will prove the first phenomenon *of clairvoyance*; namely, *the power of foretelling events relative to themselves and others*."

He paused for a moment, performed a few more manipulations, and then said, "Can you tell me any thing in reference to future events which are likely to happen to myself?"

"Within a week from this moment you will hear of the death of a relation!" replied Ellen in slow and measured terms.

"Of what sex is that relation?"

"A lady: she is now dangerously ill."

"How old is she?"

"Between sixty and seventy. I can see her lying upon her sick-couch with two doctors by her side. She has just undergone a most painful operation."

"It is perfectly true," whispered the Professor to his friends, "that I have an aunt of that age; but I am not aware that she is even ill—much less at the point of death."

"It is wonderful—truly wonderful!" exclaimed several voices, in a perfect enthusiasm of admiration.

"Let us now test her in reference to the second phenomenon I mentioned," said the Professor; "which will show *the power of describing places she has never visited, and houses whose interiors she has never seen.*"

"Ah! that will be curious, indeed," cried several guests.

"Perhaps you, Mr. Wilmot," said the Professor, addressing a gentleman standing next to him, "will have the kindness to examine the patient relative to your own abode."

"Certainly," replied Mr. Wilmot; then, turning towards Ellen, he said, "Will you visit me at my house?"

"With much pleasure," was her immediate answer.

"Where is it situated?"

"In Park Lane."

"Come in with me. What do you see?"

"A splendid hall, with a marble table between two pillars on one side, and a wide flight of stairs, also of marble, on the other."

"Come with me into the dining room of my house. Now what do you see?"

"Seven large pictures."

"Where are the windows?"

"There are three at the bottom of the room."

"What colour are the curtains?"

"A rich red."

"What is the subject of the large picture facing the fire-place?"

"The battle of Trafalgar."

"How do you know it is that battle?"

"Because I can read on the flag of one of the ships the words, '*England expects that every man will do his duty.*'"

"I shall not ask her any more questions," said Mr. Wilmot, evidently quite amazed by these answers. "Every one of her replies is true to the very letter. And I think," he added, turning towards the other guests, "that you all know me well enough to believe me, when I declare most solemnly that this young person has never, to my knowledge, been in my house in her life."

A murmur of satisfaction arose amongst the guests, who were all perfectly astounded at the phenomena now illustrated—although they had come, as before said, with a predisposition in favour of Mesmerism.

"We will have another proof yet," said the Professor. "Perhaps Mr. Parke will have the kindness to question the patient."

Mr. Parke stepped forward, and said, "Will you do me the favour to walk with me to my house."

"Thank you, I will," answered Ellen, still apparently remaining in a profound mesmeric sleep.

"Where is my house?"

"In Mortimer Street, Cavendish Square."

"How many windows has it in front?"

"Thirteen."

"Where are the two statues of Napoleon?"

"In the library."

"What else do you see in that room?"

"Immense quantities of books on shelves in glass cases."

"Are there any pictures?"

"Yes—seven."

"What is the subject of the one over the mantel-piece?"

"A beautiful view of London, by moonlight, from one of the bridges."

"Wonderful!" ejaculated Mr. Parke. "All she has said is perfectly correct. It is not necessary to ask her any more questions on this subject."

"Gentlemen," said the Professor, casting a triumphant glance around him, "I am delighted to perceive that you are satisfied with this mode of illustrating the phenomena of *clairvoyance*. I will now prove to you that the patient *can read a book held open behind her head*."

He then performed some more manipulations to plunge his patient into as deep a mesmeric sleep as possible, although she had given no symptom of an inclination to awake throughout the preceding examination. Having thus confirmed, as he said, her perfect state of *coma*, the Professor took up a book —apparently pitched upon at random amongst a heap of volumes upon the table; and, holding it open behind the head of the patient, he said, "What is this?"

"A book," was the immediate reply.

"What book?"

"Milton's *Paradise Lost*."

"At what page have I opened it?"

"I can read pages 110 and 111."

"Read a few lines."

Ellen accordingly repeated the following passage in a slow and beautifully mellifluous tone:—

> "Now morn, her rosy steps in th' eastern clime
> Advancing, sowed the earth with orient pearl,
> When Adam waked, so 'customed, for his sleep
> Was airy light, from pure digestion bred,
> And temperate vapours bland, which th' only sound
> Of leaves and fuming rills, Aurora's fan
> Lightly dispersed, and the shrill matin song
> Of birds on every bough."

"That is sufficient," cried several voices. "Do not fatigue her. We are perfectly satisfied. It is really marvellous. Who will now dare to doubt the phenomena of *clairvoyance*?"

"Let us take a picture," said the Professor; "*and she will delineate all the leading points in it*."

The mesmerist took an engraving from a portfolio, and held it behind Ellen's head.

"What is this?" he demanded.

"A picture."

"What is the subject?"

"I do not know the subject; but I can see two figures in the fore-ground, with a camel. The back-ground has elevated buildings. Oh! now I can see it plainer: it is a scene in Egypt; and those buildings are the pyramids."

"Extraordinary!" cried Mr Wilmot.

"And that little hesitation was a proof of the fact that she could really see the picture," added Mr. Parke.

"Wonderful! extraordinary!" exclaimed numerous voices.

At this moment a servant entered the room and delivered a letter to his master, the Professor, stating that it had just been left by a friend from Paris.

The mesmerist was about to open it, when a sudden idea seemed to strike him.

"Gentlemen," he exclaimed, throwing the letter upon the table, "the arrival of this missive affords me an opportunity of proving another phenomenon belonging to *clairvoyance. The patient shall read this letter through the envelope.*"

"But if its contents be private?" said a guest.

"Then I am surrounded by gentlemen of honour, who will not publish those contents," returned the professor with a smile.

A murmur of approbation welcomed this happy compliment of the Frenchman.

The mesmerist held the letter at a short distance from Ellen's countenance, and said, "What is this?"

"A letter," she replied. "It is written in French." "Read it," cried the mesmerist.

"The writing is obscure, and the lines seem to cross each other."

"That is because the letter is in an envelope and folded," said the Professor. "But try and read it."

Ellen then distinctly repeated the contents of the letter, of which the following is a translation:—

"*Paris.*

Honoured Sir,—I have to acquaint you with the alarming illness of my beloved mistress, your aunt Madame Delabarre. She was taken suddenly ill four days ago. Two eminent physicians are in constant attendance upon her. It is believed that if she does not get better in a few days, the medical attendants will perform an operation upon her. Should your leisure and occupation permit, you would do well to hasten to France to comfort your venerable relative.

"Your humble servant,

"FELICIE SOLIVEAU."

"Ah! my poor aunt! my poor aunt!" cried the Professor: "she is no more! It was her death that the patient foretold ere now! Yes—the two physicians—the painful operation—Oh! my poor aunt!"

The mesmerist tore open the letter, hastily glanced over it, and handed it to the gentleman who stood nearest to him. This individual perused it attentively, and, turning towards the other guests, said, "It is word for word as the patient read it."

The enthusiasm of the disciples of mesmerism present was only damped by the grief into which the Professor was now plunged by the conviction of the death of his venerable aunt. They, therefore, briefly returned their best thanks for the highly satisfactory illustrations of the truths of mesmeric phenomena which they had witnessed upon the occasion, and took their leave, their minds filled with the marvels that had been developed to them.

The moment the guests and the reporters had taken their departure, the Professor hastened up to Ellen, took her by the hand, and exclaimed in a transport of joy, "You may rise, my good young lady; it is all over! You acquitted yourself admirably! Nothing could be better. I am delighted with you! My fortune is made—my fortune is made! These English blockheads bite at anything!"

Ellen rose from the chair in which she had feigned her mesmeric sleep, and was by no means displeased with the opportunity of stretching her limbs, which were dreadfully cramped through having remained an hour in one unchanged position. The Professor compelled her to drink a glass of wine to refresh her; and in a few minutes she was perfectly at her ease once more.

"Yes," repeated the mesmerist; "you conducted yourself admirably. I really could not have anticipated such perfection at what I may call a mere rehearsal of your part. You remembered every thing I had told you to the very letter. By cleverly selecting to examine you, those persons whose houses I have visited myself, and the leading features of which I am able to explain to you beforehand, I shall make you accomplish such wonders in this respect, that even the most sceptical will be astounded. You have an excellent memory; and that is the essential. Moreover, I shall never mislead you. The book and the print agreed upon between us during the day, shall always be chosen for illustration at the lecture. By the bye, your little hesitation about the engraving was admirable. You may always introduce that *piece of acting* into your *part*: it appears true. The part then is not over-done. I give you great credit for the idea. In a few days I shall tell all my friends that I have received a letter announcing my aunt's death; and that her demise took place at the very moment when you beheld her death-bed in your mesmeric slumber. This will astound them completely. On the next occasion we must introduce into our comedy the scene of *the patient describing what takes place in another room, with a wall intervening*; and as we will settle before-hand all that I shall do in another apartment, upon the occasion, that portion of the task will not be difficult."

"But suppose, sir," said Ellen, "that a gentleman, concerning whose house you have given me no previous description, should wish to examine me,— what must I do in such a case?"

"Remain silent," answered the Professor.

"And would not this excite suspicion?"

"Not a bit of it. I have my answer ready:—'*There is no magnetic affinity, no mesmeric sympathy, between you and your interlocutor.*' That is the way to stave off such a difficulty; and it applies equally to a stranger holding books or prints for you to read with the back of your head."

"I really can scarcely avoid laughing when I think of the nature of the farce," observed Ellen.

"And yet this is not the only doctrine with which the world is duped," said the Professor. "But it is growing late; and you are doubtless anxious to return home. I am so well pleased with you, that I must beg you to accept this five-pound note as an earnest of my liberal intentions. You were very perfect with the poetry and the letter—the letter, by the bye, from my poor old aunt, whose existence is only in my own imagination!—Indeed, altogether, I am delighted with you!"

Ellen received the money tendered her by the mesmerist, and took her departure.

Thus successfully terminated her first essay as a patient to a Professor of Animal Magnetism!

CHAPTER LXXXVIII.
THE FIGURANTE.

THE wonders performed by the Professor of Mesmerism produced an immense sensation. The persons who had been admitted to the "private exhibition," did not fail to proclaim far and wide the particulars of all that they had witnessed; and, as a tale never loses by repetition, the narrative of those marvels became in a very few days a perfect romance. The reporters of the press, who had attended the exhibition, dressed up a magnificent account of the entire proceedings, for the journals with which they were connected; and the fame of the Professor, like that of one of the knights of the olden time, was soon "bruited abroad through the length and breadth of the land."

At length a public lecture was given, and attended with the most complete success. Ellen had an excellent memory; and her part was enacted to admiration. She recollected the most minute particulars detailed to her by the Mesmerist, relative to the interior of the houses of his friends, the contents of letters to be read through envelopes, the subjects of prints, and the lines of poetry or passages of prose in the books to be read when placed behind her. Never was a deception better contrived: the most wary were deluded by it; and the purse of the Professor was well filled with the gold of his dupes.

But all things have an end: and the deceit of the Mesmerist was not an exception to the rule.

One evening, a gentleman—a friend of the Professor—was examining Ellen, who of course was in a perfect state of *coma*, respecting the interior of his library. The patient had gone through the process of questioning uncommonly well, until at length the gentleman said to her, "Whereabouts does the stuffed owl stand in the room you are describing?"

In the abstract there was nothing ludicrous in this query: but, when associated with the absurdity of the part which Ellen was playing, and entering as a link into the chain of curious ideas that occupied her mind at the moment, it assumed a shape so truly ridiculous that her gravity was completely overcome She burst into an immoderate fit of laughter: her eyes opened wide —the perfect state of coma vanished in a moment—the *clairvoyance* was forgotten—the catalepsy disappeared—and the patient became un-mesmerised in a moment, in total defiance of all the prescribed rules and regulations of Animal Magnetism!

Laughter is catching. The audience began to titter—then to indulge in a half-suppressed cachinnation;—and at length a chorus of hilarity succeeded the congenial symphony which emanated from the lips of the patient.

The Professor was astounded.

He was, however, a man of great presence of mind: and he instantaneously pronounced Ellen's conduct to be a phenomenon in Mesmerism, which was certainly rarely illustrated, but for which he was by no means unprepared.

But all his eloquence was useless. The risible inclination which now animated the great majority of his audience, triumphed over the previous prejudice in favour of Mesmerism; the charm was dissolved—the spell was annihilated—"the pitcher had gone so often to the well that it got broken at last"—the voice of the Professor had lost its power.

No sooner did the hilarity subside a little, when it was renewed again; and even the friends and most staunch adherents of the Professor looked at each other with suspicion depicted upon their countenances.

What reason could not do, was effected by ridicule: Mesmerism, like the heathen mythology, ceased to be a worship.

The Professor grew distracted. Confusion ensued; the audience rose from their seats; groupes were formed; and the proceedings of the evening were freely discussed by the various different parties into which the company thus split.

Ellen took advantage of the confusion to slip out of the room; and in a few moments she left the house.

Her occupation was now once more gone; and she resolved to pay another visit to the old hag.

Accordingly, in a few days she again sought the miserable court in Golden Lane.

[...]

"In a word, can you find me any more employment?"

"I know no more Mesmerists," answered the old hag, in a surly tone.

"Then you can do nothing for me?"

"I did not say that—I did not say that," cried the hag. "It is true I can get you upon the stage; but perhaps that pursuit will not please you."

"Upon the stage!" ejaculated Ellen. "In what capacity?"

"As a *figurante*, or dancer in the ballet, at a great theatre," replied the old woman.

"But I should be known—I should be recognised," said Ellen.

"There is no chance of that," returned the hag. "Dressed like a sylph, with rouge upon your cheeks, and surrounded by a blaze of light, you would be altogether a different being. Ah! it seems that I already behold you upon the stage—the point of admiration for a thousand looks—the object of envy and desire, and of every passion which can possibly gratify female vanity."

For some moments Ellen remained lost in thought. The old woman's offer pleased her: she was vain of her beauty; and she contemplated with delight the opportunity thus presented to her of displaying it with brilliant effect. She already dreamt of success, applause, and showers of nosegays; and her countenance gradually expanded into a smile of pleasure.

"I accept your proposal," she said.

[...]

CHAPTER XC.
MARKHAM'S OCCUPATIONS.

SINCE the period when Markham had made so great a sacrifice of his pecuniary resources, in order to effect the liberation of Count Alteroni from a debtor's prison, he had devoted himself to literary pursuits. He aspired to the honours of authorship, and composed a tragedy.

All young authors, while yet nibbling the grass at the foot of Parnassus (and how many never reach any higher!) attempt either poetry or the drama. They invariably fix upon the most difficult tasks; and yet they did not begin learning Greek with Euripides, nor enter upon their initiation into the mysteries of the Latin tongue with Juvenal.

There is also another fault into which they invariably fall;—and that is an extraordinary tendency to those meretricious ornaments which they seem to mistake for fine writing. Truth and nature may be regarded as a noble flock, furnishing the richest fleece to mankind; but when a series of good writers have exhausted their fleece in weaving the fabrics of genius, their successors are tempted to have recourse to swine for a supply of materials; and we know, besides, that in this attempt, as in the rude dramas called "Moralities" in the middle ages, there is great cry and little wool. It is also liable to the objection that no skill in the workmanship, or adjustment in the machinery, can give it the beauty and perfection of the raw material which nature has appropriated to the purpose of clothing her favoured offspring.

Too many writers of the present day, instead of attempting to rival their predecessors in endeavouring to fabricate the genuine fleece derived from this flock of truth and nature, into new and exquisite forms, are engaged in shearing the swine. In this labour they can obtain, at best, nothing more than erroneous principles of science, worthless paradoxes, unnatural fictions, tinsel poetry and prose, and un-numbered crudities.

Richard Markham was not exempted from these faults. He wrote a tragedy —abounding in beauties, and abounding in faults.

The most delicious sweets, used in undue proportions with our food and drink, soon become in a high degree offensive and disgusting. Markham heaped figure upon figure—crammed his speeches with metaphors—and travelled many thousands of miles out of his way in search of a similitude, when he had a much better and more simple one close at hand. Nevertheless, his tragedy contained proofs of a brilliant talent, and, with much judicious pruning, every element of triumphant success.

Having obtained the address of the private residence of the manager of one of the principal metropolitan theatres, Richard sent his tragedy to the great man. He, however, withheld his real name, for he had determined to commence his literary career under a feigned one; so that, in case he should prove unsuccessful, his failure might not become known to his friends the Monroes, or reach the ears of his well-beloved Isabella. For the same reason he did not give his proper address in the letter which accompanied the drama; but requested that a reply might be sent to *Edward Preston*.

[...]

He did not mention to a single soul—not even to Monroe or the faithful Whittingham—the circumstance of his authorship. He reflected that if he succeeded, it would then be time to communicate his happiness; but, that if he failed, it would be useless to wound others by imparting to them his disappointments. He had ceased to be sanguine about any thing in this world; for he had met with too many misfortunes to anticipate much success in life; and his only ambition was to obtain an honourable livelihood.

Scarcely a week had elapsed after Markham had sent his drama to the manager, when he received a letter from this gentleman. The contents were laconic enough, but explicit. The manager "had perused the tragedy with feelings of extreme satisfaction;"—he congratulated the writer upon "the skill which he had made his combinations to produce stage effect;"—he suggested "a few alterations and considerable abbreviations;" and concluded by stating that "he should be most happy to introduce so promising an author to the public." A postscript appointed a time for an interview at the manager's own private residence.

At eleven o'clock the next morning Markham was ushered into the presence of the manager.

The great man was seated in his study, dressed in a magnificent Turkish dressing-gown, with a French skull-cap upon his head, and red morocco slippers upon his feet. He was a man of middle age—gentlemanly and affable in manner—and possessed of considerable literary abilities.

"Sit down, sir—pray, sit down," said the manager, when Markham was introduced. "I have perused your tragedy with great attention, and am pleased with it. I am, moreover, perfectly willing to undertake the risk of bringing it out, although tragedy is at a terrible discount now-a-days. But, first and foremost, we must make arrangements about terms. What price do you put upon your manuscript?"

"I have formed no idea upon that subject," replied Markham. "I would rather leave myself entirely in your hands."

"Nay—you must know the hope you have entertained in this respect?" said the manager.

"To tell you the candid truth, this is my first essay," returned Markham; "and I am totally unacquainted with the ordinary value of such labour."

"If this be your first essay, sir," said the manager, surveying Markham with some astonishment, "I can only assure you that it is a most promising one. But once again—name your price."

"The manner in which you speak to me shows that if I trust to your generosity, I shall not do wrong."

"Well, Mr. Preston," cried the manager, pleased at this compliment, "I shall use you in an equally liberal manner. You must be informed that you will have certain pecuniary privileges, in respect to any provincial theatres at which your piece may be performed should it prove successful; and you will also have the benefit of the publication of the work in a volume. What, then, should you say if I were to give you fifty guineas for the play, and five guineas a-night for every time of its performance, after the first fortnight?"

"I should esteem your offer a very liberal one," answered Richard, overjoyed at the proposal.

"In that case the bargain is concluded at once, and without any more words," said the manager; then, taking a well-filled canvass bag from his desk, he counted down fifty guineas in notes, gold, and silver.

Markham gave a receipt, and they exchanged undertakings specifying the conditions proposed by the manager.

"When do you propose to bring out the piece?" inquired Richard, when this business was concluded.

"In about six weeks," said the manager. "Shall you have any objection to attend the rehearsals, and see that the gentlemen and ladies of the company fully appreciate the spirit of the parts that will be assigned to them?"

"I shall not have the least objection," answered Markham; "but I am afraid that my experience—"

"Well, well," said the manager, smiling, "I will not press you. Leave it all to me—I will see justice done to your design, which I think I understand pretty well. If I want you I will let you know; and if you do not hear from me, you will see by the advertisements in the newspapers for what night the first representation will be announced."

Markham expressed his gratitude to the manager for the kindness with which he had received him, and then took his leave, his heart elated with hope, and his mind relieved from much anxiety respecting the future.

[...]

CHAPTER XCI.
THE TRAGEDY.

At length the evening, upon which the tragedy was to be represented for the first time, arrived.

Markham in the mean time had seen little of the manager, and had not attended a single rehearsal, his presence for that purpose not having been required. Moreover, true to his original intentions, he had not acquainted a soul with his secret relative to the drama. The manager still knew him only as Edward Preston; and the advertisements in the newspapers had announced the "forth-coming tragedy" as one that had "emanated from the pen of a young author of considerable promise, but who had determined to maintain a strict *incognito* until the public verdict should have been pronounced upon his piece."

A short time before the doors opened, Richard proceeded to the theatre, and called upon the manager, who received him in his own private apartment.

"Well, Mr. Preston," said the theatrical monarch, "this evening will decide the fate of the tragedy. A few hours, and we shall know more."

"I hope you still think well of it," returned Markham.

"My candid opinion is that the success will be triumphant," said the manager. "I have spared no expense to get up the piece well; and I am very sanguine. Besides, I have another element of success."

"What is that?" inquired Richard.

"My principal ballet-dancer, who is a beautiful creature and a general favourite—Miss Selina Fitzherbert—"

"I have heard of her fame," said Markham, "but have never seen her. Strange as it may appear, I never visit theatres—I have not done so for years."

"You will visit them often enough if your productions succeed," observed the manager with a smile. "But, as I was saying, Miss Fitzherbert has lately manifested a passionate desire to shine in tragedy; and she will make her *debut* in that sphere tonight, in your piece. She will play the *Baron's Daughter*."

"Which character does not appear until the commencement of the third act," said Markham.

"Precisely," observed the manager. "But time is now drawing on. Where will you remain during the performance?"

"I shall proceed into the body of the house," returned Markham, "and take my seat in one of the central boxes—I mean those precisely fronting the stage. I shall be able to judge of the effect better in that part of the house than elsewhere."

"As you please," said the manager. "But mind and let me see you after the performance."

Richard promised compliance with this request, and then proceeded into the house, where he took a seat in the centre of the amphitheatre.

The doors had been opened a few minutes previously, and the house was filling fast. By half-past six it was crowded from pit to roof. The boxes were filled with elegantly-dressed ladies and fashionable gentlemen: there was not room to thrust another spectator into any one point at the moment when the curtain drew up.

The overture commenced. How long it appeared to Markham, passionately fond of music though he was!

At length it ceased; and the First Act commenced.

For some time a profound silence pervaded the audience:—not a voice, not a murmur, not a sigh, gave the slightest demonstration of either approbation or dislike.

But, at length, at the conclusion of a most impressive soliloquy, which was delivered by the hero of the piece, one universal burst of applause broke forth; and the theatre rang with the sounds of human tongues and the clapping of hands. When the First Act ended, the opinion of the audience was decisive in favour of the piece; and the manager felt persuaded that "it was a hit."

This was one of the happiest moments of Markham's existence—that existence which had latterly presented so few green spots to please the mental eye of the wanderer in the world's desert. His veins seemed to run with liquid fire!—a delirium of joy seized upon him—he was inebriated with excess of bliss.

Around him the spectators were expressing their opinions of the first act, little suspecting that the author of the piece was so near. All those sentiments were unequivocally in favour of the tragedy.

The Second Act began—progressed—terminated.

No pen can describe the enthusiasm with which the audience received the development of the drama, nor the interest which it seemed to excite.

Inspired by the applause that greeted them, the performers exerted all their efforts; and the excellence of the tragedy, united with the talent of the actors and the beauty of the scenery, achieved a triumph not often witnessed within the walls of that or any other theatre.

The Third Act commenced. Selina Fitzherbert appeared upon the stage; and her presence was welcomed with rapturous applause.

She came forward, and acknowledged the kindness of the audience with a graceful curtsey.

Markham surveyed her with interest, in consequence of the manner in which her name had been mentioned to him by the manager;—but that interest grew more profound, and was gradually associated with feelings of extreme surprise, suspense, and uncertainty, for he fancied that if ever he saw Ellen Monroe in his life, there was she—or else her living counterpart—before him—an actress playing a part in his own drama!

He was stupefied;—he strained his eyes—he leant forward—he borrowed the opera-glass of a gentleman seated next to him;—and the more he gazed, the more he felt convinced that he beheld Ellen Monroe in the person of Selina Fitzherbert.

At length the actress spoke: wonder upon wonder—it was Ellen's voice—her intonation—her accent—her style of speaking.

Markham was amazed—confounded.

He inquired of his neighbour whether Selina Fitzherbert was the young lady's real name, or an assumed one.

The gentleman to whom he spoke did not know.

"How long has she been upon the stage?"

"Between two and three months; and, strange to say, it is rumoured that she only took two months to render herself so proficient a dancer as she is. But she now appears to be equally fine in tragedy. Listen!"

Markham could ask no more questions; for his neighbour became all attention towards the piece.

Richard reviewed in a moment, in his mind, all the principal appearances and characteristics of Ellen's life during the last few months, the lateness of her hours—the constancy of her employment—and a variety of circumstances, which only now struck him, but which tended to ratify his suspicion that she was indeed Selina Fitzherbert.

[...]

The moment the curtain fell Markham hastened behind the scenes, and encountered Ellen in one of the slips.

Hastily grasping her by the hand, he said in a low but hurried tone "Do not be alarmed—I know all—I am here to thank you—not to blame you."

"Thank *me*, Richard!" exclaimed the young actress, partially recovering from the almost overwhelming state of alarm into which the sudden apparition of Markham had thrown her: "why should you thank *me*?"

"Thank you, Ellen—Oh! how can I do otherwise than thank you?" said Markham. "You have carried my tragedy through the ordeal—"

"*Your* tragedy, Richard?" cried Miss Monroe, more and more bewildered.

"Yes, *my* tragedy, Ellen—it is mine! But, ah! there is a call for you—"

A moment's silence had succeeded the flattering expression of public opinion which arose at the termination of the performance; and then arose a loud cry for Selina Fitzherbert.

This was followed by a call for the author, and then a thousand voices ejaculated—"Selina Fitzherbert and the Author! Let them come together!"

The manager now hastened up to the place where Ellen and Richard were standing, and where the above hurried words had been exchanged between them.

"You must go forward, Miss Fitzherbert—and you too, Mr. Preston—"

Ellen glanced with an arch smile towards Richard, as much as to say, "*You* also have taken an assumed name."

Markham begged and implored the manager not to force him upon the stage;—but the call for "Selina Fitzherbert and the Author" was peremptory; and the "gods" were growing clamorous.

Popular will is never more arbitrary than in a theatre.

Markham accordingly took Ellen's hand:—the curtain rose, and he led her forward.

The appearance of that handsome couple—a fine dark-eyed and genteel young man leading by the hand a lovely woman,—a successful author, and a favourite actress,—this was the signal for a fresh burst of applause.

Richard was dazzled with the glare of light, and for some time could see nothing distinctly.

Myriads of human countenances, heaped together, danced before him; and yet the aspect and features of none were accurately delineated to his eyes. He could not have selected from amongst those countenances, even that of his long-lost brother, or that of his dearly beloved Isabella, had they been both or either of them prominent in that multitude of faces.

And Isabella *was* there, with her parents—impelled by the curiosity which had taken so many thither that evening.

Her surprise, and that of her father and mother, may therefore well be conceived, when, in the author of one of the most successful and beautiful dramatic compositions of modern times, they recognised Richard Markham!

[...]

The manager bowed and retired.

Fresh applause welcomed the announcement of the tragic author's name; and a thousand voices exclaimed, "Bravo, Edward Preston!"

By this time Markham had recovered his presence of mind and self-possession: and his joy was extreme when he suddenly recognised Isabella in a box close by the stage.

Oh! that was a glorious moment for him: *she* was there—*she* beheld his triumph—and doubtless *she* participated in his own happy feelings.

"Bravo, Edward Preston!" was re-echoed through the house.

And then a dead silence prevailed.

All were anxious to hear Richard speak.

But just at the moment when he was about to acknowledge the honours conferred upon him and his fair companion by the audience, a strange voice broke upon the stillness of the scene.

"It is false! his name is not Preston—"

"Silence!" cried numerous voices.

"His name is—"

"Turn out that brawler! turn him out!"

"His name is—"

"Hold your tongue!"

"Silence!"

"Turn him out! turn him out!"

"His name is Richard Markham—the Forger!"

A burst of indignation, mingled with strong expressions of incredulity, rose against the individual, who, from an obscure nook in the gallery, had interrupted the harmony of the evening.

"It is true—I say! he is Richard Markham who was condemned to two years' imprisonment for forgery!" thundered forth the hoarse and unpleasant voice.

A piercing scream—the scream of a female tone—echoed through the house: all eyes were turned towards the box whence it issued; and a young lady with flaxen hair and pale complexion, was seen to sink senseless in the arms of the elderly gentleman who accompanied her.

And in another part of the house a young lady also sank, pale, trembling, and overcome with feelings of acute anguish, upon her father's bosom.

So deeply did that dread accusing voice affect the sensitive and astonished Mary-Anne, and the faithful Isabella!

All was now confusion. The audience rose from their seats in all directions; and the theatre suddenly appeared to be converted into a modern Babel.

Overwhelmed with shame, and so bewildered by this cruel blow, that he knew not how to act, Markham stood for some moments like a criminal before his judges. Ellen, forgetting where she was, clung to him for support.

At length, the unhappy young man seized Ellen abruptly by the hand, and led her from the public gaze.

The curtain fell as they passed behind the scenes.

The audience then grew more clamorous—none scarcely knew why. Some demanded that the man who had caused the interruption should be arrested by the police; but those in the gallery shouted out that he had suddenly disappeared. Others declared that the accusation ought to be investigated;—people in the pit maintained that, even if the story were true, it had nothing to do with the success of the accused as a dramatic author;—and gentlemen in the boxes expressed their determination never to support a man, in a public institution and in a public capacity, who had been condemned to infamous penalties for an enormous crime.

[...]

And then commenced a riot in the theatre. The respectable portion of the audience escaped from the scene with the utmost precipitation:—but the occupants of the upper region, and some of the tenants of the pit, remained to exhibit their inclination for what they were pleased to term "a lark." The benches were torn up, and hurled upon the stage:—hats and orange-peel flew about in all directions;—and serious damage would have been done to the theatre, had not a body of police succeeded in restoring order.

In the mean time Markham and Ellen had been conducted to the Green

Room, where a glass of wine was administered to each to restore their self-possession.

The manager was alone with them; and when Richard had time to collect his scattered ideas, he seemed to awake as from a horrible dream. But the ominous countenance of the manager met his glance;—and he knew that it was all a fearful reality.

Then did Markham bury his face in his hands, and weep bitterly—bitterly.

"Alas! young man," said the manager, "it was an evil day for both you and me, when you sought and I accorded my patronage. This business will no doubt injure me seriously. You are a young man of extraordinary talent;—but it will not avail you in this sphere again. You have enjoyed one signal triumph—you have experienced a most heart-rending overthrow. Never did defeat follow upon conquest so rapidly."

[...]

"You gave me fifty guineas for that fatal—fatal drama," said Richard, after a long pause. "The money shall be returned to you to-morrow."

"No, my young friend,—that must not be done!" exclaimed the manager, taking Richard's hand. "Your noble conduct in this respect raises you fifty per cent. in my opinion."

"Yes—he is noble, he is generous!" cried Ellen. "He has been a benefactor to myself and my father: it is at his house that we live; and never until this evening were we aware of each other's avocations, in respect to the stage."

[...]

But before they separated, the two young people agreed with each other that the strictest silence should be preserved at the Place, not only with respect to the events of that evening, but also in regard to the nature of the avocations in which they had both lately been engaged.

Markham succeeded in escaping unobserved from the theatre;—and, humiliated, cast down, heartbroken,—bending beneath an insupportable burden of ignominy and shame,—with the fainting form of Isabella before his eyes, and the piercing shriek of Mary-Anne, whom he had also recognised, in his ears,—he pursued his precipitate retreat homewards.

But what a dread revelation had been made to him that evening! His mortal enemy—his inveterate foe had escaped from the death which, it was hitherto supposed, the miscreant had met in the den of infamy near Bird-Cage Walk some months previously:—his ominous voice still thundered in Markham's ears;—and our unhappy hero once more saw all his prospects ruined by the unmitigated hatred of the Resurrection Man.

[The recurrent 'New Year's Day' theme is one of the simple devices used by Reynolds to structure the text; a rhetorical account of the state of the poor at different periods recurs as a motif at several stages of the plot, indicating how little has changed in the state of the poor. The chapter entitled 'Female Courage' includes a remarkable account of the purchase of male clothing by Ellen Monroe: she walks the streets of London in her disguise.]

CHAPTER XCVII.
ANOTHER NEW YEAR'S DAY.

IT was the 1st of January, 1840.

[...]

Year after year rolls away; and yet how slowly does civilisation accomplish its task of improving the condition of the sons and daughters of toil.

For in the present day, as it was in the olden time, the millions labour to support the few; and the few continue to monopolise the choicest fruits of the earth.

The rights of labour are denied; and the privileges of birth and wealth are dominant.

And ever, when the millions, bowed down by cares, and crushed with incessant hardships, raise the voice of anguish to their taskmasters, the cry is, "*Toil! toil!*"

And when the poor labourer, with the sweat standing in large drops upon his brow, points to his half-starved wife and little ones, and demands that increase of his wages which will enable him to feed them adequately, and clothe them comfortably, the only response that meets his ears is still, "*Toil! toil!*"

And when the mechanic, pale and emaciated, droops over his loom, and in a faint tone beseeches that his miserable pittance may be turned into a fair remuneration for that hard and unceasing work which builds up the fortunes of his employer, the answer to his pathetic prayer is, "*Toil! toil!*"

And when the miner, who spends his best days in the bowels of the earth, hewing the hard mineral in dark subterranean caves at the peril of his life, and in positions which cramp his limbs, contract his chest, and early prostrate his energies beyond relief,—when *he* exalts his voice from those hideous depths, and demands the settlement of labour's rights upon a just basis, the only echo to his petition is, "*Toil! toil!*"

Yes—it is ever "Toil! toil!" for the millions while the few repose on downy couches, feed upon the luxuries of the land and water, and move from place to place in sumptuous equipages!

It was the 1st of January, 1840.

[...]

CHAPTER CIV.
FEMALE COURAGE.

HOLYWELL STREET was once noted only as a mart for second-hand clothing, and booksellers' shops dealing in indecent prints and volumes. The reputation it thus acquired was not a very creditable one.

Time has, however, included Holywell Street in the clauses of its Reform Bill. Several highly respectable booksellers and publishers have located themselves in the place that once deserved no better denomination than "Rag Fair." The unprincipled vendors of demoralizing books and pictures have, with few exceptions, migrated into Wych Street or Drury Lane; and even the two or three that pertinaciously cling to their old temples of infamy in Holywell Street, seem to be aware of the incursions of respectability into that once notorious thoroughfare, and cease to outrage decency by the display of vile obscenities in their windows.

The reputation of Holywell Street has now ceased to be a by-word: it is respectable; and, as a mart for the sale of literary wares, threatens to rival Paternoster Row.

It is curious to observe that, while butchers, tailors, linen-drapers, tallow-manufacturers, and toy-vendors, are gradually dislodging the booksellers of Paternoster Row, and thus changing the once exclusive nature of this famous street into one of general features, the booksellers, on the other hand, are gradually ousting the old-clothes dealers of Holywell Street.

As the progress of the American colonist towards the far-west drives before it the aboriginal inhabitants, so do the inroads of the bibliopoles menace the Israelites of Holywell Street with total extinction.

Paternoster Row and Holywell Street are both losing their primitive features: the former is becoming a mart of miscellaneous trades; the latter is rising into a bazaar of booksellers.

Already has Holywell Street progressed far towards this consummation. On the southern side of the thoroughfare scarcely a clothes shop remains; those on the opposite side wear a dirty and miserably dilapidated appearance. The huge masks, which denote the warehouse where masquerading and fancy-attire may be procured on sale or hire, seem to "grin horribly a ghastly smile," as if they knew that their occupation was all but gone. The red-haired ladies who stand at their doors beneath a canopy of grey trousers with black seats, and blue coats with brown elbows—a distant imitation of Joseph's garment of many colours—seem dispirited and care-worn, and no longer watch, with the delighted eyes of maternal affection, their promising offspring playing in the gutters. Their glances are turned towards the east—a sure sign that they meditate an early migration to the pleasant regions which touch upon the Minories.

Holywell Street is now a thoroughfare which no one can decry on the score of reputation: it is, however, impossible to deny that, were the southern range of houses pulled down, the Strand would reap an immense advantage, and a fine road would be opened from the New Church to Saint Clement Danes.

It was about half-past seven in the evening that Ellen Monroe, dressed in the most simple manner, and enveloped in a large cloak, entered Holywell Street.

Her countenance was pale; but its expression was one of resolution and firmness.

She walked slowly along from the west end of the street towards the eastern extremity, glancing anxiously upon the countenances of those traders who stood in front of the second-hand clothes shops.

At length she beheld a female—one of the identical ladies with red hair above alluded to—standing on the threshold of one of those warehouses.

Ellen looked upwards, and perceived all kinds of articles of male attire suspended over the head of this female, and swinging backwards and forwards, like so many men hanging, upon the shop-front.

Ellen paused—glanced wistfully at the Jewess, and appeared to hesitate.

Her manner was so peculiar, that, although the clothes vendors do not usually solicit the custom of females, the Jewess immediately exclaimed in a sharp under-tone, "Sell or buy, ma'am?"

Ellen turned, without another moment's hesitation, into the shop.

"I wish to purchase a complete suit of male attire—for myself," said Miss Monroe. "Serve me quickly—and we shall not dispute about the price."

These last words denoted a customer of precisely the nature that was most agreeable to the Jewess. She accordingly bustled about her, ransacked drawers and cupboards, and spread such a quantity of coats, trousers, and waistcoats, before Ellen, that the young lady was quite bewildered.

"Select me a good suit which you think will fit me," said Miss Monroe, after a moment's hesitation; "and allow me to try it on in a private room."

"Certainly, ma'am," answered the Jewess; and, having looked out a suit, she conducted Ellen up stairs into her own sleeping-apartment.

"And now I require a hat and a pair of boots," said Ellen;—"in a word, every thing suitable to form a complete male disguise. I am going to a masquerade," she added, with a smile.

The Jewess made no reply: it did not concern her, if her customer chose to metamorphose herself, so long as *she* was paid; and she accordingly hastened to supply all the remaining apparel necessary to complete the disguise.

She then left Ellen to dress herself at leisure.

And soon that charming form was clothed in the raiment of the other sex: those delicate feet and ankles were encased in heavy boots; thick blue trousers hampered the limbs lately so supple in the voluptuous dance; a coarse shirt and faded silk waistcoat imprisoned the lovely bosom; a collar and black neckcloth concealed the swan-like neck and dazzling whiteness of the throat; and a capacious frock coat concealed the admirable symmetry of the faultless figure. The hair was then gathered up in a manner which would not betray the sex of the wearer of those coarse habiliments, especially when the disguise was aided by the darkness of the night, and when that luxuriant mass was covered with the broad-brimmed and somewhat slouching hat which the Jewess had provided for the purpose.

Ellen's toilette was thus completed, and she then descended to the shop.

The Jewess—perhaps not altogether unaccustomed to such occurrences—made no comment, and took no impertinent notice of the metamorphosed lady. She contented herself with asking a handsome price for the clothes and accommodation afforded; and Ellen paid the sum without a murmur, merely observing that she should send for her own apparel next day.

Miss Monroe then left the shop, and issued from Holywell Street just as the church clocks in the neighbourhood struck eight.

The reader has, doubtless seen enough of her character to be well aware that she had acquired a considerable amount of fortitude and self-possession from the various circumstances in which she has been placed: she was not, therefore, now likely to betray any diffidence or timidity as she threaded, in male attire, the crowded streets of the metropolis. She threw into her gait as much assurance as possible; and thus, without exciting any particular notice, she pursued her way towards the eastern districts of the great city.

The weather was cold and damp; but the rain, which had fallen in torrents the day before, had apparently expended its rage for a short interval. A sharp wind, however, swept through the streets; and Ellen pitied the poor shivering, half-naked wretches, whom she saw huddling upon steps, or crouching beneath archways, as she passed along.

[...]

In a few minutes, a tall man, wrapped up in a large cloak, came up to the spot where she was standing.

"Is that you, Filippo?" said Ellen.

"Yes, Miss; I am here in obedience to your commands," returned Mr. Greenwood's Italian valet.

[...]

"I told you in my note not to be surprised if you should find me disguised in male attire; I moreover requested you to arm yourself with pistols. Have you complied with this desire on my part?"

"I have, Miss," answered Filippo.

[...]

"Give me one of your pistols."

"But, Miss Monroe—"

"Pray do not refuse me! I am not a coward; and I must inform you that I learned to fire a pistol at the theatre."

The Italian handed the young lady one of his loaded weapons.

She concealed it beneath the breast of her coat; and her heart palpitated with pride and satisfaction.

Ellen and the Italian then quickened their pace, and proceeded rapidly towards Globe Town.

[Ellen Monroe and her father hear that Richard has an appointment to meet his long lost brother by a canal bank at night. They suspect a trick, and Ellen follows him, with Greenwood's valet Filippo. The Resurrection Man, who is lying in wait, ties Richard up, and leaves him for dead in the canal.]

CHAPTER CV.
THE COMBAT.

IN spite of the suspicions entertained by Mr. Monroe and Ellen concerning the genuineness of the appointment for which Markham was engaged, the young man was too devotedly attached to the memory of his brother not to indulge in the most wild and sanguine hopes.

[...]

When he reached the banks of the canal, he was struck by the lonely and deserted nature of the spot. The sward was damp and marshy with the late heavy rains: the canal was swollen, and rolled, muddy and dark, between its banks, the pale and sickly moon vainly wooing its bosom to respond to the caresses of its beams by a reflective kiss.

[...]

He had been at his post about half an hour when footsteps suddenly fell upon his ears.

He stopped, and listened.

The steps approached; and in a few moments he beheld, through the obscurity of the night, a person advancing towards him.

"True to your appointment, sir," said the individual, when he came up to the spot where Richard was standing.

"I told you that I should not fail," answered Markham. [...] "But what of my brother? will he come? is he near? Speak!"

[...]

Approaching footsteps were heard; and in a minute or two another form emerged from the gloom of night.

Markham's heart palpitated violently.

"Here is your brother, sir," said the Buffer.

"Eugene—dear Eugene!" cried Richard, springing forward to catch his brother in his arms.

"Brother indeed!" muttered the ominous voice of the Resurrection Man; and at the same moment Richard was pinioned from behind by the Buffer, who skilfully wove a cord around his arms, and fastened his elbows together.

"Villains!" ejaculated Richard, struggling with all his might—but vainly, for the Resurrection Man, whose voice he had immediately recognised but too well, threw him violently upon the damp sod.

"Now, my lad," cried the Resurrection Man, "your fate is decided. In a few minutes you'll be at the bottom of the canal, and then—"

[...]

The Resurrection Man darted upon Richard Markham.

In another moment there was a splash of water; a cry of horror issued from the lips of Ellen; [...]

"The villains!—they have drowned him!" exclaimed Filippo; and, without an instant's hesitation, he plunged into the canal.

[...]
"He is lost—he is gone!" said Filippo, who was swimming about on the surface of the water as skilfully as if it were his native element.
[...]
At that moment a faint cry for help echoed over the bosom of the canal.
[...]
[Ellen] beheld a black object appear on the surface of the water—then disappear again in an instant.
[...]
The brave Italian, though well-nigh exhausted, dived fearlessly; and to the infinite joy of Ellen, re-appeared upon the surface, exclaiming, "He is saved—he is saved!"
[...]
Markham was insensible; but Filippo placed his hand upon the young man's breast, and said, "He lives!"
"Heaven be thanked!" ejaculated Ellen, solemnly.
[...]

The attentions of those who hung over him were redoubled; and Filippo was about to propose to convey him to the nearest dwelling, when he gasped violently, and murmured, "Where am I?"

"Saved!" answered Ellen. "None but friends are near you."

[...]

[Chapter CVIII gives an account of the practices of a body-snatcher in horrific detail. Tidkins is represented as a professional dealer in the trade, much concerned with his financial returns. The literal resurrection of the 'corpse' at the conclusion of the scene is the result of a 'trance-like state' into which the victim has fallen.]

CHAPTER CVIII.
THE EXHUMATION.

THE night was fine—frosty—and bright with the lustre of a lovely moon.

Even the chimneys and gables of the squalid houses of Globe Town appeared to bathe their heads in that flood of silver light.

The Resurrection Man and the Buffer pursued their way towards the cemetery.

For some minutes they preserved a profound silence: at length the Buffer exclaimed, "I only hope, Tony, that this business won't turn out as bad as the job with young Markham three nights ago."

"Why should it?" demanded the Resurrection Man, in a gruff tone.

"Well, I don't know why," answered the Buffer. "P'rhaps, after all, it was just as well that feller escaped as he did. We might have swung for it."

"Escape!" muttered the Resurrection Man, grinding his teeth savagely. "Yes—he did escape *then*; but I haven't done with him yet. He shall not get off so easy another time."

"I wonder who those chaps was that come up so sudden?" observed the Buffer, after a pause.

"Friends of his, no doubt," answered Tidkins. "Most likely he suspected a trap, or thought he would be on the right side. But the night was so plaguy dark, and the whole thing was so sudden, it was impossible to form an idea of who the two strangers might be."

"One on 'em was precious strong, I know," said the Buffer. "But, for my part, I think you'd better leave the young feller alone in future. It's no good standing the chance of getting scragged for mere wengeance. I can't understand that sort of thing. If you like to crack his crib for him and hive the swag, I'm your man; but I'll have no more of a business that's all danger and no profit."

"Well, well, as you like," said the Resurrection Man, impatiently. "Here we are; so look alive."

They were now under the wall of the cemetery.

The Buffer clambered to the top of the wall, which was not very high; and the Resurrection Man handed him the implements and tools, which he dropped cautiously upon the ground inside the enclosure.

He then helped his companion upon the wall; and in another moment they stood together within the cemetery.

"Are you sure you can find the way to the right grave?" demanded the Buffer in a whisper.

"Don't be afraid," was the reply: "I could go straight up to it blindfold."

They then shouldered their implements, and the Resurrection Man led the way to the spot where Mrs. Smith's anonymous lodger had been buried.

"I'm afeard the ground's precious hard," observed the Buffer, when he and his companion had satisfied themselves by a cautious glance around that no one was watching their movements.

The eyes of these men had become so habituated to the obscurity of night, in consequence of the frequency with which they pursued their avocations during the darkness which cradled others to rest, that they were possessed of the visual acuteness generally ascribed to the cat.

"We'll soon turn it up, let it be as hard as it will," said the Resurrection Man, in answer to his comrade's remark.

Then, suiting the action to the word, he began his operations in the following manner.

He measured a distance of five paces from the head of the grave. At the point thus marked he took a long iron rod and drove it in an oblique direction through the ground towards one end of the coffin. So accurate were his calculations relative to the precise spot in which the coffin was embedded in the earth, that the iron rod struck against it the very first time he thus sounded the soil.

"All right," he whispered to the Buffer.

He then took a spade and began to break up the earth just at that spot where the end of the iron rod peeped out of the ground.

"Not so hard as you thought," he observed. "The fact is, the whole burial-place is so mixed up with human remains, that the clay is too greasy to freeze very easy."

"I s'pose that's it," said the Buffer.

The Resurrection Man worked for about ten minutes with a skill and an effect that would have astonished even Jones the grave-digger himself, had he been there to see. He then resigned the spade to the Buffer, who took his turn with equal ardour and ability.

When *his* ten minutes elapsed, the resurrectionists regaled themselves each with a dram from Tidkins' flask; and this individual then applied himself once more to the work in hand. When he was wearied, the Buffer relieved him; and thus did they fairly divide the toil until the excavation of the ground was completed.

This portion of the task was finished in about forty minutes. An oblique channel, about ten feet long, and three feet square at the mouth, and decreasing only in length, as it verged towards the head of the coffin at the bottom, was now formed.

The Resurrection Man provided himself with a stout chisel, the handle of which was covered with leather, and with a mallet, the ends of which were also protected with pieces of the same material. Thus the former instrument when struck by the latter emitted but little noise.

He then descended into the channel which terminated at the very head of the coffin.

Breaking away the soil that lay upon that end of the coffin, he inserted the chisel into the joints of the wood, and in a very few moments knocked off the board that closed the coffin at that extremity.

The wood-work of the head of the shell was also removed with ease—for Banks had purposely nailed those parts of the two cases very slightly together.

The Resurrection Man next handed up the tools to his companion, who threw him down a strong cord.

The end of this rope was then fastened under the armpits of the corpse as it lay in its coffin.

This being done, the Buffer helped the Resurrection Man out of the hole.

"So far, so good," said Tidkins: "it must be close upon one o'clock. We have got a quarter of an hour left—and that's plenty of time to do all that's yet to be done."

The two men then took the rope between them, and drew the corpse gently out of its coffin—up the slope of the channel—and landed it safely on the ground at a little distance from the mouth of the excavation.

The moon fell upon the pale features of the dead—those features which were still as unchanged, save in colour, as if they had never come in contact with a shroud—nor belonged to a body that had been swathed in a winding-sheet!

The contrast formed by the white figure and the black soil on which it was stretched, would have struck terror to the heart of any one save a resurrectionist.

Indeed, the moment the corpse was thus dragged forth from its grave, the Resurrection Man thrust his hand into its breast, and felt for the gold.

It was there—wrapped up as the undertaker had described.

"The blunt is all safe, Jack," said the Resurrection Man; and he secured the coin about his person.

They then applied themselves vigorously to shovel back the earth; but, when they had filled up the excavation, a considerable quantity of the soil still remained to dispose of, it being impossible, in spite of stamping down, to condense the earth into the same space from which it was originally taken.

They therefore filled two sacks with the surplus soil, and proceeded to empty them in different parts of the ground.

Their task was so far accomplished, when they heard the low rumble of wheels in the lane outside the cemetery.

To bundle the corpse neck and heels into a sack, and gather up their implements, was the work of only a few moments. They then conveyed their burdens between them to the wall overlooking the lane, where the well-known voice of Mr. Banks greeted their ears, as he stood upright in his cart peering over the barrier into the cemetery.

"Got the blessed defunct?" said the undertaker, interrogatively.

"Right and tight," answered the Buffer; "and the tin too. Now, then, look sharp—here's the tools."

"I've got 'em," returned Banks.

"Look out for the stiff 'un, then," added the Buffer; and, aided by the Resurrection Man, he shoved the body up to the undertaker, who deposited it in the bottom of his cart.

The Resurrection Man and the Buffer then mounted the wall, and got into the vehicle, in which they laid themselves down, so that any person whom they might meet in the streets through which they were to pass would only see one individual in the cart—namely, the driver. Otherwise, the appearance of three men at that time of night, or rather at that hour in the morning, might have excited suspicion.

Banks lashed the sides of his horse; and the animal started off at a round pace.

Not a word was spoken during the short drive to the surgeon's residence in the Cambridge Road.

When they reached his house the road was quiet and deserted. A light glimmered through the fanlight over the door; and the door itself was opened the moment the cart stopped.

The Resurrection Man and the Buffer sprang up; and, seeing that the coast was clear, bundled the corpse out of the vehicle in an instant; then in less than half a minute the "blessed defunct," as the undertaker called it, was safely lodged in the passage of the surgeon's house.

Mr. Banks, as soon as the body was removed from his vehicle, drove rapidly away. His portion of the night's work was done; and he knew that his accomplices would give him his "reg'lars" when they should meet again.

The Resurrection Man and the Buffer conveyed the body into a species of out-house, which the surgeon, who was passionately attached to anatomical studies, devoted to purposes of dissection and physiological experiment.

In the middle of this room, which was about ten feet long and six broad, stood a strong deal table, forming a slightly inclined plane. The stone pavement of the out-house was perforated with holes in the immediate vicinity of the table, so that the fluid which poured from subjects for dissection might escape into a drain communicating with the common sewer. To the ceiling, immediately above the head of the table, was attached a pulley with a strong cord, by means of which a body might be supported in any position that was most convenient to the anatomist.

The Resurrection Man and his companion carried the corpse into this dissecting-room, and placed it upon the table, the surgeon holding a candle to light their movements.

"Now, Jack," said Tidkins to the Buffer, "do you take the stiff 'un out of the sack, and lay him along decently on the table ready for business, while I retire a moment to this gentleman's study and settle accounts with him."

"Well and good," returned the Buffer. "I'll stay here till you come back."

The surgeon lighted another candle, which he placed on the window-sill, and then withdrew, accompanied by the Resurrection Man.

The Buffer shut the door of the dissecting-room, because the draught caused the candle to flicker, and menaced the light with extinction. He then proceeded to obey the directions which he had received from his accomplice.

The Buffer removed the sack from the body, which he then stretched out at length upon the inclined table, taking care to place its head on the higher extremity and immediately beneath the pulley.

"There, old feller," he said, "you're comfortable, at any rate. What a blessin' it would be to your friends, if they was ever to find out that you'd been had up again, to know into what skilful hands you'd happened to fall!"

Thus musing, the Buffer turned his back listlessly towards the corpse, and leant against the table on which it was lying.

"Let me see," he said to himself, "there's thirty-one pounds that was buried along with *him*, and then there's ten pounds that the sawbones is a paying now to Tony for the *snatch*; that makes forty-one pounds, and there's three to go shares. What does that make? Threes into four goes once—threes into eleven goes three and two over—that's thirteen pounds a-piece, and two pound to split—"

The Buffer started abruptly round, and became deadly pale. He thought he heard a slight movement of the corpse, and his whole frame trembled.

Almost at the same moment some object was hurled violently against the window; the glass was shivered to atoms; the candle was thrown down and extinguished; and total darkness reigned in the dissecting-room.

"Holloa!" cried the Buffer, turning sick at heart; "what's that?"

Scarcely had these words escaped his lips when he felt his hand suddenly grasped by the cold fingers of the corpse.

"O God!" cried the miscreant; and he fell insensible across the body on the table.

[In Chapter CXIII, Isabella Alteroni reveals that her father, who has been released from a debtor's prison by the secret intervention of Richard Markham, is in fact Alberto, Prince of Castelcicala. Castelcicala was an actual Italian state, and a Prince of Castelcicala lived in London in exile until his death in 1832.]

CHAPTER CXIII.
THE LOVERS.

THE morning, which succeeded the night that witnessed the incidents just detailed, was clear, frosty, and fine. It was one of those winter mornings when the soil is as hard as iron, but on which the sun shines with gay light if not with genial heat. On such a morning we walk abroad with a consciousness that the exercise benefits us: we feel the blood acquiring a more rapid circulation in our veins; we soon experience a pleasant glow pervading the frame; our spirits become exhilarated; and we learn that even Winter has its peculiar charms.

Such was the feeling that animated Richard Markham, as, after alighting from a public vehicle at Richmond, he proceeded rapidly along a by-road that led through the fields at the back of Count Alteroni's mansion.

His cheeks were tinged with a glow that set off his handsome features to the greatest advantage: his dark eyes sparkled with an expression of joy and hope; a smile played upon his lip; and he walked with his head erect as if he felt proud of his existence—because that existence, in spite of its vicissitudes, was protected by some auspicious star.

O Love! art thou not a star full of hope and promise, like that which guided the sages of the East to the cradle of their Redeemer?—like the welcome planet which heralds the dauntless mariner over the midnight seas?—like the twinkling orb which points the right track to the Arab wanderer of the desert?

Richard Markham pursued his way—his soul full of hope, and love, and bliss.

At a distance of about a quarter of a mile on his right hand, the mansion of Count Alteroni soon met his eyes, surrounded by the evergreens that, in contrast with the withered trees elsewhere, gave to the spot where it stood the air of an oasis in the midst of a desert.

Markham's heart beat quickly when that well-known dwelling met his view; and for a moment a shade of melancholy passed over his countenance, for he recalled to mind the happy hours he had once spent within its walls.

But that transitory cloud vanished from his brow, when his eye caught a glimpse, in another instant, of a sylph-like form that was threading a leafless grove at a little distance.

Richard redoubled his steps, and was led, by the circuitous winding of the path that he was pursuing, somewhat nearer to the Count's mansion.

In a few minutes he reached the very spot where, in the preceding spring, he had accidentally encountered Isabella, and where she assured him of her unchanged and unchangeable love.

He is now on that spot once more :—he pauses—looks around—and Isabella again approaches.

Richard rushes forward, and clasps the beauteous Italian maiden in his arms.

"Isabella—dearest Isabella! What good angel prompted you to grant me this interview?" he exclaimed, when the first effusion of joy was over.

"Do you think me indiscreet, Richard?" asked the signora, taking his arm, and glancing timidly towards his countenance.

"Indiscreet, my sweet girl!" cried her lover: "Oh! how can you suppose that I would entertain a harsh feeling with regard to that goodness on your part which doubtless instigated you to afford me the happiness of this meeting?"

"But when we met here—seven or eight months ago, Richard," said Isabella, "I told you that never—never would I consent to a stolen interview. And now—you may imagine—"

"I imagine that you love me, Isabella—love me as I love you," exclaimed Markham; "and what other idea can occupy my thoughts when that one is present? Oh! you know not the ineffable joy—the unequalled pleasure which I experienced when your letter reached me yesterday. I recognised your handwriting immediately; and I seized the letter with avidity, when it was brought to me in my study. And then, Isabella—will you believe me when I tell you that I trembled to open it? I laid it upon the table—my hand refused to break the seal. Pardon me—forgive me, if for a moment I feared—"

"That I had forgotten my vows—my plighted affection," faltered Isabella, reproachfully.

"Again I say pardon—forgive me, dearest girl; but—oh! I have been so very unfortunate!"

"Think not of the past, Richard," said Isabella, tenderly.

"The past! Oh! how can I cease to ponder upon the past, when it has nearly bereaved me of all hope for the future?" exclaimed Markham, in an impassioned tone.

"Not *all* hope," murmured Isabella; "since hope still remains to *me*!"

"Angel that thou art!" cried Richard, pressing the maiden's hand fondly. "How weak I am, since it is from thee that moral courage ever is imparted."

"You were speaking of my letter," said Isabella, with a smile.

"True! But so many emotions—joy and hope—sorrowful reminiscences and brighter prospects, bewilder me! I will, however, try to talk calmly! When your letter came, I feared to open it for some moments: I dreaded a new calamity! But at length I called all my firmness to my aid; and a terrible weight was taken from my soul, when my eye glanced at the first lines of that letter which suddenly became as dear and welcome as a reprieve to the condemned criminal. Then, when I saw that my beloved Isabella still thought of me—still loved me—"

"Oh, I did not tell you *that* in my letter," exclaimed Isabella, with a smile of bewitching archness.

"No—but I divined it—I gathered it from the words in which you conveyed to me your desire to see me—from the manner in which you said that at eleven o'clock this morning you should walk in the very place where we had met accidentally once before—oh! I suddenly became a new being: never was my heart so light!"

"And yet I said in my letter, Richard, that I wished to see you upon a matter of business—"

"Ah! Isabella, destroy not the charm which makes me happy! Let no cold thought of worldly things chill the heavenly fervour of our affection. Were it not for that love which reciprocally exists between us, how should I have supported the misfortunes that have multiplied upon me?"

"Again I say, Richard, allude not to the past. Alas! bitter—bitter were the tears that I wept on that fatal night when—"

"When I was publicly disgraced at the theatre—in the midst of a triumph. Yes—Isabella, you were there—there, where my shame was consummated!"

"Accident had led us to the theatre that evening," answered Isabella. "My father had heard that a new tragedy, of which grand hopes were entertained, was to be produced; and he insisted that I should accompany him and my mother. I was compelled to assent to his desire—although I prefer retirement and tranquillity to society and gaiety. You may conceive our astonishment—you may imagine *my* surprise and *my* joy, when you came forward to acknowledge the congratulations offered for a triumph so brilliantly achieved. And then—but let us leave that subject—my blood turns cold when I think of it!"

"Oh! go on—speak of it, speak of it!" exclaimed Markham, enthusiastically; "for although the reminiscence of that fearful scene be like pouring molten lead upon an open wound, still it is sweet—it is sweet, Isabella, to receive sympathy from such lips as yours."

"Alas! I have little more to say—except that the sudden intervention of that terrible man seemed to strike me as with the arrow of death; and I became insensible. Then, Richard,—*then*," continued Isabella, in a low and tremulous tone, "my mother suspected my secret—or rather received a confirmation of the suspicion which she had long entertained!"

"And she shuddered at the mere idea?" exclaimed Markham, interrogatively.

"No, Richard: my mother is kind and good—and, you know, was always well disposed towards you: I have told you that much before! She said little—and of that no matter! But my father—my father—"

"He discovered *our* secret also!" exclaimed Richard. "Oh! did he not curse me?"

"He was cool and calm, when—on the following morning—he spoke to me upon the subject. I answered him frankly: I admitted my attachment for you."

"What did he say, Isabella! Tell me every thing—suppress not a word!"

"Oh, heavens! he made me very miserable," returned Isabella, tears trickling down her countenance. "But wherefore distress both yourself and me with a recapitulation of what ensued? Suffice it to say, that I collected all the arguments in my memory—and they were not a few; [...]"

"Dearest girl!" exclaimed Markham, rapturously.

"[...] when I saw that I had made a profound impression on him, I turned the conversation upon the momentary reverse of fortune which had plunged him into a debtors' prison—"

"Isabella!" cried Markham, in surprise.

"And then I boldly declared my conviction that the unknown friend who had released him—the anonymous individual who had thrown open to him the gate leading to liberty—the nameless person, that had done so generous a deed, and accomplished it in a manner as delicate as it was noble,—was none other than Richard Markham!"

The tone of the Italian maiden had become more and more impassioned as she proceeded; and when she uttered the last words of the foregoing sentence, she turned upon him on whose arm she leant, a countenance glowing with animation, and radiant with gratitude and love.

"Oh, Isabella! you told your father *that*!" cried Markham. "And yet—you knew not—"

"My suspicion amounted almost to a certainty," interrupted Isabella: "and now I doubt no longer. Oh! Richard—if ever for one moment I had wavered in my love for you,—if ever an instant of coldness, arising from worldly reflections, had intervened to make me repent my solemn vows to you,—that *one* deed of yours—that noble sacrifice of your property, made to release my revered parent from a gaol,—that—that alone would have rendered my heart unalterably thine!"

"Beloved girl—this moment is the happiest of my life!" exclaimed Markham; and tears of joy filled his eyes, as he pressed the maiden once more to his heart.

"Yes, Richard," continued Isabella, after a long pause; and now her splendid countenance was lighted up with an expression of dignity and generous pride, and the timid, bashful maiden seemed changed into a lady whose brow was encircled with a diadem; "yes, Richard, if ever I felt that no deed nor act of mine shall separate us eternally—if ever I rejoiced in the prospect of possessing wealth, and receiving lustre from my father's princely rank—"

"Isabella!" exclaimed Richard, dropping the arm on which the Italian lady was leaning, and stepping back in the most profound astonishment: "Isabella, what mean you?"

"I mean," continued the signora, casting upon him a glance of deep tenderness and noble pride; "I mean that henceforth, Richard, I can have no secret from you,—that I must now disclose what has often before trembled upon my tongue; a secret which my father would not, however, as yet, have revealed to the English public generally,—the secret of his rank; for he whom the world knows as the Count Alteroni, is Alberto, Prince of Castelcicala!"

[...]

[There follows a further example of the interpolation of first-person low-life narratives into the text. The employment of child labour in mines was the theme of a number of novels concerned with social problems in the 1840s. A footnote to Chapter CXVI identifies the Report of the Children's Employment Commission of 1842 as the source of many of the factual statements in this narrative. In order to explain the quality of the language, the author remarks that he has 'taken the liberty materially to correct and amend' the original. Meg Flathers, or the Rattlesnake, later becomes the mistress of Anthony Tidkins, the Resurrection Man.]

CHAPTER CXVI.
THE RATTLESNAKE'S HISTORY.

"I WAS born in a coal-mine in Staffordshire. My father was a married man, with five or six children by his wife: my mother was a single woman, who worked for him in the pit. I was, therefore, illegitimate; but this circumstance was neither considered disgraceful to my mother nor to myself, morality being on so low a scale amongst the mining population generally, as almost to amount to promiscuous intercourse. My mother was only eighteen when I was born. She worked in the pit up to the very hour of my birth; and when she found the labour-pains coming on, she threw off the belt and chain with which she had been dragging a heavy corf (or wicker basket), full of coal, up a slanting road,—retired to a damp cave in a narrow passage leading to the foot of the shaft, and there gave birth to her child. That child was myself. She wrapped me up in her petticoat, which was all the clothing she had on at the time, and crawled with me, along the passage, which was about two feet and a half high, to the bottom of the shaft. There she got into the basket, and was drawn up a height of about two hundred and thirty feet—holding the rope with her right hand, and supporting me on her left arm. She often told me those particulars, and said how she thought she should faint as she was ascending in the rickety vehicle, and how difficult she found it to maintain her hold of the rope, weak and enfeebled as she was. She, however, reached the top in safety, and hastened home to her miserable hovel—for she was an orphan, and lived by herself. In a week she was up again, and back to her work in the pit; and she hired a bit of a girl, about seven or eight years old, to take care of me.

"How my infancy was passed I, of course, can only form an idea by the mode of treatment generally adopted towards babies in the mining districts and under such circumstances as those connected with my birth. My mother would, perhaps, come up from the pit once, in the middle of the day, to give me my natural nourishment; and when I screamed during her absence, the little girl, who acted as my nurse, most probably thrust a teaspoonful of some strong opiate down my throat to make me sleep and keep me quiet. Many children are killed by this treatment; but the reason of death, in such cases, is seldom known, because the Coroner's assistance is seldom required in the mining districts.

"When I was seven years old, my mother one day told me that it was now high time for me to go down with her into the pit, and earn some money by my own labour. My father, who now and then called to see me of a Sunday, and brought me a cake or a toy, also declared that I was old enough to help my mother. So it was decided that I should go down into the pit. I remember that I was very much frightened at the idea, and cried very bitterly when the dreaded day came. It was a cold winter's morning—I recollect that well; and the snow was very thick upon the ground. I shivered with chilliness and terror as my mother led me to the pit. She gave me a good scolding because I whimpered; and then a good beating because I cried lustily. But every thing combined to make me afraid. It was as early as five in that cold wintry morning that I was proceeding to a scene of labour which I knew to be far, far under the earth. The dense darkness of the hour was not even relieved by the white snow upon the ground; but over the country were seen blazing fires on every side,—fires which appeared to me to be issuing from the very bowels of the earth, but which were in reality burning upon the surface, for the purpose of converting coal into coke: there were also blazing fields of bituminous shale; and all the tall chimneys of the great towers of the iron furnaces vomited forth flames,—the whole scene thus forming a picture well calculated to appal and startle an infant mind.

"I remember at this moment what my feelings were then—as well as if the incident I am relating had only occurred yesterday. During the day-light I had seen the lofty chimneys giving vent to columns of dense smoke, the furnaces putting forth torrents of lurid flame, and the coke-fires burning upon the ground: but that was the first time I had ever beheld those meteors blazing amidst utter darkness; and I was afraid—I was afraid.

"The shaft was perfectly round, and not more than four feet in diameter. The mode of ascent and descent was precisely that of a well, with this difference—that, instead of a bucket there was a stout iron bar about three feet long attached in the middle, and suspended horizontally, to the end of the rope. From each end of this bar hung chains with hooks, to draw up the baskets of coal. This apparatus was called the *clatch-harness*. Two people ascended or descended at a time by these means. They had to sit cross-legged, as it were, upon the transverse bar, and cling to the rope. Thus, the person who got on first sate upon the bar, and the other person sate a-straddle on the first one's thighs. An old woman presided at the wheel which wound up or lowered the rope sustaining the clatch-harness; and as she was by no means averse to a dram, the lives of the persons employed in the mine were constantly at the mercy of that old drunken harridan. Moreover, there seemed to me to be great danger in the way in which the miners got on and off the clatch-harness. One moment's giddiness—a missing of the hold of the rope—and down to the bottom of the shaft headlong! When the clatch-harness was drawn up to the top, the old woman made the handle fast by a bolt drawn out from the upright post, and then, grasping a hand of both persons on the harness at the same time, brought them by main force to land. A false step on the part of that old woman,—the failure of the bolt which stopped the rotatory motion of the roller on which the rope was wound,—or the slipping of the hands which she grasped in hers,—and a terrible accident must have ensued!

"But to return to my first descent into the pit. My mother, who was dressed in a loose jacket, open in front, and trousers (which, besides her shoes, were the only articles of clothing on her, she wearing neither shift nor stockings), leapt upon the clatch-iron as nimbly as a sailor in the rigging of his ship. She then received me from the outstretched arm of the old woman, and made me sit in the easiest and safest posture she could imagine. But when I found myself being gradually lowered down into a depth as black as night, I felt too terror-struck even to cry out; and had not my mother held me tight with one hand, I should have fallen precipitately into that hideous dark profundity.

"At length we reached the bottom, where my mother lifted me, half dead with giddiness and fright, from the clatch-iron. I felt the soil cold, damp and muddy, under my feet. A lamp was burning in a shade suspended in a little recess in the side of the shaft; and my mother lighted a bit of candle which she had brought with her, and which she stuck into a piece of clay to hold it by. Then I perceived a long dark passage, about two feet and a half high, branching off from the foot of the shaft. My mother went on her hands and knees, and told me to creep along with her. The passage was nearly six feet wide; and thus there was plenty of room for me to keep abreast of her. Had not this been the case, I am sure that I never should have had the courage either to precede, or follow her; for nothing could be more hideous to my infantine imagination than that low, yawning, black-mouthed cavern, running into the very bowels of the earth, and leading I knew not whither. Indeed, as I walked in a painfully stooping posture along by my mother's side, my fancy conjured up all kinds of horrors. I trembled lest some invisible hand should suddenly push forth from the side of the passage, and clutch me in its grasp: I dreaded lest every step I took might precipitate me into some tremendous abyss or deep well: I thought that the echoes which I heard afar off, and which were the sounds of the miner's pickaxe or the rolling corves on the rails, were terrific warnings that the earth was falling in, and would bury us alive: then, when the light of my mother's candle suddenly fell upon some human being groping his or her way along in darkness, I shuddered at the idea of encountering some ferocious monster or hideous spectre:—in a word, my feelings, as I toiled along that subterranean passage, were of so terrific a nature that they produced upon my memory an impression which never can be effaced, and which makes me turn cold all over as I contemplate those feelings now!

"You must remember that I had been reared in a complete state of mental darkness; and that no enlightened instruction had dispelled the clouds of superstition which naturally obscure the juvenile mind. I could not read: I had not even been taught my alphabet. I had not heard of such a name as JESUS CHRIST; and all the mention of GOD that had ever met my ears, was in the curses and execrations which fell from the lips of my father, my mother, her acquaintances, and even the little girl who had nursed me. You cannot wonder, then, if I was so appalled, when I first found myself in that strange and terrific place.

"At length we reached the end of that passage; and struck into another, which echoed with the noise of pickaxes. In a few moments I saw the *undergoers* (or miners) lying on their sides, and with their pickaxes breaking away the coal. They did not work to a greater height than two feet, for fear, as I subsequently learnt, that they should endanger the security of the roof of the passage, the seam of coal not being a thick one. I well remember my infantine alarm and horror when I perceived that these men were naked—stark naked. But my mother did not seem to be the least abashed or dismayed: on the contrary, she laughed and exchanged a joke with each one as we passed. In fact, I afterwards discovered that Bet Flathers was a great favourite with the miners.

"Well, we went on, until we suddenly came upon a scene that astonished me not a little. The passage abruptly opened into a large room,—an immense cave, hollowed out of the coal in a seam that I since learnt to be twenty feet in thickness. This cave was lighted by a great number of candles; and at a table sate about twenty individuals—men, women, and children—all at breakfast. There they were, as black as negroes—eating, laughing, chattering, and drinking. But, to my surprise and disgust, I saw that the women and young girls were all naked from the waist upwards, and many of the men completely so. And yet there was no shame—no embarrassment! But the language that soon met my ears!—I could not comprehend half of it, but what I *did* understand, made me afraid!

"My mother caught me by the hand, and led me to the table, where I found my father. He gave us some breakfast; and in a short time, the party broke up—the men, women, and children separating to their respective places of labour. My mother and myself accompanied one of the men, for my mother had ceased to work for my father, since she had borne a child to him, as his wife had insisted upon their separation in respect to labour in the mine.

"The name of the man for whom my mother worked was Phil Blossom. He was married, but had no children. His wife was a cripple, having met with some accident in the mine, and could not work. He was therefore obliged to employ some one to carry his coal from the place where he worked, to the cart that conveyed it to the foot of the shaft. Until I went down into the mine, my mother had carried the coal for him, and also *hurried* (or dragged) the cart; but she now made me fill one cart while she hurried another. Thus, at seven years old, I had to carry about fifty-six pounds of coal in a wooden *bucket*. When the passage was high enough I carried it on my back; but when it was too low, I had to drag or push it along as best I could. Some parts of the passages were only twenty-two inches in height; this was where the workings were in very narrow seams; and the difficulty of dragging such a weight, at such an age, can be better understood than explained. I can well recollect that when I commenced that terrible labour, the perspiration, commingling with my tears, poured down my face.

"Phil Blossom worked in a complete state of nudity; and my mother stripped herself to the waist to perform her task. She had to drag a cart holding seven hundredweight, a distance of at least two hundred yards—for our was a very extensive pit, and had numerous workings and cuttings running a considerable way underground. The person who does this duty is called a *hurrier*: the process itself is termed *tramming*; and the cart is denominated a *skip*. The work was certainly harder than that of slaves in the West Indies, or convicts in Norfolk Island. My mother had a girdle round her waist; and to that girdle was fastened a chain, which passed between her legs and was attached to the skip. She then had to go down on her hands and knees, with a candle fastened to a strap on her forehead, and drag the skip through the low passages, or else to maintain a curved or stooping posture in the high ones.

"Phil Blossom was what we called a *getter*. He first made a long straight cut with a pickaxe underneath the part of the seam where he was working: this was called *holing*; and as it was commenced low down, the getter was obliged to lie flat on his back or on his side, and work for a long time in that uneasy manner.

"I did as well as I could with the labour allotted to me; but it was dreadful work. I was constantly knocking my head against the low roofs of the passages or against the rough places of the sides: at other times I fell flat on my face, with the masses of coal upon me; or else I got knocked down by a cart, or by some collier in the dark, as I toiled along the passages, my eyes blinded with my tears or with the dust of the mine.

"Many—many weeks passed away; and at length I grew quite hardened in respect to those sights and that language which had at first disgusted me. I became familiar with the constant presence of naked men and half-naked women; and the most terrible oaths and filthy expressions ceased to startle me. I walked boldly into the great cavern which I have before described, and which served as a place of meeting for those who took their meals in the mine. I associated with the boys and girls that worked in the pit, and learnt to laugh at an obscene joke, or to practise petty thefts of candles, food, or even drink, which the colliers left in the cavern or at their places of work. The mere fact of the boys and girls in mines all meeting together, without any control,—without any one to look after them,—is calculated to corrupt all those who may be well disposed.

"I remained as a carrier of coal along the passages till I was ten years old. I was then ordered to convey my load, which by this time amounted to a hundred weight on each occasion, up a ladder to a passage over where I had hitherto worked. This load was strapped by a leather round my forehead; and, as the ladder was very rudely formed, and the steps were nearly two feet apart, it was with great difficulty that I could keep my balance. I have seen terrible accidents happen to young girls working in that way. Sometimes the strap, or tagg, round one persons's forehead has broken, and the whole load has fallen on the girl climbing up behind. Then the latter has been precipitated to the bottom of the dyke, the great masses of coal falling on the top of her. On other occasions I have seen the girls lose their balance, and fall off the ladder—their burden of coals, as in the other case, showering upon them or their companions behind. The work was indeed most horrible: a slave-ship could not have been worse.

"If I did not do exactly as Phil Blossom told me, the treatment I received from him was horrible: and my mother did not dare interfere, or he would serve her in the same manner. He thrashed me with his fist or with a stick, until I was bruised all over. My flesh was often marked with deep wales for weeks together. One day he nipped me with his nails until he actually cut quite through my ear. He often pulled my hair till it literally gave way in his hand; and sometimes he would pelt me with coals. He thought nothing of giving me a kick that would send me with great violence across the passage, or dash me against the opposite side. On one occasion he was in such a rage, because I accidentally put out the candle which he had to light him at his work, that he struck a random blow at me with his pickaxe in the dark, and cut a great gash in my head. All the miners in pits *baste* and *bray*—that is, beat and flog—their helpers.

"You would be surprised if I was to tell you how many people in the pit were either killed or severely injured, by accidents, every year. But there are so many dangers to which the poor miners are exposed! Falling down the shaft,—the rope sustaining the clatch-harness breaking,—being drawn over the roller,—the fall of coals out of the corves in their ascent,—drowning in the mines from the sudden breaking in of water from old workings,—explosion of gas,—choke-damp,—falling in of the roofs of passages,—the breaking of ladders or well-staircases,—being run over by the tram-waggons, or carts dragged by horses,—the explosion of gunpowder used in breaking away huge masses of coal,—and several other minor accidents, are all perpetually menacing the life or limbs of those poor creatures who supply the mineral that cheers so many thousands of fire-sides!

"Deaths from accidents of this nature were seldom, if ever, brought under the notice of the coroner: indeed, to save time, it was usual to bury the poor victims within twenty-four or thirty-six hours after their decease.

"I earned three shillings a week when I was ten years old, and my mother eleven. You may imagine, then, that we ought to have been pretty comfortable; but our household was just as wretched as any other in the mining districts. Filth and poverty are the characteristics of the collier population. Nothing can be more wretched—nothing more miserable than their dwellings. The huts in which they live are generally from ten to twelve feet square, each consisting only of one room. I have seen a man and his wife and eight or ten children all huddling together in that one room; and yet they might have earned, by their joint labour, thirty-shillings or more a week. Perhaps a pig, a jackass, or fowls form part of the family. And then the furniture!—not a comfort—scarcely a necessary! And yet this absence of even such articles as bedsteads, is upon principle: colliers do not like to be encumbered with household goods, because they are often obliged to *flit*—that is, to leave one place of work and seek for another. Such a thing as drainage is almost completely unknown in these districts; and all the filth is permitted to accumulate before the door. The colliers are a dirty set of people; but, poor creatures! how can they well be otherwise? They descend into the mines at a very early hour in the morning: they return home at a very late hour in the evening, and they are then too tired to attend to habits of cleanliness. Besides, it is so natural for them to say, '*Why should we wash ourselves to-night, since to-morrow we must become black and dirty again?*' or '*Why should we wash ourselves just for the sake of sleeping with a clean skin?*' As for the boys and girls, they are often so worn out—so thoroughly exhausted, that they go to rest without their suppers. They cannot keep themselves awake when they get home. I know that this was often and often my case; and I have preferred—indeed, I have been compelled by sheer fatigue, to go to bed before my mother could prepare any thing to eat.

"Again, how can the collier's home possibly be comfortable? He makes his wife and children toil with him in the mine: he married a woman from the mine; and neither she nor her daughters know any thing of housekeeping? How can disorder be prevented from creeping into the collier's dwelling, when no one is there in the day-time to attend to it? Then all the money which they can save from the *Tommy-shop*, (of which I shall speak presently) goes for whiskey. Husband and wife, sons and daughters all look after the whiskey. The habits of the colliers are hereditarily depraved: they are perpetuated from father to son, from mother to daughter; none is better nor worse than his parents were before him. Rags and filth—squalor and dissipation—crushing toil and hideous want—ignorance and immorality; these are the features of the collier's home, and the characteristics of the collier's life.

"Our home was not a whit better than that of any of our fellow-labourers; nor was my mother less attached to whiskey than her neighbours.

"But the chief source of poverty and frequent want—amounting at times almost to starvation—amongst persons earning a sufficiency of wages, is the *truck system*. This atrociously oppressive method consists of paying the colliers wages in goods, or partly in goods, through the medium of the tommy-shop. The proprietor of a tommy-shop has an understanding with the owners of the mines in his district; and the owners agree to pay the persons in their employment once a month, or once a fortnight. The consequence is that the miners require credit during the interval; and they are compelled to go to the tommy-shop, where they can obtain their bread, bacon, cheese, meat, groceries, potatoes, chandlery, and even clothes. The proprietor of the tommy-shop sends his book to the clerk of the owner of the mine the day before the wages are paid; and thus the clerk knows how much to stop from the wages of each individual, for the benefit of the shopkeeper. If the miners and their wives do not go to the tommy-shop for their domestic articles, they instantly lose their employment in the mine, in consequence of the understanding between their employer and the shopkeeper. Perhaps this would not be so bad if the tommy-shops were honest; because it is very handy for the collier to go to a store which contains every article that he may require. But the tommy-shop charges twenty-five or thirty per cent. dearer than any other tradesman; so that if a collier and his family can earn between them thirty shillings a week, he loses seven or eight shillings out of that amount. In the course of a year about twenty pounds out of his seventy-five go to the tommy-shop for nothing but interest on the credit afforded! That interest is divided between the tommy-shop-keeper and the coal-mine proprietor.

"In the district where my mother and I lived, there was no such thing at all as payment of wages in the current money of the kingdom. The tommy-shop-keeper paid the wages for the proprietors once a month: and how do you think he settled them? In ticket-money! This coinage consisted of pewter medals, or markers, with the sum they represented, and the name of the tommy-shop on them. [...]

"The wages, in my time, were subject to great changes: I have known men earn twenty-five shillings a week at one time, and twelve or fifteen at another. And out of that they were obliged to supply their own candles and grease for the wheels of the carts or *trams*. The cost of this was about three-pence a day. Then, again, the fines were frequent and vexatious: it was calculated that they amounted to a penny a day per head. These sums all went into the coffers of the coal-owners.

"Such was the state of superstitious ignorance which prevailed in the mines, that every one believed in ghosts and spirits. Even old men were often afraid to work in isolated places; [...] It was stated that the spectres of the deceased haunted the scenes of their violent departures from this world.

"By the time I was twelve years old I was as wild a young she-devil as any in the mines. Like the other females, I worked with only a pair of trousers on. [...] I may as well observe that a stranger visiting a mine, and seeing the boys and girls all huddling together, half-naked, in the caves or obscure nooks, could not possibly tell one sex from the other. I must say that I think, with regard to bad language and licentious conduct, the girls were far—far worse than the boys. [...]

It was at that period—I mean when I was twelve years old—that I determined to abandon the horrible life to which my mother had devoted me. [...] I saw nine out of ten of my fellow-labourers pining away. Some were covered with disgusting boils, caused by the constant dripping of the water upon their naked flesh in the pits. I saw young persons of my own age literally growing old in their early youth,—stooping, asthmatic, consumptive, and enfeebled. When they were washed on Sundays, they were the pictures of ill-health and premature decay. Many actually grew deformed in stature; and all were of stunted growth. It is true that their muscles were singularly developed; but they were otherwise skin and bone. The young children were for the most part of contracted features, which, added to their wasted forms, gave them a strange appearance of ghastliness, when cleansed from the filth of the mine. The holers, or excavators, were bow-legged and crooked; the hurriers and trammers knock-kneed and high-shouldered. Many—very many of the miners were affected with diseases of the heart. Then, who ever saw a person employed in the pits, live to an advanced age? A miner of fifty-five was a curiosity: the poor creatures generally drooped at five-and-thirty, and died off by forty. They invariably seemed oppressed with care and anxiety: jollity was unknown amongst them. I have seen jolly-looking butchers, blacksmiths, carpenters, plough-men, porters, and so on: but I never beheld a jolly-looking miner. [...]

"I pondered seriously upon all this; and every circumstance that occurred, and every scene around me, tended to strengthen my resolution to quit an employment worse than that of a galley-slave. [...] when I saw [my mother's] bald head—her scalp thickened, inflamed, and sometimes so swollen, that it was like a bulb filled with spongy matter, and so painful that she could not bear to touch it,—when I heard her complain of the dreadful labour of pushing the heavy corves and trams with her sore head,—when I perceived […] her chest torn with a sharp hacking cough, accompanied by the expectoration of a large quantity of matter of a deep black colour, called by colliers the *black-spit*; […]—I shuddered at the bare idea of devoting my youth to that horrible toil, and then passing to the grave while yet in the prime of life!

"I thought of running away, and seeking my fortune elsewhere. I knew that it was no use to acquaint my mother with my distaste for the life to which she had devoted me: she would only have answered my objections by means of blows. But while I was still wavering what course to pursue, a circumstance occurred which I must not forget to relate.

"One morning my candle had accidentally gone out, and I was creeping along the dark passage to the spot where Phil Blossom was working, to obtain a light from his candle, when I heard him and my mother conversing together in a low tone, but with great earnestness of manner. Curiosity prompted me to stop and listen. 'Are you sure that is the case?' said Phil.—'Certain,' replied my mother. 'I shall be confined in about five months.'—'Well,' observed Phil, 'I don't know what's to be done. My old woman will kick up the devil's delight when she hears of it. I wish she was out of the way: I would marry you if she was.'—Then there was a profound silence for some minutes. It was broken by the man, who said, 'Yes, if the old woman was out of the way you and I might get married, and then we should live so comfortable together. I'm sure no man can be cursed with a wife of worse temper than mine.'—'Yes,' returned my mother, 'she is horrible for that.'—'Do you think there would be much harm in pushing her down a shaft, or shoving her head under the wheel of your tram, Bet?' asked Phil, after another pause.—'There would be no harm,' said my mother, 'if so be we weren't found out'.—'That's exactly what I mean,' observed Phil.—'But then,' continued my mother, 'if she didn't happen to *die* at once, she might peach, and get us both into a scrape.'—'So she might,' said Phil.—'I'll tell you what we might do,' exclaimed my mother, in a joyful tone: 'doesn't your wife come down at one to bring you your dinner?'—'Yes,' replied Phil Blossom: 'that's all the old cripple is good for.'—'Well, then,' pursued my mother, 'I'll tell you how we can manage this business.'—Then they began to whisper, and I could not gather another word that fell from their lips.

"I was so frightened at what I had heard that I crept quickly but cautiously back again to my place of labour, and sate down on the lower steps of the ladder, in the dark—determined to wait till some one should come, rather than go and ask Phil Blossom for a light. I had suddenly acquired a perfect horror of that man. I had understood that my mother was with child by him; and I had heard them coolly plotting the death of the woman who was an obstacle to their marriage. At my age, such an idea was calculated to inspire me with terror. I think I sate for nearly an hour in the dark, my mind filled with thoughts of a nature which may be well understood. At length a young woman, bearing a corf, came with a light; and I was no longer left in obscurity. I then plucked up my courage, took my basket, and went to Phil Blossom for a load of coal. My mother was not there; and he was working with his pickaxe as coolly as possible. He asked me what had made me so long in returning for a load; and I told him I had fallen down a few steps of the ladder and hurt myself. He said no more on the subject; and I was delighted to escape without a braying or basting. While I was loading my corf, he asked me if I should like to have him for a father-in-law. I said 'Yes' through fear, for I was always afraid of his *nieves*, as the colliers call their clenched fists. He seemed pleased; and, after a pause, said that if ever he was my father-in-law, I should always take my *bait* (or meals) with him in the cavern. I thanked him, and went on with my work; but I pretty well comprehended that the removal of Phil's wife by some means or another had been resolved on.

"Shortly before one o'clock that same day my mother came to the place where I was carrying the coals, and gave me a *butter-cake* (as we called bread and butter), telling me that she was going up out of the mine, as she must pay a visit to the tommy-shop for some candles and grease. [...] then the creaking of the wheel and roller was heard. 'Here comes some one's bait, I dare say,' observed one of the half-marrows [as we called the young lads who pushed the trams].—'I wish it was mine,' said another; 'but I never get anything to eat from breakfast-time till I go home at night.'—Scarcely were these words spoken when a piercing scream alarmed us: there was a rushing sound—the chains of the harness clanked fearfully—and down came a woman with tremendous violence to the bottom of the pit, the clatch rattling down immediately after her. A cry of horror burst from us all; the poor creature had fallen at our very feet. We rushed forward; but she never moved. The back part of her head was smashed against a piece of hard mineral at the bottom of the shaft. Her countenance had escaped injury; and as I cast a hasty glance upon it, I recognised the well-known face of Phil Blossom's crippled wife!

"One of the boys instantly hastened to acquaint him with the accident. He came to the spot where his wife lay a mangled heap, stone dead; and he began to bewail his loss in terms which would have been moving had I not been aware of their hypocrisy. The half-marrows were, however, deceived by that well-feigned grief, and did all they could to console him. I said nothing: I was confounded!

"In due time the cause of the *accident* was ascertained. It appeared that my mother had gone up the shaft, but when she got to the top she struck her foot so forcibly against the upright post of the machinery, that she lamed herself for the time. The old woman who presided over the machinery (as I have before said) very kindly offered to go to the tommy-shop for her, on condition that she would remain there to work the handle for people coming up or going down. This was agreed to. The very first person who wanted to go down was Mrs. Blossom; and my mother alleged that the handle unfortunately slipped out of her hand as she was unwinding the rope. This explanation satisfied the overseer of the mine: the intervention of the coroner was not deemed necessary;—my mother appeared much afflicted at the *accident*: Phil Blossom mourned the death of his wife with admirable hypocrisy;—the corpse was interred within forty-eight hours;—and thus was Phil's wife removed without a suspicion being excited!

"I was now more than ever determined to leave the mine. I saw that my mother was capable of any thing; and I trembled lest she should take it into her head to rid herself of me. One day she told me that she was going to be married to Phil Blossom: [...] Accordingly, one Sunday, when I was washed quite clean, I left the hovel which my mother occupied, and set out on my wanderings.

"I had not a penny in my pocket, nor a friend on the face of the earth to whom I could apply for advice, protection, or assistance. All that stood between me and starvation, that I could see, was a piece of bread and some cheese, which I had taken with me when I left home. I walked as far as I could without stopping, and must have been about six miles from the pit where I had worked, when evening came on. It was November, and the weather was very chilly. I looked round me, almost in despair, to see if I could discover an asylum for the night. Far behind me the tremendous chimneys and furnaces vomited forth flames and volumes of smoke; and the horizon shone as if a whole city was on fire: but in the spot where I then found myself, it was drear, dark, and lonely. I walked a little farther, and, to my joy, espied a light. I advanced towards it, and soon perceived that it emanated from a fire burning in a species of cave overhung by a high and rugged embankment of earth belonging to a pit that had most probably ceased to be worked. Crouched over this fire was a lad of about fifteen, clothed in rags, dirty, emaciated, and with starvation written upon his countenance. I advanced towards him, and begged to be allowed to warm myself by his fire. He answered me in a kind and touching manner; and we soon made confidants of each other. I told him my history. [...]

"In less than an hour Skilligalee and myself became intimate friends. Varied and many were the plans which we proposed to earn a livelihood; but all proved hopeless when we remembered our penniless condition, and Skilligalee pointed to his rags. At length he exclaimed in despair, '*There is nothing left to do but to rob.*'—'*I am afraid that this is our only resource,*' was my reply. [...]

"'*Come with me,*' said Skilligallee. I did not ask any questions, but followed him. He led the way in silence for upwards of half an hour, and at length lights suddenly shone between a grove of trees. Skilligalee leapt over a low fence, and then helped me to climb it. We were then in a meadow planted with trees—a sort of park, which we traversed, guided by the lights, towards a large house. We next came to a garden; and, having passed through this enclosure, we reached the back part of the premises. Skilligalee went straight up to a particular window, which he opened. He then crept through, and told me to wait outside. In a few minutes he returned to the window, and handed me out a large bundle, wrapped up in a table-cloth. He then crept forth, and closed the window. We beat a retreat from the scene of our plunder; and returned to the cave. The fire was still blazing, and Skilligalee fed it with more fuel, which he obtained by breaking away the wood from an old ruined cabin close by.

"We next proceeded to open the bundle, which I found to contain a quantity of food, six silver forks, and six spoons. Skilligalee then told me that the mansion which we had just robbed was the dwelling of the owner of the mine wherein he had worked for seven years, and where he had been so cruelly treated by the pit-man to whom he had been apprenticed. He said that he had sometimes been sent with messages to the proprietor, from the overseer in the mine, and that the servants on those occasions had taken him into the kitchen and given him some food. He had thus obtained a knowledge of the premises. 'Last night', he added, 'I was reduced by hunger to desperation, and I went with the intention of breaking into the pantry. To my surprise I found the window open, the spring-bolt being broken. My courage, however, failed me; and I returned to this cave to suffer all the pangs of hunger. To-night you came: companionship gave me resolution; and we have got wherewith to obtain the means of doing something for an honest livelihood.'

"We then partook of some of the cold meat and fine white bread which the pantry had furnished; and, while we thus regaled ourselves, we debated what we should do with the silver forks and spoons. I said before that I was decently dressed; but my companion was in rags. It was accordingly agreed that I should go to the nearest town in the morning, dispose of the plate purchase some clothes for Skilligallee, and then rejoin him at the cave. [...]

"[...] In an hour I reached the town, and went to a pawnbrokers's shop. [...] The pawnbroker questioned me so closely that I began to prevaricate: he called in a constable, and gave me into custody. I was taken before the magistrate; but I refused to answer a single question, being determined not to betray my accomplice. The magistrate remanded me for a week; and I was sent to prison. There I herded with juvenile thieves and prostitutes; and I cared little for my incarceration, because I was tolerably, and, at all events, regularly fed. When I was had up again, the owner of the mansion which I had helped to rob, was there to identify his property. I, however, still persisted in my refusal to answer any questions: I was resolved not to criminate Skilligallee; and I also felt desirous of being sent back to gaol, as I was certain of there obtaining a bed and a meal. In vain did the magistrate impress upon me the necessity of giving an explanation of the manner in which the plate came into my possession, for both he and the owner of the property were inclined to believe that I was only a tool, and not the original thief; I remained dumb, and was remanded for another week.

"At the expiration of that period, I was again placed before the magistrate; and, to my surprise, I found Skilligalee in the court. He was still clothed in his rags, and looked more wretched and famished than when I first saw him. I gave him a look, and made a sign to assure him that I would not betray him; but the moment the case was called, he stood forward and declared that he alone was guilty,—that he had robbed the house, and that I was merely an instrument of whom he had made use to dispose of the proceeds of the burglary. I was overcome by this generosity on his part; and both the magistrate and the owner of the property were struck by the avowal. The latter declared that he did not wish to prosecute: the former accordingly indicated a summary sentence of imprisonment for a few weeks upon Skilligalee. He then questioned me about my own condition; and I told him that I had worked in a mine, but that I had been compelled to run away from home in consequence of the ill treatment I received at the hands of my mother. I expressed my determination to put an end to my life sooner than return to her; and the gentleman, whose house had been robbed, offered to provide for me at his own expense, if the magistrate would release me. This he agreed to do; and the gentleman placed me as a boarder in a school kept in the town by two elderly widows.

"This school was founded for the purpose of furnishing education to the children of pit-men who were prudent and well disposed enough to pay a small stipend for that purpose, that stipend being fixed at a very low rate, as the deficiency in the amount required to maintain the establishment was supplied by voluntary contribution. There were only a few boarders—and they were all girls: the great majority of the pupils consisted of day-scholars. At this school I stayed until I was sixteen, when the gentleman who had placed me there took me into his service as housemaid.

"During the whole of that period I had never heard of my mother, or Phil Blossom. I now felt some curiosity to discover what had become of them; so, one day, having obtained a holiday for the purpose, I went over to the pit where I had myself passed so many miserable years. The same old woman, who had presided at the handle of the roller that raised or lowered the clatch-harness, during the period of my never-to-be-forgotten apprenticeship, was there still. She did not recognise me—I was so altered for the better. Clean, neatly dressed, stout, and tall, I could not possibly be identified with the dirty, ragged, thin, and miserable-looking creature who had once toiled in that subterranean hell. I accosted the old woman, and asked her if a woman named Betsy Flathers or Blossom worked in the mine. "Bet Blossom!" ejaculated the old woman: 'why, she's been dead a year!'—'Dead!' I echoed. 'And how did she die?'—'By falling down the shaft, to be sure,' answered the old woman.—Although I entertained little affection for my mother, absence and a knowledge of her character having destroyed all feelings of that kind, I could not hear this intelligence without experiencing a severe shock.—'Yes,' continued the old woman, 'it was a sort of judgment on her, I suppose, for she herself let a poor creature fall down some four or five years ago, when she took my place at the handle here for a few minutes while I went to the tommy-shop for her. She married the husband of the woman who was killed by the fall; and every body knew well enough afterwards that there wasn't quite so much neglect in the affair as she had pretended at the time, but a something more serious still. However, there was no proof; and so the thing was soon forgot. Well, one day, about a year ago, as I said just now, Phil Blossom came up to me and asked me to run to the tommy-shop to fetch him some candles. I told him to mind the wheel, and he said he would. It seems that a few minutes after I had left on his errand, his wife came up the clatch;

and, according to what a lad, who looked up the shaft at the time, says, she had just reached the top, when she fell, harness and all, the whole pit echoing with her horrible screams. She died the moment she touched the bottom. Phil Blossom was very much cut up about it; but he swore that the handle slipped out of his hand, and then went whirling round and round with such force that he couldn't catch it again. [...] 'And what has become of Phil Blossom?' I inquired.—The old woman pointed down the shaft, as much as to say that he was still working in the mine.—'Did they have any children?' I asked.—'Bet had one, I believe,' said the old woman; 'but it died a few days after it was born, through having too large a dose of Godfrey's Cordial administered to make it sleep.'—I gave the old woman a shilling, and turned away from the place, by no means anxious to encounter Phil Blossom, who, I clearly perceived, had rid himself of my mother by the same means which she had adopted to dispose of his first wife.

"As I was returning to my master's house, I had to cross a narrow bridge over a little stream. I was so occupied with the news I had just heard, I did not perceive that there was another person advancing from the opposite side, until I was suddenly caught in the arms of a young man in the very middle of the bridge. I gave a dreadful scream; but he burst out into a loud laugh, and exclaimed, 'Well, you need n't be so frightened at a mere joke.' I knew that voice directly; and glancing at the young man, who was tolerably well dressed, I immediately recognised my old friend Skilligalee. It was then my turn to laugh, which I did very heartily, because he had not the least notion who I was. I, however, soon told him; and he was quite delighted to meet me. We walked together to the very identical cave where we had first met when boy and girl. Now he was a tall young man, and had improved wonderfully. He told me that he had become acquainted with some excellent fellows when he was in prison, and that he had profited so well by their advice and example, that he led a jovial life, did no work, and always had plenty of money. I asked him how he managed; and he told me, after some hesitation, that he had turned housebreaker. There was scarcely a gentleman's house within twelve miles round, that he had not visited in that quality. [...]

"[...] Skilligalee was delighted to see me again; and he proposed that I should leave service, and live with him. I consented; and—"

[Here the Rattlesnake's narrative breaks off.]

[Among the institutions that were attacked for their hypocrisy and disregard for the sufferings of the poor is the Church. The Reverend Reginald Tracy, vicar of St. David's ... a church 'not a hundred miles from Russell or Tavistock Square', is dissolute and sexually licentious. In Chapter CXXIX, he pursues Cecilia, wife of Lord Harborough, one of the aristocrats who first befriended, than deceived, Richard Markham. In Chapter CXXXI, his uncontrollable desires lead him to examine a statue of a semi-naked woman, which then comes alive.]

CHAPTER CXXIX.
THE FALL.

REGINALD TRACY returned to his own abode, his breast agitated with a variety of conflicting feelings.

He pushed his old housekeeper, who announced to him that dinner was ready, rudely aside, and hurried up to his own chamber.

There he threw himself upon his knees, and endeavoured to pray to be released from temptation.

For he now comprehended all the dangers which beset him, although he suspected not the perfidy and artifice of the tempter.

But not a word of supplication could he utter from the mouth which still burned with the thrilling kisses of the beautiful Cecilia.

He rose from his knees, and paced the room wildly,—at one moment vowing never to see that syren more,—at another longing to rush back to her arms.

The animal passions of that man were strong by nature and threatened to be insatiable whenever let loose; but they had slumbered from his birth, beneath the lethargic influence of high principle and asceticism.

Moreover, they had never been tempted until the present time; and now that temptation came so suddenly, and in so sweet a guise,—came with such irresistible blandishments,—came, in a word, so accompanied with all that could flatter his vanity or minister unto his pride,—that he knew not how to resist its influence.

And at one moment that man of unblemished character and lofty principle fell upon his knees, grovelling as it were at the foot-stool of Him whom he served,—anxious, yearning to crave for courage to escape from the peril that awaited him,—and yet unable to breathe a syllable of prayer. Then he walked in a wild and excited manner up and down, murmuring the name of Cecilia,—pondering upon her charms,—plunging into voluptuous reveries and dreams of vaguely comprehended bliss,—until his desires became of that fiery, hot, and unruly nature, which triumphed over all other considerations.

It was an interesting—and yet an awful spectacle, to behold that man, who could look back over a life of spotless and unblemished purity, now engaged in a terrific warfare with the demons of passion that were raging to cast off their chains, and were struggling furiously for dominion over the proud being who had hitherto held them in silence and in bondage.

But those demons had acquired strength during their long repose; and now that the day of rebellion had arrived, they maintained an avenging and desperate conflict with him who had long been their master. They were like a people goaded to desperation by the atrocities of a blood-thirsty tyrant: they fought a battle in which there was to be no quarter, but wherein one side or the other must succumb.

Hour after hour passed; and still he sustained the conflict with the new feelings which had been excited within him, and which were rapidly crushing all the better sentiments of his soul. At length he retired to bed, a prey to a mental uneasiness which amounted to a torture.

His sleep was agitated and filled with visions by no means calculated to calm the fever of his blood. He awoke in the morning excited, unsettled, and with a desperate longing after pleasures which were as yet vague and undefined to him.

But still a sense of the awful danger which menaced him stole into his mind from time to time; and he shuddered as if he were about to commit a crime.

He left the table, where the morning's meal was untasted, and repaired to his study. But his books had no longer any charm for him: he could not settle his mind to read or write.

He went out, and rambled in all directions, reckless whither he went—but anxious to throw off the spell which had fallen upon him.

Vain was this attempt.

The air was piercing and cold; but his brow was burning. He felt that his cheeks were flushed; and his eyes seemed to shoot forth fire.

"My God! what is the matter with me?" he exclaimed, in his anguish, as he entered Hyde Park, the comparative loneliness of which at that season he thought calculated to soothe his troubled thoughts. "I have tried to pray—and last night, for the first time in my life, I sought my pillow, unable to implore the blessings of my Maker. Oh! what spell has overtaken me? what influence is upon me? Cecilia—Cecilia—is it indeed thou that hast thus changed me?"

He went on,—now musing upon all that had passed within the few preceding day,—now breaking forth into wild and passionate exclamations.

He left the Park, and walked rapidly through the streets of the West End.

"No," he said within himself, "I will never see her more. I will conquer these horrible feelings—I will triumph over the mad desires, the fiery cravings which have converted the heaven of my heart into a raging hell! Oh! why is she so beautiful? why did she say that she loved me? Was it to disturb me in my peaceful career—to wean me from my God? No—no: she yielded to an impulse which she could not control;—she loves me—she loves me,—she loves me!"

There was a species of insanity in his manner as he thus addressed himself, —not speaking with the lips, but with the heart; [...]

"[...] but I must fly from her—I must avoid her as if she were a venomous serpent. I dare not trust myself again in her presence: and not for worlds— not for worlds would I be with her alone once more. No,—I must forget her—I must tear her image from my heart—I must trample it under foot!"

He paused as he spoke: he stood still—for he was exhausted.

But how was it that the demon of mischief had, with an under-current of irresistible influence, carried him on, in spite of the forceful flow of the above reflections, to the very goal of destruction!

He was in Tavistock Square.

He was at the door of Lady Cecilia Harborough's house.

And now for one minute a terrific conflict again raged within him. It seemed as if he collected all his remaining courage to struggle with the demons in his heart; but he was weak with the protracted contest—and they were more powerful than ever.

"I will see her once more," he said, yielding to the influence of his passions: "I will tell her that I stand upon an abyss—I will implore her to have mercy upon me, and permit me to retreat ere yet it be too late!"

His good genius held him faintly back; but his passions goaded him on; he obeyed the latter impulse; he rushed up the steps and knocked at the door.

"Even now I might retreat," he said to himself: "there is still time! I will—I will!"

He turned, and was already half-way down the steps, when the door was opened.

His good resolutions vanished, and he entered the house.

In a few moments more he was in the presence of Lady Cecilia,—Lady Cecilia—looking more bewitching, more captivating than ever!

She had expected him, and had resolved that this visit, on his part, should crown her triumph.

It was in a small parlour adjoining her own boudoir that she received him.

The luxurious sofa was placed near the cheerful fire: the heavy curtains were drawn over the windows in such a manner as to darken the room.

Cecilia was attired in a black silk dress, that she had purposely chosen to enhance the transparent brilliancy of her complexion, and to display the dazzling whiteness of a bust, which, though of small proportions, was of perfect contour.

She was reclining languidly upon the cushions which were piled on one end of the sofa, and her little feet peeped from beneath the skirts of her dress.

She did not rise when Reginald entered the room, but invited him to take a seat near her upon the sofa.

So bewitchingly beautiful did she appear, as the strong glare of the fire played upon her countenance, amidst the semi-obscurity of the room, that he could not resist the signal.

He accordingly sate down by her side.

[...]

"I was on the point of asking what *you* would think—what opinion you would form of *me*, if I were to confess that I also dared to love you?"

"I should reply that such happiness never could descend upon me," said Cecilia.

"And yet it is true—it is true! I cannot conceal it from myself," exclaimed Reginald, giving way to the influence of his emotions: "it is true that I love you!"

"Oh! am I indeed so blest?" faltered Cecilia. "Tell me once more that you love me!"

"Love you!" cried the rector, unable to wrestle longer with his mad desires: "I worship—I adore you—I will die for you!"

He caught her in his arms, and covered her with burning and impassioned kisses.

★ ★ ★ ★ ★ ★
  ★ ★ ★ ★ ★

Oh, Reginald! and hast thou at length fallen? Have a few short days sufficed to undo and render as naught the purity—the chastity of years?

Where was thy guardian angel in that hour?

Whither had fled that proud virtue which raised thee so high above thy fellow-men, and which gave to thine eloquence the galvanic effect of the most sublime truth?

Look back—look back, with bitterness and sorrow, upon the brilliant career through which thou hast run up to this hour, and curse the madness that prompted thee to darken so bright a destiny!

For thou hast plucked thine own crown of integrity from thy brow, and hast trampled it underfoot.

Henceforth, in thine own heart, wilt thou know thyself as a hypocrite and a deceiver!

⋆ ⋆ ⋆ ⋆ ⋆ ⋆
 ⋆ ⋆ ⋆ ⋆ ⋆

[...]
Again he looked upwards; and the dense sombre clouds, which rolled rapidly like huge black billows over each other, imparted fresh terrors to his guilty soul.

Then his feverish and excited imagination began to invest those clouds with fantastic shapes; and he traced in the midst of the heavens a mighty black hand, the fore-finger of which pointed menacingly *downwards*.

[...]
Suddenly a deafening peal of thunder burst above him: he looked frantically up—the hand appeared to wave in a convulsive manner—then the clouds parted, rolling pell-mell over each other,—and the terrific sign was broken into a hundred moving masses.

[...]
Oh! His punishment had already begun!

⋆ ⋆ ⋆ ⋆ ⋆ ⋆
 ⋆ ⋆ ⋆ ⋆ ⋆

Weak, wearied, subdued,—drenched with the rain that had accompanied the storm; and in state of mind bordering upon madness and despair, the wretched man reached his home at four o'clock in the morning.

[...]

CHAPTER CXXXI.
THE STATUE.

THE old woman led the way at a rapid pace towards Golden Lane, the rector following her at a little distance.

[...]
The hag chuckled:—the sound was between a hollow laugh and a death-rattle; and it seemed horrible to the ears of Reginald Tracy.

The old woman then slowly ascended the narrow and dark staircase, until she reached the landing, where she drew a key from her pocket, and leisurely applied it to the lock of a door.

She fumbled about so long with the key, muttering to herself all the while, that Reginald thought she would never open the door, and he offered to assist her.

But at that moment the key turned in the lock, and the door was slowly opened.

The hag beckoned the rector to follow her; and he found himself in a tolerably large room, decently furnished, and with an excellent fire burning in the grate.

There were no candles lighted; nor did the hag offer to provide any;—but the contents of the apartment were plainly visible by means of the strong glare of the fire.

Heavy curtains of a dark colour covered the windows: the floor was carpeted; the chairs and tables were of plain but solid material; and a large mirror stood over the mantel.

At the farther end of the room was a second door, which was now closed, but evidently communicated with an inner chamber.

"I gave the poor artist the best rooms in my house," observed the hag, as she placed a chair near the fire for the rector. "The statue stands in the adjoining chamber; you can inspect it at once, while I—"

She mumbled the remainder of the sentence in such a way that it was wholly unintelligible to the rector, and then left the room.

For a few minutes Reginald stood before the fire, uncertain what course to pursue. He now began to think that the entire proceeding was somewhat extraordinary; and the singular manner in which the old hag had left him, inspired him with a feeling not entirely free from alarm.

But for what purpose could he have been inveigled thither, if it were not really to behold the marvellous statue? and, perhaps, after all, the old woman had only left him in order to fetch the candles or to summon the artist? Moreover, had she not informed him that the statue was in the next room, and that he might inspect it at once? It was therefore easy to satisfy himself whether he had been deceived or not.

Ashamed of his transient fears, he threw off his hat and cloak, and advanced towards the door communicating with the inner chamber.

Even then he hesitated for a minute as his fingers grasped the handle; but, at length, he boldly entered the room.

The moment the door was thrown open, he perceived by the light of the fire which burned in the front apartment, that the inner one was a small and comfortably fitted-up bed-chamber. It was involved in a more than semi-obscurity; but not to such an extent as to conceal from Reginald Tracy's penetrating glance the semblance of a female form standing upon a low pedestal in the most remote corner of the room.

"I am not then deceived!" he exclaimed aloud, as he advanced nearer towards the statue.

By this time his eyes had become accustomed to the obscurity of the chamber, into which the glimmer of the fire threw a faint but mellowed light. Still, in somewhat bold relief, against the dark wall, stood the object of his interest,—seeming a beautiful model of a female form, the colouring of which was that of life. It was naked to the middle; the arms were gracefully rounded; and one band sustained the falling drapery which, being also coloured, produced upon the mind of the beholder the effect of real garments.

Lost in wonder at the success with which the sculptor had performed his work,—and experiencing feelings of a soft and voluptuous nature,—Reginald drew closer to the statue. At that moment the light of the fire played upon its countenance; and it seemed to him as if the lips moved with a faint smile. Then, how was his surprise increased, when the conviction flashed to his mind that the face he was gazing upon was well known to him!

"O Cecilia, Cecilia!" he ejaculated aloud: "hast thou sent thy statue hither to compel me to fall at its feet and worship the senseless stone, while thou—the sweet original—art elsewhere, speculating perhaps upon the emotions which this phantasmagorian sport was calculated to conjure up within me! Ah! Cecilia, if thou wast resolved to subdue me once more—if thou couldst not rest until I became thy slave again,—oh! why not have invited me to meet thine own sweet self, instead of this speechless, motionless, passionless image,—a counterpart of thee only in external loveliness! Yes—there it is perfect:—the hair—the brow—the eyes—the mouth—Heavens! those lips seem to smile once more; those eyes sparkle with real fire! Cecilia—Cecilia—"

And Reginald Tracy was afraid—he scarcely knew wherefore: the entire adventure of the evening appearing to be a dream.

"Yes—yes!" he suddenly exclaimed, after having steadfastly contemplated the form before him for some moments,—standing at a distance of only three or four paces,—afraid to advance nearer, unwilling to retreat altogether,— "yes!" he exclaimed, "there is something more than mere senseless marble here! The eyes shoot fire—the lips smile—the bosom heaves—Oh! Cecilia—Cecilia, it is yourself!"

As he spoke he rushed forward: the statue burst from chill marble into warmth and life;—it was indeed the beauteous but wily Cecilia—who returned his embrace and hung around his neck;—and the rector was again subdued—again enslaved!

* * * * * *
 * * * * *

"And you will pardon me for the little stratagem which I adopted to bring you back to my arms?" said Cecilia.

"How can I do otherwise than pardon you?" murmured the rector, whose licentious soul was occupied only with gross delights, and who would at that moment have dared exposure and disgrace rather than tear himself away from the syren on whose bosom his head was pillowed. "Oh! Cecilia, I have had a violent struggle with my feelings; but I shall now contend against them no more. No! from this instant I abandon all hope of empire—all wish for dominion over myself: I yield myself up to the pleasures of love and to thee! Sweet Cecilia, thou hast taught me how ineffable is the bliss which mortals may taste in this world;—and after all, the sure present is preferable to the uncertain future!"

[...]

* * * * * *

The barrier was now completely broken down; and the rector gave way to the violence of the passion which hurried him along.

That man, so full of vigour, and in the prime of his physical strength, abandoned himself without restraint to the fury of those desires which burnt the more madly—the more wildly, from having been so long pent-up.

Day after day did he meet his guilty paramour; and on each occasion did he reflect less upon the necessity of caution. He passed hours and hours together with her at her abode; and at length he ventured to receive her at his own residence, when his housekeeper had retired to rest.

But he did not neglect his professional duties on the Sabbath;—and he now became an accomplished hypocrite. He ascended the pulpit as usual, and charmed thousands with his discourse as heretofore. Indeed his eloquence improved, for the simulated earnestness which displaced the tone of heart-felt conviction that he had once experienced, seemed more impassioned, and was more impressive than the natural ebullition of his feelings.

Thus as he progressed in the ways of vice, his reputation increased in sanctity.

But the moment he escaped from the duties of his profession, he flew to the arms of her who had seduced him from his career of purity; and so infatuated was he with her who had been his tutoress in the ways of amorous pleasure, that he joyfully placed his purse at the disposal of her extravagance.

Thus was Lady Cecilia triumphant in all points with regard to the once immaculate, but now sensual and voluptuous rector of Saint David's.

[The Victorian interest in the Gypsy as an image of freedom is well documented. In Chapter CXXXIV, Gypsy life is represented as well ordered, although it is an element of the social 'other' constructed in this text. The Traveller who appears in the gypsy King Zingary's Palace in disguise is Crankey Jem, the arch-enemy of the Resurrection Man. The Holy Land is a part of the notorious rookery of St Giles, where criminals took refuge in a maze of backyards and passages, riddled with secret boltholes and trapdoors, and almost impenetrable by the forces of law and order.]

CHAPTER CXXXIV.
THE PALACE IN THE HOLY LAND.

THE wanderer amidst the crowded thoroughfares of the multitudinous metropolis cannot be unacquainted with that assemblage of densely populated streets and lanes which is situate between High Street (St. Giles's) and Great Russell Street (Bloomsbury).

The district alluded to is called the Holy Land.

There poverty hides its head through shame, and crime lurks concealed through fear;—there everything that is squalid, hideous, debauched, and immoral, makes its dwelling;—there woman is as far removed from the angel as Satan is from the God-head, and man is as closely allied to the brute as the idiot is to the baboon;—there days are spent in idleness, and nights in dissipation;—there no refinement of habit or speech is known, but male and female alike wallow in obscene debauchery and filthy ideas;—there garments are patched with pieces of various dyes, and language is disfigured with words of a revolting slang;—there the natural ruffianism and brutal instincts of the human heart are unrepressed by social ties or conventional decencies;—there infamy is no disgrace, crime no reproach, vice no stain.

Such is the Holy Land.

In a dark and gloomy alley, connecting two of the longer streets in this district, stood a large house four storeys high, and with windows of such narrow dimensions that they seemed intended to admit the light of day only by small instalments.

[…]

The interior of the house resembled a small barrack. The apartments on the ground floor were used as day-rooms or refectories, and were fitted up with long tables and forms. The floors were strewed with sand; and the appearance of the place was more cleanly and comfortable than might have been expected in such a neighbourhood. The lower panes of the windows were smeared with a whitewash, which prevented passers-by from peering from the street into the apartments.

The upper storeys were all used as dormitories, some being allotted to the male and others to the female inmates of the house.

[…]

We have now endeavoured to furnish the reader with an idea of King Zingary's Palace in the Holy Land.

[…]

It was ten o'clock at night; and the king of the gipsies was presiding at the banqueting-table in his Palace.

Upwards of sixty gipsies, male and female, were assembled round the board. These consisted of the chiefs of the different districts into which the gipsy kingdom was divided, with their wives and daughters.

[…]

With all the solemn gravity of a chairman at a public dinner, Zingary rapped his knuckles upon the table, and commanded those present to fill their glasses.

The order was obeyed by both men and women; and the king then spoke as follows:—

"Most loyal and dutiful friends, this is the hundred and thirty-first anniversary of the institution of that custom in virtue of which the provincial rulers of the united races of Egyptians and Bohemians in England assemble together once every year at the Palace.

[…]

"Ours is indeed a happy life," continued Zingary. "When roving over the broad country, we enjoy a freedom unknown to the rest of the world. No impost or taxes have we then to pay: we drink of the stream at pleasure, and never feel alarmed lest our water should be cut off. We can choose pleasant paths, yet pay no paving-rate. The sun lights us by day, and the stars by night; and no one comes to remind us that we owe two quarters' gas. We pitch our tents where we will, but are not afraid of a ground-landlord. We do not look forward with fear and trembling to Lady-Day or Michaelmas, for the broker cannot distress us. […] In fine, we are as free and independent as the inhabitants of the desert. A health, then, to the united races of the Zingarees!"

[…]

The Traveller meantime disguised himself in a manner which would have defied the penetrating eyes of even a parent, had he met his own mother; and from morning until evening did he prowl about London, in search of the *one individual* against whom he nourished the most terrible hatred.

[…]

EPILOGUE TO VOLUME I.

THUS far have we pursued our adventurous theme; and though we have already told so much, how much more does there remain yet to tell!

Said we not, at the outset, that we would introduce our readers to a city of strange contrasts? and who shall say that we have not fulfilled our promise?

But as yet we have only drawn the veil partially aside from the mighty panorama of grandeur and misery which it is our task to display:—the reader has still to be initiated more deeply into the MYSTERIES of LONDON.

We have a grand moral to work out—a great lesson to teach every class of society;—a moral and a lesson whose themes are:

WEALTH. | POVERTY.

For we have constituted ourselves the scourge of the oppressor, and the champion of the oppressed: we have taken virtue by the hand to raise it, and we have seized upon vice to expose it; we have no fear of those who sit in high places; but we dwell emphatically upon the failings of the educated and the rich, as on the immorality of the ignorant and poor.

We invite all those who have been deceived to come around us, and we will unmask the deceiver;—we seek the company of them that drag the chains of tyranny along the rough thoroughfares of the world, that we may put the tyrant to shame;—we gather around us all those who suffer from vicious institutions, that we may expose the rottenness of the social heart.

Crime, oppression, and injustice prosper for a time; but, with nations as with individuals, the day of retribution must come. Such is the lesson which we have yet to teach.

And let those who have perused what we have already written, pause ere they deduce therefrom a general moral;—for as yet they cannot anticipate our design, nor read our end.

[...]

For the word "LONDON" constitutes a theme whose details, whether of good or of evil, are inexhaustible: nor knew we, when we took up our pen to enter upon the subject, how vast—how mighty—how comprehensive it might be!

[...]

END OF THE FIRST VOLUME.

THE

MYSTERIES OF LONDON.

BY

GEORGE W. M. REYNOLDS.

WITH NUMEROUS ILLUSTRATIONS.

VOLUME II.

[Richard sees the Resurrection Man by chance in Tottenham Court Road, and pursues him, with the help of the police, into the worst slums of the East End. In an odd scene, he enters a house which is decorated and furnished as a Museum of Crime. It belongs to the Public Executioner, who is training his humpbacked son, Gibbet, in his craft. The hangman, like the body-snatcher, was a traditional figure of horror in popular consciousness.]

CHAPTER CXXXVIII.
A PUBLIC FUNCTIONARY.

URGED by that sense of duty to which we have before alluded, and which prompted him to neglect no step that might lead to the discovery of a great criminal's lurking-place, Richard accompanied the police officer to various houses where the dregs of the population herded together.

The inspection of a plague-hospital could not have been more appalling: the scrutiny of a lazar-house could not have produced deeper disgust.

In some the inmates were engaged in drunken broils, the women enacting the part of furies: in others the females sang obscene songs, the men joining in the chorus.

Here a mother waited until her daughter should return with the wages of prostitution, to purchase the evening meal: there a husband boasted that his wife was enabled, by the liberality of a paramour, to supply him with ample means for his night's debauchery.

In one house which our hero and the constable visited, three sisters of the respective ages of eleven, thirteen, and fourteen, were comparing the produce of their evening's avocations,—the avocations of the daughters of crime!

And then those three children, having portioned out the necessary amount for their suppers and their lodging that night, and their breakfast next morning, laughed joyously as they perceived how much they had left to purchase gin!

For GIN is the deity, and INTEMPERANCE is the hand-maiden, of both sexes and nearly all ages in that district of London.

What crimes, what follies have been perpetrated for Gin! A river of alcohol rolls through the land, sweeping away health, honour, and happiness with its remorseless tide. The creaking gibbet, and the prison ward—the gloomy hulk, and the far-off penal isle—the debtors' gaol, and the silent penitentiary—the tomb-like workhouse, and the loathsome hospital—the galling chain, and the spirit-breaking tread-wheel—the frightful mad-cell, and the public dissecting-room—the death-bed of despair, and the grave of the suicide, are indebted for many, many victims to thee, most potent GIN!

O GIN! the Genius of Accidents and the Bad Angel of Offences worship thee! Thou art the Juggernaut beneath whose wheels millions throw themselves in blind adoration.

The pawnbroker points to thee and says, "Whilst thy dominion lasts, I am sure to thrive."

The medical man smiles as he marks thy progress, for he knows that thou leadest a ghastly train,—apoplexy, palsy, dropsy, delirium tremens, consumption, madness.

The undertaker chuckles when he remembers thine influence, for he says within himself, "Thou art the Angel of Death."

And Satan rejoices in his kingdom, well-knowing how thickly it can be populated by thee!

Yes—great is thy power, O GIN: thou keepest pace with the progress of civilisation, and thou art made the companion of the Bible. For when the missionary takes the Word of God to the savage in some far distant clime, he bears the fire-water with him at the same time. While his right hand points to the paths of peace and salvation, his left scatters the seeds of misery, disease, death, and damnation!

Yes—great is thy power, O GIN!

[…]

But to continue.

The clock of St. Giles's Church proclaimed the hour of midnight; and though our hero and the constable had visited many of the low dens and lodging-houses in the Holy Land, still their search was without success.

[...]

At that moment a violent scream issued from the upper part of the house close to which Markham and the constable were standing.

[...]

The policeman and our hero hurried up the narrow stairs, lighted by the officer's bull's-eye; and speedily reached the room whence the screams had emanated.

But we must pause for a moment to describe that apartment, and to give the reader some idea of the inmates of the house to which we have introduced him.

The room was situated at the top of the house, and bore the appearance of a loft, their being no ceiling to conceal the massive beams and spars which supported the angular roof.

From one of the horizontal beams hung a stuffed figure, resembling a human being, and as large as life. It was dressed in a complete suit of male attire; and a white mask gave it the real but ghastly appearance of a dead body. It was suspended by a thick cord, or halter, the knot of which being fastened beneath the left ear, made the head incline somewhat over the right shoulder; and it was waving gently backwards and forwards, as if it had been recently disturbed. The arms were pinioned behind; and the hands, which were made more or less life-like by means of dingy white kid gloves, were curled up as it were in a last convulsion. In a word, it presented the exact appearance of a man hanging.

Markham started back when his eyes first fell on this sinister object; but a second glance convinced him that the figure was only a puppet.

This second survey brought to his view other features, calculated to excite his wonder and curiosity, in that strange apartment.

The figure already described was suspended in such a way that its lower extremity was about a foot from the ground; but it was concealed nearly up to the knee by a small scaffold, or large black box, it having been suffered to fall that much through a trap-door made like a drop in the platform of that diminutive stage.

From this strange spectacle,—which, in all respects, was a perfect representation of an execution—Markham's eyes wandered round the loft.

The walls—the rough brick-work of which was smeared over with whitewash,—were covered with rude pictures, glaringly coloured and set in common black wooden frames. The pictures were such as are sold in low neighbourhoods for a few pence each, and represented scenes in the lives of remarkable highwaymen, murderers, and other criminals who had ended their days upon the scaffold. The progress of Jack Sheppard to the gibbet at Tyburn,—the execution of Jonathan Wild,—Turpin's ride to York,—Sawney Bean and his family feasting off human flesh in their cave,—Hunt and Thurtell throwing the body of Mr. Weare into the pond,—Corder murdering Maria Martin at the Red Barn,—James Greenacre cutting up the corpse of Hannah Brown, —such were the principal subjects of that Gallery of Human Enormity.

But as if these pictorial mementos of crime and violent death were not sufficient to gratify the strange taste of the occupants of that apartment, some hand, which was doubtless the agent of an imagination that loved to "sup full of horrors," had scrawled with a burnt stick upon the wall various designs of an equally terrific nature. Gibbets of all forms, and criminals in all the different stages of their last minutes in this life, were there represented. The ingenuity of the draughtsman had even suggested improvements in the usual modes of execution, and had delineated drops, halters, and methods of pinioning on new principles!

Every thing in that spacious loft savoured of the scaffold!

Oh! had the advocates of capital punishment but been enabled to glance upon that scene of horrors, they would have experienced a feeling of dire regret that any system which they had supported could have led to such an exhibition!

But to proceed.

On a rude board, which served as a mantel over the grate, was a miniature gibbet, about eight inches high, and suspended to the horizontal beam of which was a mouse—most scientifically hung with a strong piece of pack-thread.

The large silver watch belonging to the principal inmate of the house was suspended to a horizontal piece of wood, with an oblique supporter, projecting from the wall above the fire-place.

In one corner of the room was a bed, over which flowed curtains of a coarse yellow material; and even these were suspended to a spar arranged and propped up like the arm of a gibbet.

A table, on which the supper things still remained, and half a dozen chairs, completed the contents of this strange room.

And now a few words relative to the inmates of that house.

The hump-backed lad who had rushed down the stairs in the manner already described, was about seventeen or eighteen years of age, and so hideously ugly that he scarcely seemed to belong to the human species. His hair was fiery red, and covered with coarse and matted curls a huge head that would not have been unsuitable for the most colossal form. His face was one mass of freckles; his eyes were of a pinkish hue; his eyebrows and lashes were white; and his large teeth glittered like dominoes between his thick and blueish lips. His arms were long like those of a baboon; but his legs were short; and he was not more than four feet and a half high. In spite of his hideous deformity and almost monstrous ugliness, there was an air of good-nature about him, combined with an evident consciousness of his own repulsive appearance, which could not do otherwise than inspire compassion —if not interest.

The moment the policeman, who entered the room first, made his appearance upon the threshold, a young female precipitated herself towards him, exclaiming, "For God's sake protect me—but do not, do not hurt my uncle!"

This girl was about sixteen years of age, and, though not beautiful, possessed a countenance whose plaintive expression was calculated to inspire deep interest in her behalf. She was tall, and of a graceful figure: her hair was light chesnut; her eyes dark blue, and with a deep melancholy characterising their bashful glances; her teeth were small, white, and even. Although clad in humble attire, there was something genteel in her appearance,—something superior to the place and society in which we now find her.

The man from whose cruel blows she implored protection, was of middle height, rather stoutly built, with a pale countenance, and an expression of stern hard-heartedness in his large grey eyes and compressed lips. He was dressed in a suit which evidently had never been made for him,—the blue frock coat being too long in the sleeves, the waistcoat too wide round the waist, and the trousers scarcely reaching below the knees.

[...]

The constable repeated a caution to the ruffian who had ill-used them, and then took his departure, followed by Richard Markham.

When they were once more in the street, our hero said to his companion, "Who is that man?"

"THE PUBLIC EXECUTIONER," was the reply.

[Richard Markham continues his pursuit of the Resurrection Man through the streets of London, and is accosted by Crankey Jem, who has been staying in the Gypsy Palace under the pseudonym of the Traveller. He informs Richard that he has killed Anthony Tidkins with a dagger, and he invites Richard to visit the Palace to confirm his story.]

CHAPTER CXL.
INCIDENTS IN THE GIPSY PALACE.

For a few moments Richard remained rooted to the spot where the returned convict had left him. He was uncertain how to proceed.

Warned by the desperate adventure which had nearly cost him his life at Twig Folly, he feared lest the present occurrence might be another scheme of the Resurrection Man to ensnare him.

Then he reflected that the individual who had just left him, had met him accidentally, and had narrated to him circumstances which had every appearance of truth.

[...]

This reflection decided him; and, without further hesitation, he knocked boldly at the front door of the Gipsies' Palace.

Some minutes elapsed ere his summons appeared to have created any attention within; and he was about to repeat it, when the door slowly moved on its hinges.

[...]

"Who are you?" demanded the gruff voice of the porter.

"I seek a few hours' of repose and rest," answered Markham.

"Who sent you here?"

"A person who is a friend to you."

[...]

"You may enter," he said. "The Zingarees never refuse hospitality when it can be safely granted."

[...]

The porter closed both doors with great care.

"Follow me," said the man.

He then led the way up stairs to the first floor, and conducted our hero into a room where there were several beds, all of which were unoccupied.

[...]

But to the surprise and annoyance of Markham, the gipsy locked the door of the apartment.

As the key turned with a grating sound, a tremor crept over Richard's frame; and he almost repented having sought the interior of an abode the character and inmates of which were almost entirely unknown to him.

[...]

He proceeded to examine the room in which he appeared to be a prisoner.

[...]

He tried the door—it was indeed fastened: he examined the windows—they were not barred, but were of a dangerous height from the back-yard on which they looked.

[...]

His eye chanced to fall upon a long nail in the wall opposite to the bed from which he had just risen.

A scheme which had already suggested itself to his mind, now assumed a feasible aspect:—he knew that the door was only locked, and not bolted; and that nail seemed to promise the means of egress.

[...]

Having extracted the nail from the wall, he proceeded to pick the lock of the room-door—an operation which he successfully achieved in a few minutes.

Without a moment's hesitation, he issued from the room, bearing the candle in his hand.

As he crossed the landing towards the staircase, which he resolved to ascend, his foot came in contact with some object.

He picked it up: it was an old greasy pocket-book, tied loosely round with a coarse string, and as Markham raised it, a letter dropped out.

Richard was in the act of replacing the document in the pocket-book, which he intended to leave upon the stairs, so as to attract the notice of the inmates of the house, when the address on the outside of the letter caught his eyes.

The candle nearly fell from his hand, so great was the astonishment which immediately seized upon him.

That address consisted simply of the words "ANTHONY TIDKINS!"—but the handwriting—Oh! there was no possibility of mistaking *that*! Markham knew it so well; and though years had elapsed since he had last seen it, still it was as familiar to him as his own—the more so, as it remained unchanged in style;—for it was the writing of his brother Eugene.

With a hasty but trembling hand he opened the letter, the wafer of which had already been broken;—he did not hesitate to read the contents;—judging by his own frank and generous heart, he conceived that such a licence was permitted between brothers. [...]

But all that the letter contained was this:—

"Come to me to-night without fail, between eleven and twelve. Knock in the usual manner."

Richard examined the handwriting with the most minute attention; and the longer he scrutinised it, the more he became confirmed in his belief that it was Eugene's.

But Eugene a patron of the greatest miscreant that had ever disgraced human nature! Was such a thing possible?

The letter bore no date—no signature—and was addressed from no place. It had no post-mark upon it, and had, therefore, been delivered by a private hand.

"Oh!" thought Richard within himself, "if my unhappy brother have really been the victim, the associate, or the employer of that incarnate demon, may God grant that the wretch is indeed no more—for the sake of Eugene!"

And then his curiosity to ascertain the truth relative to the alleged assassination of Tidkins, became more poignant.

[He searches the house, and finds evidence which seems to confirm Crankey Jem's account.]

He was about to leave the last room, when the appearance of one of the beds attracted his attention; and on a closer examination, he perceived that it was saturated with blood. Moreover, on a chair close by, there were pieces of linen rag, on which large stains of gore were scarcely dry, together with lint and bandages—unquestionable proofs that a wound had very recently been dressed in that apartment.

"No—that self-accuser has not deceived me!" thought Markham, as he contemplated these objects.

"All circumstances combine to bear evidence to the truth of his assertion! Doubtless the gipsies have departed, carrying away the corpse with them!" [...]

But suddenly he asked himself—"Am I certain that he is no more? That lint to stanch the blood—those bandages to bind the wound,—do they not rather bear testimony to a blow which was not fatal, but left life behind it? And yet, for what purpose could a body be removed—save for secret interment? Oh! if that man be yet alive—" [...]

[Richard slips away, without disturbing the gypsies.]

[Chapter CXLVI reverts to the Reverend Tracy, who has now turned his attentions to Ellen Monroe. In a salacious scene, he spies on her and the child she has borne secretly, while she is in the 'bathing-room'.]

CHAPTER CXLVI.
THE BATH.—THE HOUSEKEEPER.

IT was scarcely light when the rector of Saint David's rose from a couch where visions of a most voluptuous nature had filled his sleep.

Having hastily dressed himself, he descended from his room with the intention of seeking the fine frosty air of the garden to cool his heated brain.

But as he proceeded along a passage leading to the landing of the first flight of stairs, he heard a light step slowly descending the upper flight; and the next moment, the voice of Ellen speaking fondly to her child, fell upon his ear.

For nurses and mothers will talk to babes of even a few months old—although the innocents comprehend them not!

Reginald stepped into the recess formed by the door of one of the bed-chambers in that spacious mansion; and scarcely had he concealed himself there when he saw Ellen, with the child in her arms, pass across the landing at the end of the passage, and enter a room on the other side.

She wore a loose dressing-gown of snowy whiteness, which was confined by a band round her delicate waist, and was fastened up to the throat: her little feet had been hastily thrust into a pair of buff morocco slippers; and her long shining hair flowed over her shoulders and down her back.

The licentious eyes of the clergyman followed her from the foot of the stairs to the room which she entered; and even plunged with eager curiosity into that chamber during the moment that the door was open as she went in.

That glance enabled him to perceive that there was a bath in the apartment to which Ellen had proceeded with her child.

Indeed, the young lady, ever since her residence at Markham place, had availed herself of the luxury of the bathing-room which that mansion possessed:

and every morning she immersed her beautiful person in the refreshing element, which she enjoyed in its natural state in summer, but which was rendered slightly tepid for her in winter.

When the rector beheld her descend in that bewitching *negligee*,—her hair unconfined, and floating at will—her small, round, polished ankles glancing between the white drapery and the little slippers,—and the child, with merely a thick shawl thrown about it, in her arms,—and when he observed the bath in that chamber which she entered, he immediately comprehended her intention.

Without a moment's hesitation he stole softly from the recess where he had concealed himself, and approached the door of the bath-room.

His greedy eyes were applied to the key-hole; and his licentious glance plunged into the depths of that sacred privacy.

The unsuspecting Ellen was warbling cheerfully to her child.

She dipped her hand into the water, which Marian had prepared for her, and found the degree of heat agreeable to her wishes.

Then she placed the towels near the fire to warm.

Reginald watched her proceedings with the most ardent curiosity: the very luxury of the unhallowed enjoyment which he experienced caused an oppression at his chest; his heart beat quickly; his brain seemed to throb with violence.

The fires of gross sensuality raged madly in his breast.

Ellen's preparations were now completed.

With her charming white hand she put back her hair from her forehead.

Then, as she still retained the child on her left arm, with her right hand she loosened the strings which closed her dressing-gown round the neck and the band which confined it at the waist.

While thus occupied, she was partly turned towards the door; and all the treasures of her bosom were revealed to the ardent gaze of the rector.

His desires were now inflamed to that pitch when they almost become ungovernable. He felt that could he possess that charming creature, he would care not for the result—even though he forced her to compliance with his wishes, and murder and suicide followed,—the murder of her, and the suicide of himself!

He was about to grasp the handle of the door, when he remembered that he had heard the key turn in the lock immediately after she had entered the room.

He gnashed his teeth with rage.

And now the drapery had fallen from her shoulders, and the whole of her voluptuous form, naked to the waist, was exposed to his view.

He could have broken down the door, had he not feared to alarm the other inmates of the house.

He literally trembled under the influence of his fierce desires.

How he envied,—Oh! how he envied the innocent babe which the fond mother pressed to that bosom—swelling, warm, and glowing!

And now she prepared to step into the bath: but, while he was waiting with fervent avidity for the moment when the whole of the drapery should fall from her form, a step suddenly resounded upon the stairs.

He started like a guilty wretch away from the door: and, perceiving that the footsteps descended from the upper flight, he precipitated himself down the stairs.

Rushing across the hall, he sought the garden, where he wandered up and down, a thousand wild feelings agitating his breast.

He determined that Ellen should be his; but he was not collected enough to deliberate upon the means of accomplishing his resolution,—so busy was his imagination in conjuring up the most voluptuous idealities, which were all prompted by the real scene the contemplation whereof had been interrupted.

He fancied that he beheld the lovely young mother immersed in the bath —the water agitated by her polished limbs—each ripple kissing some charm, even as she herself kissed her babe!

Then he imagined he saw her step forth like a Venus from the ocean—her cheeks flushed with animation—her long glossy hair floating in rich undulations over her ivory shoulders.

"My God!" he exclaimed, at length, "I shall grow mad under the influence of this fascination! One kiss from her lips were worth ten thousand of the meretricious embraces which Cecilia yields so willingly. Oh! Ellen would not surrender herself without many prayers—much entreaty—and, perhaps, force;—but Cecilia falls into my arms without a struggle! Enjoyment with her is not increased by previous bashfulness;—she does not fire the soul by one moment of resistance. But Ellen—so coy, so difficult to win,—so full of confidence in herself, in spite of that one fault which accident betrayed to me,—Ellen, so young and inexperienced in the ways of passion,—Oh! she were a conquest worth every sacrifice that man could make!"

[...]

[Ellen Monroe dresses as a Circassian slave in order to attend a masquerade without being recognized. The episode is a further example of the motif of deceptive surfaces which recurs so often in this narrative. All the participants at the ball are disguised, and the archaic language affected by Ellen is another mode of deception.]

CHAPTER CXLIX.
THE MASQUERADE.

THE evening of the masquerade arrived.

It is not our intention to enter into a long description of a scene the nature of which must be so well known to our readers.

Suffice it to say that at an early hour Old Drury was, within, a blaze of light. The pit had been boarded over so as to form a floor level with the stage, at the extremity of which the orchestra was placed. The spacious arena thus opened, soon wore a busy and interesting appearance, when the masques began to arrive; and the boxes were speedily filled with ladies and gentlemen who, wearing no fancy costumes, had thronged thither for the purpose of beholding, but not commingling with, the diversions of the masquerade.

To contemplate that blaze of female loveliness which adorned the boxes, one would imagine that all the most charming women of the metropolis assembled there by common consent that night; and the traveller, who had visited foreign climes, must have been constrained to admit that no other city in the universe could produce such a brilliant congress.

For the fastidious elegancies of fashion, sprightliness of manners, sparkling discourse, and all the refinements of a consummate civilisation, which are splendid substitutes for mere animal beauty, the ladies of Paris are unequalled; —but for female loveliness in all its glowing perfection—in all its most voluptuous expansion, London is the sovereign city that knows in this respect no rival.

In sooth, the scene was ravishing and gorgeous within Old Drury on the night of which we are writing.

The spacious floor was crowded with masques in the most varied and fanciful garbs.

There were Turks who had never uttered a "Bismillah," and Shepherdesses who had seen more of mutton upon their tables than ever they had in the fields;—Highlanders who had never been twenty miles north of London, and Princesses whose fathers were excellent aldermen or most conscientious tradesmen;—Generals without armies, and Flower-Girls whose gardens consisted of a pot of mignonette on the ledge of their bed-room windows;— Admirals whose nautical knowledge had been gleaned on board Gravesend steamers, and Heathen Goddesses who were devoted Christians;—Ancient Knights who had not even seen so much as the Eglintoun Tournament, and Witches whose only charms lay in their eyes;—and numbers, of both sexes, attired in fancy-dresses which were very fanciful indeed.

Then there was all the usual fun and frolic of a masquerade;—friends availing themselves of their masks and disguises to mystify each other,—witticism and repartee, which if not sharp nor pointed, still served the purpose of eliciting laughter,—and strange mistakes in respect to personal identity, which were more diverting than all.

There was also plenty of subdued whispering between youthful couples; for Love is as busy at masquerades as elsewhere.

The brilliancy of the dresses in the boxes, and the variety of those upon the floor, combined with the blaze of light and the sounds of the music formed a scene at once gay, exhilarating, and ravishing.

At about a quarter before ten o'clock, a masque, attired in the sombre garb of a Carmelite Friar, with his cowl drawn completely over his face, and a long rosary hanging from the rude cord which girt his waist, entered the theatre.

He cast a wistful glance, through the slight opening in his cowl, all around; and, not perceiving the person whom he sought, retired into the most obscure nook which he could find, but whence he could observe all that passed.

At five minutes to ten, a lady, habited as a Circassian slave, and wearing an ample white veil, so thick that it was impossible to obtain a glimpse of her countenance, alighted from a cab at the principal entrance of the theatre.

Lightly she tripped up the steps; but as she was about to enter the vestibule, her veil caught the buttons of a lounger's coat, and was drawn partly off her face.

She immediately re-adjusted it—but not before a gentleman, masked, and in the habit of a Greek Brigand, who was entering at the time, obtained a glimpse of her features.

"What? Ellen *here!*" murmured the Greek Brigand to himself: "I must not lose sight of her!"

Ellen did not however notice that she had been particularly observed; much less did she suspect that she was recognised.

But as she hastened up the great staircase, the Greek Brigand followed her closely.

Although her countenance was so completely concealed, her charming figure was nevertheless set off to infinite advantage by the dualma which she wore, and which, fitting close to her shape, reached down to her knees. Her ample trousers were tied just above the ankle where the graceful swell of the leg commenced; and her little feet were protected by red slippers.

The Brigand who had recognised her, and now watched her attentively, was tall, slender, well made, and of elegant deportment.

Ellen soon found herself in the midst of the busy scene, where her graceful form and becoming attire immediately attracted attention.

"Fair eastern Lady," said an Ancient Knight in a buff jerkin and plumed tocque, "if thou hast lost the swain that should attend upon thee, accept of my protection until thou shalt find him."

"Thanks for thy courtesy, Sir Knight," answered Ellen, gaily: "I am come to confess to a holy father whom I see yonder."

"Wilt thou then abjure thine own creed, and embrace ours?" asked the Knight.

"Such is indeed my intention, Sir Knight," replied Ellen; and she darted away towards the Carmelite Friar whom she had espied in his nook.

The Ancient Knight mingled with a group of Generals and Heathen Goddesses, and did not offer to pester Ellen with any more of his attentions.

"Sweet girl," said Reginald Tracy (whom the reader has of course recognised in the Carmelite Friar), when Ellen joined him, "how can I sufficiently thank you for this condescension on your part."

"I am fully recompensed by the attention you have shown to the little caprice which prompted me to choose this scene for the interview that you desired," answered Ellen.

Both spoke in a subdued tone—but not so low as to prevent the Greek Brigand, who was standing near, from overhearing every word they uttered.

"Mr. Tracy," continued Ellen, "why did you entrust your message of love to another? why could you not impart with your own lips that which you were anxious to communicate to me?"

"Dearest Ellen," answered the rector, "I dared not open my heart to you in person—I was compelled to do so by means of another."

"If your passion be an honourable one," said Ellen, "there was no need to feel shame in revealing it."

"My passion is most sincere, Ellen. I would die for you! Oh! from the first moment that I beheld you by your father's sick-bed, I felt myself drawn towards you by an irresistible influence; and each time that I have since seen you has only tended to rivet more firmly the chain which makes me your slave. Have I not given you an unquestionable proof of my sincerity by meeting you *here?*"

"A proof of your desire to please me, no doubt," said Ellen. "But what proof have I that your passion is an honourable one? You speak of its sincerity

—you avoid all allusion to the terms on which you would desire me to return it."

"What terms do you demand?" asked the rector. "Shall I lay my whole fortune at your feet? Shall I purchase a splendid house, with costly appointments, for you? In a word, what proof of my love do you require?"

"Are you speaking as a man who would make a settlement upon a wife, or as one who is endeavouring to arrange terms with a mistress?" demanded Ellen.

"My sweet girl," replied Reginald, know you not that, throughout my career, I have from the pulpit denounced the practice of a man in holy orders marrying, and that I have more than once declared—solemnly declared—my intention of remaining single upon principle? You would not wish me to commit an inconsistency which might throw a suspicion upon my whole life?"

"Then, sir, by what right do you presume that I will compromise my fair fame for your sake, if you tremble to sacrifice your reputation for mine?" asked Ellen. "Is every compromise to be effected by poor woman, and shall man make no sacrifice for her? Are you vile, or base, or cowardly enough to ask me to desert home and friends to gratify your selfish passion, while you carefully shroud your weakness beneath the hypocritical cloak of a reputed sanctity? Was it to hear such language as this that I agreed to meet you? But know, sir, that you have greatly—oh! greatly mistaken *me*. By the most unmanly—the most disgraceful means you endeavoured to wring from me, a few days ago, a secret which certain expressions of mine, incautiously uttered over what I conceived to be my father's death-bed, had perhaps made you more than half suspect. Those words, which escaped me in a moment of bitter anguish, you treasured up, and converted them into the text for a sermon which you preached me."

"Ellen," murmured the rector; "why these reproaches?"

"Oh! why these reproaches?—I will tell you," continued the young lady, whose bosom palpitated violently beneath the dualma. "Do you think that you did well to press me to reveal the secret of my shame? Do you think that you adopted an honourable means to discover it? When you address me in that saintly manner—a manner which I now know to have been that of a vile hypocrisy—I actually believed you to be sincere; for the time I fancied that a man of God was offering me consolation. Nevertheless, think you that my feeling were not wounded? But an accident made you acquainted with that truth which you vainly endeavoured to extort from me! And now you perhaps believe that I cannot read your heart. Oh! I can fathom its depths but too well. You cherish the idea that because I have been frail once, I am fair game for a licentious sportsman like you. You are wrong, sir—you are wrong. I never erred but once—but once, mark you;—and then not through passion —nor through love—nor in a moment of surprise. I erred deliberately—no matter why. The result was the child whom you have seen. But never, never will I err more—no, not even though tempted, *as I have been*, by the father of my child! You sent to me a messenger—the same filthy hag who pandered to my first, my only disgrace,—you sent her as your herald of love. Ah! sir, you must have already plunged into ways at variance with the sanctity of your character—or you could not have known *her*! [...]"

The individual in the garb of the Greek Bandit drew a pace or two nearer as these words met his ears.

Neither the rector nor Ellen observed that he was paying any attention to them: on the contrary, he appeared to be entirely occupied in contemplating the dancers from beneath his imperious mask.

"Ellen, what means all this?" asked Reginald: "are you angry with me? You alarm me!"

"Suffer me to proceed, that you may understand me fully," said Ellen. "You mercilessly sought to cover me with humiliation, when you rudely probed that wound in my heart, the existence of which an unguarded expression of mine had revealed to you. Your conduct was base—was cowardly; and, as a woman, I eagerly embraced the opportunity to avenge myself."

"To avenge yourself!" faltered Reginald, nearly sinking with terror as these words fell upon his ears. "Yes—to avenge myself," repeated Ellen hastily. "When your messenger—that vile agent of crime—proposed to me that I should grant you an interview, I bethought myself of this ball which I had seen announced in the newspapers. It struck me that if I could induce you— you, the man of sanctity—to clothe yourself in the mummery of a masque and meet me at a scene which you and your fellow-ecclesiastics denounce as one worthy of Satan, I should hurl back with tenfold effect that deep, deep humiliation which you visited upon me. It was for this that I made the appointment here to-night—for this that I retired early to my chamber, and thence stole forth unknown to my father and my benefactor—for this that I now form one at an assembly which has no charms for me! My intention was to seize an opportunity to tear your disguise from you, and allow all present to behold amongst them the immaculate rector of Saint David's. But I will be more merciful to you than you were to me: I will not inflict upon you that last and most poignant humiliation!"

"My God! Miss Monroe, are you serious?" said the rector, deeply humbled; "or is this merely a portion of the pastime?"

"Does it seem sport to you?" asked Ellen: "if so, I will continue it, and wind it up with the scene which I had abandoned."

"For heaven's sake, do not expose me, Miss Monroe!" murmured Reginald, now writhing in agony at the turn which the matter had taken. "Let me depart—and forget that I ever dared to address you rudely."

"Yes—go," said Ellen: "you are punished sufficiently. You possess the secret of my frailty—I possess the secret of your hypocrisy: beware of the use you make of your knowledge of me, lest I retaliate by exposing you."

There was something very terrible in the lesson which that young woman gave the libidinous priest on this occasion; and he felt it in its full force.

Cowering within himself, he uttered not another word, but stole away, completely subdued—cruelly humiliated.

Ellen lingered for a few moments on the spot where she had so effectually chastised the insolent hypocrite; and then hastily retired.

The Greek Brigand made a movement as if he were about to follow her; but, yielding to a second thought, he stopped, murmuring, "By heavens! she is a noble creature!"

[A foreigner calls at Markham Place and requests a few moments' private conversation with Richard. He proposes that Richard should become engaged in the opposition to the despotic rule of the Grand Duke in Castelcicala. The Duke has 'destroyed the freedom of the press, suppressed political meetings, and threatened martial law'.]

CHAPTER CLV.
PATRIOTISM.

It was late in the evening [...] [when] a foreigner called at Markham Place, and requested a few moments' private conversation with our hero.

The request was immediately acceded to; and the foreigner was shown into the library.

He was a man of middle age, with a dark complexion, and was dressed with considerable taste. His air was military, and his manners were frank and open.

He addressed Richard in bad English, and tendered an apology for thus intruding upon him.

Markham, believing him, by his accent and appearance, to be an Italian, spoke to him in that language; and the foreigner immediately replied in the same tongue with a fluency which convinced our hero that he was not mistaken relative to the country to which his visitor belonged.

"The object of my visit is of a most important and solemn nature," said the Italian; "and you will excuse me if I open my business by asking you a few questions."

"This is certainly a strange mode of proceeding," observed our hero; "but you are aware that I must reserve to myself the right of replying or not to your queries, as I may think fit."

"Undoubtedly," said the Italian. "But I am a man of honour; and should our interview progress as favourably as I hope, I shall entrust you with secrets which will prove my readiness to look upon you in the same light."

"Proceed," said Richard: "you speak fairly."

"In the first place, am I right in believing that you were once most intimate with a certain Count Alteroni who resides near Richmond?"

"Quite right," answered Richard.

"Do you, or do you not, entertain good feelings towards that nobleman?"

"The best feelings—the most sincere friendship—the most devoted attachment," exclaimed our hero.

"Are you aware of any particulars in his political history?"

"He is a refugee from his native land," he replied.

"Does he now bear his true name?" he continued.

"If you wish me to place confidence in you," said Richard, "you will yourself answer me one question, before I reply to any farther interrogatory on your part."

"Speak," returned the Italian stranger.

"Do you wish to propose to me any thing whereby I can manifest my attachment to Count Alteroni, without injury to my own character or honour?" demanded Richard.

"I do," said the stranger solemnly. "You can render Count Alteroni great and signal services."

"I will then as frankly admit to you that I am acquainted with *all* which relates to *Count Alteroni*," said Richard, dwelling upon the words marked in italics.

"With *all* which relates to *Prince Alberto of Castelcicala*?" added the stranger, in a significant whisper. "Do we understand each other?"

"So far that we are equally well acquainted with the affairs of his Highness the Prince," answered Richard.

"Right. You have heard of General Grachia?" said the foreigner.

"He is also an exile from Castelcicala," returned Markham.

"He is in England," continued the foreigner. "I had the honour to be his chief aide-de-camp, when he filled the post of Minister of War; and I am Colonel Morosino."

Richard bowed an acknowledgment of this proof of confidence.

"General Grachia," proceeded Morosino, "reached England two days ago. His amiable family is at Geneva. The general visited Prince Alberto yesterday, and had a long conversation with his Highness upon the situation of affairs in Castelcicala. The Grand Duke is endeavouring to establish a complete despotism, and to enslave the country. One province has already been placed under martial law; and several executions have taken place in Montoni itself. The only crime of the victims was a demand for a Constitution. General Grachia represented to his Highness Prince Alberto the necessity of taking up arms in defence of the liberties of the Castelcicalans against the encroachments of despotism. The reply of the Prince was disheartening to his friends and partizans. '*Under no pretence,*' said he, '*would I kindle civil war in my native country.*'"

"He possesses a truly generous soul," said Richard.

"He is so afraid of being deemed selfish," observed the Colonel; "and no one can do otherwise than admire that delicacy and forbearance which shrink from the idea of even appearing to act in accordance with his own personal interests. The Prince has everything to gain from a successful civil war; hence he will not countenance that extremity."

"And what does General Grachia now propose?" asked Markham.

"You are aware that when Prince Alberto was exiled from Castelcicala for having openly proclaimed his opinions in favour of a Constitution and of the extension of the popular liberties, numbers of his supporters in those views were banished with him. *We know* that there cannot be less than two thousand Castelcicalan refugees in Paris and London. Do you begin to comprehend me?"

"I fear that you meditate proceedings which are opposed to the wishes of his Highness Prince Alberto," said Markham.

"The friends of Castelcicalan freedom can undertake what in them would be recognised as *pure patriotism*, but which in Prince Alberto would be deemed the result of his own *personal interests* or *ambition.*"

"True," said Richard: "the distinction is striking."

"The Prince, moreover, in an audience which he accorded to General Gracchia yesterday evening, used these memorable words:—'*Were I less than I am, I would consent to take up arms in defence of the liberties of Castelcicala; but, being as I am, I never will take a step which the world unanimously attribute to selfishness.*'"

"Those were noble sentiments!" ejaculated Markham: "well worthy of him who uttered them."

"And worthy of serving as rules and suggestions for the patriots of Castelcicala!" cried Colonel Morosino. "There are certain times, Mr. Markham," he continued, "when it becomes a duty to take up arms against a sovereign who forgets *his duty* towards his subjects. Men are not born to be slaves; and they are bound to resist those who attempt to enslave them."

"Those words have often been uttered by a deceased friend of mine—Thomas Armstrong," observed Richard.

"Thomas Armstrong was a true philanthropist," said the Colonel; "and were he alive now, he would tell you that subjects who take up arms against a bad prince are as justified in so doing as the prince himself could be in punishing those who violate the laws."

"In plain terms," said Richard, "General Grachia intends to espouse the popular cause against the tyranny of the Grand Duke?"

"Such is his resolution," answered Colonel Morosino. "And now that you have heard all these particulars, you will probably listen with attention to the objects of my present visit."

"Proceed, Colonel Morosino," said Richard. "You must be well aware that, as one well attached to his Highness Prince Alberto, I cannot be otherwise than interested in these communications."

"I shall condense my remarks as much as possible," continued the officer. "General Grachia purports to enter into immediate relations with the Castelcicalans now in London and Paris. Of course the strictest secrecy is required. The eventual object will be to purchase two or three small ships which may take on board, at different points, those who choose to embark in the enterprise; and these ships will have a common rendezvous. When united, they will sail for Castelcicala. A descent upon that territory would be welcomed with enthusiasm by nine-tenths of the population; and the result," added Morosino, in a whisper,—"the inevitable result must be the dethronement of the Grand Duke and the elevation of Alberto to the sovereign seat."

"That the project is practicable, I can believe," said Markham; "that it is just, I am also disposed to admit. But do you not think a bloodless revolution might be effected?"

"We hope that we shall be enabled successfully to assert the popular cause without the loss of life," returned Morosino. "But this can only be done by means of an imposing force, and not by mere negotiation."

"You consider the Grand Duke to be so wedded to his despotic system?" said Markham, interrogatively.

"What hope can we experience from so obstinate a sovereign, and so servile an administration as that of which Signor Pisani is the chief?" demanded the Colonel. "And surely you must allow that patriotism must not have too much patience. By allowing despots to run their race too long, they grow hardened and will then resist to the last, at the sacrifice of thousands of lives and millions of treasure."

"Such is, alas! the sad truth," said Richard. "At the same time a fearful responsibility attaches itself to those who kindle a civil war."

"Civil wars are excited by two distinct motives," returned the Colonel. "In one instance they are produced by the ambition of aspirants to power: in the other, they take their origin in the just wrath of a people driven to desperation by odious tyranny and wrong. The latter is a sacred cause."

"Yes—and a most just one," exclaimed Markham. "If then, I admit that your projects ought to be carried forward, in what way can my humble services be rendered available?"

"I will explain this point to you," answered Colonel Morosino. "General Grachia, myself, and several stanch advocates of constitutional freedom, met to deliberate last evening upon the course to be pursued, after the General had returned from his interview with the Prince at Richmond. We sat in deliberation until a very late hour; and we adopted the outline of the plans already explained to you. We then recognised the necessity of having the cooperation of some intelligent, honourable and enlightened Englishman to aid us in certain departments of our preliminary arrangements. We must raise considerable sums of money upon certain securities which we possess; we must ascertain to what extent the laws of this country will permit our meetings, or be calculated to interfere with the progress of our measures; we must purchase ships ostensibly for commercial purposes; and we must adopt great precautions in procuring from outfitters the arms, clothing, and stores which we shall require. In all these proceedings we require the counsel and aid of an Englishman of honour and integrity."

"Proceed, Colonel Morosino," said Richard, seeing that the Italian officer paused.

"We then found ourselves at a loss where to look for such a confidential auxiliary and adviser; when one of our assembly spoke in this manner:—'I came to this country, as you well know, at the same time as his Highness the Prince. From that period until the present day I have frequently seen his Highness; and I became aware of the acquaintance which subsisted between his Highness and an English gentleman of the name of Richard Markham, who was introduced to his Highness by the late Thomas Armstrong. I am also aware that a misunderstanding arose between the Prince and Mr. Markham: the nature of that misunderstanding I never learnt; but I am aware that, even while it existed, Richard Markham behaved in the most noble manner in a temporary difficulty in which his Highness was involved. I also know that the motive which led to that misunderstanding have been completely cleared away, and that the Prince now speaks in the highest terms of Mr. Richard Markham. Address yourself, then, to Mr. Markham: he is a man of honour; and with him your secret is safe, even if he should decline to meet your views.' Thus spoke our friend last night; and now the cause and object of my visit are explained to you."

"You have spoken with a candour and frankness which go far to conquer any scruples that I might entertain in assisting you," said Richard. "At the same time, so important a matter demands mature consideration. Should I consent to accept the office with which you seek to honour me, I should not be a mere lukewarm agent: I should enter heart and soul into your undertaking; nor should I content myself with simply succouring you in an administrative capacity. Oh! no," added Richard, enthusiastically, as he thought of Isabella, "I would accompany you on your expedition when the time came, and I would bear arms in your most righteous cause."

"Generous young man!" cried the Colonel, grasping our hero's hand with true military frankness:" God grant that your answer may be favourable to us. But pray delay not in announcing your decision."

"This time to-morrow evening I will be prepared to give you an answer," returned Markham.

The Colonel then took his leave, saying, "To-morrow evening I will call again."

[Richard continues his pursuit of the Resurrection Man, and falls in with the Gypsies. Zingary, King of the Gypsies, and his son Morcar, who becomes Richard's right-hand man in Castelcicala, give an account of Gypsy history and inform him that Tidkins is still alive.]

CHAPTER CLXIII.
THE ZINGAREES.

THE old farmer had offered to convey Richard to Hounslow in his own spring-cart, or to provide him with a guide to conduct him thither; but our hero felt so confident of being enabled to find his way back to the town, that he declined both offers.

He walked on, across the fields, pondering upon various subjects,—Isabella, his brother, Reginald Tracy's crimes, and the frightful suicide of Lady Cecilia Harborough,—and with his mind so intent upon these topics, that some time elapsed ere he perceived that he had fallen into a wrong path.

He looked around; but not an object of which he had taken notice in the morning, when proceeding to the farm could he now discover.

Thus he had lost the only means which could assist his memory in regaining the road.

As he stood upon a little eminence, gazing around to find some clue towards the proper direction which he should follow, a light blue wreath of smoke, rising from behind a hill at a short distance, met his eyes.

"There must be a dwelling yonder," he said to himself; "I will proceed thither, and ask my way; or, if possible, obtain a guide."

Towards the light blue cloud which curled upwards, Markham directed his steps; but when he reached the brow of the hill, from the opposite side of which the smoke at first met his eye, he perceived, instead of a cottage as he expected, an encampment of gipsies.

A covered van stood near the spot where two men, two women, and a boy were partaking of a meal, the steam of which impregnated the air with a powerful odour of onions.

The caldron, whence the mess was served up in earthenware vessels, was suspended by means of stakes over a cheerful wood-fire.

We need attempt no description of the persons of those who were partaking of the repast: it will be sufficient to inform the reader that they consisted of King Zingary, Queen Aischa, Morcar, Eva, and this latter couple's son.

They were, however, totally unknown to Richard: but the moment he saw they were of the gipsy tribe, he determined to glean from them any thing which they might know and might choose to reveal concerning the Resurrection Man.

He therefore accosted them in a civil manner, and, stating that he had lost his way, inquired which was the nearest path to Hounslow.

"It would be difficult to direct you, young gentleman, by mere explanation," answered Zingary, stroking his long white beard in order to impress

Richard with a sense of veneration; "but my grandson here shall show you the way with pleasure."

"That I will, sir," exclaimed the boy, starting from the ground, and preparing to set off.

"But perhaps the gentleman will rest himself, and partake of some refreshment," observed Morcar.

"If you will permit me," said Markham, whose purpose this invitation just suited, "I will warm myself for a short space by your cheerful fire; for the evening is chilly. But you must not consider me rude if I decline your kind hospitality in respect to food."

"The gentleman is cold, Morcar," said Zingary: "produce the rum, and hand a snicker."

The King's son hastened to the van to fetch the bottle of spirits; and Markham could not help observing his fine, tall, well-knit frame, to which his dark Roman countenance gave an additional air of manliness—even of heroism.

Richard partook of the spirits, in order to ingratiate himself with the gipsies; and King Zingary then called for his "broseley."

"You appear to lead a happy life," observed Richard, by way of encouraging a conversation.

"We are our own masters, young gentleman," answered Zingary; "and where there is freedom there is happiness."

"Is it true that your race is governed by a King?" asked Markham.

"I am the King of the united races of Bohemians and Egyptians," said Zingary, in a stately manner. "This is my beloved Queen, Aischa: that is my son, Morcar; here is my daughter-in-law, Eva; and that lad is my grandson."

[...]

"I feel highly honoured by the hospitality which your Majesty has afforded me," said Richard, with a bow—an act of courtesy which greatly pleased King Zingary. "On one occasion I was indebted to some of your subjects for a night's lodging at your establishment in St Giles's."

[...]

"I must inform you," resumed Richard, "that I have suffered great and signal injuries at the hands of a miscreant, whom I one night traced to your dwelling in St Giles's."

[...]

[Said Zingary] "But I have one more question to ask our guest. Let him satisfy us how he traced Anthony Tidkins *to* the Palace, and how he learned that Anthony Tidkins was wounded *in* the Palace."

"On that head I must remain silent," said Richard. "I will not invent a falsehood, and I cannot reveal the truth. Be you, however, well assured that I never betrayed the secrets and mysteries of your establishment in Saint Giles's."

"Our guest is an honourable man," observed Morcar. "We ought to be satisfied with what he says."

"I am satisfied," exclaimed the King. "Aischa, answer you the questions which it is now the young man's turn to put to us."

"I wish to know whether Anthony Tidkins died of the wound which he received?" said Richard.

"It was my lot to attend to his wound," began Aischa. "When he was so far recovered as to be able to speak—which was about half an hour after the blood was stanched—he implored me to have him removed from the Palace. He told me a long and pathetic story of persecutions and sufferings which he had undergone; and he offered to enrich our treasury if we would take him beyond the reach of the person who had wounded him. His anxiety to get away was extreme; and it was in consequence of his representations and promises that I prevailed upon the King to issue orders to those who were to leave London with us, to hurry the departure as much as possible. That accounts for the abrupt manner in which we left at such an hour, and for the removal of the wounded man with us. In answer to your direct question, I must inform you that he did *not* die of the wound which he received."

"He did *not* die!" repeated Markham. "Then he is still alive—and doubtless as active as ever in purposes of evil."

"Is he such a bad man?" asked Aischa.

"He belongs to the atrocious gang called *Burkers*," answered Richard, emphatically.

"Merciful heavens!" cried Eva, with a shudder. "To think that we should have harboured such a wretch!"

"And to think that I should have devoted my skill to resuscitate such a demon!" exclaimed Aischa.

"The vengeance of the Zingarees will yet overtake him," said the King, calmly.

"Wherever I meet him, there will I punish him with the stoutest cudgel that I can find ready to hand," cried Morcar, with a fierce air.

"Have you then cause to complain against him?" asked Richard.

"The wretch, sir," answered Morcar, "remained nearly a month in our company, until his wound was completely healed by the skill of my mother. We treated him with as much kindness as if he had been our near and dear relative. One morning, when he was totally recovered, he disappeared, carrying away my father's gold with him."

"The ungrateful villain!" ejaculated Richard. "And he was indebted to your kindness for his life?"

"He was," returned Morcar. "Fortunately, there was but little in the treasury at the time—very little;—nevertheless, it was all we had—and he took our all."

"And you have no trace of him?" said Richard, eagerly.

"Not yet," replied Morcar. "But we have adopted measures to discover him. The King my father has sent a description of his person and the history of his treachery to every chief of our race in the kingdom; and thousands of sharp eyes are on the look-out for him through the length and breadth of the land."

"Heaven be thanked!" exclaimed Markham. "But when you discover him, hand him over to the grasp of justice, and instantly acquaint me with the fact."

"The Zingarees recognise no justice save their own," said the King, in a dignified manner. "But this much I promise you, that the moment we obtain a trace of his whereabouts, we will communicate it to you, and you may act as seemeth good to yourself. We have no sympathy in common with a cowardly murderer."

"None," added Morcar, emphatically.

"I thank you for this promise," said Richard, addressing himself to the King. "Here is my card; and remember that as anxious as I am to bring a miscreant to justice, so ready shall I be to reward those who are instrumental in his capture."

"You may rely upon us, young gentleman," said Zingary. "We will not shield a man who belongs to the miscreant gang of *Burkers*. To-morrow morning I will issue fresh instructions to the various district chiefs, but especially to our friends in London."

"And is it possible that, with no compulsory means to enforce obedience, you can dispose of thousands of individuals at will?" exclaimed Markham.

"Listen, young man," said the King; stroking his beard. "When the great Ottoman monarch, the Sultan Selim, invaded Egypt at the beginning of the sixteenth century, and put to death the Marmeluke sovereign Toumanbai,—when the chivalry of Egypt was subdued by the overwhelming multitudes of warriors who fought beneath the banner of Selim and his great Vizier Sinan-Pacha,—then did a certain Egyptian chief place himself at the head of a chosen body of Mamelukes, and proclaim death and destruction to the Ottomans. This chief was Zingarai. For some time he successfully resisted the troops of Selim; but at length he was compelled to yield to numbers; and Selim put him to death. His followers were proscribed; and those who did not fall into the hands of the Turkish conquerors escaped into Europe. They settled first in Bohemia, where their wandering mode of life, their simple manners, their happy and contented dispositions, and their handsome persons soon attracted notice. Then it was that the Bohemian maidens were proud to bestow their hands upon the fugitive followers of Zingarai; and many Bohemian men sought admittance into the fraternity. Hence the mixed Egyptian and Bohemian origin of the gipsy race. In a short time various members of this truly patriarchal society migrated to other climes; and in 1534 our ancestors first settled in England. Now the gipsy race may be met with all over the globe: in every part of Asia, in the interior of Africa, and in both the Americas, you may encounter our brethren, as in Europe. The Asiatics call us *Egyptians*, the Germans *Zinguener*, the Italians *Cingani*, the Spaniards *Gitanos*, the French *Bohemians*, the Russians *Saracens*, the Swedes and Danes *Tartars*, and the English *Gipsies*. We most usually denominate ourselves the *united races of Zingarees*. And Time, young gentleman, has left us comparatively unchanged; we preserve the primitive simplicity of our manners; our countenances denote our origin; and, though deeply calumniated—vilely maligned, we endeavour to live in peace and tranquillity to the utmost of our power. We have resisted persecution—we have outlived oppression. All Europe has promulgated laws against us; and no sovereigns aimed more strenuously to extirpate our race in their dominions than Henry the Eighth and Elizabeth of England. But as the world grows more enlightened, the prejudice against us loses its virulence; and we now enjoy our liberties and privileges without molestation, in all civilised states."

"I thank you for this most interesting account of your origin," said Richard.

"Henceforth you will know how to recognise the real truth amongst all the wild, fanciful, and ridiculous tales which you may hear or read concerning our race," proceeded Zingary. "From the two or three hundred souls who fled from Egypt and took refuge in Bohemia, as I have ere now explained to you, has sprung a large family, which has increased with each generation; and at the present moment we estimate our total number, scattered over all parts of the earth, at one million and a half."

"I was not aware that you were so numerous," said Richard, much interested by these details. "Permit me to ask whether the members in every country have one sovereign or chief, as those in England?"

"There is a King of the Zingarees in Spain; another in France; a third in Italy; and a fourth in Bohemia. In the northern provinces of European Turkey, in Hungary, and in Transylvania, there is a prince with the title of a Waiewode: the Zingarees of Northern Europe are governed by a Grand, or Great Lord."

[...]

[The Resurrection Man, now returned to his criminal gang, attempts to rob a plague ship which is anchored in the Thames, but he falls ill, and is once again left behind for dead. On board the ship are Richard Markham and his friends, in disguise. They plan to capture Tidkins. In this passage, as often, Reynolds is relying on a folk-memory of earlier horrors, rather than contemporary experience.]

CHAPTER CLXVIII.
THE PLAGUE SHIP.

It wanted half-an-hour to day-break, when the splash of oars alongside met their ears; and in a few moments, Swot, the foreman, made his appearance.

"I've got all ready for you, my boys," said that individual; "a good boat, and two stout chaps to help."

"Have they got their barkers?" demanded the Resurrection Man, thereby meaning pistols.

"A brace each," replied the foreman. "But they must only be used in case of desperation. There's a false bottom to the boat; and there I've stowed away five cutlasses."

"All right!" cried the Buffer. "Now, Moll, you make yourself comfortable till we get back again."

"You're a fool, Jack, not to let me go along with you," observed the woman.

"Nonsense," answered her husband. "Some one must stay on board to take care of the lighter."

"Well, do n't say that I'm a coward—that's all," exclaimed Moll.

"We won't accuse you of that," said the Resurrection Man. "But now let's be off. Where shall we meet you at Gravesend?"

"You know the windmill about a mile below the town," returned Swot, to whom this question was addressed. "Well, close by is the *Lobster Tavern*: and there's a little jetty where the boat can be fastened. Meet me at that tavern at ten o'clock this evening."

"Agreed," answered Tidkins.

The three men then ascended to the deck.

The dawn was at that moment breaking in the east; and every moment mast after mast on the stream, and roof after roof on the shore, appeared more palpably in the increasing light of the young day.

On board of the *Blossom*, the Black was busily employed in washing the deck, and seemed to take no notice of any thing that was passing elsewhere.

"The tide will be with us for nearly three hours," said Tidkins. "Come— we won't lose a moment."

The foreman retraced his steps across the barges to the wharf; while the Resurrection Man and the Buffer, each armed with a pair of pistols, leapt into the boat, that lay alongside the lighter.

Two stout fellows, dressed like watermen, and who were already seated in the boat, instantly plied their sculls.

The skiff shot rapidly away from the vicinity of the barges, and was soon running down the middle of the river with a strong tide.

The morning was beautiful and bright: a gentle breeze swept the bosom of the stream:—and when the sun burst forth in all its effulgent glory, a few fleecy clouds alone appeared on the mighty arch of blue above.

Here and there the mariners on board the outward-bound vessels were busy in heaving up their anchors—a task which they performed with the usual cheering and simultaneous cry,—or in loosening the canvass that immediately became swollen with the breeze.

At distant intervals some steamer, bound to a native or foreign port, walked, as it were, with gigantic strides along the water, raising with its mighty Briarean arms, a swell on either side, which made the smaller craft toss and pitch as if in a miniature whirlpool.

Alas! how many souls have found a resting-place in the depths of those waters; and the spray of the billows seems the tears which old Father Thames sheds as a tribute to their graves! Then, at dark midnight, when the wind moans over the bosom of the river, the plaintive murmurs sound as a lament for those that are gone.

[...]

The sky was covered with dense black clouds: no moon and not a star appeared.

The water seemed as dark as ink.

But the foreman knew every inlet and every jutting point which marked the course of the Thames; and, with the tiller in his hand, he navigated the boat with consummate skill.

Not a word was spoken; and the faint murmurs of the oars were drowned in the whistling of the breeze which now swept over the river.

At length the foreman said in a low whisper, "There is the light of the police-boat."

At a distance of about a quarter of a mile that light appeared, like a solitary star upon the waters.

Sometimes it moved—then stopped, as the quarantine officers rowed, or rested on their oars.

"We must now be within a few yards of the *Lady Anne*," whispered Swot, after another long pause: "take to your arms."

The Buffer cautiously raised a plank at the bottom of the boat, and drew forth, one after another, five cutlasses.

These the pirates silently fastened to their waists.

The boat moved slowly along; and in another minute it was by the side of the plague ship.

The Resurrection Man stretched out his arm, and his hand swept its slimy hull.

There was not a soul upon the deck of the *Lady Anne*; and, as if to serve the purposes of the river-pirates, the wind blew in strong gusts, and the waves splashed against the bank and the vessel itself, with a sound sufficient to drown the noise of their movements.

The bow of the *Lady Anne* lay high upon the bank: the stern was consequently low in the water.

As cautiously as possible the boat was made fast to a rope which hung over the schooner's quarter; and then the five pirates, one after the other, sprang on board.

"Holloa!" cried a boy, suddenly thrusting his head above the hatchway of the after cabin.

Long Bob's right hand instantly grasped the boy's collar, while his left was pressed forcibly upon his mouth; and in another moment the lad was dragged on the deck, where he was immediately gagged and bound hand and foot.

But this process had not been effected without some struggling on the part of the boy, and trampling of feet on that of the pirates.

Some one below was evidently alarmed, for a voice called the boy from the cabin.

Long Bob led the way; and the pirates rushed down into the cabin, with their drawn cutlasses in their hands.

There was a light below; and a man, pale and fearfully emaciated, started from his bed, and advanced to meet the intruders.

"Not a word—or you're a dead man," cried Long Bob, drawing forth a pistol.

"Rascal! what do you mean?" ejaculated the other; "I am the surgeon, and in command of this vessel. Who are you? what do you require? Do you know that the pestilence is here?"

"We know all about it, sir," answered Long Bob.

Then, dropping his weapons, he sprang upon the surgeon, whom he threw upon the floor, and whose mouth he instantly closed with his iron hand.

The pirates then secured the surgeon in the same way as they had the boy above.

"Let's go forward now," cried Swot. "So far, all's well. One of you must stay down here to mind this chap."

The Lully Prig volunteered this service; and the other pirates repaired to the cabin forward.

They well knew that the plague-stricken invalids must be *there*; and when they reached the hatchway, there was a sudden hesitation—a simultaneous pause.

The idea of the pestilence was horrible.

"Well," said the foreman, "are we afraid?"

"No—not I, by God!" ejaculated the Resurrection Man; and he sprang down the ladder.

The others immediately followed him.

But there was no need of cutlass, pistol, or violence there. By the light of the lamp suspended to a beam, the pirates perceived two wretched creatures, each in his hammock,—their cadaverous countenances covered with large sores, their hair matted, their eyes open but glazed and dim, and their wasted hands lying like those of the dead outside the coverlids, as if all the nervous energy were defunct.

Still they were alive; but they were too weak and wretched to experience any emotion at the appearance of armed men in their cabin.

The atmosphere which they breathed was heated and nauseous with the pestilential vapours of their breath and their perspiration.

"These poor devils can do no harm," said the Resurrection Man, with a visible shudder.

The pirates were only too glad to emerge from that narrow abode of the plague; and never did air seem more pure than that which they breathed when they had gained the deck.

"Now then to work," cried Swot. "Wait till we raise this hatch," he continued, stopping at that which covered the compartment of the ship where the freight was stowed away; "and we'll light the darkey when we get down below. You see, that as they had n't a light hung out before, it would be dangerous to have one above: we might alarm the police-boat or the guard ashore."

The hatch was raised without much difficulty: a rope was then made fast to a spar and lowered into the waist of the schooner; and Long Bob slid down.

In a few moments he lighted his dark lantern; and the other three descended one after the other, the Lully Prig, be it remembered, having remained in the after cabin.

And now to work they went. The goods, with which the schooner was laden, were removed, unpacked, and ransacked.

There were gums, and hides, and various other articles which the western coast of Africa produces; but the object of the pirates' enterprise and avarice was the gold-dust, which was contained in two heavy cases. These were, however, at the bottom of all the other goods; and nearly an hour passed before they were reached.

"Here is the treasure—at last!" cried Swot, when every thing was cleared away from above the cases of precious metal. "Come, Tony—do n't waste time with the brandy flask now."

"I've such a precious nasty taste in my mouth," answered the Resurrection Man, as he took a long sup of the spirit. "I suppose it was the horrid air in the fore-cabin."

"Most likely," said the foreman: "come—bear a hand, and let's get these cases ready to raise. Then Long Bob and me will go above and reeve a rope and a pulley to haul 'em up."

The four men bent forward to the task; and as they worked by the dim light of the lantern, in the depths of the vessel, they seemed to be four demons in the profundities of their own infernal abode.

Suddenly the Resurrection Man staggered, and, supporting himself against the side of the vessel, said in a thick tone, "My God! what a sudden headache I've got come on!"

"Oh! it's nothing, my dear feller," cried Swot.

"And now I'm all cold and shivering," said Tidkins, seating himself on a bale of goods; "and my legs seem as if they'd break under me."

The Buffer, the foreman, and Long Bob were suddenly and simultaneously inspired with the same idea; and they cast on their companion looks of mingled apprehension and horror.

"No—it can't be!" ejaculated Swot.

"And yet—how odd that he should turn so," said Bob, with a shudder.

"The plague!" returned the Buffer, in a tone of indescribable terror.

[...]

"The plague!" repeated the Buffer, now unable to contain his fears.

Then he hastily clambered from the hold of the schooner.

"The coward!" cried Swot: "such a prize as this is worth any risk."

But as he yet spoke, Long Bob, influenced by panic fear, sprang after the Buffer, as if Death itself were at his heels, clad in all the horrors of the plague.

"My God! don't leave me here," cried the Resurrection Man, his voice losing its thickness and assuming the piercing tone of despair.

"Every man for himself, it seems," returned Swot, whom the panic had now robbed of all his courage: and in another moment he also had disappeared.

"The cowards—the villains!" said Tidkins, clenching his fists with rage.

Then, by an extraordinary and almost superhuman effort, he raised himself upon his legs: but they seemed to bend under him.

He, however managed to climb upon the packages of goods; and, aided by the rope, lifted himself up to the hatchway. But the effort was too great for his failing strength: his hands could not retain a firm grasp of the cord; and he fell violently to the bottom of the hold, rolling over the bales of merchandize in his descent.

"It's all over!" he muttered to himself; and then he became rapidly insensible.

Meantime the Lully Prig, who was mounting sentry upon the surgeon in the after cabin, was suddenly alarmed by hearing the trampling of hasty steps over head. He rushed on deck, and demanded the cause of this abrupt movement.

"The plague!" cried the Buffer, as he leapt over the ship's quarter into the boat.

The Lully Prig precipitated himself after his comrade; and the other two pirates immediately followed .

"But we are only four!" said the Lully Prig, as the boat was pushed away from the vessel.

"Tidkins has got the plague," answered the Buffer, his teeth chattering with horror and afright.

Fortunately the police-boat was at a distance; and the pirates succeeded in getting safely away from that dangerous vicinity.

But the Resurrection Man remained behind in the plague-ship!

[In Chapter CLXXI, a group of financiers, including Greenwood, Tory Members of Parliament and some aristocrats plan to set up a fraudulent company. The placing of this scene next to that of Tidkins and his gang is intended to suggest an obvious comparison to the reader. Both groups represent the 'enemies of the people', who exploit the industrious classes.]

CHAPTER CLXXI.
MR. GREENWOOD'S DINNER-PARTY.

SOME few days after the events just related, Mr. G. M. Greenwood, M.P., entertained several gentlemen at dinner at his residence in Spring Gardens.

The banquet was served up at seven precisely:—Mr. Greenwood had gradually made his dinner hour later as he had risen in the world; and he was determined that if ever he became a baronet, he would never have that repast put on table till half-past eight o'clock.

On the present occasion, as we ere now observed, the guests were conducted to the dining-room at seven.

The thick curtains were drawn over the windows: the apartment was a blaze of light.

The table groaned beneath the massive plate: the banquet was choice and luxurious in the highest degree.

On Mr. Greenwood's right sate the Marquis of Holmesford—a nobleman of sixty-three years of age, of immense wealth, and notorious for the unbounded licentiousness of his mode of life. His conversation, when his heart was somewhat warmed with wine, bore ample testimony to the profligacy of his morals: seductions were his boast; and he frequently indulged in obscene anecdotes or expressions which even called a blush to the cheeks of his least fastidious male acquaintances.

On Mr. Greenwood's left was Sir T. M. B. Muzzlehem, Bart., M.P., and Whipper-in to the Tory party.

Next to the two guests already described, sate Sir Cherry Bounce, Bart., and the Honourable Major Smilax Dapper—the latter of whom had recently acquired a grade in the service *by purchase*.

Mr. James Tomlinson, Mr. Sheriff Popkins, Mr. Alderman Sniff, Mr. Bubble, Mr. Chouse, and Mr. Twitchem (a solicitor) completed the party.

Now this company, the reader will perceive, was somewhat a mixed one: the aristocracy of the West End, the civic authority, and the members of the financial and legal spheres, were assembled on the present occasion.

The fact is, gentle reader, that this was a "business dinner;" and that you may be no longer kept in suspense, we will at once inform you that when the cloth was drawn, Mr. Greenwood, in a brief speech, proposed "Success to the Algiers, Oran, and Morocco Railway."

The toast was drunk with great applause.

"With your permission, my lord and gentlemen," said Mr. Twitchem, the solicitor, "I will read the Prospectus."

"Yeth, wead the pwothpecthuth, by all meanth," exclaimed Sir Cherry Bounce.

"Strike me—but I am anxious to hear *that*," cried the Honourable Major Dapper.

The solicitor then drew a bundle of papers from his pocket, and in a business-like manner read the contents of one which he extracted from the parcel:—

"ALGIERS, ORAN, AND MOROCCO GREAT DESERT RAILWAY.

"(Provisionally Registered Pursuant to Act.)
"Capital £1,600,000, in 80,000 shares, of £20 each.
"Deposit £2 2s. per Share.

"COMMITTEE OF DIRECTION.

"THE MOST HONOURABLE THE MARQUIS OF HOLMESFORD, G.C.B., CHAIRMAN.

"GEORGE M. GREENWOOD, Esq., M.P., Deputy Chairman.

"Sir T. M. B. Muzzleham, Bart., M.P.
[...]
"Sylvester Popkins, Esq., Sheriff of London.
[...]
"Sir Cherry Bounce, Bart.
"The Honourable Major Smilax Dapper.
[...]

"This Railway is intended to connect the great Cities of Algiers and Morocco, passing close to the populous and flourishing town of Oran. It will thus be the means of transit for passengers and traffic over a most important section of the Great Desert, which, though placed in maps in a more southerly latitude, nevertheless extends to the District through which this Line is to pass.

"The French government has willingly accorded its countenance to the proposed scheme; and the Governor-General of Algeria has expressed his sincere wish that it may be carried into effect.

[…]

The Emperor of Morocco, on one side, and his Excellency the Governor-General of Algeria, on the other, have signified their readiness to grant a strong armed force to protect the engineers and operatives, when laying down the rails, from being devoured by wild beasts, or molested by predatory tribes.

The ex-Emir of Mascara, Abd-el-Kadir, has entered into a bond not to interfere with the works while in progress, nor to molest those who may travel by the Line when it shall be opened; and, in order to secure this important concession on the part of the ex-Emir, the Committee have agreed to make that Prince an annual present of clothes, linen, tobacco, and ardent spirit.

[…]

"By order of the Board,
"SHARPLY TWITCHEM, Secretary."

"On my thoul, there never wath any thing better—conthith, bwief, ekthplithit, and attwactive!" cried Sir Cherry.

"Sure to take—as certain as I'm in Her Majesty's service—strike me!" exclaimed Major Dapper.

"I think you ought to have thrown in something about African beauties," observed the Marquis: "they are particularly stout, you know, being all fed on a preparation of rice called *couscousou*. I really think I must pay a visit to those parts next spring."

"I will undertake to get one of the members of the government to introduce a favourable mention of the project into his speech to-morrow night, in the House," said Sir T. M. B. Muzzlehem: "but you must send him a hundred shares the first thing in the morning."

"That shall be done." answered Mr Twitchem.

"Well, my lord and gentlemen," observed Mr. Greenwood "I think that this little business looks uncommonly well. The project is no doubt feasible—I mean, the shares are certain to go off well. Mr. Bubble and Mr. Chouse will undertake to raise them in public estimation, by the reports they will circulate in Capel Court. Of course, my lord and gentlemen, when they are at a good premium, we shall all sell; and if we do not realise twenty or thirty thousand pounds each—*each*, mark me—then shall you be at liberty to say that the free and independent electors of Rottenborough have chosen as their representative a dolt and an idiot in the person of your humble servant."

[…]

"And now, my lord and gentlemen, we perfectly understand each other. Each takes as many shares as he pleases. When they reach a high premium, each may sell as he thinks fit. Then, when we have realised our profits, we will inform the shareholders that insuperable difficulties prevent the carrying out of the project,—that Abd-el-Kadir, for instance, has violated his agreement and declared against the scheme,—that the Committee of Directors will therefore retain a sum sufficient to defray the expenses already incurred, and that the remaining capital paid up shall be returned to the shareholders."

"That is exactly what, I believe, we all understand," observed Mr. Twitchem. [...]

[One of the aristocrats involved in the fraud is the Marquis of Holmesford. This character is probably based on that of a notorious rake and sensualist, the third Marquis of Hertford, who had died in 1842. He is also said to have inspired Thackeray's Lord Steyne, in *Vanity Fair*.]

CHAPTER CLXXII.
THE MYSTERIES OF HOLMESFORD HOUSE.

THE Marquis and Mr. Greenwood alighted at the door of Holmesford House—one of the most splendid palaces of the aristocracy at the West End.

The Marquis conducted his visitor into a large ante-room at the right hand of the spacious hall.

The table in the middle of the apartment was covered with the most luxurious fruits, nosegays of flowers, preserves, sweetmeats, and delicious wines.

From this room three doors afforded communication elsewhere. One opened into the hall, and had afforded them ingress: the other, on the opposite side, belonged to a corridor, with which were connected the baths; and the third, at the bottom, communicated with a vast saloon, of which we shall have more to say very shortly.

The Marquis said to the servant who conducted him and Mr. Greenwood to the ante-room, "You may retire; and let *them* ring the bell when all is ready."

The domestic withdrew.

The Marquis motioned Greenwood to seat himself at the table; and, filling two coloured glasses with real Johannisburg, he said, "We must endeavour to while away half an hour; and then I can promise you a pleasing entertainment."

The nobleman and the member of Parliament quaffed the delicious wine, and engaged in discourse upon the most voluptuous subjects.

"For my part," said the Marquis, "I study how to enjoy life. I possess an immense fortune, and do not scruple to spend it upon all the pleasures I fancy, or which suggest themselves to me. [...] I have become an Epicurean in my recreations. I invent and devise the means of inflaming my passions; and then—*then* I am young once more. You will presently behold something truly oriental in the refinements on voluptuousness which I have conceived to produce an artificial effect on the temperament when nature is languid and weak."

"Your lordship is right to fan the flame that burns dimly," observed Greenwood, who, unprincipled as he was, could not, however, avoid a feeling of disgust when he heard that old voluptuary, with one foot in the grave, thus shamelessly express himself.

"Wine and women, my dear Greenwood," continued the Marquis, "are the only earthly enjoyments worth living for. I hope to die, with my head pillowed on the naked—heaving bosom of beauty, and with a glass of sparkling champagne in my hand."

"Your lordship would then even defy the pangs of the grim monster who spares no one," said Greenwood.

[...]

Just as the aged voluptuary uttered these words, a silver bell that hung in the apartment was agitated gently by a wire which communicated with the adjoining saloon.

"Now all is in readiness!" exclaimed the Marquis: "follow me."

The nobleman opened the door leading into the saloon, which he entered, accompanied by Greenwood.

He then closed the door behind him.

The saloon was involved in total obscurity; the blackest darkness reigned there, unbroken by a ray.

"Give me your hand," said the Marquis.

Greenwood complied; and the nobleman led him to a sofa at a short distance from the door by which they had entered.

They both seated themselves on the voluptuous cushions.

For some moments a solemn silence prevailed.

At length that almost painful stillness was broken by the soft notes of a delicious melody, which, coming from the farther end of the apartment, stole, with a species of enchanting influence, upon the ear.

Gentle and low was that sweet music when it began; but by degrees it grew louder—though still soft and ravishing in the extreme.

Then a chorus of charming female voices suddenly burst forth; and the union of that vocal and instrumental perfection produced an effect thrilling —intoxicating—joyous, beyond description.

The melody created in the mind of Greenwood an anxious desire to behold those unseen choristers whose voices were so harmonious, so delightful.

The dulcet, metallic sounds agitated the senses with feelings of pleasure, and made the heart beat with vague hopes and expectations.

For nearly twenty minutes did that delicious concert last. Love was the subject of the song,—Love, not considered as an infant boy, nor as a merciless tyrant,—but Love depicted as the personification of every thing voluptuous, blissful, and enchanting,—Love, the representative of all the joys which earth in reality possesses, or which the warmest imagination could possibly conceive,

—Love apart from the refinements of sentiment, and contemplated only as the paradise of sensualities.

[...]

Twenty minutes, we said, passed with wonderful rapidity while that inspiring concert lasted.

But even then the melody did not cease suddenly. It gradually grew fainter and fainter—dying away, as it were, in expiring sounds of silver harmony, as if yielding to the voluptuous entrancement of its own magic influence.

And now, just as the last murmur floated to the ears of the raptured listeners, a bell tinkled at a distance; and in an instant—as if by magic—the spacious saloon was lighted up with a brilliancy which produced a sensation like an electric shock.

At the same time, the music struck up in thrilling sounds once more; and a bevy of lovely creatures, whom the glare suddenly revealed upon a stage at the farther end of the apartment, became all life and activity in a voluptuous dance.

Three chandeliers of transparent crystal had suddenly vomited forth jets of flame; and round the walls the illumination had sprung into existence, with simultaneous suddenness, from innumerable silver sconces.

A glance around showed Greenwood that he was in a vast and lofty apartment, furnished with luxurious ottomans in the oriental style; and with tables groaning beneath immense vases filled with the choicest flowers.

The walls were covered with magnificent pictures, representing the most voluptuous scenes of the heathen mythology and of ancient history.

The figures in those paintings were as large as life; and no prudery had restrained the artist's pencil in the delineation of the luxuriant subjects which he had chosen.

There was Lucretia, struggling—vainly struggling with the ardent Tarquin, —her drapery torn by his rude hands away from her lovely form, which the brutal violence of his mad passion had rendered weak, supple, and yielding.

There was Helen, reclining in more than semi-nudity on the couch to which her languishing and wanton looks invited the enamoured Phrygian youth, who was hastily laying aside his armour after a combat with the Greeks.

There was Messalina—that imperial harlot, whose passions were so insatiable and whose crimes were so enormous,—issuing from a bath to join her lover, who impatiently awaited her beneath a canopy in a recess, and which was surmounted by the Roman diadem.

Then there were pictures representing the various amours of Jupiter,— Leda, Latona, Semele, and Europa—the mistresses of the god—all drawn in the most exciting attitudes, and endowed with the most luscious beauties.

But if those creations of art were sufficient to inflame the passions of even that age when the blood seems frozen in the veins, how powerful must have been the effect produced by those living, breathing, moving houris who were now engaged in a rapid and exciting dance to the most ravishing music.

They were six in number, and all dressed alike, in drapery so light and gauzy that it was all but transparent, and so scanty that it afforded no scope for the sweet romancing of fancy, and left but little need for guesses.

But if their attire were thus uniform, their style of beauty was altogether different.

We must, however, permit the Marquis to describe them to Greenwood—which he did in whispers.

"That fair girl on the right," he said, "with the brilliant complexion, auburn hair, and red cherry lips, is from the north—a charming specimen of Scotch beauty. Mark how taper is her waist, and yet how ample her bust! She is only nineteen, and has been in my house for the past three years. Her voice is charming; and she sings some of her native airs with exquisite taste. The one next to her, with the brown hair, and who is somewhat stout in form, though, as you perceive, not the less active on that account, is an English girl—a beauty of Lancashire. She is twenty-two, and appeared four years ago on the stage. From thence she passed into the keeping of a bishop, who took lodgings for her in great Russell Street, Bloomsbury. The Right Reverend Prelate one evening invited me to sup there; and three days afterwards she removed to my house."

"Not with the consent of the bishop, I should imagine," observed Greenwood, laughing.

"Oh! no—no," returned the Marquis, chuckling and coughing at the same time. "The one who is next to her—the third from the left, I mean—is an Irish girl. Look how beautifully she is made. What vigorous, strong, and yet elegantly formed limbs! And what elasticity—what airy lightness in the dance! Did you observe that pirouette? How the drapery spread out from her waist like a circular fan! Is she not a charming creature?"

"She is, indeed!" exclaimed Greenwood. "Tall, elegant, and graceful."

[…]

"She seems an especial favourite, methinks," whispered Greenwood.

"Yes—I have a sneaking preference for her, I must admit," answered the Marquis. "But I also like my little French girl, who is dancing next to Kathleen. Mademoiselle Anna is an exquisite creature—and such a wanton! What passion is denoted by her burning glances! How graceful are her movements: survey her now—she beats them all in that soft abandonment of limb which she just displayed. Her mother was a widow, and sold the lovely Anna to a French Field-Marshal, when she was only fifteen. The Field-Marshal, who was also a duke and enormously rich, placed her in a magnificent mansion in the Chausseé d'Antin, and settled a handsome sum upon her. But, at his death, she ran through it all, became involved in debt, and was glad to accept my offers two years ago."

[…]

"The beauty next to her is a Spaniard. The white drapery, in my opinion, sets off her clear, transparent, olive skin, to the utmost advantage. The blood seems to boil in her veins: she is all fire—all passion. How brilliant are her large black eyes! Behold the glossy magnificence of her raven hair! Tall—

straight as an arrow—how commanding, and yet how graceful is her form! And when she smiles—now—you can perceive the dazzling whiteness of her teeth. Last of all I must direct your attention to my Georgian—"

"A real Georgian?" exclaimed Greenwood.

"A real Georgian," answered the Marquis; "and, as Byron describes his Katinka, 'white and red.' Her large melting blue eyes are full of voluptuous, lazy, indolent, but not the less impassioned love."

[...]

"What is the name of that beauty?" asked Greenwood.

"Malkhatoun," replied the Marquis; "which means *The Full Moon*. That was the name of the wife of Osman, the founder of the Ottoman empire."

"And how did you procure such a lovely creature?" inquired Greenwood, enraptured with the beauty of the oriental girl.

"Six months ago I visited Constantinople," answered the Marquis of Holmesford; "and in the Slave-Market I beheld that divinity. Christians are not allowed to purchase slaves; but a convenient native merchant was found, who bought her for me. I brought her to England; and she is well contented to be here. Her own apartment is fitted up in an oriental style; she has her Koran, and worships Alla at her leisure; and when I make love to her, she swears by the Prophet Mahommed that she is happy here. The romance of the thing is quite charming."

"Of course she cannot speak English?" said Greenwood interrogatively.

"I beg your pardon," answered the Marquis. "She has an English master, who is well acquainted with Persian, which she speaks admirably; and I can assure you that she is a most willing pupil. But of that you shall judge for yourself presently."

During this conversation, the dance proceeded.

[...]

It was now nearly two in the morning; and Greenwood intimated to the Marquis his wish to retire.

"Just as you please," replied the old voluptuary, [...] "but if you like to accept of a bed here, there is one at your service—and," he added, in a whisper, "you need not be separated from Malkhatoun."

[...]

On a signal from the Marquis, the Scotch, English, French, and Spanish girls withdrew.

"One glass of wine in honour of those houris who have just left us!" cried the nobleman, who was already heated with frequent potations, and inflamed by the contiguity of his Hibernian mistress.

"With pleasure," responded Greenwood.

The toast was drunk; and then the Marquis whispered something to Greenwood, pointing at the same time to the door which opened into the bathing rooms.

The member of Parliament nodded an enraptured assent.

[...]

Greenwood presented his hand to Malkhatoun, and led her away in obedience to the nobleman suggestion.

The door by which they left the ante-room admitted them into a passage dimly lighted with a single lamp, and where several doors opened into bathing apartments.

Into one of those rooms Greenwood and the beautiful Georgian passed.

Shortly afterwards the Marquis and Kathleen entered another.

Here we must pause: we dare not penetrate farther into the mysteries of Holmesford House.

[The criminal gang is once more in the *Boozing-Ken* on Saffron Hill. They discuss the adulteration of drink by landlords, a persistent popular grievance. The Resurrection Man, left for dead on the plague ship, re-appears in disguise and explains to his companions how he escaped.]

CHAPTER CLXXX.
THE "BOOZING-KEN" ONCE MORE.

WE must now direct our readers' attention for a short space to the parlour of the Boozing-Ken on Saffron Hill.

It was nine o'clock in the evening; and, as usual, a motley company was assembled in that place.

A dozen persons, men and women, were drinking the vile compounds which the landlord dispensed as "Fine Cordial Gin," "Treble X Ale," "Real Jamaica Rum," "Best Cognac Brandy," and "Noted Stout."

[...]

"Rum, I should think, is the best of all the spirits," said the Buffer.

"Because you like it best, perhaps?" exclaimed the old man. "Ha! ha! you do n't know that the *Fine Jamaica Rum* is nothing else but the vile low-priced Leeward Island Rum, which is in itself a stomach-burning fire-water of the deadliest quality, and which is mixed by the publican with cherry-laurel water and *devil.*"

"What's *devil?*" asked the Knacker.

"Aye, what is it, indeed. It's nothing but chilie pods infused in oil of vitriol —that's all! But now for *Best Cognac Brandy,*" continued the old man. "Do you think the brandy sold under that name ever saw France—ever crossed the sea? Not it! Aqua ammonia, saffron, mace, extract of almond cake, cherry-laurel water, *devil*, terra japonica, and spirits of nitre, make up the brandy when the British spirit has been well deluged with water. That's your brandy! Ha! ha!"

[...]

"Well, I've learnt someot tonight," said the Knacker.

"Learnt something! You know nothing about it yet," cried the old man, who was on his favourite topic. "You don't know what poison—rank poison—there is in all these cheap wines;—aye, and in the dear ones too, for that matter. Sugar of lead is a chief ingredient! I need n't tell you that sugar of lead is a deadly poison: any fool knows that. Salt enixum and slaked lime are used to clear muddy wine; and litharge gives a sweet taste to wines that are too acid. [...]"

With these words the old man rose, and shuffled out of the room.

His denunciation of the abominable system of doctoring wines, spirits, and malt liquors produced a gloomy effect upon the company whom he left behind.

[...]

The waiter entered, and whispered something to the Buffer.

"By God, how fortunate!" ejaculated this individual, his countenance suddenly assuming an expression of the most unfeigned joy. "Show him up—this minute!"

The waiter disappeared.

"Who is it?" demanded Lafleur.

"The very person we are in want of! He has turned up again:—that feller has as many lives as a cat."

"But who is it?" repeated Lafleur impatiently.

Before the Buffer could answer the question, the door was thrown open, and the Resurrection Man entered the room.

CHAPTER CLXXXI.
THE RESURRECTION MAN AGAIN.

ANTHONY TIDKINS was dressed in a most miserable manner; and his whole appearance denoted poverty and privation. He was thin and emaciated; his eyes were sunken; his cheeks hollow; and his entire countenance more cadaverous and ghastly than ever.

"My dear fellow," cried the Buffer, springing forward to meet him; "how glad I am to see you again. I really thought as how you was completely done for."

"And no thanks to you that I was n't," returned the Resurrection Man gruffly. "Did n't you leave me to die like a dog in the plague-ship?"

"I've been as sorry about that there business, Tony, ever since it happened, as one can well be," said the Buffer: "but if you remember the hurry and bustle of the sudden panic that came over us, I'm sure you won't harbour no ill-feeling."

"Well, well—the least said, the soonest's mended," growled the Resurrection Man, taking his friend's hand.

[...]

When the Resurrection Man and the Buffer were alone together, they brewed themselves strong glasses of brandy and water, lighted their pipes, and naturally began to discourse on what had passed since they last saw each other.

The Buffer related all that had occurred to him after his return to Mossop's wharf,—how he had been pursued by the three men belonging to the *Blossom*,—how one turned out to be Richard Markham, another a policeman in disguise, and the third Morcar,—how they had vainly searched the *Fairy* to discover Anthony Tidkins. [...]

"Since then," added the Buffer, "I have not been doing much, and was deuced glad when Greenwood's valet came to me last evening and made an appointment with me for to-night to talk upon some business of importance. You know what that business is; and I hope it will turn up a trump—that's all."

"Then the whole affair of the *Blossom* was a damnation plant?" cried the Resurrection Man, gnashing his teeth with rage. "And that hated Markham was at the bottom of it all? By the thunders of heaven, I'll have the most deadly vengeance! But how came you to learn that Morcar was one of the three?"

"Because I heard Markham call him by that name when they all boarded the *Fairy*; and I instantly remembered the gipsy that you had often spoken about. But what do you think? He was the Black—the counterfeit Brummagem scoundrel that could neither speak nor hear. The captain was the blue-bottle; and Markham, I s'pose, had kept down below during the time the *Blossom* was at Mossop's. It was a deuced good scheme of theirs; and if you had n't been left in the plague-ship, it might have gone precious hard with you."

"Well said, Jack," observed the Resurrection Man. "Out of evil sometimes comes good, as the parsons say. But that shan't prevent me from doing Master Richard Markham a turn yet."

"You must go to Italy, then," said the Buffer laconically.

"What gammon's that?" demanded Tidkins.

"Why, I happened yesterday morning to look at a newspaper in the parlour down stairs, and there I read of a battle which took place in some country with a cursed hard name in Italy, about three weeks ago; and what should I see but a long rigmarole about the bravery of "*our gallant fellow-countryman, Mr Richard Markham,*" and "*the great delight it would be to all the true friends of freedom to learn that he was not retained among the prisoners.*"

"But perhaps he was killed in the battle, the scoundrel?" said the Resurrection Man.

"No, he was n't," answered the Buffer; "for the moment I saw that all this nonsense was about him, I read the whole article through; and I found that he *had* been taken prisoner, but had either been let go or had made his escape. No one, however, seems to know what's become of him;—so p'r'aps he's on his way back to this country."

"I'd much sooner he'd get hanged or shot in Italy," said the Resurrection Man. "But if he ever does come home again, I'll be square with him—and no mistake."

"Now you know all that has happened to me, Tony," exclaimed the Buffer, "have the kindness to tell us how you got out of that cursed scrape in the *Lady-Anne*."

"I will," said the Resurrection Man, refilling his glass. "After you all ran away in that cowardly fashion, I tried to climb after you; but I fell back insensible. When I awoke, the broad day-light was shining overhead; and a boy was looking down at me from the deck. He asked me what I was doing there. I rose with great difficulty; but I was much refreshed with the long sleep I had enjoyed. The boy disappeared; and in a few minutes the surgeon came and hailed me down the hatchway. I begged him to help me up out of the hold, and I would tell him every thing. He ordered me to throw aside my pistols and cutlass, and he would assist me to gain the deck. I did as he commanded me. He and the boy then lowered a rope, with a noose; I put my foot in the noose, grasped the rope tight, and was hauled up. The surgeon instantly presented a pistol, and said, '*If you attempt any violence, I'll shoot you through the head.*' I declared that nothing was farther from my intention, and begged him to give me some refreshment. This request was complied with; and I then felt so much better, that I was able to walk with comparative ease. It, however, seemed as if I had just recovered from a long illness: for I was weak, and my head was giddy. I told the surgeon that I was an honest hardworking man; that I had come down to Gravesend the day before to see a friend; and had fallen in with some persons who offered me a job for which I should be well paid; that I assented, and accompanied them to their boat; that when I understood the nature of their business, I declared I would have nothing more to do with it; that they swore they would blow my brains out if I made any noise; that I was compelled to board the ship with them; that when some sudden sound alarmed them as they were examining the goods in the hold, they knocked me down with the butt-end of a pistol; and that I remembered nothing more until the boy awoke me by calling out to me from the deck. The surgeon believed my story, and said, '*A serious offence has been perpetrated, and you must declare all you know of the matter before a magistrate.*' I of course signified my willingness to do so, because I saw that the only chance of obtaining my liberty was by gaining the good opinion of the surgeon; for he had a loaded pistol in his hand—I was unarmed—and the policeboat was within hail. '*But, according to the quarantine laws,*' continued the surgeon, '*you cannot be permitted to leave the vessel for the present; and what guarantee have I for your good behaviour while you are on board?*'"

"That was a poser," observed the Buffer.

"No such thing," said the Resurrection Man. "I spoke with so much apparent sincerity, and with such humility, that I quite gained the surgeon's good opinion. [...] '*I really do believe you to be an honest man,*' exclaimed the surgeon; '*but I must adopt some precaution. You shall be at large during the day; and I think it right to give you due notice that I shall carry loaded pistols constantly with me.* [...]' I affected to thank him very sincerely for his kindness in leaving me at liberty during the day; and he then repaired to the fore-cabin to attend to his patients."

"Had n't he got the plague himself?" inquired the Buffer.

"No: but the fœtid atmosphere of the fore-cabin, to which he was compelled so frequently to expose himself, had made him as emaciated and as pale as if he had only just recovered from the malady. [...]"

"Well—and how did you escape after all?"

"I remained three or four days on board, before I put any scheme into force, although I planned a great many. At night I could do nothing, because I was a prisoner in the hold; and during the day the police-boat was constantly about, besides the sentinels on land. The surgeon always made me go down into the hold while it was still day-light; and never let me out again until after sun-rise; so that I was always in confinement during the very time that I might contrive something to effect my escape from that infernal pest-ship. But the surgeon seemed afraid to trust me when it was dark. I never passed such a miserable time in my life. The slight touch that I had experienced of the plague—for it could have been nothing else—kept me in a constant fear lest it should return with increased force. How often did I mutter the most bitter curses against you and the other pals for abandoning me; —but now, in consequence of what you told me of the plant that Markham had set a-going against me, I am not sorry to think that I was left behind in the plague-ship. One evening—I think it was the fifth after my first entrance into the vessel—I observed that it was growing darker and darker; and yet the surgeon did not appear on deck with his loaded pistol to send me below. The boy was walking about eyeing me suspiciously; and at length he went down into the after-cabin. It struck me that the surgeon was probably indulging in a nap, and that the lad would awake him. It was not quite dark; but still I fancied that it was dusk enough to leap from the bow of the ship, which part of the vessel was high and dry, without alarming the sentinels on shore. At all events the chance was worth the trial. Seizing a handspike, I hurried forward, and sprang from the ship. Then, without losing a moment, I ran along the bank towards Gravesend, as rapidly as I could. In a short time I knew that I was safe. I hurled the handspike into the Thames, and walked on to the *Lobster Tavern*. There I obtained a bed—for I had plenty of ready money in my pocket. My only regret was that I had not been able to bring away any of the gold-dust with me."

"Why did n't you knock the surgeon and the boy on the head, and help yourself?" demanded the Buffer.

"So I should if I had seen a chance," replied the Resurrection Man; "but I was so weak and feeble all the time I was on board, that I was no match even for the young lad; and the surgeon always kept at such a distance, with a loaded pistol ready cocked in his hand, when I was ordered into the hold of an evening, or called up of a morning, that there was n't a shadow of a chance. Well, I slept at the *Lobster Tavern*, and departed very early in the morning— long before it was day-light. I thought that London would be too hot for me, after every thing that had lately occurred; and I resolved to pay a visit to Walmer—my own native place. I was still too weak to walk many miles without resting; and so I took nearly four days to reach Walmer. Besides, I kept to the fields, and avoided the high road as much as possible. I took up my quarters at a small inn on the top of Walmer hill, and then made inquiries concerning all the people I had once known in or about the village. I have often related the former incidents of my life to you; and you will therefore recollect the baronet who was exchequered for smuggling, and was welcomed with open arms by his friends, when he paid the fine. You also remember all that occurred between him and me. I found that he had married his cook-maid, who ruled him with a rod of iron; and that the *'very select society'* of Walmer and Deal had all cut him on account of that connexion, which was much worse in their eyes than all the smuggling in which he had been engaged. In fact, he was a hero when prosecuted for smuggling; but now *no decent persons could associate with him*, since he had married his scullion. In a word, I learnt that he was as miserable as I could have wished him to be."

"And did n't you inquire after your friend the parson?" demanded the Buffer.

"You may be sure I did," returned the Resurrection Man. "He had made himself very conspicuous for refusing the sacrament to a young woman who was seduced by her lover, and had an illegitimate child; and the *'select society'* of Walmer greatly applauded him for his conduct. At length, about a year ago, it appears, this most particular of all clergymen was discovered by a neighbouring farmer in too close a conversation with the said farmer's wife; and his reverence was compelled to decamp, no one knows where. He, however, left his wife and children to the public charity. [...] I stayed at Walmer for nearly a week; and then departed suddenly for Ramsgate, with the contents of the landlord's till in my pocket. At Ramsgate I put up at a small public-house where I was taken dreadfully ill. For four months I was confined to my bed; and both landlord and landlady were very kind to me. At length I slowly began to recover; and, when I was well enough to walk abroad, I used to go upon the beach to inhale the sea-air. It was then summer time; and bathing was all the rage. I never was more amused in my life than to see the ladies, old as well as young, sitting on the beach, to all appearance deeply buried in the novels which they held in their hands, but in reality watching, with greedy eyes, the men bathing scarcely fifty yards off."

"You don't mean to say that?" cried the Buffer.

"I do indeed, though," returned Tidkins. "It was the commonest thing in the world for elderly dames and young misses to go out walking along the beach, or to sit down on it, close by the very spot where the men bathed, although there were plenty of other places to choose either for rambling or reading. Well, I stayed two more months at Ramsgate; and as the landlord and landlady of the public-house had behaved so kind to me, I took nothing from them when I went away. I merely left my little account unsettled. I walked over to Margate, with the intention of taking the steamer to London Bridge; but just as I was stepping on the jetty, some one tapped me on the shoulder, and, turning round, I beheld my landlord of the little inn on the top of

Walmer hill. All my excuses, promises, and entreaties were of no avail: the man collared me—a crowd collected—a constable was sent for, and I was taken before a magistrate. Of course I was committed for trial, and sent across in a cart to Canterbury gaol. There I lay till the day before yesterday, when the sessions came on. By some extraordinary circumstance or another, no prosecutor appeared before the Grand Jury; and I was discharged. I resolved to come back to London;—for, after all, London is the place for business in our way. With all its police, it's the best scene for our labours. So here I am; and the moment I set foot in this ken, I find employment waiting for me."

[…]

"Where are you hanging out now, Jack?" inquired the Resurrection Man.

"Me and Moll has got a room in Greenhill's Rents—at the bottom of Saint John's Street, you know," was the answer.

"Well, I shall sleep here to-night," said the Resurrection Man; "and by six o'clock to-morrow morning I shall expect you."

[As before, the interpolated 'New Year's Day' episode contains specific political rhetoric concerning the state of the nation; in this case a programme of self-education for the working classes is advocated. The 'New Cut' episode gives an unusually detailed and convincing account of the vitality and variety of street life and popular entertainment in a notorious London locality.]

CHAPTER CLXXXV.
ANOTHER NEW YEAR'S DAY.

It was the 1st of January, 1841.

If there be any hour in the life of man when he ought to commune with his own heart, that proper interval of serious reflection is to be found on New Year's Day.

[…]

An oligarchy has cramped the privileges and monopolised the rights of a mighty nation.

Behold the effects of its infamous Poor-Laws;—contemplate the results of the more atrocious Game-Laws;—mark the consequences of the Corn-Laws.

The Poor-Laws! Not even did the ingenuity of the Spanish or Italian Inquisitions conceive a more effectual method of deliberate torture and slow death, than the fearful system of mental-abasement and gradient starvation invented by England's legislators. When the labourer can toil for the rich no longer, away with him to the workhouse! […] When the poor widow, whose sons have fallen in the ranks of battle or in defence of the wooden walls of England, is deprived of her natural supporters, away with her to the workhouse!

The workhouse is a social dung-heap on which the wealthy and great fling those members of the community whose services they can no longer render available to their selfish purposes.

THE GAME-LAWS! Never was a more atrocious monopoly than that which reserves the use of certain birds of the air or animals of the earth to a small and exclusive class. [...] The Game-Laws have fabricated an offence which fills our prisons—as if there were not already crimes enough to separate men from their families and plunge them into loathsome dungeons. [...] The Game-Laws are a rack whereon the aristocracy loves to behold its victims writhing in tortures, and when the sufferers are compelled to acknowledge as a heinous crime a deed which has in reality no moral turpitude associated with it.

THE CORN-LAWS! [...] What! liberty in connexion with the vilest monopoly that ever mortal policy conceived? Impossible! England manufactures articles which all the civilised world requires; and other states yield corn in an abundance that defies the possibility of home consumption. And yet an inhuman selfishness has declared that England shall not exchange her manufactures for that superfluous produce.

[...]

Although our legislators—trembling at what they affect to sneer at under the denomination of "the march of intellect"—obstinately refuse to imitate enlightened France by instituting a system of national education,—nevertheless, the millions of this country are now instructing themselves!

Honour to the English mechanic—honour to the English operative: each alike seeks to taste of the tree of learning, "whose root is bitter, but whose friuts are sweet!"

Thank God, no despotism—no tyranny can arrest the progress of that mighty intellectual movement which is now perceptible amongst the industrious millions of these realms.

And how excellent are the principles of that self-instruction which now tends to elevate the moral condition of the country. It is not confined within the narrow limits which churchmen would impose: it embraces the sciences —the arts—all subjects of practical utility,—its aim being to model the mind on the solid basis of Common Sense.

[...]

There breathes not a finer specimen of the human race than a really enlightened and liberal-minded Englishman. But if *he* be deserving of admiration and applause, who has received his knowledge from the lips of a paid preceptor—how much more worthy of praise and respect is *the self-instructed mechanic!*

[...]

CHAPTER CLXXXVI.
THE NEW CUT.

AT nine o'clock on the same evening, Mr Greenwood, muffled in a cloak, alighted from a hackney-cab in the Waterloo Road at the corner of the New Cut.

That wide thoroughfare which connects the Waterloo and Blackfriars' Roads, is one of the most busy and bustling, after its own fashion, in all London.

Nowhere are the shops of a more miscellaneous nature: nowhere are the pathways so thronged with the stalls and baskets of itinerant venders.

The ingenuity of these petty provision-dealers adapts the spoilt articles of the regular fishmongers and butchers to servicable purposes in the free market of the New Cut. The fish is cut in slices and fried in an oil or butter whose rancid taste obviates the putrid flavour and smell of the comestible; and the refuse scraps from the butchers' shops are chopped up to form a species of sausage-balls called "faggots." Then the grease, in which the racy slices of fish and savoury compounds of lights and liver have been alike cooked, serves to fry large rounds of bread, which, when thus prepared, are denominated "sop in the pan." Of course these culinary delights are prepared by the vendors in their own cellars or garrets hard by; but when conveyed to the miscellaneous market in the New Cut, the luxuries impart a greasy and sickening odour to the air.

It is perfectly wonderful to behold the various methods in which the poor creatures in that throughfare endeavour to obtain an honest livelihood; and, although their proceedings elicit a smile—still, God pity them! they had better ply their strange trades thus than rob or beg!

There may be seen, for instance, a ragged urchin holding a bundle of onions in his hand, and shouting at the top of his shrill voice, "Here's a ha'porth!"— and, no matter how finely dressed the passer-by, he is sure to thrust the onions under his or her very nose, still vociferating, "Here's a ha'porth!" Poor boy! he thinks every one *must* want onions!

The immediate vicinity of the Victoria Theatre is infested with women who offer play-bills for sale, and who seem to fancy it impossible that the passers-by can be going elsewhere than to the play.

Here an orange-girl accosts a gentleman with two or three of the fruit in her hand, but with a significant look which gives the assurance that her real trade is of a less innocent nature:—there a poor woman with an array of children before her offers lucifer-matches, but silently appeals for alms.

A little farther on is a long barrow covered with toys; and a tall man without a nose, shouts at intervals, "Only a penny each! only a penny each!" Some of these gim-cracks excite astonishment by their extreme cheapness; but they are chiefly made by the convicts in Holland, and are exported in large quantities to England.

In the middle of the road, a man with stentorian voice offers "A hundred songs for a penny;" and, enumerating the list, he is sure to announce the "Return of the *H*admiral" amongst the rest.

Nearly opposite the Victoria Theatre there is an extensive cook's-shop; and around the window stands a hungry crowd feasting their eyes on the massive joints which are intended to feast the stomach.

[...]

Perhaps a new baker's shop is opened in the New Cut; and then a large placard at the window announces that "a glass of gin will be given to every purchaser of a quartern loaf." The buyers do not pause to reflect that the price of the cordial is deducted from the weight of the bread.

The pawnbrokers' shops seem to drive a most bustling trade in the New Cut; and the fronts of their establishments present a more extensive and miscellaneous assortment of second-hand garments, blankets, handkerchiefs, and sheets, than is to be seen elsewhere.

The influx and efflux of people at the public-houses and gin-shops constitute not the least remarkable feature of that neighbourhood, where everything is dirty and squalid, yet where every one appears able to purchase intoxicating liquor!

On the southern side of the New Cut there are a great many second-hand furniture shops, the sheds wherein the articles are principally exposed being built against the houses in a fashion which gives the whole, when viewed by the glaring of the gas-lights, the appearance of a bazaar or fair.

The New Cut is always crowded; but the multitude is not entirely in motion. Knots of men congregate here, and groups of women there—the posts at the corners of the alleys and courts, or the doors of the gin-shops, being the most favourite points of such assembly.

The edges of the path-ways are not completely devoted to provision dealers. Penny peep-shows, emblazoned with a coloured drawing representing the last horrible murder,—itinerant quacks with "certain remedies for the toothach,"—stalls covered with odd numbers of cheap periodical publications,— old women seated on stools, behind little trays containing combs, papers of needles, reels of cotton, pack-thread, stay-laces, bobbin, and such-like articles, —men with cutlery to sell, and who flourish in their hands small knives with innumerable blades sticking out like the quills on a porcupine,—these are also prominent features in that strange market.

In some conspicuous place most likely stands a caravan, surmounted by a picture representing a colossal giant and a giantess to match, with an assurance in large letters that the originals may be seen inside :—then, as the eye wanders from the enormous canvass to the caravan itself, and compares their sizes, the mind is left in a pleasing state of surprise how even *one* of the Brobdignab marvels—let alone *two*—could possibly stow itself away in that diminutive box.

Branching off from the New Cut, on either side, are numerous narrow streets,—or rather lanes, of a very equivocal reputation; their chief characteristics being houses of ill-fame, gin-shops, beer-shops, marine-store dealers, pawnbrokers, and barbers' establishments.

[...]

Such are the New Cut and its tributary lanes.

And it was now along the New Cut that Mr. Greenwood, enveloped in his cloak, was pursuing his way.

He scarcely noticed the turmoil, bustle, and business of that strange thoroughfare; for he was too much absorbed in his own meditations.

The truth was, that his affairs—once so gloriously prosperous—were now rendered desperate by various reverses; and he was about to seek a desperate means of retrieving them.

The reader cannot have failed to observe that the characters of George Montague Greenwood and Richard Markham stand out from our picture of London Life in strong contrast with each other; and it is not the less remarkable that while the former was rising rapidly to wealth, rank and eminence, the latter was undergoing persecutions and sinking into comparative poverty. Now—at the epoch which we are describing—the tables seem to have turned; for while George Montague Greenwood is about to seek a desperate remedy for his desperate affairs, Richard Markham is leading a gallant army over the fertile plains of Castelcicala.

The former, then, may be deemed the personification of vice, the latter the representative of virtue.

They had chosen separate paths:—the sequel will fully demonstrate which of the two characters had selected the right one.

In the meantime we will continue our narrative.

[Greenwood calls at the house of a disreputable moneylender, Mr Pennywhiffe.]

"I require your aid in a most important business," answered Greenwood, taking a chair, and throwing back his cloak. "To-morrow I must raise twenty or twenty-five thousand pounds, for three or four months—upon bills—*good bills*, Mr. Pennywhiffe."

"To be deposited?" asked that individual.

"To be deposited," replied Greenwood.

"Shall you withdraw them in time?"

"Decidedly. I will convert the money I shall thereby raise into a hundred thousand," exclaimed Greenwood.

"My commission will be heavy for such a business," observed Pennywhiffe; "and *that*, you know, is ready money."

"I am aware of it, and am come provided. Name the amount you require."

"Will two hundred hurt you?" said Pennywhiffe. "Remember—the affair is a serious one."

"You shall have two hundred pounds," exclaimed the Member of Parliament, laying his pocket-book upon the table.

[Pennywhiffe forges bills, which Greenwood will use to obtain credit.]

But now the ingenuity of Mr Pennywhiffe mainly exhibited itself. Each bill was filled up with a different ink and a different pen; and so skilful a caligrapher was he, that the most astute judge of writing could not possibly have perceived that they were all written by the same hand. Then, by the aid of red ink, a few flourishes, and little circles containing initial letters or figures as if each document corresponded with some particular entry in some particular leger or bill-book, the papers speedily assumed a very business-like appearance.

[...]

"The bills are excellent in every point save one," observed Greenwood.

"Which is that?" demanded the caligrapher.

"They look *too new*—the paper is too clean."

"I know it," returned Mr. Pennywhiffe; "but the process is not entirely complete."

He rose and threw a quantity of small coal upon the fire, so as to smother the flame, and create a dense smoke. He then passed each bill several times through the smoke, until they acquired a slightly dingy hue. Lastly, he placed them between the leaves of a portfolio scented with musk, so as to take off the odour of the smoke; and the entire process was terminated.

[...]

[In the following episode Ellen Monroe has stolen a pocketbook recording the forged bills which Greenwood intends to pass off as real. With characteristic enterprise, she has threatened to reveal the contents of the book, and has forced him to marry her in order to legitimize their child.]

CHAPTER CLXXXVII.
THE FORGED BILLS.

[...]

[A] few minutes before ten o'clock, a post-chaise stopped at the gate of the parish church of Hackney; and Mr. Greenwood alighted.

He was pale; and the quivering of his lip denoted the agitation of his mind.

The clock was striking ten, when a hackney-coach reached the same point.

Greenwood hastened to the door, and assisted Mrs. Wentworth and Ellen Monroe to descend the steps.

As he handed out the latter, he said, in a hurried whisper, "You have the pocket-book with you?"

"I have," answered Ellen.

The party then proceeded to the church, the drivers of the vehicles being directed to await their return at a little distance, so as not to attract the notice of the inhabitants.

The clergyman and the clerk awaited the arrival of the nuptial party.
The ceremony commenced—proceeded—and terminated.
Ellen was now a wife!
[...]

[Richard Markham now commands the 'Constitutionalist Army' in Castelcicala against the despotic Grand Duke, and wins a famous victory. By popular acclaim, he is appointed Regent until the return of Alberto.]

CHAPTER CLXXXIX.
THE BATTLE OF MONTONI.

THE morning of the memorable 23d of January dawned, and the bells were ringing in every tower, when three cannon gave the signal for the fight, and the battle of Montoni began.

The light troops of the Constitutionalists opened a smart fire upon the Austrians, and dislodged a strong corps from a position which it occupied on the bank of a small stream. In consequence of this first success, Richard was enabled to stretch out his right wing without restraint; and, remembering the operation effected by the Cingani at Abrantani, he instantly despatched that faithful corps, with a battalion of rifles, to make the circuit of the village, and endeavour to turn the Austrians' left flank.

The left wing of the Constitutionalists soon came to close quarters with the right wing of the enemy; and a desperate struggle ensued to decide the occupancy of the sand-banks, which were quite hard and a desirable position for artillery-pieces. Colonel Cossario, who commanded in that point, succeeded, after a desperate conflict, in repulsing the Austrians; and twenty field-pieces were dragged on the sand-banks. These speedily vomited forth the messengers of destruction; and the dread ordnance scattered death with appalling rapidity.

The Grand Duke, seeing that his cause was hopeless if that dreadful cannonade was not stopped, ordered four battalions of grenadiers to attack the position. Markham, who was riding about the field,—now issuing orders—now taking a part in the conflict,—observed the manœuvre, and instantly placed himself at the head of two regiments of cuirassiers with a view to render it abortive.

Then commenced one of the most deadly spectacles ever performed on the theatre of the world. The Grand Duke sent a strong detachment of Austrian Life-Guards to support the grenadiers; and the two squadrons of cavalry came into fearful collision. The Constitutionalists were giving way, when Markham precipitated himself into the thickest of the fight, cleared every thing before him, and seized the Austrian colours. Morcar was immediately by his side: the sword of a Life-Guard already gleamed above our hero's head

—another moment, and he would have been no more. But the faithful gipsy warded off the blow, and with another stroke of his heavy brand nearly severed the sword-arm of the Life-Guard. Richard thanked him with a rapid but profoundly expressive glance, and, retaining his hold on the Austrian banner, struck the ensign-bearer to the ground.

This splendid achievement re-animated the Constitutional cuirassiers; and the Austrian Life-Guards were shattered beyond redemption.

Almost at the same time, the Cignani and rifles effected their movement on the left wing of the enemy, and threw it into confusion. This disorder was however retrieved for about the space of two hours; when the Marquis of Estella, with his cuirassiers, was enabled to take a part in the conflict in that direction. This attack bore down the Austrians. They formed themselves into a square; but vain were their attempts to oppose the impetuosity with which the cuirassiers charged them. By three o'clock in the afternoon, the left wing of the enemy was overwhelmed so completely that all the endeavours of Marshal Herbertstein to rally his troops were fruitless.

Then, resolved to perish rather than surrender, the Austrian commander met an honourable death in the ranks of battle.

In the centre the conflict raged with a fury which seemed to leave room for doubt relative to the fortune of the day, notwithstanding the important successes already obtained by the Constitutionalists.

The Grand Duke had flown with a choice body of cavalry to support the compact masses that were now fighting for the victory: he himself rode along the ranks—encouraging them—urging them on—promising rewards.

For nearly four hours more did the battle last in this point; but at length our hero came up with his cuirassiers, all flushed with conquest elsewhere; and his presence gave a decided turn to the struggle.

Rushing precipitately on—bearing down all before them—thundering along with an irresistible impetuosity, the cuirassiers scattered confusion and dismay in the ranks of their enemies. And ever foremost in that last struggle, as in the first, the waving heron's plume which marked his rank, and the death-dealing brand which he wielded with such fatal effect, denoted the presence of Richard Markham.

He saw that the day was his own;—the Austrians were flying in all directions;—confusion, disorder, and dismay prevailed throughout their broken corps and shattered bands;—Marshal Herbertstein was numbered with the slain;—the Grand Duke fled;—and at eight o'clock in the evening Montoni was delivered.

Darkness had now fallen on the scene of carnage; but still the Constitutionalists pursued the Austrian fugitives; and numbers were taken ere they could reach the river. A comparatively small portion of the vanquished succeeded in throwing themselves into the boats that were moored on the southern bank, or in gaining the adjacent bridges; and those only escaped.

Montoni saluted its deliverance with salvoes of artillery and the ringing of bells; and the joyous sounds fell upon the ears of the Grand Duke, as, heart-broken and distracted, he pursued his way, attended only by a few faithful followers, towards the frontiers of that State from which his rashness and despotism had driven him for ever.

Meantime, Richard Markham issued the necessary orders for the safeguard of the prisoners and the care of the wounded; and, having attended to those duties, he repaired to the village before mentioned, where he established his temporary head-quarters at the *chateau* of a nobleman devoted to the Constitutional cause

Then, in the solitude of the chamber to which he had retired, and with a soul full of tenderness and hope, as in the morning in the grove of Legino,—he addressed a letter to the Princess—the only joy of his heart, the charming and well-beloved Isabella:—

Head Quarters, near Montoni. Jan. 23.
"Eleven at night.

"Long ere this will reach thee, dearest one, thou wilt have heard, by means of telegraphic dispatch through France, of the great victory which has made me master of Castelcicala. If there be any merit due unto myself, in consummating this great aim, and conducting this glorious cause to its final triumph, it was thine image, beloved Isabella, which nerved my arm and gave me intelligence to make the combinations that have led to so decided an end. [...]

To-morrow I shall write at great length to your honoured father, whom in the morning it will be my pleasing duty to proclaim ALBERTO I. GRAND DUKE OF CASTELCICALA.

"Although men now call me *Marquis of Estella*, to thee, dearest I am simply

"RICHARD,"

Our hero despatched this letter in one to Signor Viviani at Pinella, by especial courier. He next wrote hasty accounts of the great victory which he had gained, to the chief authorities of the various cities and towns which had first declared in his favour, as before mentioned; and these also were instantly sent off by messengers.

Then soon did rumour tell the glorious tale how Montoni was delivered; and how the mighty flood of Austrian power, which had dashed its billows against the walls of the ducal capital, was rolled back over the confines of Castelcicala into the Roman States never to return.

We shall not dwell upon the particulars of that night which succeeded the battle. Our readers can imagine the duties which devolve upon a commander after so brilliant and yet so sanguinary a day. [...]

That night Montoni was brilliantly illuminated; and the most exuberant joy prevailed throughout the capital.

The Committee of Government assembled in close deliberation, immediately after the receipt of the welcome tidings of the victory; and, although they consulted in secret, still the inhabitants could well divine the subject of their debate—the best means of testifying their own and the nation's gratitude towards that champion who had thus diffused joy into so many hearts.

[...]

Our hero came forth to meet them, at the door of the mansion where he was lodged, and received those high functionaries with his plumed hat in hand.

[...]

"We have, however, further favours to solicit at your lordship's hand. Until that Prince, who is now our rightful sovereign, can come amongst us, and occupy that throne which your hands have prepared for him, you must be our chief—our Regent. My lord, a hundred councillors, forming the Provisional Committee of Government, debated this point last evening; and not a single voice was raised in objection to that request which I, as their organ, have now proffered to your lordship."

"No," answered Richard: "that cannot be. The world would say that I am ambitious—that I am swayed by interested motives of aggrandizement. Continue, gentlemen, to exercise supreme sway, until the arrival of your sovereign."

"My lord," returned the President, "Castelcicala demands this favour at your hands."

"Then, if Castelcicala command, I accept the trust with which you honour me," exclaimed Markham; "but so soon as I shall have succeeded in restoring peace and order, you will permit me, gentlemen, to repair to England, to present the ducal diadem to your rightful liege. And one word more," continued Markham; "your troops have conducted themselves, throughout this short but brilliant campaign, in a manner which exceeds all praise. To you I commend them—you must reward them."

"Your lordship is now the Regent of Castelcicala," answered the President; "and your decrees become our laws. Order—and we obey."

"I shall not abuse the power which you place in my hands," rejoined Markham.

The President then communicated to the Regent the pleasing fact that the Lord High Admiral had that morning hoisted the tri-coloured flag and sent an officer to signify his adhesion to the victorious cause. In answer to a question from Signor Gaëtano, Richard signified his intention of entering Montoni at three o'clock in the afternoon.

The principal authorities then returned to the capital.

Long before the appointed hour, the sovereign city wore an aspect of rejoicing and happiness. Triumphal arches were erected in the streets through which the conqueror would have to pass: the troops of the garrison were mustered in the great square of the palace; and a guard of honour was despatched to the southern gate. The windows were filled with smiling faces: banners waved from the tops of the houses. The ships in the harbour and roadstead were decked in their gayest colours; and boats were constantly arriving from the fleet with provisions of all kinds for the use of the inhabitants.

The great bell in the tower of Saint Theodosia at length proclaims the hour of three.

And now—hark! the artillery roars—Montoni salutes her Regent: the guard of honour presents arms; the martial music plays a national air; and the conqueror enters the capital. The men-of-war in the roadstead thunder forth echoes to the cannon on the ramparts; and the yards are manned in token of respect for the representative of the sovereign power.

What were Richard's feelings now? But little more than two months had elapsed since he had first entered that city, a prisoner—vanquished—with shattered hopes—and uncertain as to the fate that might be in store for him. How changed were his circumstances! As a conqueror—a noble—and a ruler did he now make his appearance in a capital where his name was upon every tongue, and where his great deeds excited the enthusiasm, the admiration, and the respect of every heart.

[...]

On went the procession amidst the enthusiastic applause of the myriads collected to welcome the conquerors,—on through streets crowded to the roof-tops with happy faces,—on to the ducal palace, in whose great square ten thousand troops were assembled to receive the Regent.

Richard alighted from his horse at the gate of the princely abode, on the threshold of which the municipal authorities were gathered to receive him.

Oh! at that moment how deeply—how sincerely did he regret the loss of General Grachia, Colonel Morosino, and the other patriots who had fallen in the fatal conflict of Ossore!

[...]

[This interpolated first person narrative, told by 'Crankey Jem' to the Resurrection Man, is an unusual addition to the popular literature of transportation; the memoirs of returned convicts and a range of ballads and broadsides dealing with this topic were staples of street literature in the early nineteenth century. The mix of factual observations drawn from these sources, together with the purely mythical is typical of Reynolds's method. Port Macquarie was a convict settlement notorious for its brutality, and Norfolk Island was associated with a commandant, Major Foveaux, whose sadism was a byword among the returned convicts.]

CHAPTER CXCI.
CRANKEY JEM'S HISTORY.

"My father's name was Robert Cuffin. At the death of *his* father he succeeded to a good business as grocer and tea-dealer; but he was very extravagant, and soon became bankrupt. He obtained his certificate, and then embarked as a wine merchant. At the expiration of three years he failed again, and once more appeared in the *Gazette*. This time he was refused his certificate. He, however, set up in business a third time, and became a coal merchant. His extravagances continued: so did his misfortunes. He failed, was thrown into prison, and took the benefit of the Insolvents' Act—but not without a long remand. On his release from gaol, he turned dry-salter. This new trade lasted a short time, and ended as all the others had done. Another residence in prison—another application to the Insolvents' court—and another remand, ensued.

"My father was now about forty years of age, and completely ruined. He had no credit—no resources—no means of commencing business again. He was, however, provided with a wife and seven children—all requiring maintenance, and he having nothing to maintain them on. I was not as yet born. It appears that my father sate down one evening in a very doleful humour, and in a very miserable garret, to meditate upon his circumstances. He revolved a thousand schemes in his head; but all required some little credit or capital where with to make a commencement; and he had neither. At length he started up, slapped his hand briskly upon the table, and exclaimed, 'By heavens, I've got it!'—'Got what?' demanded his wife.—'A call!' replied my father.—'A call!' ejaculated his better half, in astonishment.—'Yes; a call,' repeated my father; 'a call from above to preach the blessed Gospel and cleanse the unsavoury vessels of earth from their sinfulness.'—His wife began to cry, for she thought that distress had turned his brain; but he soon convinced her that he was never more in earnest in his life. He desired her to make the room look as neat as possible, and get a neighbour to take care of the children for an hour or two in the evening, when he should return with a few friends. He then went out, and his wife obeyed his instructions. Sure enough, in the evening, back came my father with a huge Bible under one arm and a Prayer-Book under the other, and followed by half-a-dozen demure-looking ladies and gentlemen, who had a curious knack of keeping their eyes incessantly fixed upwards—or heaven-wards as my father used to express it.

"Well, the visitors sate down; and my father, whose countenance had assumed a most wonderful gravity of expression since the morning, opened the prayer-meeting with a psalm. He then read passages from the two sacred books he had brought with him; and he wound up the service by an extemporaneous discourse, which drew tears from the eyes of his audience.

"The prayer-meeting being over, an elderly lady felt herself so overcome with my father's convincing eloquence, that a considerate old gentleman sent for a bottle of gin; and thus my father's 'call' was duly celebrated.

"To be brief—so well did my father play his cards, he soon gathered about him a numerous congregation; a chapel was hired somewhere in Goodman's Fields; and he was now a popular minister. His flock placed unbounded confidence in him—nay almost worshipped him; so that, thanks to their liberality, he was soon provided with a nicely-furnished house in the immediate vicinity of the chapel. Next door to him there dwelt a poor widow, named Ashford, and who had a very pretty daughter called Ruth. These families were amongst the most devoted of my father's flock; and in their eyes the reverend preacher was the pattern of virtue and holiness. The widow was compelled to take a little gin at times 'for the stomach's sake!' but one day she imbibed too much, fell down in a fit, and died. Father preached a funeral sermon, in which he eulogised her as a saint; and he afforded an asylum to the orphan girl. Ruth accordingly became an inmate of my father's house.

"And now commences the most extraordinary portion of the history of my father's life. You will admit that the suddenness of his 'call' was remarkable enough; but this was nothing to the marvellous nature of a vision which one night appeared to him. Its import was duly communicated to Miss Ashford next day; and the young lady piously resigned herself to the fate which my father assured her was the will of heaven. In a few months the consequences of the vision developed themselves; for Miss Ashford was discovered to be in the family-way. My father's lawful wife raised a storm which for some time seemed beyond the possibility of mitigation; the deacons of the chapel called, and the elders of the congregation came to investigate the matter. My father received them with a countenance expressive of more than ordinary demureness and solemnity. A conclave was held—explanations were demanded of my father. Then was it that the author of my being rose, and, in a most impressive manner, acquainted the assembly with the nature of his vision. 'The angel of the Lord,' he said, 'appeared to me one night, and ordered me to raise up seed of righteousness, so that when the Lord calls me unto himself, fitting heirs to carry on the good work which I have commenced, may not fail. I appealed to the angel in behalf of my own lawfully begotten offspring; but the angel's command brooked not remonstrances, and willed that I should raise up seed of Ruth Ashford: for she is blessed, in that her name is Ruth.'—This explanation was deemed perfectly satisfactory: and, when the deacons and elders had departed, my father succeeded some how or another not only in pacifying his wife, but also in reconciling her to the amour which he still carried on with Miss Ashford.

"Thus my father preserved both his mistress and his sanctity—at least for some considerable time longer. The fruit of that amour was myself; and my name is consequently Ashford—James Ashford—although my father insisted upon calling me Cuffin. Time wore on; but by degrees the jealousies which my father had at first succeeded in appeasing, developed themselves in an alarming manner between the wife and the mistress. Scenes of violence occurred at the house of his Reverence; and the neighbours began to think that their minister's amour was not quite so holy in its nature as he had represented it. The congregation fell off; and my father's reputation for sanctity was rapidly wearing out. Still he would not part with my mother and me; and the result was that his lawful wife left the house with all her own children. My father refused to support them; the parish officers interfered; and the scandal was grievously aggravated. Death arrived at this juncture to carry away the principal bone of contention. My mother became dangerously ill, and after languishing in a hopeless condition for a few weeks, breathed her last.

"Having thus stated the particulars of my birth, it will not be necessary to dwell on this portion of my narrative. I will only just observe that, at the death of Miss Ashford, a reconciliation was effected between my father and his wife; and that the former contrived to maintain his post as minister of the chapel—though with a diminished flock, and consequently with a decreased revenue. Nevertheless, I obtained a smattering of education at the school belonging to the chapel, and was treated with kindness by my father, although with great harshness by his wife. Thus continued matters until I was fifteen, when my father died; and I was immediately thrust out of doors to shift for myself.

"I was totally friendless. Vainly did I call upon the deacons and elders of the congregation; even those who had adhered to my father to the very last, had their eyes opened now that he was no longer present to reason with them. They spurned me from their doors; and I was left to beg or steal. I chose the former; but one night I was taken up by a watchman (there were no police in those times) because I was found wandering about without being able to give a satisfactory account of myself. You may look astonished; but I can assure you that when a poor devil says, '*I am starving—houseless—friendless—pennyless,*' it is supposed to mean that he can't give a satisfactory account of himself! In the morning I was taken before the magistrate, and committed to the House of Correction as a rogue and vagabond.

"In prison I became acquainted with a number of young thieves and pickpockets; and, so desperate was my condition, that when the day of emancipation arrived, I was easily persuaded to join them. Then commenced a career which I would gladly recall—but cannot! Amongst my new companions I obtained the nick-name of '*Crankey,*' because I was subject to fits of deep despondency and remorse, so that they fancied I was not right in my head. In time I became the most expert housebreaker in London—Tom the Cracksman alone excepted. My exploits grew more and more daring; and on three occasions I got into trouble. The first and second times I was sent to the hulks. I remember that on my second trial a pal of mine was acquitted through a flaw in the indictment. He was charged with having broken into and burglariously entered a jeweller's shop. It was, however, proved by one of the prosecutor's own witnesses that the shop door had been accidentally left unlocked and unbolted, and that consequently he had entered without any violence at all. Thanks to the laws, he escaped on that ground, although judge and jury were both convinced of his guilt. Time wore on; and I formed new acquaintances in the line to which I was devoted. These were Tom the Cracksman, Bill Bolter, Dick Flairer, the Buffer, and the Resurrection Man. With them I accomplished many successful burglaries; but at length I got into trouble a third time, and a stop was put to my career in London. It was in the year 1835 that the Resurrection Man and I broke into a jeweller's shop in Princes Street, Soho. We got off with a good booty. The Resurrection Man went over to the Mint: I let Dick Flairer into the secret, gave him a part of my share in the plunder, and then took to a hiding-place which there is in Chick Lane, Smithfield. Now I knew that Dick was stanch to the back-bone; and so he proved himself—for he brought me my food as regularly as possible; and at the end of a week, the storm had blown over enough to enable me to leave my hiding-place. I hastened to join the Resurrection Man in the Mint, where I stayed two or three days. Then the miscreant sold me, in order to save himself; and we were both committed to Newgate. Tidkins turned King's Evidence; and I was sentenced to transportation for life. The Resurrection Man was discharged at the termination of the business of the sessions.

"Myself and several other convicts, who were sentenced at the same session, were removed from Newgate to the Penitentiary at Millbank. Amongst the number were two persons whose names you may have heard before, because their case made a great noise at the time. These were Robert Stephens and Hugh Mac Chizzle, who were the principal parties concerned in a conspiracy to pass a certain Eliza Sydney off as a young man, and defraud the Earl of Warrington out of a considerable property. We remained about a fortnight in the Penitentiary, and were then transferred to the convict-ship at Woolwich. But before we left Millbank, we were clothed in new suits of grey, or pepper-and-salt, as we called the colour; and we were also ironed. The convict-ship was well arranged for its miserable purpose. On each side of the between-decks were two rows of sleeping-berths, one above the other: each berth was about six feet square, and was calculated to hold four convicts, eighteen inches of space to sleep in being considered ample room enough for each individual. The hospital was in the fore-part of the vessel, and was separated from the prison by means of a bulk-head, in which partition there were two strong doors, forming a means of communication between the two compartments. The fore and main hatchways, between decks, were fitted up with strong wooden stanchions round them; and in each of those stanchions there was a door with three padlocks, to let the convicts in and out, and secure them effectually at night.

[...]

"It was in January, 1836, that we sailed for Sydney. Although I had no wife,—no children,—and, I may almost say, no friend that I cared about,— still my heart sank within me, when, from the deck of convict-ship, I caught a last glimpse of the white cliffs of Old England. [...]

"The guard, under the command of a commissioned officer, consisted of thirty-one men, who did duty on the quarter-deck in three alternate watches. A sentry, with a drawn cutlass, stood at each hatchway; and the soldiers on watch always had their fire-arms loaded.

"When we had been to sea a little time, most of the convicts relapsed into their old habits of swearing, lying, and obscene conversation. They also gambled at pitch and toss, the stakes being their rations. Thieving prevailed to a very great extent; for the convict who lost his dinner by gambling, was sure to get one by stealing. They would often make wagers amongst themselves as to who was the most expert thief; and when the point was put to a practical test, dreadful quarrels would arise, the loser of the wager, perhaps, discovering that he himself was the victim of the trial of skill, and that his hoard of lime-juice, sugar, tobacco, or biscuit had disappeared. Stephens, who was at the same mess with myself, did all he could to discourage these practices; but the others pronounced him "*a false magician*," and even his friend, Mac Chizzle, turned against him. So at last he gave up the idea of introducing a reformation amongst his brethren in bondage. The fact is, that any convict who attempts to humbug the others by pretensions to honesty, or who expresses some superior delicacy of sentiment, which, of course, in many instances is actually experienced, had better hang himself at once. The equality of the convict-ship is a frightful equality,—the equality of crime,—the levelling influence of villainy,—the abolition of all social distinctions by the hideous free-masonry of turpitude and its consequent penalties! And yet there *is* an aristocracy, even in the prison of the convict-ship,—an aristocracy consisting of the oldest thieves, in contra-distinction to the youngest; and of *townies*, in opposition to *yokels*. The deference paid by the younger thieves to the elder ones is astonishing; and that man who, in relating his own history, can enumerate the greatest number of atrocities, is a king amongst convicts. Some of the best informed of the convicts wrote slang journals during the passage, and read them once a-week to the rest. They generally referred to the sprees of the night, and contained some such entries as this:—'*A peter cracked and frisked, while the cobbles dorsed; Sawbones came and found the glim doused; fadded the dobbins in a yokel's crib, while he blew the conkey-horn; Sawbones lipped a snitch; togs leered in yokels's downy; yokel screwed with the darbies.*' The exact meaning of this is:—'A chest broken open and robbed while the convicts slept: surgeon came in and found the lamp put out; the thief thrust the clothes which he had stolen into a countryman's berth, while he was snoring fast asleep; the surgeon ordered a general search; the clothes were found in the countryman's bed; and the countryman was put into irons.'

"I must observe, that while the ship was still in the Thames, none of the convicts would admit that they deserved their fate. They all proclaimed themselves much-injured individuals, and declared that the Home Secretary was certain to order a commutation of their sentence. The usual declarations were these:—'I am sure never to see New South Wales. The prejudice of the judge against me at the trial was evident to all present in the court. The jury were totally misled by his summing-up. My friends are doing every thing they can for me; and I am sure to get off.'—Out of a hundred and ten convicts, at least a hundred spoke in this manner. But the ship sailed,—England was far behind,—and *not one single convict* had his hopes of a commuted sentence gratified. Then, when those hopes had disappeared, they all opened their budget of gossip most freely, and related their exploits in so frank a manner, that it was very easy to perceive the justice of the verdicts which had condemned them.

"The voyage out was, on the whole, a tolerably fine one. It lasted four months and a half; and it was, consequently, in the middle of May that we arrived in sight of Sydney. But, when thus at the point of destination, the sea became so rough, and the wind blew such 'great guns,' that the captain declared there was mischief at hand. The convicts were all ordered into the prison, the ports of which were closed; and the heat was stifling. The tempest came with appalling violence. Crash went every loose thing on board,—the timbers creaked as if they would start from their settings,—the ropes rattled, —and the wind whistled horribly through the rigging. The ship was lifted to an immense height, and then by the fall of the mountain wave, was plunged into the depths of the trough of the sea;—at one moment dipping the studding-sail boom into the water,—and the next lying nearly on its beam ends on the opposite side. I afterwards learnt from a sailor, that the waves were forty feet high, twenty below the ordinary level of the sea, and twenty above it. Thus, when we were in the trough, they were forty feet above our heads! Towards evening the storm subsided; and early next morning Sydney broke more clearly upon our view.

"Sydney is beautifully situated. It possesses a fine ascent from a noble harbour; and its bays, its coves, its gardens, its gentlemen's seats, form a pleasing spectacle. Then its forests of masts—the Government-house, with its beautiful domain—the numerous wharfs—the thousands of boats upon the glassy water—and Wooloomooloo, with its charming villas and its windmills,—all these combine to enhance the interest of the scene. The town itself is far more handsome than I had expected to find it. The shops are very fine—particularly the silversmiths', the haberdashers', and confectioners', which would not disgrace the West End of London. They are mostly lighted with gas, and in the evening have a brilliant appearance. There is an astonishing number of grog-shops—nearly two hundred and fifty, for a population of 30,000 souls. George Street and Pitt Street are the principal thoroughfares: and the rents are so high that they average from three to five hundred pounds a-year. There are no common sewers in Sydney; and, although the greater portion of the town stands upon a height, yet many of the principal streets are perfectly level, and the want of a vent for the foul water and other impurities is sadly felt. I may add, that the first appearance of Sydney and its inhabitants does not impress a stranger with the idea of being in a country so far away from Europe; the language, the manners, and the dress of the people being so closely similar to those of England. But wait a little while, and a closer observation produces a different effect. Presently you will see the government gangs of convicts, marching backwards and forwards from their work in single military file,—solitary ones straggling here and there, with their white woollen Paramatta frocks and trousers, or grey or yellow jackets with duck overalls, all daubed over with broad arrows and initial letters to denote the establishment to which they belong,—and then the gaol-gang, moving sulkily along with their jingling leg-chains,—all these sad spectacles telling a tale of crime and its effects, and proclaiming trumpet-tongued the narrative of human degradation!

"The ship entered the harbour; our irons had already been put on again some days previously; and we were all landed under the care of the guard. We were marched to the gaol-yard; and there our clothes were all daubed over with broad arrows and the initials P. B.—meaning '*Prisoner's Barracks,*' to which establishment we were conducted as soon as the ceremony of painting our garments was completed. This barrack had several large day-rooms and numerous sleeping wards, the bedsteads being arranged in two tiers, or large platforms, but without separation. In every room there was a man in charge who was answerable for the conduct of the rest; but no one ever thought of complaining of the misbehaviour of his companions. A tread-mill was attached to the building: there were moreover several solitary cells—a species of punishment the horrors of which no tongue can describe.

"In the course of a few days we were all divided into sections, according to the degrees of punishment which we were to undergo. Stephens and MacChizzle were kept at Sydney: I was sent with some thirty others to Port Macquarie—a place about two hundred and sixty miles, as the crow flies, to the north of Sydney.

"The scenery is magnificent in the neighbourhood of Macquarie Harbour: but the life of the convict—oh! that is fearful in the extreme! I know that I was a great criminal—I know that my deeds demanded a severe punishment; but death had been preferable to a doom like that! Compelled to endure every kind of privation,—shut out from the rest of the world,—restricted to a very limited quantity of food, which *never* included fresh meat,—kept in chains and under a military guard with fixed bayonets and loaded fire-arms, —with no indulgence for good conduct, but severe penalties, even flogging or solitary confinement, for the smallest offenses,—constantly toiling in the wet, at felling timber and rolling it to the water,—forced to support without murmuring the most terrible hardships,—how did I curse the day when I rendered myself liable to the discipline of this hell upon earth! I will give you an idea of the horrors of that place:—during the six months that I remained there, nineteen deaths occurred amongst two hundred and twenty convicts; and of those *nineteen*, only five were from natural causes. Two were drowned, four were killed by the falling of trees, three were shot by the military, and five were murdered by their comrades! And why were those murders perpetrated? Because the assassins were tired of life, but had not the courage to commit suicide; and therefore they accomplished crimes which were sure to be visited by death upon the scaffold!

"The chain-gang to which I belonged was stationed at Philip's Creek; and our business was to supply timber for the ship-builders on Sarah's Island. We were lodged in huts of the most miserable description; and though our toils were so long and arduous, our rations were scarcely sufficient to keep body and soul together. The timber we cut was principally Huon pine; no beasts of burden were allowed; and we had to roll the trunks of trees to an immense distance. What with the humid climate, the want of fresh meat, and the severity of the labour, no man who fell ill ever entertained a hope of recovery. Talk of the civilised notions of the English—talk of the humane principles of her penal laws,—why, the Inquisition itself could not have been more horrible than the doom of the convict at Macquarie Harbour! Again I say, it was true that we were great criminals; but surely some adequate mode of punishment —some mode involving the means of *reformation*—might have been devised, without the application of so much real physical torture! I have heard or read that when the Inquisition put its victims to the rack, it afterwards remanded them to their dungeons, and allowed them leisure to recover and be cured;— but in the penal settlement of Port Macquarie those tortures were renewed daily—and they killed the miserable sufferers by inches!

"Our rations consisted daily of one pound and a half of flour, from which twelve per cent. of bran had been subtracted, one pound and a half of salt meat, and half an ounce of soap. No tea—no vegetables. The flour was made into cakes called *damper*, cooked in a frying-pan; and this wasteful mode of preparing it greatly diminished its quantity. Besides, divide those rations into three parts, and you will find that the three meals are little enough for men toiling hard from sunrise to sunset. The convict who did not keep a good look-out on his provisions was certain to be robbed by his comrades; and some men have been plundered to such an extent as actually to have been on the very verge of starvation.

"I had not been at Macquarie Harbour more than five months, when Stephens and Mac Chizzle arrived, and were added to our chain-gang. This punishment they had incurred for having endeavoured to escape from Sydney, where they had been treated with some indulgence, in consequence of their station in life previous to their sentence in England. So miserable was I, with hard work and scanty food, that I resolved to leave the place, or perish in the attempt. I communicated my design to Stephens and Mac Chizzle; and they agreed to accompany me. Escape from Macquarie was known to be a most difficult undertaking; and few convicts who essayed it were ever able to reach the settlements in other parts of the Colony. They were either murdered by their comrades for a supply of food, or perished in the bush. Formidable forests had to be traversed; and the chance of catching kangaroos was the only prospect of obtaining the means of existence. Nevertheless, I resolved to dare all those horrors and fearful risks, rather than remain at Philip's Creek. Five or six others, in addition to Stephens and Mac Chizzle, agreed to adopt this desperate venture with me; and one night we stole away—to the number of ten —from the huts.

"Yes—we thus set out on this tremendous undertaking, each individual possessing no more food than was sufficient for a single meal. And ere the sun rose all our store was consumed; and we found ourselves in the middle of a vast forest—without a guide—without victuals—almost without a hope! Convicts are not the men to cheer each other: misfortunes have made them selfish, brutal, and sulky. We toiled on in comparative silence. One of my companions, who had been ten years at Maquarie Harbour, was well acquainted with the mode in which the natives search for traces of the opossum, and when hunger began to press upon us, he examined every tree with a hollow limb, and also the adjacent trees for marks of the opossum's claws. For, I must tell you, that this animal is so sagacious, that it usually runs up a neighbouring tree and thence jumps to the one wherein its retreat is, in order to avoid being traced. The convict to whom I have alluded, and whose name was Blackley, at length discovered the trail of an opossum, and clambered up the tree in which its hole was found, by means of successive notches in the bark, to place the great toe in. Having reached the hole, he probed it with a long stick, and found that there actually was an opossum within. Thrusting in his hand, he seized the animal by the tail, pulled it out, and killed it by a swinging dash against the trunk of a tree. But this was little enough among so many. We, however, made a fire, cooked it, and thus contrived just to mitigate the terrible cravings of hunger. The flesh of the opossum is like that of a rabbit, and is therefore too delicate to enable a hearty appetite to make a good meal on a tenth portion of so small an animal.

"On the following day Blackley managed to kill a kangaroo, weighing about sixty pounds; and thus we were supplied with food for three or four days, acting economically. The flesh of the kangaroo is much like venison, and is very fine eating. We continued our way amidst the forest, which appeared endless; and in due time the kangaroo's flesh was consumed. Blackley was unwearied in his exertions to provide more food; and so much time was wasted in these endeavours, that we made but little progress in our journey. And now, to our terror, Blackley could find no more opossums—could kill no more kangaroos. We grew desperate: starvation was before us. Moody—sulky—glaring on each other with a horribly significant ferocity, we dragged ourselves along. Four days elapsed—and not a mouthful of food had we touched. On the fifth night we made a fire, and sate round it at considerable distances from each other. We all endeavoured to remain awake: we trembled at the approach of drowsiness—*for we knew the consequences of sleep in our desperate condition.* There we sate—none uttering a word,—with cracked and bloody lips—parched throats—eyes glowing with cannibal fires,—our minds a prey to the most appalling thoughts. At length Mac Chizzle, the lawyer, fell back in a sound slumber, having no doubt found it impossible to bear up against the weariness which was creeping over him. Then Blackley rose, and went farther into the wood. It required no ghost to tell us that he had gone to cut a club for a horrible purpose. The most breathless silence prevailed. At length there was a strange rustling amongst the trees at a little distance; and then cries of indescribable agony fell upon our ears. These tokens of distress were in the voice of Blackley, who called us by name, one after another. A vague idea of the real truth rivetted us to the spot; and in a short time the cries ceased altogether. Oh! what a night of horror was that! An hour had elapsed since Blackley's disappearance; and we had ceased to trouble ourselves concerning his fate:—our own intolerable cravings for food were the sole objects of our thoughts. Nor was Mac Chizzle doomed to escape death. A convict named Felton determined to execute the purpose which Blackley had entertained—though in a different manner. Afraid to venture away from the party to cut a bludgeon, he drew a large clasp-knife from his pocket, and plunged the long sharp blade into the breast of the sleeper. A cry of horror burst from Stephens and myself; and we rushed forward—now that it was unfortunately too late—to save the victim. We were well aware of the man's intentions when he approached his victim; but it was not until the blow was struck that we had the courage to interfere. It was, however, as I have said—too late! Mac Chizzle expired without a groan.

"I cannot dwell upon this scene: depraved—wicked—criminal as I was in many respects, my soul revolted from the idea of cannibalism, now that the opportunity of appeasing my hunger by such horrible means was within my reach. Stephens and I retired a little from the rest, and turned our backs upon the frightful work that was in progress. Again I say—oh! the horrors of that night! I was starving—and food was near. But what food? The flesh of a fellow-creature! In imagination I followed the entire process that was in operation so close behind me; and presently the hissing of the flesh upon the embers, and the odour of the awful cookery, convinced me that the meal would soon be served up. Then how did I wrestle with my own inclinations! And Stephens, I could well perceive, was also engaged in a terrific warfare with the promptings of hunger. But we resisted the temptation: yes—we resisted it;—and our companions did not trouble themselves to invite us to their repast.

"At length the morning dawned upon that awful and never-to-be-forgotten night. The fire was now extinguished; but near the ashes lay the entrails and the head of the murdered man. The cannibals had completely anatomised the corpse, and had wrapped up in their shirts (which they took off for the purpose) all that they chose to carry away with them. Not a word was spoken amongst us. The last frail links of sympathy—if any really had existed—seemed to have been broken by the incidents of the preceding night. Six men had partaken of the horrible repast; and they evidently looked on each other with loathing, and on Stephens and myself with suspicion. We all with one accord cut thick sticks, and advanced in the direction whence Blackley's cries had proceeded a few hours previously. His fate was that which we had suspected: an enormous snake was coiled around the wretch's corpse—licking it with its long tongue, to cover it with saliva for the purpose of deglutition. We attacked the monstrous reptile, and killed it. Its huge coils had actually squeezed our unfortunate comrade to death! Then—for the first time for many, many years—did a religious sentiment steal into my soul; and I murmured to myself: '*Surely this was the judgement of God upon a man who had meditated murder.*'

"That same day Stephens and myself gave our companions the slip, and struck into another direction together. We were fortunate enough to kill a kangaroo; and we made a hearty meal upon a portion of its flesh. Then how did we rejoice that we had withstood the temptation of the cannibal banquet! [...] Prudence now compelled us to separate; for though we had rid ourselves of our chains, we were still in our convict garb; and it was evident that two persons so clad were more likely to attract unpleasant notice, than one individual skulking about by himself. We accordingly parted; and from that moment I have never heard of Stephens. Whether he succeeded in escaping from the colony altogether, or whether he took to the bush again and perished, I know not:—that he was not retaken I am sure, because, were he captured, he would have been sent to Norfolk Island; and that he did *not* visit that most horrible of all the penal settlements—at least during a period of eighteen months after our escape from Macquarie—I am well aware, for reasons which I shall soon explain.

"In fact, I was not long at large after I separated with Stephens. My convict-dress betrayed me to a party of soldiers: I was arrested, taken to Sydney, tried, and sentenced to transportation to Norfolk Island. Before I left England in 1836, and since my return towards the end of 1839, I have heard a great many persons talk about Norfolk Island; but no one seemed to know much about it. I will therefore tell you something concerning it now.

"A thousand miles to the eastward of Sydney there are three islands close together. As you advance towards them in a ship from Sydney, Philip Island, which is very high land, and has a bold peak to the south, comes into view: close beyond it the lower hills of Norfolk Island, crowned with lofty pines, appear in sight; and between those two islands is a small and sterile speck called Nepean Island. Norfolk Island is six miles and a half long, and four broad—a miserable dot in the ocean compared to the vast tract of Australia. [...] The Norfolk Island pine shoots to a height of a hundred feet,—sometimes growing in clumps, elsewhere singly, on the grassy parts of the island, even to the very verge of the shore, where its roots are washed by the sea at high water. The apple-fruited guava, the lemon, grapes, figs, coffee, olives, pomegranates, strawberries, and melons have been introduced, and are cultivated successfully. The island is every where inaccessible, save at an opening in a low reef fronting the little bay; and that is the point where the settlement is situated. [...] The convicts are principally employed in quarrying stone; and as no gunpowder is used in blasting the rocks, and the stone is raised by means of levers, the labour is even more crushing than that of wood-felling at Port Macquarie. The prisoners, moreover, have to work in irons; and the food is not only insufficient, but bad—consisting only of dry maize bread and hard salt meat. Were it not for the supply of wild fruits in the island, the scurvy would rage like a pestilence. Between Macquarie Harbour and Norfolk Island I can only draw this distinction—that the former is *Purgatory*, and the latter *Hell!*
[...]

[He escapes from Norfolk Island by stealing a boat, and sails to Van Diemen's Land, where he claims to have been shipwrecked, and returns to England undetected, intending to take revenge on the Resurrection Man.]

[The Mint is another of the London rookeries which form one extreme of the moral topography of the city. As in the case of the Holy Land, there is some irony in the naming here.

The organization of thieves described has some foundation in reality.]

CHAPTER CXCII.
THE MINT.—THE FORTY THIEVES.

READER, if you stroll down that portion of the Southwark Bridge Road which lies between Union Street and Great Suffolk Street, you will perceive, midway, and on your left hand, a large mound of earth heaped on an open space doubtless, intended for building-ground.

At the southern extremity of this mound (on which all the offal from the adjacent houses is thrown, and where vagabond boys are constantly collected) is the entrance into an assemblage of miserable streets, alleys, and courts, forming one of the vilest, most dangerous, and most demoralised districts of this huge metropolis.

The houses are old, gloomy, and sombre. Some of them have the upper part, beginning with the first floor, projecting at least three feet over the thoroughfares—for we cannot say over the pavement. Most of the doors stand open, and reveal low, dark and filthy passages, the mere aspect of which compels the passer-by to get into the middle of the way, for fear of being suddenly dragged into those sinister dens, which seem fitted for crimes of the blackest dye.

This is no exaggeration.

Even in the day-time one shudders at the cut-throat appearance of the places into the full depths of whose gloom the eye cannot entirely penetrate. But, by night, the Mint,— for it is of this district that we are now writing,— is far more calculated to inspire the boldest heart with alarm, than the thickest forest or the wildest heath ever infested by banditti.

The houses in the Mint give one an idea of those dens in which murder may be committed without the least chance of detection. And yet that district swarms with population. But of what kind are its inhabitants? The refuse and the most criminal of the metropolis.

[...]

In passing through the mazes of the Mint—especially in Mint Street itself—you will observe more ill-looking fellows and revolting women in five minutes than you will see either on Saffron Hill or in Bethnal Green in an hour. Take the entire district that is bounded on the north by Peter Street, on the south by Great Suffolk Street, on the east by Blackman Street and High Street, and on the west by the Southwark Bridge Road,—take this small section of the metropolis, and believe us when we state that within those limits there is concentrated more depravity in all its myriad phases, than many persons could suppose to exist in the entire kingdom.

The Mint was once a sanctuary, like Whitefriars; and, although the law has deprived it of its ancient privileges, its inhabitants still maintain them, by a tacit understanding with each other, to the extent of their power. [...]

There is no part of Paris that can compare with the Mint in squalor, filth, or moral depravity;—no—not even the street in the Island of the City, where Eugene Sue has placed his celebrated *tapis-franc*.

Let those who happen to visit the Mint, after reading this description thereof, mark well the countenances of the inhabitants whom they will meet in that gloomy labyrinth. Hardened ruffianism characterises the men;—insolent, leering, and shameless looks express the depravity of the women;—the boys have the sneaking, shuffling manner of juvenile thieves;—the girls, even of a tender age, possess the brazen air of incipient profligacy.

It was about nine o'clock in the evening when the Resurrection Man, wrapped in a thick and capacious pea-coat, the collar of which concealed all the lower part of his countenance, turned hastily from the Southwark Bridge Road into Mint Street.

[The Resurrection Man visits a low tavern which is the centre of a criminal organization, the Forty Thieves. This group, under the control of their chief the Bully Grand, control all underworld activities in the East End, through a network of contacts. In every district there is a 'boozing-ken' or alehouse which is the centre of criminal activity, and the whole is governed by a complex set of rules, reminiscent of the Masons. Tidkins joins their regular meeting.]

It was a fortnightly meeting of the society when the Resurrection Man visited the house in the Mint, on the occasion of which we were ere now speaking.

The Forty Thieves were all gathered around a board formed of several rude deal tables placed together, and literally groaning beneath the weight of pewter-pots, bottles, jugs, &c.

[...]

"Have you any information to give me?" inquired Tidkins in a low tone.

"Plenty—but not at this moment, Mr. Tidkins. Take a glass of something to dispel the cold; and by-and-bye we will talk on matters of business. There is plenty of time; and many of my young friends here would no doubt be proud to give you a specimen of their vocal powers." [...]

[...]

Mr. Lipkins—a sharp-looking, hatchet-faced, restless-eyed youth of about sixteen—did not require much pressing ere he favoured his audience with the following sample of vocal melody:—

THE SIGN OF THE FIDDLE.

There's not in all London a tavern so gay,
As that where the knowing ones meet of a day:
So long as a farthing remains to my share,
I'll drink at that tavern, and never elsewhere.

Yet it is not that comforts there only combine,
Nor because it dispenses good brandy and wine;
'Tis not the sweet odour of pipe nor cigar—
Oh! no—'tis a something more cozie by far!

'Tis that friends of the light-fingered craft are all nigh,
Who'd drink till the cellar itself should be dry,
And teach you to feel how existence may please,
When pass'd in the presence of cronies like these.

Sweet Sign of the Fiddle! how long could I dwell
In thy tap full of smoke, with the friends I love well;
When baliffs no longer the alleys infest,
And duns, like their bills, have relapsed into rest!

"Bravo!" "Brayvo!" "Bra-ah-vo!" echoed on all sides, when this elegant effusion was brought to a close.
[…]
"Now for your information," said the Resurrection Man, somewhat impatiently. "In the first place, have you discovered any thing concerning Crankey Jem Cuffin?"
"My emissaries have been successful in every instance," answered Tunks, with a complacent smile. "A man exactly corresponding with your description of Crankey Jem dwells in an obscure court in Drury Lane. Here is the address."
[…]
"Your lads are devilish sharp fellows, Bully Grand," said the Resurrection Man, approvingly.
[…]
Shortly afterwards the Resurrection Man took his leave of the Bully Grand, and left the head-quarters of the Forty Thieves.
[…]

[Henry Holford once again enters Buckingham Palace; he overhears further conversation concerning Victoria's tendency to depression. There is also reference to the domestic problems resulting from the gender of the monarch; Albert 'did not feel himself to be his wife's equal', thus contradicting the conventional ordering of power in the Victorian household. After his discovery and expulsion from the Palace, Holford makes an attempt on the life of the Queen, which is foiled by Crankey Jem.]

CHAPTER CXCIII.
ANOTHER VISIT TO BUCKINGHAM PALACE.

It was the evening following the one the incidents of which occupied the preceding chapter.

Beneath a sofa in the Ball Room of Buckingham Palace, Henry Holford lay concealed.

It would be a mere repetition of statements made in former portions of this work, were we to describe the means by which the young man obtained access to the most private parts of the royal dwelling. We may, however, observe that he had paid frequent visits to the palace since the occasion when we first saw him enter those sacred precincts at the commencement of January, 1839; and that he was as familiar with the interior of the sovereign's abode, even to its most retired chambers, as any of its numerous inmates.

He had run many risks of discovery; but a species of good fortune seemed to attend upon him in these strange and romantic ventures; and those frequent alarms had never as yet terminated in his detection. Thus he became emboldened in his intrusions; and he now lay beneath the sofa in the Ball Room, with no more apprehension than he would have entertained if some authority in the palace had actually connived at his presence there.

It was nine o'clock in the evening; and the Ball Room was brilliantly illuminated.

But as yet the low-born pot-boy was its sole occupant.

Not long, however, was he doomed to that solitude. By a strange coincidence, the two noble ladies whose conversation had so much interested him on the occasion of his first visit to the palace, entered the room shortly after nine o'clock. He recognised their voices immediately; and he was delighted at their arrival, for their former dialogues had awakened the most lively sentiments of curiosity in his mind. But since his intrusion in January, 1839, he had never seen nor heard them in his subsequent visits to the royal dwelling, until the present occasion; and now, as they advanced through the room together, he held his breath to catch the words that fell from them.

"The dinner-party was tiresome to-day, my dear countess," observed the duchess: "her Majesty did not appear to be in good spirits."

"Alas!" exclaimed the lady thus addressed, "our gracious sovereign's melancholy fits occur at less distant intervals as she grows older."

"And yet her Majesty has every earthly reason to be happy," said the duchess. "The Prince appears to be devotedly attached to her; and the Princess Royal is a sweet babe."

"Worldly prosperity will not always ensure felicity," returned the countess; "and this your grace must have perceived amongst the circle of your acquaintance. Her Majesty is a prey to frequent fits of despondency, which are distressing to the faithful subjects who have the honour to be near the royal person. She will sit for an hour at a time, in moody contemplation of that sweet babe;

and her countenance then wears an expression of such profound—such plaintive—such touching melancholy, that I have frequently wept to behold her thus."

"What can be the cause of this intermittent despondency?" inquired the duchess.

"It is constitutional," answered the countess. "The fit comes upon her Majesty at moments when she is surrounded by all the elements of pleasure, happiness, and joy. It is a dark spirit against which no mind, however powerful, can wrestle. The only method of mitigating the violence of its attacks is the bustle of travelling:—then novelty, change of scene, exercise, and the demonstrations of popular devotion seem to relieve our beloved sovereign from the influence of that morbid, moody melancholy."

"I believe that when we conversed upon this topic on a former occasion,—it must be at least two years ago,—your ladyship hinted at the existence of hereditary idiosyncrasies in the Royal Family?" observed the duchess, inquiringly. "Indeed," added her grace, hastily, "I well remember that you alluded to the unfortunate attachment of George the Third for a certain Quakeress—"

"Yes—Hannah Lightfoot, to whom the monarch, when a prince, was privately united," answered the countess. "His baffled love—the necessity which compelled him to renounce one to whom he was devotedly attached—and the constant dread which he entertained lest the secret of this marriage should transpire, acted upon his mind in a manner that subsequently produced those dread results which are matters of history."

"You allude to his madness," said the duchess, with a shudder.

"Yes, your grace—that madness which is, alas! hereditary," replied the countess solemnly. "But George the Third had many—many domestic afflictions. Oh! if you knew all, you would not be surprised that he had lost his reason! The profligacy of some of his children—most of them—was alone sufficient to turn his brain. Many of those instances of profligacy have transpired; and although the public have not been able to arrive at any positive proofs respecting the matters, I can nevertheless assure your grace that such proofs *are* in existence—and in my possession!"

"Your ladyship once before hinted as much to me; and I must confess that without having any morbid inclination for vulgar scandal, I feel some curiosity in respect to these matters."

"Some day I will place in your hand papers of a fearful import, in connexion with the Royal Family," returned the countess. "Your grace will then perceive that profligacy the most abandoned—crimes the most heinous—vices the most depraved, characterised nearly all the children of George the Third. There is one remarkable fact relative to that prince's marriage with Hannah Lightfoot. The Royal Marriage Act was not passed until *thirteen years after this union*, and could not therefore set it aside; and yet *Hannah Lightfoot was still living when the prince espoused Charlotte Sophia Princess of Mecklenburgh Strelitz in 1761.*"

"Is this possible?" exclaimed the duchess, profoundly surprised.

"It is possible—it is true!" said the countess emphatically. "In 1772 the Royal Marriage Act was passed, and provided that no member of the Royal Family should contract a marriage without the sovereign's consent. This measure was enacted for several reasons; but principally because the King's two brothers had formed private matrimonial connexions,—the Duke of Cumberland with Mrs. Horton, a widow—and the Duke of Gloucester with the widow of the Earl of Waldegrave."

"The act certainly appears to me most cruel and oppressive," said the duchess; "inasmuch as it interferes with the tenderest affections and most charming of human sympathies—feelings which royalty has in common with all the rest of mankind."

"I cordially agree with your grace," observed the countess. "The law is barbarous—monstrous—revolting; and its evil effects were evidenced by almost every member of the family of George the Third. In the first place, the Prince of Wales (afterwards George the Fourth) was privately united to Mrs. Fitzherbert, at the house of that lady's uncle, Lord Sefton. Fox, Sheridan, and Burke were present at the ceremony, in addition to my mother and several relations of the bride. Mr. Fox handed her into the carriage; and the happy pair proceeded to Richmond, where they passed a week or ten days. Queen Charlotte was made acquainted with the marriage: she sent for her son, and demanded an explanation. The prince avowed the truth. Your grace has, of course, read the discussion which took place in connexion with this subject, in the House of Commons, in 1787. Mr. Rolle, the member for Devonshire, mysteriously alluded to the union: Mr. Fox rose up, and denied it; but from that day forth Mrs. Fitzherbert never spoke to Fox again. Sheridan let the truth escape him:—he said, '*A lady who has been alluded to, is without reproach, and is entitled to the truest and most general respect.*' How would Mrs. Fitzherbert have been without reproach, or entitled to respect, if she were *not* married to the prince? But I have proofs—convincing proofs—that such an union did actually take place, although it was certainly null and void in consequence of the Marriage Act."

"It nevertheless subsisted according to the feelings and inclinations of the parties interested," said the duchess; "and it was based on *honour*, if on no legal principle."

"Alas!" whispered the countess, casting a rapid glance around; "the word *honour* must not be mentioned in connexion with the name of George the Fourth. It pains me to speak ill of the ancestors of our lovely queen; but—if we converse on the subject at all—truth must influence our observations."

[...]

The reader may probably deem it somewhat extraordinary that ladies attached to the Court should thus freely discuss the most private affairs, and canvass the characters of deceased members of the Royal Family. But we can positively assert that no-where are scandal and tittle-tattle more extensively indulged in, than amongst the members of that circle of courtiers and female sycophants who crowd about the sovereign.

The conversation of the duchess and countess was not renewed on the present occasion; for while they were yet plunged each in the depths of her own particular meditations, the regal train entered the Ball Room.

And all this while Henry Holford remained concealed beneath the sofa!

Victoria leant upon the arm of her consort; and the illustrious party was preceded by the Lord Chamberlain and the Lord Steward. The Queen and the Prince proceeded to the reserved seats which were slightly elevated in a recess, and were covered with white satin embroidered in silver.

Then the magnificent Ball-Room presented a truly fairy spectacle. Plumes were waving, diamonds were sparkling, bright eyes were glancing, and music floated on the air. The spacious apartment was crowded with nobles and gentlemen in gorgeous uniforms or court-dresses; and with ladies in the most elegant attire that French fashions could suggest or French milliners achieve. All those striking or attractive figures, and all the splendours of their appearance, were multiplied by the brilliant mirrors to an illimitable extent.

The orchestra extended across one end of the Ball-Room; and the musicians had entered by a side-door almost at the same moment that the royal procession made its appearance.

In the rooms adjoining, the Corps of Gentlemen-at-arms and the Yeomen of the Guard were on duty; and in the hall the band of the Royal Regiment of Horse Guards was in attendance.

The Queen and the Prince danced in the first quadrille; and afterwards they indulged in their favourite waltz—the *Frohsinn mein Ziel*. At the termination of each dance the royal party passed into the Picture Gallery, where they promenaded amidst a wilderness of flowers and aromatic shrubs. Then indeed the odour-breathing exotics—the whispering leaves—the light of the pendent lamps, mellowed so as to give full effect to the portraits of those who were once famous or once beautiful—the ribboned or gartered nobles—the blaze of female loveliness—the streams of melody—the presence of all possible elements of splendour, harmony, and pleasure, combined to render the whole scene one of enchantment, and seemed to realize the most glowing and brilliant visions which oriental writers ever shadowed forth!

The dancing was renewed in the Ball-Room: and as the beauteous ladies of the court swam and turned in graceful mazes, it appeared as if the art had become elevated into the harmony of motion. Dancing there was something more than mechanical: it was a true, a worthy, and a legitimate sister of poetry and music.

At twelve o'clock the doors of the supper-room were thrown open; and in that gorgeous banqueting-hall the crimson draperies, the service of gold, and the massive table ornaments were lighted up by Chinese lanterns and silver candelabra of exquisite workmanship. A splendid row of gold cups was laid on each side of the table. On the right of each plate stood a decanter of water, a finger-glass half filled with tepid water, a champagne glass, a tumbler, and three wine-glasses. Numerous servants in magnificent liveries were in attendance. No one asked for any thing: the servants offered the various dishes, of which the guests partook or which they rejected according to their taste. No healths were drunk during the Queen's presence; nor was the ceremony of taking wine with each other observed—not even on the part of the gentleman with the lady whom he had handed into the room. The domestics whose especial duty it was to serve the wine, never filled a glass until it was quite empty; nor did any guest ask for wine, but, when the servant approached him, merely stated the kind of wine he chose.

After sitting for about an hour, the Queen rose, and was conducted to the Yellow Drawing-Room by Prince Albert, the guests all rising as the royal couple retired.

Then the servants filled the glasses, and the Lord Steward said, "The Queen!" The health was drunk standing, in silence, and with a gentle inclination of the head. In a few minutes afterwards the gentlemen conducted the ladies into the Yellow Drawing-Room, where coffee and liqueurs were served.

The harp, piano, and songs by some of the ladies, occupied another hour; at the expiration of which the guests took their departure.

Holford had now been concealed nearly five hours beneath the sofa in the ball-room; and he was cramped, stiff, and wearied. During that interval he had experienced a variety of emotions:—wonder at the strange revelations which he had heard from the lips of the countess,—ineffable delight in contemplating the person of his sovereign,—envy at the exalted prosperity of Prince Albert,—thrilling excitement at the fairy-like aspect of the enchanting dance,—sensations of unknown rapture occasioned by the soft strains of the music,—and boundless disgust for his own humble, obscure, and almost serf-like condition.

During those intervals when the royal party and the guests were promenading in the Picture-Gallery or were engaged in the supper-apartment and the drawing-room, Holford longed to escape from his hiding-place and retreat to the lumber-closet where he was in the habit of concealing himself on the occasion of his visits to the palace; but there were too many persons about to render such a step safe.

It was not, therefore, until a very late hour,—or rather an early one in the morning,—that he was able to enter the supper-room and help himself to some of the dainties left upon the board; having done which, he retreated to his nook in the most retired part of the palace.

CHAPTER CXCIV.
THE ROYAL BREAKFAST.

HOLFORD did not immediately close his eyes in slumber.

Although his education had been miserably neglected, he possessed good natural abilities; and his reflections at times were of a far more philosophical nature than could have been anticipated.

The gorgeous scenes which he had just witnessed now led him to meditate upon the horrible contrasts which existed elsewhere, not only in the great metropolis, but throughout the United Kingdom,—and many, very many of which he himself had seen with his own eyes, and felt with his own experience.

At that moment when festivity was highest, and pleasure was most exciting in the regal halls, there were mothers in naked attics, dark cellars, or even houseless in the open streets,—mothers who pressed their famished little ones to their bosoms, and wondered whether a mouthful of food would ever pass their lips again.

While the royal table groaned beneath the weight of golden vessels and the choicest luxuries which earth's fruitfulness, heaven's bounty, or man's ingenuity could supply,—while the raciest produce of fertile vineyards sparkled in the crystal cups,—at that same period, how many thousands of that exalted lady's subjects moistened their sorry crust with tears wrung from them by the consciousness of ill-requited toil and the pinching gripe of bitter poverty!

Delicious music here, and the cries of starving children there;—silver candelabra pouring forth a flood of lustre in a gorgeous saloon, and a flickering rushlight making visible the naked and damp-stained walls of a wretched garret;—silks and satins, rags and nudity;—luxurious and pampered indolence; crushing and ill-paid labour;—homage and reverence, ill-treatment and oppression;—the gratification of every whim, the absence of every necessary;—not a care for to-morrow here, not a hope for to-morrow there;—a certainty of a renewal of this day's plenty, a total ignorance whence the next day's bread can come;—mirth and laughter, moans and sorrowing;—a palace for life on one hand, and an anxiety lest even the wretched hovel may not be changed for a workhouse to-morrow;—these are the appalling contrasts which our social sphere presents to view!

Of all this Holford thought as he lay concealed in the lumber-room of the royal dwelling.

But at length sleep overtook him.

It was still dark when he awoke. At first he thought that he must have slumbered for many hours—that a day had passed, and that another night had come;—but he felt too little refreshed to remain many instants in that opinion. Moreover, as he watched the window, he observed a faint, faint gleam of light —or rather a mitigation of the intenseness of the gloom without—slowly appearing; and he knew that the dawn was at hand.

He was nearly frozen in that cheerless room where he had slept: his teeth chattered—his limbs were benumbed. He longed for some new excitement to elevate his drooping spirits, and thus impart physical warmth to his frame.

Suddenly a thought struck him: he would penetrate into the royal breakfast-room! He knew that the Queen and Prince Albert frequently partook of the morning meal together; and he longed to listen to their conversation when thus *tête-à-tête*.

Scarcely had he conceived this project when he resolved to execute it. The interior of the palace—even to its most private apartments and chambers—was as we have before stated, perfectly familiar to him. Stealing from the place where he had slept, he proceeded with marvellous caution to the point of his present destination; and in about ten minutes he reached the breakfast-room in safety.

The twilight of morning had now penetrated through the windows of this apartment; for the heavy curtains were drawn aside, a cheerful fire burnt in the grate, and the table was already spread.

A friendly sofa became Holford's hiding-place.

Shortly after eight o'clock a domestic entered with the morning ministerial paper, which he laid upon the table, and then withdrew.

Five minutes elapsed, when the door was thrown open, and the Queen entered, attended by two ladies. These were almost immediately dismissed; and Victoria seated herself near the fire, to read the journal. But scarcely had she opened it, ere Prince Albert made his appearance, followed by a gentleman in waiting, who humbly saluted her Majesty and retired.

Servants immediately afterwards entered, and placed upon the table the materials for a sumptuous breakfast, having performed which duty they immediately left the room.

The Queen and her consort were now alone—or at least, supposed themselves to be so; and their conversation soon flowed without restraint.

But such an empire—such a despotism does the habitual etiquette of Courts establish over the natural freedom of the human mind, that even the best and most tender feelings of the heart are to a certain extent subdued and oppressed by that chilling influence. The royal pair were affectionate to each other: still their tenderness was not of that lively, unembarrassed, free, and cordial nature which subsists at the domestic hearth elsewhere. There seemed to be a barrier between the frank and open interchange of their thoughts; and even though that barrier were no thicker than gauze, still it existed. Their words were to some degree measured—scarcely perceptibly so, it is true—nevertheless, the fact *was* apparent in the least, least degree; and the effect was also in the least, least degree unpleasant.

The Queen was authoritative in the enunciation of her opinion upon any subject; and if the Prince differed from her, he expressed himself with restraint. In fact, he did not feel himself his wife's equal. Could a listener, who did not see them as they spoke, have deadened his ear to those intonations of their voices which marked their respective sex, and have judged only by their words, he would have thought that the Queen was the *husband,* and the Prince the *wife.*

The Prince appeared to be very amiable, very intelligent; but totally inexperienced in the ways of the world. The Queen exhibited much natural ability and an elegant taste: nevertheless, she also seemed lamentably ignorant of the every-day incidents of life. We mean that the royal pair manifested a reluctance to believe in those melancholy occurrences which characterise the condition of the industrious millions. This was not the result of indifference, but of sheer ignorance.

[The royal couple begin to study the morning papers.]

"On this page," continued the Queen, turning the paper upon the table, "there is an article entitled '*Death from Starvation*;' another headed '*Dreadful Condition of the Spitalfield's Weavers*;' a third called '*Starving State of the Paisley Mechanics*;' and a fourth entitled '*Awful Distress in the Manufacturing Districts*;' and I perceive numerous short paragraphs all announcing similar calamities."

"The English papers are always full of such accounts," observed the Prince.

"And yet I would have you know that England is the richest, most prosperous, and happiest country on the face of the earth," returned the Queen, somewhat impatiently. "You must not take these accounts literally as you read them. My Ministers assure me that they are greatly exaggerated. It appears—as the matter has been explained to me—that the persons who furnish these narratives are remunerated according to quantity; and they therefore amplify the details as much as possible."

"Still those accounts must be, to a certain extent, based on truth?" said Prince Albert, half inquiringly.

"Not nearly so much as you imagine. My Ministers have satisfied me on that head; and they must know better than you. Take, for instance, the article headed '*Dreadful Condition of the Spitalfields' Weavers.*' You may there read that the weavers are in an actual state of starvation. This is only newspaper metaphor: the writer means his readers to understand that the weavers are not so well off as they would wish to be. Perhaps they have not meat every day—perhaps only three or four times a week: but they assuredly have plenty of bread and potatoes—because bread and potatoes are so cheap!"

[...]

The Queen smiled, and continued:—

"You remember the paragraph which the Secretary of State pointed out a few days ago: it was in the *Morning Post*, if you recollect. That journal—which, by the bye, circulates entirely amongst the upper servants of the aristocracy, and nowhere else—declared '*that so great is the devotion of my loyal subjects that, were such a sacrifice necessary, they would joyfully throw themselves beneath the wheels of my state-carriage, even as the Indians cast themselves under the car of Juggernaut.*' I never in my life saw but that one number of the *Post*: its circulation, I am told, is confined entirely to the servants of the aristocracy; still it seems in that instance to express the sentiments of the entire nation. You smile, Albert?"

"I was only thinking whether the paragraph to which you have alluded, was another specimen of newspaper metaphor," answered the Prince, with some degree of hesitation.

"Not at all," returned the Queen, quickly; "the Editor wrote precisely as he thought. He must know the real sentiments of the people, since he is a man of the people himself. I have been assured that he was once the headbutler in a nobleman's family: hence his success in conducting a daily newspaper exclusively devoted to the interests and capacities of upper-servants."

"I thought that English Editors were generally a better class of men?" observed the Prince.

"So they are for the most part," replied the Queen: "graduates at the Universities—barristers—and highly accomplished gentlemen. But in the case of the *Morning Post* there seems to be an exception. We were, however, conversing upon the distress in the country—for there certainly is some little distress here and there; although the idea of people actually dying of starvation in a Christian land is of course absurd. I am really bewildered, at times, with the reasons of, and the remedies proposed for, that distress. If I ask the Home Secretary, he declares that the people are too obstinate to understand what comfortable places the workhouses are;—if I ask the Colonial Secretary, he assures me that the people are most wilfully blind to the blessings of emigration: if I ask the Foreign Secretary, he labours to convince me that the distracted state of the East reacts upon this country; and if I ask the Bishop of London he expresses his conviction that the people require more churches."

"For my part, I do not like to interfere in these matters," said the Prince; "and therefore I never ask any questions concerning them."

"And you act rightly, Albert, for you certainly know nothing of English politics. I observe by the newspapers that the country praises your forbearance in this respect. You are a Field-Marshal, and Chief Judge of the Stannaries Court—and—"

"And a Knight of the Garter," added the Prince.

"Yes—and a Learned Doctor of Laws," continued the Queen : "any thing else?"

"Several things—but I really forget them all now," returned the Prince.

[...]

The royal pair then conversed upon a variety of topics which would afford little interest to the reader; and shortly after nine her Majesty withdrew.

Prince Albert remained in the room to read the newspaper.

Henry Holford had listened with almost breathless attention to the conversation which we have recorded.

The Prince had drawn his chair more closely to the fire, after the Queen left the room; and he was now sitting within a couple of yards of the sofa beneath which Holford lay concealed.

The pot-boy gently drew aside the drapery which hung from the framework of the sofa to the floor, and gazed long and intently on the Prince. His look was one in which envy, animosity, and admiration were strangely blended. He thought within himself, "Why are you so exalted, and I so abased? And yet your graceful person—your intelligent countenance—your handsome features, seem to fit you for such an elevated position. Nevertheless, if I had had your advantages of education—"

The meditations of the presumptuous youth were suddenly and most disagreeably checked:—the Prince abruptly threw aside the paper, and his eyes fell on the human countenance that was gazing up at him from beneath the sofa.

His Royal Highness uttered an exclamation of surprise—not altogether unmingled with alarm; and his first impulse was to stretch out his hand towards the bell-rope. But, yielding to a second thought, he advanced to the sofa, exclaiming, "Come forth—whoever you may be."

Then the miserable pot-boy dragged himself from his hiding-place, and in another moment stood, pale and trembling, in the presence of the Prince.

"Who are you?" demanded his Royal Highness in a stern tone :"what means this intrusion? how came you hither?"

Henry Holford fell at the feet of the Prince, and confessed that, urged by an invincible curiosity, he had entered the palace on the preceding evening; but he said nothing of his previous visits.

For a few moments Prince Albert seemed uncertain how to act : he was doubtless hesitating between the alternatives of handing the intruder over to the officers of justice, or of allowing him to depart unmolested.

After a pause, he questioned Holford more closely, and seemed satisfied by the youth's assurance that he had really entered the palace through motives of curiosity, and not for any dishonest purpose.

The Prince accordingly determined to be merciful.

"I am willing," he said, "to forgive the present offence; you shall be suffered to depart. But I warn you that a repetition of the act will lead to a severe punishment. Follow me."

The Prince led the way to an ante-room where a domestic was in waiting.

"Conduct this lad as privately as you can from the palace," said his Royal Highness. "Ask him no questions—and mention not the incident elsewhere."

The Prince withdrew; and the lacquey led Henry Holford through various turnings in the palace to the servants' door opening into Pimlico.

Thus was the pot-boy ignominiously expelled from the palace, and never —never in his life had he felt more thoroughly degraded—more profoundly abased—more contemptible in his own eyes, than on the present occasion!

CHAPTER CCXI.
THE DEED.

CRANKEY JEM was at dinner, in the afternoon of the day which followed the night of Holford's sad historical studies, when the young man entered his room.

"Oh! so you've turned up at last," said Jem, pointing to a seat, and pushing a plate across the table in the same direction. "What have you been doing with yourself for the last two days? But sit down first, and get something to eat; for you look as pale and haggard as if you'd just been turned out of a workhouse."

[...]

"I say, Jem," exclaimed Henry Holford, abruptly, "I wish you would lend me your pistols for a few hours."

"And what do you want with pistols, young feller?" demanded the returned convict, laying down his knife, and looking Holford full in the face.

"A friend of mine has made a wager with another man about hitting a halfpenny at thirty paces," said Henry, returning the glance in a manner so confident and unabashed, that Jem's suspicions were hushed in a moment.

"Yes—you shall have the pistols till this evening," said he: "but mind you bring 'em back before dusk."

With these words, he rose, went to a cupboard, and produced the weapons.

"I'll be sure to bring them back by the time you go out," said Holford. "Are they loaded?"

"No," answered Jem. "But here's powder and ball, which you can take along with you."

"I wish you would load them all ready," observed Holford. "I—I don't think my friend knows how."

"Not know how to load a pistol—and yet be able to handle one skilfully!" ejaculated Jem, his vague suspicions returning.

"Many persons learn to fire at a mark at Copenhagen House, or a dozen other places about London," said the young man, still completely unabashed; "and yet they can't load a pistol for the life of them."

"Well—that's true enough," muttered Jem.

Still he was not quite reassured; and yet he was unwilling to task Holford with requiring the pistols for any improper purpose. The young lad's reasons might be true—they were at least feasible; and Jem was loth to hurt his feelings by hinting at any suspicion which the demand for the weapons had occasioned. Moreover, it would be churlish to refuse the loan of them—and almost equally so to decline loading them;—and the returned convict possessed an obliging disposition, although he had been so much knocked about in the world. He was also attached to Henry Holford, and would go far to serve him.

Nevertheless, he still hesitated.

"Well—won't you do what I ask you, Jem?" said Holford, observing that he wavered.

"Is it really for your friends?" demanded the man, turning short round upon the lad.

"Don't you believe me?" cried Holford, now blushing deeply. "Why, you cannot think that I'm going to commit a highway robbery or a burglary in the day-time—even if I ever did at all?"

"No—no," said Jem; "but you seemed so strange—so excited—when you first came in—"

"Ha! ha!" cried Holford, laughing: "you thought I was going to make away with myself! No, Jem—the river would be better than the pistol, if I meant *that*."

"Well—you must have your will, then," said Crankey Jem; and, turning to the cupboard, he proceeded to load the pistols.

But still he was not altogether satisfied!

Holford rose from his seat with an assumed air of indifference, and approached the table where the little models of the ships were standing.

A few minutes thus elapsed in profound silence.

"They're all ready now," said Jem, at length; "and as your friends don't know how to load them, it's no use your taking the powder and ball. I suppose they'll fire a shot each, and have done with it?"

"I suppose so," returned Holford, as he concealed the pistols about his person. "I shall see you again presently. Good bye till then."

"Good bye," said Jem.

But scarcely had Holford left the room a minute, when the returned convict followed him.

The fact was that there shot forth a gleam of such inexpressible satisfaction from Holford's eyes, at the moment when he grasped the pistols, that the vague suspicions which had already been floating in the mind of Crankey Jem seemed suddenly to receive confirmation—or at least to be materially strengthened; and he feared lest his young friend meditated self-destruction.

"The pistols are of no use to him," muttered Jem, as he hastened down the stairs, slouching his large hat over his eyes; "but if he is bent on suicide, the river is not far off. I don't like his manner at all!"

When he gained the street, he looked hastily up and down, and caught a glimpse of Holford, who was just turning into Russell Street, leading from Drury Lane towards Covent Garden.

"I will watch him at all events," thought Crankey Jem. "If he means no harm, he will never find out that I did it; and if he does, I may save him."

Meantime, Holford, little suspecting that his friend was at no great distance behind him, pursued his way towards St. James's Park.

Now that his mind was bent upon a particular object, and that all considerations had resolved themselves into that fixed determination, his countenance, though very pale, was singularly calm and tranquil; and neither by his face nor his manner did he attract any particular notice as he wandered slowly along.

He gained the Park, and proceeded up the Mall towards Constitution Hill. Crankey Jem followed him at a distance.

"Perhaps, after all, it is true that he has got some friends to meet," he muttered to himself; "and it may be somewhere hereabouts that he is to join them."

Holford stopped midway in the wide road intersecting Constitution Hill, and lounged in an apparently indifferent manner against the fence skirting the Green Park.

There were but few persons about, in that particular direction, at the time, —although the afternoon was very fine, and the sun was shining brightly through the fresh, frosty air.

It was now three o'clock; and some little bustle was visible amongst those few loungers who were at the commencement of the road, and who were enabled to command a view of the front of the palace.

They ranged themselves on one side:—there was a trampling of horses; and in a few moments a low open phaeton, drawn by four bays, turned rapidly from the park into the road leading over Constitution Hill.

"They are coming!" murmured Holford to himself, as he observed the equipage from the short distance where he was standing

Every hat was raised by the little group at the end of the road, as the vehicle dashed by—for in it were seated the Queen and her illustrious husband.

By a strange coincidence Her Majesty was sitting on the left hand of Prince Albert, and not on the right as usual: she was consequently nearest to the wall of the palace-gardens, while the Prince was nearest to the railings of the Green Park.

And now the moment so anxiously desired by Holford, was at hand:—the phaeton drew nigh.

He hesitated:—yes—he hesitated;—but it was only for a single second.

"Now to avenge my expulsion from the palace!—now to make my name a subject for history!" were the thoughts that, rapid as lightning, flashed across his mind.

Not another moment did he waver; but, advancing from the railings against which he had been lounging, he drew a pistol from his breast and fired it point-blank at the royal couple as the phaeton dashed past.

The Queen screamed and rose from her seat; and the postillions stopped their horses.

"Drive on!" cried the Prince, in a loud tone, as he pulled her Majesty back upon the seat; and his countenance was ashy pale.

Holford threw the first pistol hastily away from him, and drew forth the second.

But at that moment a powerful grasp seized him from behind,—his arm was knocked upwards,—the pistol went off into the air,—and a well-known voice cried in his ears, "My God! Harry, what madness is this?"

Several other persons had by this time collected on the spot; and the most cordial shouts of "God save the Queen!" "God save the Prince!" burst from their lips.

Her Majesty bowed in a most graceful and grateful manner: the Prince raised his hat in acknowledgment of the sympathy and attachment manifested towards his royal spouse and himself;—and the phaeton rolled rapidly away towards Hyde Park, in obedience to the wishes of the Queen and the orders of the Prince.

"What madness is this, I say, Harry?" repeated Crankey Jem, without relaxing his hold upon the would-be regicide.

But Holford hung down his head, and maintained a moody silence.

"Do you know him?" "Who is he?" were the questions that were now addressed to Crankey Jem from all sides.

But before he could answer his interrogators, two policemen broke through the crowd, and took Holford into custody.

"We must take him to the Home Office," said one of the officers, who was a serjeant, to his companion.

"Yes, Mr. Crisp," was the reply.

"And you, my good feller," continued the serjeant, addressing himself to Crankey Jem, "had better come along with us—since you was the first to seize on this here young miscreant."

"I'd rather not," said Jem, now terribly alarmed on his own account: "I—"

"Oh! nonsense," cried Mr. Crisp. "The Home Secretary is a wery nice genelman, and will tell you how much obleeged he is to you for having seized—But, I say," added Mr. Crisp, changing his tone and assuming a severe look as he gazed on the countenance of the returned convict, "what the deuce have we here?"

"What, Mr. Crisp?" said the policeman, who had charge of Holford.

"Why! if my eyes does n't deceive me," cried the serjeant, "this here feller is one James Cuffin, generally known as Crankey Jem—and he's a 'scaped felon."

With these words Mr. Crisp collared the poor fellow, who offered no resistance.

But large tears rolled down his cheeks!

Policemen and prisoners then proceeded across the park to the Home Office, followed by a crowd that rapidly increased in numbers as it rolled onwards.

[In Chapter CCXXIII, Richard Markham finally marries Isabella, and the couple become the Prince and Princess of Montoni.]

CHAPTER CCXXIII.
THE MARRIAGE.

THE happy morning dawned.

The weather was mild and beautiful; the sky was of a cloudless azure; and all nature seemed to smile with the gladness of an early spring.

Markham rose at seven o'clock, and dressed himself in plain clothes; but upon his breast he wore the star which denoted his princely rank.

And never had he appeared so handsome;—no—not even when, with the flush of his first triumph upon his cheeks, he had entered the town of Estella and received the congratulations of the inhabitants.

When he descended to the breakfast-room, he found Mr. Monroe, Ellen, and Katherine already assembled: they too were attired in a manner which showed that they were not to be omitted from the bridal party.

At eight o'clock the Grand-Duke's carriage drove up to the door; and in a few minutes our hero and his friends were on their way to Richmond.

"Strange!" thought Ellen to herself; "that I should have passed my honey-moon of twenty-four hours with *him* in the same neighbourhood whither Richard is now repairing to fetch his bride."

The carriage rolled rapidly along; and as the clock struck nine it dashed up the avenue to the door of the now royal dwelling.

Richard and his companions were ushered into the drawing-room, where the Grand-Duke and the Duchess, with the *aides-de-camp*, and a few select guests, were awaiting their arrival. The reception which Mr. Monroe, Ellen, and Katherine experienced at the hands of the royal pair was of a most cordial kind, and proved how favourably our hero had spoken of them.

In a short time Isabella made her appearance, attended by her bridesmaids —the two daughters of an English peer.

Richard hastened to present his friends to the Princess; and the cordiality of the parents underwent no contrast on the part of the daughter;—but if she were more courteous—nay, kind—in her manner to either, that preference was shown towards Ellen .

And it struck the young lady that such slight preference *was* evinced towards her; for she turned a quick but rapid glance of profound gratitude upon Richard, as much as to say, "'Tis you whom I must thank for this!"

How lovely did Isabella seem—robed in virgin white, and her cheeks suffused with blushes! There was a charm of ineffable sweetness—a halo of innocence about her, which fascinated the beholder even more than the splendour of her beauty. As she cast down her eyes, and the long slightly-curling black fringes reposed upon her cheeks, there was an air of purest chastity in her appearance which showed how nearly allied her heart was to the guilelessness of angels. And then her loveliness of person—Oh! that was of a nature so ravishing, so enchanting, as to inspire something more than mere admiration—something nearer resembling a worship. Poets have compared eyes to stars—teeth to ivory—lips to coral—bosoms to snow;—they have likened symmetry of form to that of sylphs, and lightness of step to that of fairies;—but poor, poor indeed are all similitudes which we might call to our aid to convey an idea of the beauty of this charming Italian maiden, now arrayed in her bridal vestment!

The ceremony was twofold, Richard being a Protestant and Isabella a Roman Catholic. A clergyman of the Church of England therefore united them, in the first instance, by special licence, at the Grand-Duke's mansion. The bridal party immediately afterwards entered the carriages, which were in readiness, and repaired to the Roman Catholic chapel at Hammersmith, where the hands of the young couple were joined anew according to the ritual of that creed.

And now the most exalted of Richard's earthly hopes were attained;—the only means by which his happiness could be ensured, and a veil drawn over the sorrows of the past, were accomplished. When he looked back to the period of his first acquaintance with Isabella,—remembered how ridiculously insignificant was once the chance that his love for her would ever terminate in aught save disappointment,—and then followed up all the incidents which had gradually smoothed down the difficulties that arose in his path until the happy moment when he knelt by her side at the altar of God,—he was lost in astonishment at the inscrutable ways of that Providence which had thus brought to a successful issue an aspiration that at first wore the appearance of a wild and delusive dream!

On the return of the bridal party to the mansion near Richmond, a splendid banquet was served up; and if there were a sentiment of melancholy which stole upon the happiness of any present, it was on the part of Isabella and her parents at the idea of separation.

At length the *dejeuner* is over; and Isabella retires with her mother and bridesmaids to prepare for her departure. The Grand-Duke takes that opportunity to thrust a sealed packet into our hero's hand. A few minutes elapse—Isabella returns—the farewells take place—and the bridegroom conducts his charming bride to the carriage. Mr. Monroe, Ellen, and Catherine follow in a second chariot.

It was four o'clock in the afternoon when Richard assisted his lovely young wife to alight at the door of his own mansion; and now Markham Place becomes the residence of the Prince and Princess of Montoni.

Vain were it to attempt to describe the delight of the old butler when he beheld his master bring home that beauteous, blushing bride; and—as he said in the course of the day to Mr. Monroe, "It was only, sir, a doo sense of that comportance which belongs to a man in my situation of authority over the servants that perwented me from collapsing into some of them antics that I indulged in when we heerd of Master—I mean of his Highness's successes in Castle Chichory, and when he came home the day before yesterday. But I won't do it, sir—I won't do it; although I don't promise, Mr. Monroe," he added, in a mysterious whisper, "that I shan't go to bed rayther jolly to-night with champagne."

★   ★   ★   ★   ★   ★
  ★   ★   ★   ★   ★

[…]
On the following morning, after breakfast, Richard conducted his lovely bride over the grounds belonging to the Place; and when they had inspected the gardens, he said, "I will now lead you to the hill-top, beloved Isabella, where you will behold those memorials of affection between my brother and myself, which mark the spot where I hope again to meet him."

They ascended the eminence: they stood between the two trees.

But scarcely had Richard cast a glance towards the one planted by the hand of Eugene, when he started, and dropped Isabella's arm.

She threw a look of intense alarm on his countenance; but her fears were immediately succeeded by delight when she beheld the unfeigned joy that was depicted on his features.

"Eugene is alive! He has been hither again—he has revisited this spot!" exclaimed Richard. "See, Isabella—he has left that indication of his presence."

The Princess now observed the inscriptions upon the tree.

They stood thus:—

EUGENE.
Dec. 25, 1836.

EUGENE.
May 17*th*, 1838.

EUGENE
March 6, 1841.

"Eugene was here yesterday," said Richard. "Oh! he still thinks of me— he remembers that he has a brother. Doubtless he has heard of my happiness —my prosperity: perhaps he even learnt that yesterday blest me with your hand, dearest Isabel and that inscription is a congratulation—a token of his kind wish alike to you and to me."

Isabella partook of her husband's joy; and after lingering for some time upon the spot, they retraced their steps to the mansion.

The carriage was already at the door: they entered it; and Richard commanded the coachman to drive to Woolwich.

On their arrival at the wharf where Richard had landed only two days previously, they found a barge waiting to convey them on board the Castelcicalan steamer.

The Grand-Duke and Grand-Duchess, with their suite, received them upon the deck of the vessel.

The hour of separation had come: Alberto and his illustrious spouse were about to return to their native land to ascend a throne.

The Grand-Duke drew Richard aside, and said, "My dear son, you remember your promise to repair to Montoni so soon as the time of appointment with your brother shall have passed."

"I shall only be too happy to return, with my beloved Isabella, to your society," answered Markham. "My brother will keep his appointment; for yesterday he revisited the spot where that meeting is to take place, and inscribed his name upon the tree that he planted."

"That is another source of happiness for you, Richard," said the Grand-Duke; "and well do you deserve all the felicity which this world can give."

"Your Serene Highness has done all that is in mortal power to ensure that felicity," exclaimed Markham. "You have elevated me to a rank only one degree inferior to your own;—you have bestowed upon me an inestimable treasure in the person of your daughter;—and you yesterday placed in my hands a decree appointing me an annual income of twenty thousand pounds from the ducal treasury. Your Serene Highness has been too liberal:—a fourth part will be more than sufficient for all our wants. Moreover, from certain hints which Signor Viviani dropped when I was an inmate of his house at Pinalla—and subsequently, after his arrival at Montoni to take the post of Minister of Finance which I conferred upon him, and which appointment has met the approval of your Serene Highness—I am justified in believing that in July, 1843, I shall inherit a considerable fortune from our lamented friend Thomas Armstrong."

"The larger your resources, Richard, the wider will be the sphere of your benevolence," said the Grand-Duke; then, by way of cutting short our hero's remonstrances in respect to the annual revenue, his Serene Highness exclaimed, "But time presses: we must now say farewell."

We shall not dwell upon the parting scene. Suffice it to say that the grief of the daughter in separating from her parents was attempered by the conviction that she remained behind with an affectionate and well-beloved husband; and the parents sorrowed the less at losing their daughter, because they knew full well that she was united to one possessed of every qualification to ensure her felicity.

And now the anchor was weighed; the steam hissed through the waste-valves as if impatient of delay; and the young couple descended the ship's side into the barge.

The boat was pushed off—and the huge wheels of the steamer began to revolve on their axis, ploughing up the deep water.

The cannon of the arsenal thundered forth a parting salute in honour of the sovereign and his illustrious spouse who were returning to their native land from a long exile.

The ship returned the compliment with its artillery, as it now sped rapidly along.

And the last waving of the Grand-Duchess's handkerchief, and the last farewell gesture on the part of the Grand-Duke met the eyes of Isabella and Richard during an interval when the wind had swept away the smoke of the cannon.

The Prince and Princess of Montoni landed at the wharf, re-entered their carriage, and were soon on their way back to Markham Place.

[The Resurrection Man returns to his house in Globe Town, only to discover that the secret hiding-place of his money has been discovered by Crankey Jem. The sub-plots involving the Marquis of Holmesford and Greenwood also move towards their resolution. Holmesford dies in sensual excess, while Greenwood is revealed as a cheat and a fraud.]

CHAPTER CCXXXIX.
THE RESURRECTION MAN'S RETURN HOME.

As the Resurrection Man hurried through the fields, amidst the darkness of the night, he vented in horrible imprecations the rage he experienced at the failure of a scheme to which he had devoted so much time and trouble.

[...]

And it was to [his house in Globe Town] that he was now repairing. [...] Abandoning, therefore, all his long-nourished schemes of vengeance against the Prince of Montoni, the Rattlesnake, and Crankey Jem, Tidkins was now intent only on securing his treasure, and taking his departure for America with the least possible delay.

It was about two o' clock in the morning when the Resurrection Man, sinking with the fatigues of his long and circuitous journey round all the northern outskirts of London, arrived at his own house.

Wearied as he was, he wasted no time in snatching a temporary repose: a glass of spirits recruited his strength and invigorated his energies; and, with his bunch of keys in is hand, he repaired from his own chamber to the rooms on the ground-floor.

It will be remembered that on a former occasion,—on his return home, in the middle of the month of March, after his escape from the Middlesex House of Correction,—the Resurrection Man had perceived certain indications which led him to imagine that the step of an intruder had visited the ground-floor and the subterranean part of his house. His suspicions had fallen upon Banks; but an interview with this individual convinced him that those suspicions were unfounded; for although he did not question him point-blank upon the subject, yet his penetration was such, that he could judge of the real truth by the undertaker's manner.

Since that period Tidkins had visited his house in Globe Town on several occasions—indeed, as often as he could possibly get away from Ravensworth Hall for the greater portion of a day; and, perceiving no farther indications of the intrusion of a stranger, he became confirmed in the belief which had succeeded his first suspicions, and which was that he had been influenced by groundless alarms.

But now, the moment he put the key into the lock of the door in the alley, he uttered a terrible imprecation—for the key would not turn, and there was evidently something in the lock!

Hastily picking the lock with one of those wire-instruments which are used for the purpose by burglars, he extracted from it a piece of a key which had broken in the wards.

Fearful was now the rage of the Resurrection Man; and when he had succeeded in opening the door, he precipitated himself madly into that department of his abode.

But what pen can describe his savage fury, when, upon lighting a lantern, he saw the trap raised, and the brick removed from the place in the chimney where it covered the secret means of raising the hearth-stone?

Plunging desperately down into the subterranean, at the risk of breaking his neck, Tidkins felt like one on whose eyes a hideous spectre suddenly bursts, when he beheld the door of a cell—the very cell in which his treasure was concealed—standing wide open!

Staggering now, as a drunken man—and no longer rushing wildly along, —but dragging himself painfully,—Tidkins reached that cell.

His worst fears were confirmed: the stone in the centre was removed from its place;—and his treasure was gone!

Yes:—money-bags and jewel-casket—the produce of heaven only knows how much atrocity and blackest crime—had disappeared.

This was the second time that his hoarded wealth was snatched from him.

Then did that man—so energetic in the ways of turpitude, so strong in the stormy paths of guilt,—then did he sink down, with a hollow groan, upon the cold floor of the cell.

For a few minutes he lay like one deprived of sense and feeling, the only indications of life being the violent clenching of his fists, and the demoniac workings of his cadaverous countenance.

Cadaverous!—never did the face of a wretched being in the agonies of strangulation by hanging, present so appalling—so hideous an appearance!

But in a short time the Resurrection Man started up with a savage howl and a terrible imprecation: his energies—prostrated for a period—revived; and his first idea, when arousing from that torpor, was vengeance—a fearful vengeance upon the plunderer.

But who was that plunderer? Whose hand had suddenly beggared him?

His suspicions instantly fixed themselves upon two persons—the only two of his accomplices who were acquainted with the mysteries of the subterranean.

These were Banks and the Buffer.

He was about to turn from the cell, and repair forthwith—even at that hour—to the dwelling of the undertaker, when his eyes suddenly fell upon some letters scrawled in chalk upon the pavement, and which the position of the lantern had hitherto prevented him from observing.

He stooped down, and read the words—"JAMES CUFFIN."

The mystery was solved: his mortal enemy, Crankey Jem, had robbed him of his treasure!

Dark—terribly ominous and foreboding—was now the cloud which overspread the countenance of the Resurrection Man.

"Had I ten times the wealth I have lost," he muttered to himself, with a hyena-like growl, "I would not quit this country till I had wreaked my vengeance upon that man! But this is now no place for me: he has tracked me here—he may set the traps upon me. Let us see if the Bully Grand cannot discover his lurking hole."

With these words,—and now displaying that outward calmness which often covers the most intensely concentrated rage,—the Resurrection Man quitted the subterranean, carefully securing the doors behind him,

He purposely broke a key in the lock of the door leading into the dark alley, so as to prevent the intrusion of any of the neighbours, should their curiosity tempt them to visit the place; for he made up his mind not to return thither again so long as Jem Cuffin was alive and able to betray him.

Having provided himself with a few necessaries, he closed the up-stairs rooms, and then took his departure.

He bent his steps towards the house of the undertaker in Globe Lane; and, knocking him up, obtained admittance and a bed.

When he awoke from a sound sleep, into which sheer fatigue plunged him in spite of the unpleasant nature of his thoughts, it was broad-daylight.

[He determined to devote himself 'heart and soul' to a search after 'that scoundrel Crankey Jem'.]

CHAPTER CCLII.
DEATH OF THE MARQUIS OF HOLMESFORD.

WE have described at great length, in a former portion of our narrative, the voluptuous attractions of that department of Holmesford House which may very properly be denominated "the harem".

The reader doubtless remembers the vast and lofty room which we depicted as being furnished in the most luxurious oriental style, and which was embellished with pictures representing licentious scenes from the mythology of the ancients.

To that apartment we must now once more direct attention.

Grouped together upon two ottomans drawn close to each other, five beautiful women were conversing in a tone so low that it almost sank to a whisper; while their charming countenances wore an expression of mingled suspense and sorrow.

They were all in *deshabillée*, though it was now past four o'clock in the afternoon.

This negligence, however, extended only to their attire; for each of those lovely creatures had bathed her beauteous form in a perfumed bath, and had arranged her hair in the manner best calculated to set off its luxuriance to advantage and at the same time to enhance the charms of that countenance which it enclosed.

But farther than this the toilette of those five fascinating girls had not progressed; and the loose morning-wrappers which they wore, left revealed all the glowing beauties of each voluptuous bust.

There was the Scotch charmer, with her brilliant complexion, her auburn hair, and her red cherry lips:—there was the English girl—the pride of Lancashire—with her brown hair, and her robust but exquisitely modelled proportions:—and next to her, on the same ottoman, sate the Irish beauty, whose sparkling black eyes denoted all the fervour of sensuality.

On the sofa facing these three women, sate the French wanton, her taper fingers playing with the gold chain which, in the true spirit of coquetry, she had thrown negligently round her neck, and the massive links of which made not the least indentation upon the plump fullness of her bosom. By her side was the Spanish houri, her long black ringlets flowing on the white drapery which set off her transparent olive skin to such exquisite advantage.

This group formed an assemblage of charms which would have raised palpitations and excited mysterious fires in the heart of the most heaven-devoted anchorite that ever vowed a life of virgin-purity.

And the picture was the more fascinating—the more dangerous, inasmuch as its voluptuousness was altogether unstudied at this moment, and those beauteous creatures noticed not, in their sisterly confidence towards each other, that their glowing and half-naked forms were thus displayed almost as it might have seemed in a spirit of competition and rivalry.

But what is the topic of their discourse? and wherefore has a shade of melancholy displaced those joyous smiles that were wont to play upon lips of coral opening above teeth of pearls?

Let us hear them converse.

"This illness is the more unfortunate for us," said the Scotch girl, "because it arrived so suddenly."

"And before the Marquis had made his will," added the French-woman.

"Yes," observed the English beauty,—"it was only yesterday afternoon that he assured us he should not fail to take good care of us all whenever he did make his will."

"And now he will die intestate, as the lawyers say," murmured the Scotch girl; "and we shall be sent forth into the world without resources."

"Oh! how shocking to think of!" cried the Spaniard. "I am sure I should die if I were forced to quit this charming place."

[...]

Scarcely were these words uttered, when the door of the apartment opened abruptly, and the Marquis made his appearance.

[...]

Indeed, it was with the greatest difficulty that the young women could restrain a murmur of surprise—almost of disgust—when, as he drew nearer towards them, they beheld the fearful ravages which a few hours' illness had made upon his face. The extent of those inroads was moreover enhanced by the absence of his false teeth, which he had not time to fix in his mouth ere he escaped from the thraldom of his physicians: so that the thinness of his cheeks was rendered almost skeleton-like by the sinking in of his mouth.

The superb dressing-gown seemed a mockery of the shrivelled and wasted form which it loosely wrapped; and as the old nobleman staggered towards his mistresses, whose first ebullition of joy at his appearance was so suddenly shocked by the ghastly hideousness of his aspect, they had not strength nor presence of mind to hasten to meet him.

Kathleen was the first to conquer her aversion and dismay; and she caught the Marquis in her arms just at the instant when, overcome by the exertions of the last few minutes, he was about to sink beneath the weight of sheer exhaustion.

Then the other women crowded forward to lend their aid; and the old nobleman was placed, upon one of the luxurious ottomans.

He closed his eyes, and seemed to breathe with great difficulty.

"Oh! my God—he is dying!" exclaimed Kathleen: "ring for aid—for the physicians—"

"No—no!" murmured the Marquis, in a faint tone; and, opening his eyes once more, he gazed around him—vacantly at first, then more steadily,—until he seemed to recover visual strength sufficient to distinguish the charming countenances that were fixed upon him with mournful interest: "no, my dear girls," he continued, his voice becoming a trifle more powerful; "the doors of this room must not be opened again so long as the breath remains in my body—for I am come," he added with a smile the ghastliness of which all his efforts could not subdue,—"I am come to die amongst you!"

"To die—here—amongst us!" ejaculated all the women (save Kathleen), shrinking back in terror and dismay.

"Yes, my dear girls," returned the Marquis: "and thus will my hope and my prophecy be fulfilled. But let us not trifle away the little time that remains to me. Kathleen, my charmer—I am faint—my spirit seems to be sinking:—give me wine!"

"Wine, my lord?" she repeated, in a tone of kind remonstrance.

"Yes—wine—delicious, sparkling wine!" cried the nobleman, raising himself partially up on the cushions of the sofa. "Delay not—give me champagne!"

The French and Spanish girls hastened to a splendid buffet near the stage at the end of the room, and speedily returned to the vicinity of the ottoman, bearing between them a massive silver salver laden with bottles and glasses.

The wine was poured forth: the Marquis desired Kathleen to steady his hand as he conveyed the nectar to his lips; and he drained the glass of its contents.

A hectic tinge appeared upon his cheeks; his eyes were animated with a partial fire; and he even seemed happy, as he commanded his ladies to drink bumpers of champagne all round.

"Consider that I am going on a long journey, my dear girls," he exclaimed, with a smile; "and do not let our parting be sorrowful. Kathleen, my sweet one, come nearer: there—place yourself so that I may recline my head on your bosom—and now throw that warm, plump, naked arm over my shoulder. Oh! this is paradise!"

And for a few minutes the hoary voluptuary whose licentious passions were dominant even in death, closed his eyes and seemed to enjoy with intense gratification all the luxury of his position.

It was a painful and disgusting sight to behold the shrivelled, haggard, and attenuated countenance of the dying sensualist, pressing upon that full and alabaster globe so warm with health, life, and glowing passions;—painful and disgusting, too, to see that thin, emaciated, and worn-out frame reclining in the arms of a lovely girl in the vigour and strength of youth:—hideous—hideous to view that contiguity of a sapless, withered trunk and a robust and verdant tree!

"Girls," said the Marquis, at length opening his eyes, but without changing his position, "it is useless to attempt to conceal the truth from you: you know that I am dying! Well—no matter: sooner or later Death must come to all! My life has been a joyous—a happy one; and to you who solace me in my dissolution, I am not ungrateful. Anna, dearest—thrust your hand into the pocket of my dressing-gown."

The French-woman obeyed this command, and drew forth a sealed packet, addressed to the five ladies by their christian and surnames.

"Open it," said the Marquis. "Two months ago I made this provision for you, my dear girls—because, entertaining foolish apprehensions relative to making my will, I felt the necessity of at least taking care of you."

While the nobleman was yet speaking, Anna had opened the packet, whence she drew forth a number of Bank-notes.

There were ten—each for a thousand pounds; and a few words written within the envelope specified that the amount was to be equally divided amongst the five ladies.

"Oh! my dear Marquis, how liberal!" exclaimed the French girl, her countenance becoming radiant with joy.

"How generous!" cried the English beauty.

"How noble!" ejaculated the Scotch charmer.

"It is more than generous and noble—it is princely!" said the Spanish houri.

Kathleen simply observed, "My dear lord, I thank you most unfeignedly for this kind consideration on your part."

The Marquis made no reply; but taking the delicate white hand of the Irish girl, as he lay pillowed upon her palpitating breast, he gently slipped upon one of her taper fingers a ring of immense value.

He then squeezed her hand to enjoin silence; and this act was not perceived by the other ladies, who were too busily employed in feasting their eyes upon the Bank-notes to pay attention to aught beside.

"Come—fill the glasses!" suddenly exclaimed the Marquis, after a short pause: "I feel that my strength is failing me fast—the sand of my life's hour-glass is running rapidly away!"

The French girl—to whose mind there was something peculiarly heroical and romantic in the conduct of the Marquis—hastened to obey the order which had been specially addressed to her; and the sparkling juice of Epernay again moistened the parched throat of the dying man, and also enhanced the carnation tints upon the cheeks of the five youthful beauties.

"And now, my charmers," said the nobleman, addressing himself to the French and Spanish women, "gratify me by dancing some pleasing and voluptuous measure,—while you, my loves," he added, turning his glazing eyes upon the Scotch and English girls, "play a delicious strain,—so that my spirit may ebb away amidst the soothing ecstasies of the blissful scene!"

The Marquis spoke in a faint and tremulous voice, for he felt himself growing every moment weaker and weaker; and his head now lay, heavy and motionless, upon the bosom of the Irish girl, whose warm and polished arm was thrown around him.

The Scotch and English girls hastened to place themselves, the former before a splendid harp, and the latter at a pianoforte, the magnificent tones of which had never failed to excite the admiration of all who ever heard them.

Then the French and Spanish women commenced a slow, languishing, and voluptuous dance, the evolutions of which were well adapted to display the fine proportions of their half-naked forms.

A smile relaxed the features of the dying man; and his glances followed the movements of those foreign girls who vied with each other in assuming the most lascivious attitudes.

By degrees, that exciting spectacle grew indistinct to the eyes of the Marquis; and the music no longer fell upon his ears in varied and defined tones, but with a droning monotonous sound.

"Kathleen—Kathleen," he murmured, speaking with the utmost difficulty, "reach me the glass—place the goblet to my lips—it will revive me for a few minutes—"

The Irish girl shuddered in spite of herself—shuddered involuntarily as she felt the cheek of the Marquis grow cold and clammy against her bosom.

"Kathleen—dear Kathleen," he murmured in a whisper that was scarcely audible; "give me the goblet!"

Conquering her repugnance, the Irish girl, who possessed a kind and generous heart, reached a glass on the table near the sofa; and, raising the nobleman's head, she placed the wine to his lips.

With a last—last expiring effort, he took the glass in his own hand, and swallowed a few drops of its contents:—his eyes were lighted up again for a moment, and his cheek flushed; but his head fell back heavily upon the white bosom.

Kathleen endeavoured to cry for aid—and could not: a sensation of fainting came over her—she closed her eyes—and a suffocating feeling in the throat almost choked her.

But still the music continued and the dance went on, for several minutes more.

All at once a shriek emanated from the lips of Kathleen: the music ceased —the dance was abandoned—and the Irish girl's companions rushed towards the sofa.

Their anticipations were realised: the Marquis was no more!

The hope which he had so often expressed in his life-time, was fulfilled almost to the very letter;—for the old voluptuary had "*died with his head pillowed on the naked—heaving bosom of beauty, and with a glass of sparkling champagne in his hand!*"

.

CHAPTER CCLIII.
THE EX-MEMBER FOR ROTTENBOROUGH.

It was now the middle of April, 1843.

The morning was fine, and the streets were marked with the bustle of men of business, clerks, and others repairing to their respective offices, when Mr. George Montague Greenwood turned from Saint Paul's Churchyard into Cheapside.

He was attired in a plain, and even somewhat shabby manner: there was not a particle of jewellery about him; and a keen eye might have discovered, in the *tout ensemble* of his appearance, that his toilette had been arranged with every endeavour to produce as good an effect as possible.

Thus his neckcloth was tied with a precision seldom bestowed upon a faded piece of black silk: His shirt-cuffs were drawn down so as to place an interval of snowy white between the somewhat threadbare sleeve of the blue coat and the common grey glove of Berlin wool:—a black riband hung round his neck and was gathered at the ends in the right pocket of the soiled satin waistcoat, so as to leave the beholder in a state of uncertainty whether it were connected with a watch or only an eye-glass—or, indeed, with any thing at all;—and the Oxford-mixture trousers, *rather* white at the knees, were strapped tightly over a pair of well-blacked bluchers, a casual observer would certainly have taken for Wellingtons.

In his hand he carried a neat black cane; and his gait was characterised by much of the self-sufficiency which had marked it in better days. It was, however, far removed from a swagger: Greenwood was too much of a gentleman in his habits to fall into the slightest manifestation of vulgarity.

His beautiful black hair, curling and glossy, put to shame the brownish hue of the beaver hat which had evidently seen some service, and had lately been exposed to all the varieties of weather peculiar to this capricious climate. His face—eminently handsome, as we have before observed—was pale and rather thin; but there was a haughty assurance in the proud curl of the upper lip, and a fire in his large dark eyes, which showed that hope was not altogether a stranger to the breast of Mr. George Montague Greenwood.

It was about a quarter past nine in the morning when this gentleman entered the great thoroughfare of Cheapside.

Perhaps there is no street in all London which presents so many moral phases to the eyes of the acute beholder as this one, and at that hour; inasmuch as those eyes may single out, and almost read the pursuit of, every individual forming an item in the dense crowd that is then rolling onward to the vicinity of the Bank of England.

For of every ten persons, nine are proceeding in that direction.

Reader, let us pause for a moment and examine the details of the scene to which we allude: for Greenwood has slackened his pace—his eye has caught sight of Bow clock—and he perceives that he is yet too early to commence the visits which he intends to make in certain quarters.

And first, gentle reader, behold that young man with the loose taglioni and no undercoat: he has a devil-may-care kind of look about him, mingled with an air of seediness, as if he had been up the best part of the night at a free-and-easy. He is smoking a cigar—at that hour of the morning! It is impossible to gaze at him for two seconds, without being convinced that he is an articled clerk to an attorney, and that he does n't care so long as he reaches the office just five minutes before the "governor" arrives.

But that old man, with a threadbare suit of black, and the red cotton handkerchief sticking so suspiciously out of his pocket, as if he had something wrapped up in it,—who is he? Mark how he shuffles along, dragging his heavy high-lows over the pavement at a pace too speedy for his attenuated frame: and see with what anxiety he looks up at the clock projecting out far over-head, to assure himself that he shall yet be at his office within two minutes of half-past nine—or else risk his place and the eighteen shillings a week which it brings him in, and on which he has to support a wife and large family. He is a copying clerk in a lawyer's office—there can be no doubt of it; and the poor man has his dinner wrapped up in his pocket-handkerchief!

Do you observe that proud, pompous-looking stout man, with the large yellow cane in his hand, and the massive chain and seals hanging from his fob? He is a stockbroker who, having got up a bubble Railway Company, has enriched himself in a single day, after having struggled against difficulties for twenty years. But, see—a fashionably-dressed gentleman, with a *little* too much jewellery about his person, and a *rather* too severe swagger in his gait, overtakes our stout friend, and passes his arm familiarly in his as he wishes him "good morning." There is no mistake about this individual: he is the Managing-Director of the stockbroker's Company, and was taken from a three-pair back in the New Cut to preside at the Board.

[...]

But we must abandon any farther scrutiny of the several members of the crowd in Cheapside—at least for the present; because it is now half-past nine o'clock, and Mr. Greenwood has reached Cornhill.

Here he paused—and sighed,—sighed deeply.

That sigh told a long and painful history,—of how he had lately been rich and prosperous—how he had lost all by grasping at more—how he was now reduced almost to the very verge of penury—and how he wondered whether he should ever be wealthy and great again!

"Yes—yes: I *will* be!" he said to himself—speaking not with his lips, but with that silent though emphatic tongue which belongs to the soul. "My good star cannot have deserted me for ever! But this day must show!"

Then, calling all his assurance to his aid, he turned into the office of a well-known merchant and capitalist on Cornhill.

The clerks did not immediately recognise him; for the last time he had called there, it was at four in the afternoon and he had alighted from an elegant cab: whereas now it was half-past nine in the morning, and he had evidently come on foot. But when he demanded, in his usual authoritative tone, whether their master had arrived yet, they recollected him, and replied in the affirmative.

Greenwood accordingly walked into the merchant's private office.

[...]

The merchant affected not to perceive the out-stretched hand; nor did he return the bland smile with which Mr. Greenwood accosted him. But, just raising his eyes from the morning paper which lay before him, he said in a cold tone, "Oh! Mr. Greenwood, I believe? Pray, sir, what is your business?"

The ex-member for Rottenborough took a chair uninvited, and proceeded to observe in a confidential kind of whisper,—"The fact is, my dear sir, I have conceived a magnificent project for making a few thousands into as many millions, I may say; and as on former occasions you and I have done *some* little business together—and I have put a *few* good things in your way—I thought I would give you the refusal of my new design."

"I am really infinitely obliged to you, Mr. Greenwood—"

"Oh! I knew you would be, my dear sir!" interrupted the ex-member. "The risk is nothing—the gains certain and enormous. You and I can keep it all to ourselves; and—"

"You require me to advance the funds, I presume?" asked the merchant, eyeing his visitor askance.

"Just so—a few thousands only—to be repaid out of the first proceeds, of course," returned Greenwood.

"Then, sir, I beg to decline the speculation," said the merchant, drily.

"Speculation! it is *not* a speculation," cried Greenwood: "it is a certainty."

"Nevertheless, sir, I must decline it; and as my time is very much occupied—"

"Oh! I shall not intrude upon you any longer," interrupted Greenwood, indignantly; and he strode out of the office.

[…]

[H]is anger had, however, cooled and his spirits revived by the time he reached Birchin Lane, where dwelt another of his City acquaintances.

This individual was a capitalist who had once been saved from serious embarrassment, if not from total ruin, by a timely advance of funds made to him by Greenwood; and though the capitalist had paid enormous interest for the accommodation, he had nevertheless always exhibited the most profound gratitude towards the ex-member for Rottenborough.

It was, therefore, with great confidence that Greenwood entered the private office of the capitalist.

"Ah, my dear fellow," cried the latter, apparently overjoyed to see his visitor. […]

Greenwood addressed him in terms similar to those which he had used with the merchant a few minutes previously.

[…]

"Then, in plain terms," continued Greenwood, "do me the service of advancing two or three thousand pounds to set my new project in motion."

"Impossible, Greenwood—impossible!" cried the capitalist, buttoning up his breeches-pockets. "Things are in such a state that I would not venture a penny upon the most feasible speculation in the world."

"Perhaps you will lend me a sum—"

"Lend! Ah! ha! Now, really, Greenwood, this is too good! Lend, indeed! What—when we are all in the borrowing line in the City!"—and the capitalist chuckled, as if he had uttered a splendid joke.

[…]

"[B]ut I declare most solemnly that fifty pounds at this moment would be of the greatest service to me."

"Nothing gives me more pain than to refuse a friend like you," answered the capitalist: "but, positively, I could not part with a shilling to-day to save my own brother from a gaol."

Greenwood rose, put on his hat, and left the office without uttering another word.

[...]

He could now no longer remain blind to the cruel conviction that the extremities of his position were well known in the City, and that the hopes with which he had sallied forth three hours previously were mere delusive visions.

Still he was resolved to leave no stone unturned in the endeavour to retrieve his ruined fortunes; but feeling sick at heart and the prey to a deep depression of spirits, he plunged hastily into a public-house to take some refreshment.

And now behold the once splendid and fastidious Greenwood,—the man who had purchased the votes of a constituency, and had even created a sensation within the walls of Parliament,—the individual who had discounted bills of large amount for some of the greatest peers of England, and whose luxurious mode of living had once been the envy and wonder of the fashionable world,—behold the ex-member for Rottenborough partaking of a pint of porter and a crust of bread and cheese in the dingy parlour of a public house!

[...]

No wonder, then, that the bitter—bitter tears started from his eyes; and, though he immediately checked that first ebullition of heart-felt anguish yet the effort only caused the storm of emotions to rage the more painfully within his breast.

For, in imagination, he cast his eyes towards a mansion a few miles distant; and there he beheld *one* whose condition formed a striking contrast with his own—*one* who had suddenly burst from obscurity and created for himself as proud a name as might be found in Christendom,—a young man whose indomitable energies and honourable aspirations had enabled him to lead armies to conquest, and who had taken his place amongst the greatest Princes in the universe!

The comparison which Greenwood drew—despite of himself—between the elevated position of Richard Markham and his own fallen, ruined lot, produced feelings of so painful—so exquisitely agonizing a nature, that he could endure them no longer. He felt that they were goading him to madness—the more so because he was alone in that dingy parlour at the time, and was therefore the least likely to struggle against them successfully.

Hastily quitting the public-house, he rushed into the street, where the fresh air seemed to do him good.

[...]

[H]e composed his countenance as well as he could ere he entered the office of a wealthy stockbroker in Moorgate Street.

The stockbroker was lounging over the clerks' desk, conversing with a merchant whom Greenwood also knew; and the moment the ex-member for Rottenborough entered, the two City gentlemen treated him to a long, impertinent, and contemptuous stare.

"Ah!" said Greenwood, affecting a pleasant smile, which, God knows! did not come from the heart; "you do not appear to recollect me? Am I so very much changed as all *that?*"

"Well—it *is* Greenwood, pos-i-tive-ly!" drawled the stockbroker, turning towards his friend the merchant in a manner that was equivalent to saying, " I wonder at his impudence in calling here."

[...]

"You are disposed to be facetious, gentlemen," said the object of this intended witticism but really galling insult: "I presume that my long absence from the usual City haunts—"

"I can assure you, Greenwood," interrupted the stockbroker, "that the City has got on uncommonly well without you. The Bank has n't stopped payment—bills are easy of discount—money is plentiful—"

"And yet," said Greenwood, determined to receive all this sarcasm as quietly as a poor devil ought to do when about to make a proposal requiring an advance of funds,—"and yet a certain capitalist—a very intimate friend of mine, in Birchin Lane—assured me just now that money was very scarce."

"Ha! ha! ha!" laughed the stockbroker.

"He! he! he!" chuckled the merchant.

"Why, the fact is, Greenwood," continued the broker, "your *very intimate friend* the capitalist was here only a quarter of an hour ago; and he delighted us hugely by telling us how you called upon him this morning with a scheme that would make millions, and ended by wanting to borrow fifty pounds of him."

"He! he! he!" again chuckled the merchant.

"Ha! ha! ha!" once more laughed the stockbroker; and, taking his friend's arm, he led him into his private office, the two continuing to laugh and chuckle until the door closed behind them.

[...]

[In the closing chapters of Volume II, all the plots and sub-plots move towards resolution. Tidkins meets a suitable fate and dies blinded by an explosion in his own cellar, in which he has been trapped by Crankey Jem. Greenwood's true identity is finally revealed, and he dies in the arms of his brother after being attacked by his ex-valet, Lafleur.]

CHAPTER CCLVII.
THE REVENGE.

IT was about eleven o'clock in the night of the first Saturday of June, that the Resurrection Man—the terrible Anthony Tidkins—issued from the dwelling of Mr. Banks, the undertaker in Globe Lane, Globe Town.

Mr. Banks followed him to the threshold, and, ere he bade him good night, said, as he retained him by the sleeve, "And so you are determined to go back to the old crib?"

"Yes—to be sure I am," returned Tidkins. "I've been looking after that scoundrel Crankey Jem for the last two years, without even being able so much as to hear of him. The Bully Grand has set all his Forty Thieves to work for me; and still not a trace—not a sign of the infernal villain!"

"Well," observed Banks, "it does look as if the cussed wessel had made hisself scarce to some foreign part, where it's to be hoped he's dead, buried, and resurrectionised by this time."

"Or else he's living like a fighting-cock on all the tin he robbed me of," exclaimed Tidkins, with a savage growl. "But I'm sure he's not in London; and so I do n't see any reason to prevent me from going back to my old crib. I shall feel happy again there. It's now two years and better since I left it—and I'm sick of doing nothing but hunt after a chap that's perhaps thousands of miles off."

"And all that time, you see," said Banks, "you've been doing no good for yourself or your friends; and if it was n't for them blessed coffins on economic principles, which turn me in a decent penny, I'm sure I do n't know what would have become of me and my family."

"You forget the swag we got from the old woman in Golden Lane," whispered Tidkins, impatiently. "Did n't I give you a fair half, although you never entered the place, but only kept watch outside?"

"Yes—yes," said Mr. Banks; "I know you treated me very well, Tony—as you've always done. But I'm sorry you used the wicked old creetur as you did."

"Why did she resist, then, damn her!" growled the Resurrection Man.

"Ah! well-a-day," moaned the hypocritical undertaker: "she's a blessed defunct now—a wenerable old carkiss—and all packed up nice and cosy in a hospital coffin too! But they can't get up them coffins as well as me: I can beat 'em all at that work—'cause its the economic principles as does it."

"Hold your stupid tongue, you infernal old fool!" muttered Tidkins; "and get yourself to bed at once, so that you may be up early in the morning and come to me by eight o'clock."

"You do n't mean to do what you was telling me just now?" said Banks, earnestly. "Depend upon it, he'll prove too much for you."

"Not he!" exclaimed Tidkins. "I've a long—long score to settle up with him; and if he has neither seen nor heard of me for the last two years, it was only because I wanted to punish Crankey Jem first."

"And now that you can't find that cussed indiwidual," said Banks, "you mean to have a go in earnest against the Prince?"

"I do," answered Tidkins, with an abruptness which was in itself expressive of demoniac ferocity. "You come to me to-morrow morning; and see if I won't invent some scheme that shall put Richard Markham in my power. I tell you what it is, Banks," added the Resurrection Man, in a hoarse—hollow whisper, "I hate that fellow to a degree I cannot explain; and depend upon it, he shall gnash his teeth in one of the dark cells yonder before he's a week older."

"And what good will that do you?" asked the undertaker.

"What good!" repeated Tidkins, scornfully: then, after a short pause, he turned towards Banks, and said in a low voice, "We'll make him pay an immense sum for his ransom—a sum that shall enrich us both, Ned: and then—"

"And then?" murmured Banks, interrogatively.

"And then—when I've got all I can from him," replied Tidkins, "*I'll murder him!*"

With these words—uttered in a tone of terrible ferocity—the Resurrection Man hastened away from the door of the undertaker's dwelling.

The sky was overcast with dark clouds of stormy menace: the night was dark; and big drops of rain began to patter down, as Tidkins hurried along the streets leading towards his own abode—that abode which he was now on the point of revisiting after an absence of two years!

At length he reached the house; and though he stopped for a few minutes to examine its outward appearance from the middle of the street, the night was so dark that he could not distinguish whether its aspect had undergone any change.

Taking from his pocket the door-key, which he had carefully retained ever since he abandoned the place after the discovery of the loss of his treasure, he soon effected an entrance into the house.

Having closed the door, he immediately lighted a lantern which he had brought with him; and then, holding it high above his head, he hastily scrutinized the walls, the stairs, and as much of the landing above the precipitate steps, as his range of vision could embrace.

There was not the least indication of the presence of intruders: the dust had accumulated upon the stairs, undisturbed by the print of footsteps; and the damp had covered the walls with a white mildew.

Tidkins was satisfied with this scrutiny, and ascended to the first-floor rooms, the doors of which were closed—as if they had never been opened during his absence of two years.

The interior appearance of the two chambers was just the same as when he was last there—save in respect to the ravages of the damp, the accumulation of the dust, and the effects of the rain which had forced its way through the roof.

"Well, nothing has been disturbed up here—that's certain enough," said Tidkins to himself. "Now for a survey of the vaults."

Taking from a shelf the bunch of skeleton-keys, which had suffered grievously from the damp, the Resurrection Man descended the stairs, issued forth into the street, and turned up the alley running along the side of the house.

His first attempt to open the door in that alley was unsuccessful, there being evidently some impediment in the lock: but a moment's reflection reminded him that he himself had broken a key in the lock, ere he had quitted the premises at the end of May, 1841.

Nearly ten minutes were occupied in picking the lock, which was sadly rusted; but at length this task was accomplished—and the Resurrection Man entered the ground-floor of his abode.

The condition in which he had found the lock of the door in the alley would have been a sufficient proof, in the estimation of any less crafty individual, that no intrusive footstep had disturbed that department of the dwelling: but Tidkins was resolved to assure himself on all points relative to the propriety of again entrusting his safety to that abode.

"I think it's all right," he muttered, holding up his lantern, and glancing around with keen looks. "Still the lock might have been picked since I was here last, and another key purposely broken in it to stave off suspicion. At any rate, it is better to examine every nook and corner of the whole place—and so I will!"

He entered the front room on the ground-floor: the resurrection tools and house-breaking implements, which were piled up in that chamber, had not been disturbed. Huge black cob-webs, dense as filthy rags, were suspended from mattock to spade, and from crow-bar to long flexible iron rod.

Tidkins turned with an air of satisfaction into the back room, where the dust lay thick upon the floor, and the walls were green with damp.

"Yes—it *is* all right!" he exclaimed, joyfully. "no one has been here during my absence. I suppose that villain Jem Cuffin was content with all the gold and jewels he got, and took no farther steps to molest me. But, by Satan! if ever I clap my eyes on him again!"—and the Resurrection Man ground his teeth furiously together. "Well," he continued, speaking aloud to himself in a musing strain, "it's a blessing to be able to come back and settle in the old crib! There's no place in London like it: the house in Chick Lane is nothing to it. And now that I *have* returned," he added, his hideous countenance becoming ominously dark and appallingly threatening, as the glare of the lantern fell upon it,—"one of these deep, cold, cheerless dungeons shall soon become the abode of Richard Markham!"

As he uttered these last words in a loud, measured, and savage voice, the Resurrection Man raised the stone-trap, and descended into the subterranean.

The detestable monster gloated in anticipation upon the horrible revenge which he meditated; and as he now trod the damp pavement of the vaulted passage, he glanced first at the four doors on the right, then at the four doors on the left, as if he were undecided in which dungeon to immure his intended victim.

At length he stopped before one of the doors, exclaiming, "Ah! this must be the cell! It's the one, as I have been told, where so many maniacs dashed their brains out against the wall, when this place was used as an asylum—long before my time."

Thus musing, Tidkins entered the cell, holding the lantern high up so as to embrace at a glance all the gloomy horrors of its aspect.

"Yes—yes!" he muttered to himself: "this is the one for Richard Markham! All that he has ever done to me shall soon be fearfully visited on his own head! Ah, ah! we shall see whether his high rank—his boasted virtues—his immense influence—and his glorious name can mitigate one pang of all the sufferings that he must here endure! Yes," repeated Tidkins, a fiendish smile relaxing his stern countenance,—"*this* is the dungeon for Richard Markham!"

"No—it is *thine!*" thundered a voice; and at the same moment the door of the cell closed violently upon the Resurrection Man.

Tidkins dropped the lantern, and flung himself with all his strength against the massive door;—but the huge bolt on the outside was shot into its iron socket too rapidly to permit that desperate effort to prove of the least avail.

Then a cry of mingled rage and despair burst from the breast of the Resurrection Man,—a cry resembling that of the wolf when struck by the bullet of the hunter's carbine!

"The hour of vengeance is come at last!" exclaimed Crankey Jem, as he lighted the candle in a small lantern which he took from his pocket. "There shall you remain, Tidkins—to perish by starvation—to die by inches—to feel the approach of Death by means of such slow tortures that you will curse the day which saw your birth!"

"Jem, do not say all that!" cried the Resurrection Man, from the interior of the dungeon. "You would not be so cruel? Let me out—and we will be friends."

"Never!" ejaculated Cuffin. "What! have I hunted after you—dogged you—watched you—then lost sight of you for two years—now found you out again—at length got you into my power—and all this for nothing?"

"Well, Jem—I know that I used you badly," said the Resurrection Man, in an imploring tone: "but forgive me—pray forgive me! Surely you were sufficiently avenged by plundering me of my treasure—my hoarded gold—my casket of jewels?"

"Miserable wretch!" cried Crankey Jem, in a tone of deep disgust: "do not imagine that I took your gold and your jewels to enrich myself. No: had I been starving, I would not have purchased a morsel of bread by means of their aid! Two hours after I had become possessed of your treasure, I consigned it all—yes, all—gold and jewels—to the bed of the Thames!"

"Then are you not sufficiently avenged?" demanded Tidkins, in a voice denoting how fiercely rage was struggling with despair in his breast.

"Your death, amidst lingering tortures, will alone satisfy me!" returned Crankey Jem. "Monster that you are, you shall meet the fate which you had reserved for an excellent nobleman whose virtues are as numerous as your crimes!"

"What good will my death do you, Jem?" cried Tidkins, his tone now characterised only by an expression of deep—intense—harrowing despair.

"What good would the death of Richard Markham have done *you*?" demanded James Cuffin. "Ah! you cannot answer that question! Of what advantage is your cunning now? But listen to me, while I tell you how I have succeeded in over-reaching you at last. One night—more than two years ago—I was watching for you in the street. I had found out your den—and I was waiting your return, to plunge my dagger into your breast. But when you did come home that night, you was not alone. Another man was with you; and a woman, blindfolded, was being dragged between you up the alley. I watched—you and the man soon afterwards reappeared; but the woman was not with you. Then I knew that she was a prisoner, or had been murdered; and I thought that if I could place you in the hands of justice, with the certainty of sending you to the scaffold, my revenge would be more complete. But my plan was spoilt by the silly affair of young Holford; for I was locked up in prison on account of that business. But I got my liberty at last; and that very same night I returned to this house. I knew that you had been arrested and was in Coldbath Fields; and so I resolved to examine the entire premises. By means of skeleton keys I obtained an easy entrance into the lower part of the house; and, after a little careful search, I discovered the secret of the trap-door. I visited the cells; but the woman was not in any of them. And now you know how I came to discover the mysteries of your den, Tidkins; and you can guess how at another visit I found the hiding-place of your treasure."

"Jem, one word!" cried the Resurrection Man, in a hoarse—almost hollow tone. "You have got me in your power—do you mean to put your dreadful threat into execution?"

"No persuasion on earth can change my mind!" returned the avenger, in a terrible voice. "Hark! this is a proof of my determination!"

A dead silence prevailed in the subterranean for two or three minutes; and then that solemn stillness was broken by the sounds of a hammer, falling with heavy and measured cadence upon the head of a large nail.

"Devil!" roared the Resurrection Man, from the interior of the cell.

Crankey Jem was nailing up the door!

It must be supposed that this appalling conviction worked the mind of the immured victim up to a pitch of madness; for he now threw himself against the door with a fury that made it crack upon its hinges—massive and studded with iron nails though it were!

But Crankey Jem pursued his awful task; and as nail after nail was driven in, the more demoniac became the feelings of his triumph.

Tidkins continued to rush against the door, marking the intervals of these powerful but desperate attempts to burst from his living tomb, with wild cries and savage howls such as Cuffin had never before heard come from the breast of a human being.

At length the last nail was driven in; and then the struggles against the door ceased.

"Now you can understand that I am determined!" cried the avenger. "And here shall I remain until all is over with you, Tidkins. No! I shall now and then steal out for short intervals at a time, to procure food—food to sustain *me*, while *you* are starving in your coffin!"

"Infernal wretch!" shouted Tidkins: "you are mistaken! I will not die by starvation, if die I must. I have matches with me—and in a moment I can blow the entire house—aye, and half the street along with it—into the air!"

"You will not frighten me, Tidkins," said Crankey Jem, in a cool and taunting tone.

"Damnation!" thundered the Resurrection Man, chafing against the door like a maddened hyena in its cage: "will neither prayers nor threats move you? Then must I do my worst!"

Crankey Jem heard him stride across the dungeon; but still the avenger remained at his post,—leaning against the door, and greedily drinking in each groan—each curse—each execration—and each howl, that marked the intense anguish endured by the Resurrection Man.

Presently James Cuffin heard the sharp sound of a match as it was drawn rapidly along the wall.

He shuddered—but moved not.

Solemn was the silence which now prevailed for a few moments: at length an explosion—low and subdued, as of a small quantity of gunpowder—took place in the cell.

But it was immediately followed with a terrific cry of agony; and the Resurrection Man fell heavily against the door.

"My eyes! my eyes!" he exclaimed, in a tone indicative of acute pain: "O God! I am blinded!"

"Sight would be of no use in that dark dungeon," said Crankey Jem, with inhuman obduracy of heart towards his victim.

"Are you not satisfied now, demon—devil—fiend!" almost shrieked the Resurrection Man. "The powder has blinded me, I say!"

"It was damp, and only exploded partially," said the avenger. "Try again!"

"Wretch!" exclaimed Tidkins; and James Cuffin heard him dash himself upon the paved floor of the cell, groaning horribly.

★   ★   ★   ★   ★   ★

Ten days afterwards, Crankey Jem set to work to open the door of the dungeon.

This was no easy task; inasmuch as the nails which he had driven in were strong, and had caught a firm hold of the wood.

But at length—after two hours' toil—the avenger succeeded in forcing an entrance into the cell.

He knew that he incurred no danger by this step: for, during that interval of ten days, he had scarcely ever quitted his post outside the door of the dungeon;—and there had he remained, regaling his ears with the delicious music formed by the groans—the prayers—the screams—the shrieks—the ravings—and the curses of his victim.

At length those appalling indications of a lingering—slow—agonizing death,—the death of famine,—grew fainter and fainter; and in the middle of the ninth night they ceased altogether.

Therefore was it that on the morning of the tenth day, the avenger hesitated not to open the door of the dungeon.

And what a spectacle met his view when he entered that cell!

The yellow glare of his lantern fell upon the pale, emaciated, hideous countenance of the Resurrection Man, who lay on his back upon the cold, damp pavement—a stark and rigid corse!

Crankey Jem stooped over the body, and examined the face with a satisfaction which he did not attempt to subdue.

The eyes had been literally burnt in their sockets; and it was true that the Resurrection Man was blinded, in the first hour of his terrible imprisonment, by the explosion of the gunpowder in an iron pipe running along the wall of the dungeon!

The damp had, however, rendered that explosion only partial: had the train properly ignited, the entire dwelling would have been blown into the air.

★ ★ ★ ★ ★ ★
 ★ ★ ★ ★ ★

A few hours afterwards, the following letter was delivered at Markham Place by the postman:—

"Your mortal enemy, my lord, is no more. My vengeance has overtaken him at last. Anthony Tidkins has died a horrible death:—had he lived, you would have become his victim.
"JAMES CUFFIN."

CHAPTER CCLVIII.
THE APPOINTMENT KEPT.

It was the 10th of July, 1843.

The bell upon the roof of Markham Place had just proclaimed the hour of nine, and the morning was as bright and beautiful as the cheerful sun, the cloudless sky, and the gentle breeze could render a summer-day,—when a party of eight persons ascended the hill on which stood the two trees.

Those emblems of the fraternal affection of early years were green, verdant, and flourishing; and on the one which had been planted by the hands of the long-lost brother, were the following inscriptions:—

EUGENE.
Dec. 25, 1836.

EUGENE.
May 17*th*, 1838.

EUGENE.
March 6, 1841.

EUGENE.
July 1*st*, 1843.

This last inscription, as the reader will perceive, had only been very recently added; and Richard regarded it as a promise—a pledge—a solemn sign that the appointment would be kept.

It was nine o'clock in the evening when the parting between the brothers took place in the year 1831; and, although it was impossible to determine at what hour of the day on which the twelve years expired, Eugene would return, nevertheless Richard, judging by his own anxiety to clasp a brother in his arms, felt certain that this brother would not delay the moment that was to re-unite them.

Accordingly, at nine o'clock on the morning of the 10th of July, 1843, the Prince, repaired to the eminence on which he hoped—oh! how fondly hoped —full soon to welcome the long-lost Eugene.

His seven companions were the Princess Isabella, Ellen, Mr. Monroe, Katherine, Mario Bazzano, Eliza Sydney, and the faithful Whittingham.

Richard could not conceal a certain nervous suspense under which he laboured; for although he felt assured of Eugene's appearance, yet so long a period had elapsed since they had parted, and so many vicissitudes might have occurred during the interval, that he trembled lest the meeting should be characterised by circumstances which would give his brother pain.

The Princess Isabella, naturally anxious to become acquainted with her brother-in-law, also looked forward to the return of the long-lost one with emotions which enabled her to comprehend those that animated her husband; and pressing his hand tenderly as they seated themselves on the bench between the trees, she whispered, "Be of good cheer, Richard: your brother will keep the appointment—and oh! what joy for us all!"

[...]

And Ellen—poor Ellen!—how difficult for her was the task of concealing all the emotions which agitated her bosom now! But she nevertheless derived much encouragement and hope from the frequent looks of profound meaning which were directed towards her by Eliza Sydney.

[...]

Mr. Monroe and Whittingham shared to a considerable degree the suspense which now animated them all.

★   ★   ★   ★   ★   ★

It was about a quarter past nine o'clock, when Mr. Greenwood halted by the road-side, at a spot which commanded a view of the hill-top whereon stood the two trees.

He was on foot; and though he had so far recovered from his recent accident as to exhibit only a very trifling lameness in his gait, still the short walk which he had taken from Islington to the immediate vicinity of Markham Place, compelled him to pause and rest by the way-side.

He looked towards the hill, and could plainly distinguish the number of persons who were stationed on that eminence.

A deadly pallor overspread his countenance; and tears started from his eyes.

But in a few moments he exercised a violent effort over his emotions, and exclaimed aloud, with a kind of desperate emphasis, "I have promised *her* to go through the ordeal—and I must nerve myself to do so! Ah! Ellen," he added, his voice suddenly changing to a plaintive tone, "you have forced me to love you—you have taught me to bless the affectionate care and solicitude of woman!"

This apostrophe to his wife seemed to arouse all the better feelings of his soul; and without farther hesitation, he pursued his way towards the hill.

In a few minutes he reached a point where the road took a sudden turn to the right, thus running round all one side of the base of the eminence, and passing by the mansion itself.

There he paused again;—for although the party assembled on the hill were plainly perceived by him, he was yet unseen by them—a hedge concealing him from their view.

"Oh! is the dread ordeal so near at hand?" he exclaimed, with a temporary revival of bitterness of spirit. "Scarcely separated from *him* by a distance of two hundred yards—a distance so soon cleared—and yet—and yet—"

At that instant he caught sight of the figure of his wife, who, having advanced a few paces in front of her companions, stood more conspicuously than they upon the brow of the hill.

"She anxiously awaits my coming!" he murmured to himself. "Oh! why do I hesitate?"

And, as he spoke, he was about to emerge from the shade of the high hedge which concealed him,—about to turn the angle of the road, whereby he would immediately be perceived by those who stood on the hill,—when his attention was suddenly called elsewhere.

For, no sooner had the words—"Oh! why do I hesitate?" issued from his lips, than a post-chaise, which was dashing along the road towards London at a rapid rate, upset only a few paces from the spot where he had paused to glance towards the hill.

One of the fore-wheels of the vehicle had come off; and the chaise rolled over with a heavy crash.

The postilion instantly stopped his horses; while a man—the only traveller whom the vehicle contained—emerged from the door that was uppermost, and which he had contrived to open.

All this occurred so rapidly that the traveller stood in the road a few instants after the upsetting of the chaise.

Greenwood drew near to inquire if he were hurt: but, scarcely had his eyes caught a glimpse of that man's features, when he uttered a cry of mingled rage and delight, and sprang towards him.

For that traveller was Lafleur!

"Villain!" cried Greenwood, seizing hold of the Frenchman by the collar: "to you I owe all my misfortunes! Restore me the wealth of which you vilely plundered me!"

"Unhand me," exclaimed the ex-valet; "or, by heaven—"

"Wretch!" interrupted Greenwood: "it is for me to threaten!"

Lafleur gnashed his teeth with rage, and endeavoured to shake off his assailant with a sudden and desperate effort to hurl him to the ground.

But Greenwood, weakened though he was by illness, maintained his hold upon the Frenchman, and called for assistance.

The postilion knew not whose part to take, and therefore remained neutral.

Lafleur's situation was most critical; but he was not the man to yield without a desperate attempt to free himself.

Suddenly taking a pistol from his pocket, he aimed a furious blow, with the butt-end of the weapon, at the head of Greenwood, whose hat had fallen off in the struggle.

The blow descended with tremendous force: and in the next moment Greenwood lay senseless on the road, while Lafleur darted away from the spot with the speed of lightning.

For an instant the postilion hesitated whether to pursue the fugitive or attend to the wounded man; but he almost immediately decided in favour of the more humane course.

Upon examination he found that Greenwood's forehead had received a terrible wound, from which the blood was streaming down his temples.

He was moreover quite senseless; and the postilion, after binding the wound with a handkerchief, vainly endeavoured to recover him.

"Well, it won't do to let the poor gentleman die in this way," said the man to himself; and, after an instant's reflection, he remembered that Markham Place was close at hand.

Depositing Greenwood as comfortably as he could on the cushions which he took from the chaise, he hastened to the mansion, and related to the servants all that had occurred.

Without a moment's hesitation,—well knowing that their conduct would be approved of by their excellent master,—three stout footmen hastened, with the means of forming a litter, to the spot where the postilion had left Greenwood.

On their arrival they found that he had to some extent recovered his senses; and a cordial, which one of the footmen poured down his throat, completely revived him.

But, alas! he was aroused only to the fearful conviction that he had received his death-blow; for that mysterious influence which sometimes warns the soul of its approaching flight, was upon him!

"My good friends," he said, in a faint and languid tone, "I have one request to make—the request of a dying man!"

"Name it, sir," returned the senior footman; "and command us as you will."

"I conjure you, then," exclaimed Greenwood, speaking with more strength and animation than at first,—"I conjure you to remove me on that litter which your kindness has prepared, to the spot where your master, his family, and friends are now assembled. You hesitate! Oh! grant me this request, I implore you—and the Prince will not blame you!"

The servants were well aware of the motive which had induced their master and his companions to repair to the hill-top thus early on this particular day;

and the urgent request of Greenwood now excited a sudden suspicion in their minds.

But they did not express their thoughts: there was no time to waste in question or comment—for the wounded gentleman, who had proffered so earnest a prayer, was evidently in a dying state.

Exchanging significant glances, the servants placed Greenwood upon the litter; and, aided by the postilion, set out with their burden towards the hill.

The angle of the road was passed; and the party bearing the wounded man, suddenly appeared to the view of those who were stationed on the hill.

"Merciful heaven!" exclaimed Richard, with a shudder: "what can this mean?"

"Be not alarmed," said Ellen: "it can have no reference to Eugene. Doubtless some poor creature has met with an accident—"

"But my own servants are the bearers of that litter which is approaching!" cried the Prince, now becoming painfully excited. "A man is stretched upon it—his head is bandaged—he lies motionless—Oh! what terrible fears oppress me!"

And as he uttered these words, Richard sank back almost fainting upon the seat.

The gallant warrior, whose heart had never failed in the thickest of the battle—whose courage was so dauntless when bullets were flying round him like hail—and whose valour had given him a name amongst the mightiest generals of the universe,—this man of a chivalrous soul was subdued by the agonizing alarm that had suddenly menaced all his fond fraternal hopes with annihilation!

For so ominous—so sinister appeared to be the approach of a litter at the very moment when he was anxiously awaiting the presence of a long-lost brother, that his feelings experienced a revulsion as painful as it was sudden.

And now for a few moments the strange spectacle of the litter was forgotten by those who crowded round our hero in alarm at the change which had come over him.

Even Ellen turned away from the contemplation of that mournful procession which was toiling up the hill;—for she had seen Greenwood on the preceding evening—she had left him in good health—she had raised his spirits by her kind attentions and her loving language—and she did not for one moment apprehend that *he* could be the almost lifeless occupant of that litter!

"Pardon me, sweet Isabella—pardon me, dear Kate—and you also, my devoted friends," said Richard, at the expiration of a few minutes: "I am grieved to think that this weakness on my part should have distressed you—and yet I cannot be altogether ashamed of it!"

"Ashamed!" repeated Isabella, tenderly: "Oh! no, Richard—that word can never be associated with act or feeling on your part! For twelve years you have been separated from your brother—that last inscription on his own tree promises his return—and your generous heart is the prey of a suspense easily aggravated by the slightest circumstance of apparent ill omen."

"You describe my feelings exactly, dearest Isabel," said Markham, pressing with the tenderest warmth the hand of his lovely young wife.

"Because I know your heart so well," answered the Princess, with a sweet smile.

"Let us not believe in omens of an evil nature," said Katherine. "Some poor creature has met with an accident—"

"But wherefore should the servants bring him hither?" asked Richard.

This question produced a startling effect upon all who heard it: and no wonder that it did so—for the consideration which it involved had escaped all attention during the excitement of the last few minutes.

"Oh! heavens—now I am myself alarmed!" whispered Ellen to Eliza Sydney. "And yet it is foolish—"

At that moment the litter had approached so near the brow of the hill, that as Ellen glanced towards it while she spoke, her eyes obtained a full view of the countenance of him who lay stretched upon that mournful couch.

A piercing shriek burst from her lips; and she fell back, as if suddenly shot through the heart, into the arms of Eliza Sydney.

Richard sprang forward: a few steps brought him close by the litter, which the bearers now placed upon the ground *beneath the foliage of the very tree whereon the inscriptions were engraved*!

One look—one look was sufficient!

"Eugene—my brother Eugene!" exclaimed our hero, in a tone of the most intense anguish, as he cast himself on his knees by the side of the litter, and threw his arms around the dying man. "Oh! my God—is it thus that we meet? You are wounded, my dearest brother: but we will save you—we will save you! Hasten for a surgeon—delay not a moment—it is the life of my brother which is at stake!"

"Your brother, Richard!" cried Isabella, scarcely knowing what she said in that moment of intense excitement and profound astonishment: "your brother, my beloved husband? Oh! no—there is some dreadful mistake—for he whom you thus embrace is Mr. George Montague Greenwood!"

"Montague—Greenwood!" ejaculated Richard, starting as if an ice-bolt had suddenly entered his heart. "No—no—impossible, Isabella! Tell me—Eugene—tell me—you cannot be he of whom I have heard so much?"

"Yes, Richard—I am that villain!" answered Eugene, turning his dying countenance in an imploring manner towards his brother. "But do not desert me—do not spurn me—do not even upbraid me *now!*"

"Never—never!" cried the Prince, again embracing Eugene with passionate —almost frantic warmth. "Upbraid you, my dearest brother! Oh! no—no! Forget the past, Eugene—let it be buried in oblivion. And look up, my dear—dear brother: they are all kind faces which surround you!"

[…]

"And you, too, Isabella—for *you* also are my sister now," continued Eugene, extending his hand towards her: "do you pardon him who once inflicted so much injury upon your father?"

"You are my husband's brother—and you are therefore mine, Eugene," answered the Princess, tears trickling down her countenance. "None but affectionate relatives and kind friends now surround you; and your restoration to health shall be our earnest care!"

"Alas! there is no hope of recovery!" murmured Eugene.

"Yes—there *is* hope, my dearest husband!" exclaimed Ellen, who, having regained her consciousness through the kind attentions of Eliza Sydney, now flew to the litter.

"Your husband, Ellen!" cried Mr. Monroe and Richard as it were in the same breath.

"Yes—Eugene is my husband—my own, much-loved husband!" ejaculated Ellen: "and now you can divine the cause which led to the maintenance of that secret until this day!"

"And you, Mr. Monroe," said Eugene, a transient fire animating his eyes, as he clasped Ellen in his arms, "may be proud of your daughter—you also, Richard, may glory in her as a sister—for she has taught me to repent of my past errors—she has led me to admire and worship the noble character of Woman! But our child, Ellen—where is my boy—my darling Richard?"

"We will remove you into the house, Eugene," said his wife, bending over the litter with the tenderest solicitude;" and there you shall embrace your boy!"

"No—no—leave me here!" exclaimed her husband: "it is so sweet to lie beneath the foliage of this tree which bears my own name, and reminds me of my youthful days,—surrounded, too, by so many dear relatives and kind friends!"

"Amongst the latter of whom you must now reckon me," said Eliza Sydney, approaching the couch, and extending her hand to Eugene, who wrung it cordially. "Hush!" added Eliza, perceiving that he was about to address her: "no reference to the past! All that is unpleasant is forgotten:—a happy future is before us!"

"Admirable woman!" cried Eugene, overpowered by so many manifestations of forgiveness, affection, and sympathy as he had received within the last few minutes.

Mario Bazzano was then presented to his brother-in-law.

"May God bless your union with my sister!" said Eugene, in a solemn tone. "For a long time I have known that I possessed a sister—and much have I desired to see her. Richard, be not angry with me when I inform you that I was in a room adjacent to that apartment wherein the explanations relative to Katherine's birth took place between yourself and the Marquis of Holmesford;—be not angry with me, I say, that I did not discover myself, and rush into your arms,—but I was then the victim of an insatiable ambition! Do not interrupt me—I have much to say. Let some one hasten to fetch my child; and do you all gather round me, to hear my last words!"

"Your last words!" shrieked Ellen: "Oh! no—you must recover!"

"Yes—with care and attention, dearest Eugene," said Richard, his eyes dimmed with tears, "you shall be restored to us."

Katherine and Isabella also wept abundantly.

A servant had already departed to fetch a surgeon: a second was now despatched to the house for the little Richard and the young Prince Alberto.

It was at length Whittingham's turn to go forward; and, whimpering like a child, he pressed Eugene's hand warmly in his own. The old man was unable to speak—his voice was choked with emotion; but Eugene recognised him, and acknowledged his faithful attachment with a few kind words which only increased the butler's grief.

"Listen to me for a few minutes, my dearest relatives—my kindest friends," said Eugene, after a brief pause. "I feel that I am dying—I have met my fate at the hands of the villainous Lafleur, who plundered me more than two years and a half ago, and whom I encountered ere now in my way hither. Alas! I have pursued a strange career—a career of selfishness and crime, sacrificing every consideration and every individual to my own purposes—raising at one time a colossal fortune upon the ruin of thousands! I was long buoyed up by the hope of making myself a great name in the world, alike famous for wealth and rank,—that I might convince you, my brother, how a man of talent could carve out his way without friends, and without capital at the beginning! But, alas! I have for some months been convinced—thanks to the affectionate reasoning of that angel Ellen, and to the contemplation of your example, Richard, even from a distance—that talent will not maintain prosperity for ever, unless it be allied to virtue! And let me observe, Richard—as God is my witness!—that with all my selfishness I never sought to injure you! [...] The truth was revealed to me one day at the dwelling of Isabella's parents: and heaven knows how deeply I felt the villainy of my conduct, which had robbed *you*! Do not interrupt me—I conjure you to allow me to proceed! Many and many a time did I yearn to hasten to your assistance when misfortune first overtook you, Richard:—but, no—the appointment had been made for a certain day—and I even felt a secret pleasure to think that you might probably be reduced to the lowest state of penury, from which in one moment, when that day should come, I might elevate you to an enjoyment of the half of my fortune! But that I have ever loved you, Richard, those inscriptions on the tree will prove; and, moreover, I once penetrated into the home of our forefathers—the study-window was not fastened—I effected an entrance—I sought your chamber—I saw you sleeping in your bed—"

"Oh! then it was not a dream!" exclaimed Richard. "Dearest Eugene, say no more—we require no explanations—no apology for the past! Here is your child, Eugene—and mine also: your son and your little nephew are by your side!"

Eugene raised himself, by Ellen's aid, upon the litter, and embraced the two children with the most unfeigned tenderness.

For a few moments he gazed earnestly upon their innocent countenances: then, yielding to a sudden impulse, as the incidents of his own career swept through his memory, he exclaimed, "God grant that they prove more worthy of the name of *Markham* than I!"

Richard and Ellen implored him not to give way to bitter reflections for the past.

"Alas! such counsel is offered as vainly as it is kindly meant!" murmured Eugene. "My life has been tainted with many misdeeds—and not the least was my black infamy towards that excellent man, who afterwards became your friend, Richard—I mean Thomas Armstrong!"

"He forgave you—he forgave you, Eugene!" exclaimed the Prince.

"Ellen has informed me that you have in your possession a paper which he gave you on his death-bed—"

"And which is to be opened this day," added Richard.

Then, drawing forth the document, he broke the seal.

A letter fell upon the ground.

"Read it," said Eugene: "all that concerns you is deeply interesting to me."

The Prince complied with his brother's request, and read the letter aloud. Its contents were as follow:—

"I have studied human nature to little purpose, and contemplated the phases of the human character with small avail, if I err in the prediction which I am now about to record.

"*Richard, you will become a great man—as you are now a good one.*

"Should necessity compel you to open this document at any time previously to the 10th of July, 1843, receive the fortune to which it refers as an encouragement to persevere in honourable pursuits. But should you not read these words until the day named, my hope and belief are that you will be placed, by your own exertions, far beyond the want of that sum which, in either case, is bequeathed to you as a testimonial of my sincerest regard and esteem.

"Signor Viviani, banker at Pinalla, in the State of Castelcicala, or his agents, Messrs. Glyn and Co., bankers, London, will pay over to you, on presentation of this letter, the sum of seventy-five thousand pounds, with all interest, simple and compound, accruing thereto since the month of July, 1839, at which period I placed that amount in the hands of Signor Viviani.

"One word more, my dear young friend. Should you ever encounter an individual who speaks ill of the memory of Thomas Armstrong, say to him, '*He forgave his enemies!*' And should you ever meet one who has injured me, say to him, '*In the name of Thomas Armstrong I forgive you.*'

Be happy, my dear young friend—be happy!

"THOMAS ARMSTRONG."

It would be impossible to describe the emotions awakened in the breast of all those who heard the contents of this letter.

"Now, my dearest brother," exclaimed Richard, after a brief pause, "*in the name of Thomas Armstrong, you are forgiven the injury which you did to him!*"

"Thank you, dear brother, for that assurance: it relieves my mind of a heavy load! And, Richard," continued Eugene, in a voice tremulous with emotions and faint with the ebb of life's spirit, "the prediction is verified—you are a great man! The world is filled with the glory of your name—and you are as good as you are great! The appointment has been kept:—but how? We meet beneath the foliage of the two trees—you as the heir apparent to a throne—I as a ruined profligate!"

"No—no!" exclaimed the Prince; "you shall live to be rich and prosperous—"

Eugene smiled faintly.

"Merciful heavens! he is dying!" ejaculated Ellen.

And it was so!

Terrible was the anguish of those by whom he was surrounded.

Mr. Wentworth, the surgeon, appeared at this crisis; but his attentions were ministered in vain.

Eugene's eyes grew dim—still he continued sensible; and he knew that his last moments were approaching.

Richard—Ellen—Katherine—Eliza Sydney—the two children—Isabella—Mr. Monroe—and the faithful Whittingham,—all wept bitterly, as the surgeon shook his head in despair!

"My husband—my dearest husband!" screamed Ellen, wildly: "look upon me—look upon your child—oh! my God—this day that was to have been so happy!"

Eugene essayed to speak—but could not: and that was his last mortal effort. In another moment his spirit had fled for ever!

CHAPTER CCLIX.
CONCLUSION.

LAFLEUR was captured, tried, and condemned to transportation for life, for the manslaughter of Eugene Markham.

Immediately after the trial the Prince and Princess of Montoni, with the infant Prince Alberto, and accompanied by Signor and Signora Bazzano, embarked for Castelcicala in the *Torione* steam-frigate which was sent to convey them thither. We need scarcely say that the faithful Whittingham was in our hero's suite.

Eliza Sydney continues to reside at her beautiful villa near Upper Clapton; and her charitable disposition, her amiable manners, and her exemplary mode of life render her the admiration and pride of the entire neighbourhood.

[…]

King Zingary departed this life about six months ago; and Morcar is now the sovereign of the Gipsy tribe in these realms. He has already begun strenuously to exert himself in the improvement of the moral character of his people; and though he finds the materials on which he labours to make an impression somewhat stubborn, he has declared his intention of persevering in his good work. His wife Eva constantly wears round her neck the gold chain which Isabella sent her; and night and morning the son of these good people is taught to kneel down and pray for the continued prosperity and happiness of the Prince and Princess of Montoni.

[…]

And that mansion—to whom does it now belong? It is the property of Mr. Monroe, and will become Ellen's at his death: but the old man is still strong and hearty; and every fine afternoon he may be seen walking through the grounds, leaning upon the arm of his daughter or of Eliza Sydney, who is a frequent visitor at the Place.

Ellen is beautiful as ever, and might doubtless marry well, did she choose to seek society: but she has vowed to remain single for the sake of her child, who is now a blooming boy, and whom she rears with the fond hope that he will prove worthy of the name that he bears—the name of his uncle, Richard Markham.

Skilligalee and the Rattlesnake, long since united in matrimonial bonds, are leading a comfortable and steady life in Hoxton, the business of their little shop producing them not only a sufficiency for the present, but also the wherewith to create a provision for their old age.

Crankey Jem called upon them on the evening following the death of the Resurrection Man, and acquainted them with the event. From that moment nothing positive has ever been heard of James Cuffin; but it is supposed that he embarked as a common sailor in some ship bound for a long voyage.

Henry Holford remains a prisoner in Bethlem Hospital. He is in the full and unimpaired possession of his intellects, but has often and bitterly cursed the day when he listened to the whispering voice of his morbid ambition.

[...]

Colonel Cholmondeley, Sir Rupert Harborough, and Mr. Chichester are undergoing a sentence of ten years' condemnation to the galleys at Brest, for having attempted to pass forged Bank of England notes at a money-changer's shop in Paris.

[...]

Mrs. Chichester removed about two years ago to a pleasant cottage in Wales, where she dwells in the tranquil seclusion suitable to her taste.

[...]

Lady Bounce was compelled to sue for a separate maintenance about eighteen months ago, on the ground of cruelty and ill-treatment; and in this suit she succeeded.

Sir Cherry and Major Dapper continue as intimate as ever, and pursue pretty well the same unprofitable career as we have hitherto seen them following.

Mr. Banks, the undertaker of Globe Lane, carried his economic principles to such an extent that he fell into the habit of purchasing cloth to cover his coffins at a rate which certainly defied competition; but a quantity of that material having been missed from a warehouse in the City and traced to his establishment, he was compelled, although much against his inclination, to accompany an officer to Worship Street, where the porter belonging to the aforesaid warehouse was already in the dock on a charge of stealing the lost property. Vain was it that Mr. Banks endeavoured to impress upon the magistrate's mind the fact that he was as "pious and savoury a old wessel as ever made a coffin on economic principles:" the case was referred to the learned Recorder at the Old Bailey for farther investigation; and one fine morning Mr. Banks found himself sentenced to two years' imprisonment in the Compter for receiving goods knowing them to have been stolen.

[...]

John Smithers, better known to our readers as Gibbet, is the wealthiest inhabitant of a new town that has risen within these last three years in the valley of Ohio; and in a recent letter to the Prince of Montoni he declares that he is happier than he ever thought he could become.

EPILOGUE.

'Tis done: Virtue is rewarded—Vice has received its punishment.

Said we not, in the very opening of this work, that from London branched off two roads, leading to two points totally distinct the one from the other?

Have we not shown how the one winds its tortuous way through all the noisome dens of crime, chicanery, dissipation, and voluptuousness; and how the other meanders amidst rugged rocks and wearisome acclivities, but having on its way-side the resting-places of rectitude and virtue?

The youths who set out along those roads,—the elder pursuing the former path, the younger the latter,—have fulfilled the destinies to which their separate ways conducted them.

The one sleeps in an early grave: the other is the heir-apparent to a throne.

Yes: and the prophetic words of the hapless Mary-Anne are fulfilled to the letter; for now in their palace at Montoni, do the hero and heroine of our tale, while retrospecting over all they have seen and all they have passed through, devote many a kind regret to the memory of the departed girl who predicted for them all the happiness which they enjoy!

And that happiness—the world has seen no felicity more perfect.

Adored by a tender wife,—honoured by her parents, on whose brows his valour placed the diadems which they wear,—and almost worshipped by a grateful nation whom his prowess redeemed from slavery,—Richard Markham knows not a single care.

On her side,—wedded to him to whom her young heart gave its virgin love,—proud of a husband whose virtues in peace and whose glory in war have shed undying lustre on the name which he bears,—blessed, too, with a lovely boy, whose mind already develops the reflections of his father's splendid qualities, and with a charming girl, who promises to be the heiress of the mother's beauty,—can Isabella be otherwise than happy?

Kind Reader, who have borne with me so long—one word to thee.

If amongst the circle of thy friends, there be any who express an aversion to peruse this work,—fearful from its title or from fugitive report that the mind will be shocked more than it can be improved, or the blush of shame excited on the cheek oftener than the tear of sympathy will be drawn from the eye;—if, in a word, a false fastidiousness should prejudge, from its own suppositions or from misrepresentations made to it by others, a book by means of which we have sought to convey many an useful moral and lash many a flagrant abuse,—do you, kind reader, oppose that prejudice, and exclaim—"Peruse ere you condemn!"

For if, on the one side, we have raked amidst the filth and loathsomeness of society,—have we not, on the other, devoted adequate attention to its bright and glorious phases?

In exposing the hideous deformity of vice, have we not studied to develope the witching beauty of virtue?

Have we not taught, in fine, how the example and the philanthropy of one good man can "*save more souls and redeem more sinners than all the Bishops that ever wore lawn-sleeves?*"

If, then, the preceding pages be calculated to engender one useful thought —awaken one beneficial sentiment,—the work is not without its value.

If there be any merit in honesty of purpose and integrity of aim,—then is that merit ours.

And if, in addition to considerations of this nature, we may presume that so long as we are enabled to afford entertainment, our labours will be rewarded by the approval of the immense audience to whom we address ourselves, —we may with confidence invite attention to a SECOND SERIES of "THE MYSTERIES OF LONDON."

GEORGE W. M. REYNOLDS

THE END OF THE FIRST SERIES.

Appendix
Complete chapter titles and page numbers from the original issue

The Mysteries of London Series I, Volume I

		Prologue	1
Chapter	I	The Old House in Smithfield	2
	II	The Mysteries of the Old House	4
	III	The Trap-Door	6
	IV	The Two Trees	7
	V	Eligible Acquaintances	11
	VI	Mrs. Arlington	14
	VII	The Boudoir	16
	VIII	The Conversation	19
	IX	A City Man.—Smithfield Scenes	20
	X	The Frail One's Narrative	24
	XI	"The Servants' Arms"	27
	XII	The Bank Notes	30
	XIII	The Hell	32
	XIV	The Station-House	35
	XV	The Police-Office	37
	XVI	The Beginning of Misfortunes	39
	XVII	A Den of Horrors	43
	XVIII	The Boozing-Ken	45
	XIX	Morning	50
	XX	The Villa	51
	XXI	Atrocity	54
	XXII	A Woman's Mind	55
	XXIII	The Old House in Smithfield again	58
	XXIV	Circumstantial Evidence	61
	XV	The Enchantress	63
	XXVI	Newgate	67
	XXVII	The Republican and the Resurrection Man	69
	XXVIII	The Dungeon	71
	XXIX	The Black Chamber	75
	XXX	The 26th of November	78
	XXXI	Explanations	84

XXXII	The Old Bailey	86
XXXIII	Another Day at the Old Bailey	91
XXXIV	The Lesson Interrupted	93
XXXV	Whitecross Street Prison	95
XXXVI	The Execution	99
XXXVII	The Lapse of Two Years	102
XXXVIII	The Visit	104
XXXIX	The Dream	109
XL	The Speculation—An Unwelcome Meeting	111
XLI	Mr. Greenwood	115
XLII	"The Dark House"	118
XLIII	The Mummmy	122
XLIV	The Bodysnatchers	125
XLV	The Fruitless Search	128
XLVI	Richard and Isabella	131
XLVII	Eliza Sydney	133
XLVIII	Mr. Greenwood's Visitors	140
XLIX	The Document	148
L	The Drugged Wine-glass	151
LI	Diana and Eliza	154
LII	The Bed of Sickness	156
LIII	Accusations and Explanations	158
LIV	The Banker	162
LV	Miserrima!!	167
LVI	The Road to Ruin	171
LVII	The Last Resource	176
LVIII	New Year's Day	178
LIX	The Royal Lovers	182
LX	Revelations	185
LXI	The "Boozing-Ken" once more	188
LXII	The Resurrection Man's History	191
LXIII	The Plot	197
LXIV	The Counterplot	198
LXV	The Wrongs and Crimes of the Poor	202
LXVI	The Result of Markham's Enterprise	205
LXVII	Scenes in Fashionable Life	207
LXVIII	The Election	210
LXIX	The "Whippers-in"	213
LXX	The Image, the Picture, and the Statue	216
LXXI	The House of Commons	219
LXXII	The Black Chamber again	221
LXXIII	Captain Dapper and Sir Cherry Bounce	224
LXXIV	The Meeting	227
LXXV	The Crisis	230
LXXVI	Count Alteroni's Fifteen Thousand Pounds	233

LXXVII	A Woman's Secret	235
LXXVIII	Marian	237
LXXIX	The Bill.—A Father	239
LXXX	The Revelation	242
LXXXI	The Mysterious Instructions	245
LXXXII	The Medical Man	246
LXXXIII	The Black Chamber again	248
LXXXIV	The Second Examination.—Count Alteroni	250
LXXXV	A Friend in Need	254
LXXXVI	The Old Hag	256
LXXXVII	The Professor of Mesmerism	260
LXXXVIII	The Figurante	262
LXXXIX	The Mysterious Letter	266
XC	Markham's Occupations	268
XCI	The Tragedy	274
XCII	The Italian Valet	277
XCIII	News from Castelcicala	282
XCIV	The Home Office	285
XCV	The Forger and the Adulteress	290
XCVI	The Member of Parliament's Levee	293
XCVII	Another's New Year's Day	296
XCVIII	Dark Plots and Schemes	301
XCIX	The Buffer's History	304
C	The Mysteries of the Ground-floor Rooms	310
CI	The Widow	312
CII	The Reverend Visitor	314
CIII	Hopes and Fears	317
CIV	Female Courage	318
CV	The Combat	321
CVI	The Grave-digger	323
CVII	A Discovery	326
CVIII	The Exhumation	328
CIX	The Stock-Broker	331
CX	The Effects of a Trance	339
CXI	A Scene at Mr. Chichester's House	340
CXII	Viola	342
CXIII	The Lovers	346
CXIV	The Contents of the Packet	349
CXV	The Treasure—A New Idea	351
CXVI	The Rattlesnake's History	353
CXVII	The Rattlesnake	361
CXVIII	The Two Maidens	364
CXIX	Poor Ellen!	367
CXX	The Father and Daughter	369
CXXI	His Child!	371

CXXII	A Change of Fortune	373
CXXIII	Aristocratic Morals	375
CXXIV	The Intrigues of a Demirep	377
CXXV	The Reconciliation	380
CXXV	The Rector of St. David's	382
CXXVII	Blandishments	384
CXXVIII	Temptation	387
CXXIX	The Fall	389
CXXX	Mental Struggles	391
CXXXI	The Statue	394
CXXXII	An Old Friend	396
CXXXIII	Skilligalee's History	400
CXXXIV	The Palace in the Holy Land	406
CXXXV	The Proposal.—Unexpected Meetings	408
CXXXVI	The Secret Tribunal	413
	Epilogue	415

The Mysteries of London   Series I, Volume II

CXXXVII	Rat's Castle	1
CXXXVIII	A Public Functionary	4
CXXXIX	The Confidence	7
CXL	Incidents in the Gipsy Palace	10
CXLI	The Subterranean	13
CXLII	Gibbet	15
CXLIII	Morbid Feelings	18
CXLIV	The unfinished Letter	20
CXLV	Hypocrisy	23
CXLVI	The Bath.—The Housekeeper	25
CXVLII	The Rector's new Passion	28
CXLVIII	The Old Hag's Intrigue	31
CXLIX	The Masquerade	34
CL	Mrs. Kenrick	36
CLI	A mysterious Deed	39
CLII	The Death-bed	42
CLIII	Proceedings in Castelcicala	45
CLIV	Reflections.—The New Prison	47
CLV	Patriotism	50
CLVI	The Decision	52
CLVII	The Trial of Catherine Wilmot	54
CLVIII	A happy Party	58
CLIX	The Interview	60
CLX	The Rector in Newgate	63
CLXI	Lady Cecilia Harborough	66

CLXII	The Bequest	69
CLXIII	The Zingarees	71
CLXIV	The Executioner's History	75
CLXV	The Trace	79
CLXVI	The Thames Pirates	82
CLXVII	An Arrival at the Wharf	84
CLXVIII	The Plague Ship	86
CLXIX	The Pursuit	90
CLXX	The Black Veil	93
CLXXI	Mr. Greenwood's Dinner-party	95
CLXXII	The Mysteries of Holmesford House	96
CLXXIII	The Adieux	100
CLXXIV	Castelcicala	103
CLXXV	Montoni	107
CLXXVI	The Club-house	111
CLXXVII	The History of an Unfortunate Woman	115
CLXXVIII	The Tavern at Friuli	133
CLXXIX	The Journey	135
CLXXX	The "Boozing-ken" once more	138
CLXXXI	The Resurrection Man again	142
CLXXXII	Mr. Greenwood's Journey	144
CLXXXIII	Kind Friends	147
CLXXXIV	Estella	150
CLXXXV	Another New-Year's Day	155
CLXXXVI	The New Cut	158
CLXXXVII	The forged Bills	162
CLXXXVIII	The Battles of Piacere and Abrantani	165
CLXXXIX	The Battle of Montoni	172
CXC	Two of our old Acquaintances	174
CXCI	Crankey Jem's History	176
CXCII	The Mint.—The Forty Thieves	187
CXCIII	Another Visit to Buckingham Palace	192
CXCIV	The Royal Breakfast	197
CXCV	The Aristocratic Villain and the low Miscreant	200
CXCVI	The old Hag and the Resurrection Man	203
CXCVII	Ellen and Catherine	206
CXCVIII	A gloomy Visitor	208
CXCIX	The Orphan's filial Love	211
CC	A Maiden's Love	214
CCI	The handsome Stranger.—Disappointment	218
CCII	The Princess Isabella	220
CCIII	Ravensworth Hall	223
CCIV	The Bride and Bridegroom	226
CCV	The Breakfast	228
CCVI	The Patrician Lady and the Unfortunate Woman	231

CCVII	The Husband, the Wife, and the Unfortunate Woman	235
CCVIII	The Resurrection Man's House in Globe Town	238
CCIX	Alderman Sniff.—Tomlinson and Greenwood	240
CCX	Holford's Duties	245
CCXI	The Deed	248
CCXII	The Examination at the Home Office	251
CCXIII	The Tortures of Lady Ravensworth	253
CCXIV	The Duellists	255
CCXV	The Voices in the Ruins	259
CCXVI	The Progress of Lydia Hutchinson's Vengeance	262
CCXVII	The Prisoner in the Subterranean	267
CCXVIII	The veiled Visitor	269
CCXIX	The Murder	272
CCXX	The Effect of the Oriental Tobacco	275
CCXXI	The Return to England	277
CCXXII	The Arrival at Home	281
CCXXIII	The Marriage	285
CCXXIV	Mr. Banks's House in Globe Lane	288
CCXXV	The Old Hag's History	292
CCXXVI	The Marquis of Holmesford	299
CCXXVII	Coldbath Fields' Prison	303
CCXXVIII	A desperate Achievement	306
CCXXIX	The Widow	309
CCXXX	Bethlem Hospital	314
CCXXXI	Mr. Greenwood and Mr. Vernon	317
CCXXXII	Scenes at Ravensworth Hall	319
CCXXXIII	A welcome Friend	322
CCXXXIV	A Midnight Scene of Mystery	324
CCXXXV	Plots and Counterplots	327
CCXXXVI	Woman as she ought to be	332
CCXXXVII	The Jugglers	335
CCXXXVIII	The Performance	339
CCXXXIX	The Resurrection Man's Return Home	345
CCXL	A new Epoch	347
CCXLI	Crockford's	350
CCXLII	The Aunt	355
CCXLIII	The Fight.—The ruined Gamester	358
CCXLIV	The History of a Gamester	360
CCXLV	The Excursion	372
CCXLVI	The Party at Ravensworth Hall	378
CCXLVII	The Stranger who discovered the Corpse	382
CCXLVIII	An unpleasant Exposure	384
CCXLIX	The Resurrection Man's last Feat at Ravensworth Hall	388
CCXLX	Egerton's last Dinner-party	391
CCLI	The obstinate Patient	397

APPENDIX

CCLII	Death of the Marquis of Holmesford	400
CCLIII	The Ex-Member for Rottenborough	403
CCLIV	Further Misfortunes	407
CCLV	Gibbet at Markham Place	410
CCLVI	Eliza Sydney and Ellen.—The Hospital	412
CCLVII	The Revenge	415
CCLVIII	The Appointment kept	419
CCLIX	Conclusion	423
	Epilogue	424

Technical Note:

This edition reproduces the text of an early issue of *The Mysteries of London* with the imprint of George Vickers, from two volumes dated 1845 and 1846, in the private collection of the editor. Later issues bear the imprint of John Dicks, but the text is identical, although a few woodcuts are modified. Photocopied text was scanned and read using Omni-Page character recognition software.

For a complete list of KUP publications,
please write to:

Keele University Press, Keele University,
Staffordshire ST5 5BG England

Tel: 01782 583099   Fax: 01782 584120